TEMPEST AT DAWN

A NOVEL

James D. Best

Tempest at Dawn

Cover design by Jim Wood

Published by Wheatmark®
610 East Delano Street, Suite 104
Tucson, Arizona 85705 U.S.A.
www.wheatmark.com

International Standard Book Number: 978-1-60494-344-3
Library of Congress Control Number: 2009942840

For my grandchildren.
May our Constitution keep you and your children safe and free.

"The infant periods of most nations are buried in silence, or veiled in fable, and perhaps the world has lost little it should regret. But the origins of the American Republic contain lessons of which posterity ought not to be deprived."

James Madison

Contents

Historical Note

In July of 1776, thirteen North American colonies declared their independence from Great Britain. Fighting had actually started a year earlier at Concord and Lexington with "the shot heard 'round the world." War continued for seven more years until, on September 3, 1783, the Treaty of Paris finally legitimized the sovereignty claims of the United States of America. At that time, the thirteen former colonies considered themselves independent states loosely connected for self-defense.

The Articles of Confederation, the first United States Constitution, proved barely adequate during the imperative of war and a failure in peacetime. Within a few years, the military had been reduced to near extinction, depression and hyperinflation sapped hope, insurrection sprang from civil injustice, a confused government tottered perilously close to collapse, and European powers hovered like vultures, eager to devour the remains.

In the summer of 1786, a convention at Annapolis collapsed without making any recommendations to our enfeebled government. James Madison and Alexander Hamilton attended the aborted Annapolis Convention and made a pact to promote another national conference the following summer. In May of 1787, fifty-five men came to Philadelphia with a congressional charter to revise the Articles of Confederation.

Prologue

October 6, 1835

Anxiety woke me before dawn. Rolling to my side, I pulled the heavy quilt over my exposed ear. Was I ready? Had I prepared sufficiently? Would the old man reveal what I had come here to learn? He was stubborn and had frustrated many before me.

Eventually I stirred and made my way to the lamp. I fumbled to light it, then held quiet, alert to any noise in the house. Nothing. I started to dress.

I had arrived the previous night, eager to ask questions, but the old man had sent me to bed, explaining that he thought more clearly in the mornings. Now I knew this was fortuitous. If I had charged ahead, I would have blundered and disclosed my true objective. The old man knows secrets and he has documents— documents he has kept hidden from public view for fifty years. I counseled myself to be patient and approach my subject obliquely.

The events that concerned me had occurred fifty years ago, when the old man was thirty-six. He would die soon, the last witness gone. Powerful men had gathered, met in secret, and plotted to overthrow a government. When he died, no one would be left to expose what had happened behind those locked doors.

I grabbed my coat, intent on a brisk walk to clear my mind. Just before opening the bedroom door, I stopped. I had traversed the path only once. I decided to leave the lamp lit, so the spill of light would help me navigate the landing. The front door stood directly in front of the stairs, so if I found the first step, I should avoid stumbling.

Escaping the house, I discovered enough nascent light to guide my way. At the back of the estate, a horseshoe-shaped garden greeted me. Flowers and ornamental shrubs bracketed vegetables, fruit trees, and grape arbors. The garden appeared withered, prepared for winter's dormancy, but its general neatness still impressed—four acres of unruly nature rigidly ordered and groomed to match the taste of its owner.

The morning chill chased me back toward the house. A thick forest girdled a vast arc of grass spilling across the front acreage. Stately white pines lined the approach road, and clusters of trees occasionally broke the uniformity. I took a deep sniff and smelled wet foliage that carried a hint of decay.

A noise from the porch drew my attention to the mansion. I saw two people work their way across the porch. The old man shuffled unsteadily as he clung to a strong black arm. The manservant slipped a hand under the old man's elbow and lowered him into his rocker. When he had settled, the patriarch sat back to allow his servant to spread a heavy blanket across his lap.

"Thank you, Paul, I'll be fine now. Tell Sukey I'm ready for my tea."

I stood silently and watched my host tuck the blanket tight against his legs. Kneading his rheumatic hands, he gazed at the rolling mountains in the distance. Before I could decide how to signal my presence, the mistress waltzed onto the porch, breaking the old man's reverie.

"James, I know you love your morning ritual, but it's far too chilly for you to be out here. Come. I'll help you move into the sitting room."

"I'm bundled warmly. If you want to ward off my chill, hurry Sukey with my tea."

"Sukey'll be here shortly," she said, one hand on her hip, "I won't argue, but may I remind you that you barely made it through last winter? Just think how disappointed you'll be if you can't read your books."

"Clever, my dear, but I'm staying—although, I might expire right here if I don't get my tea."

"I'll see what's keeping Sukey, but breakfast will be served in the dining room." She threw this last over her shoulder as she retreated into the house.

The subject of my investigation looked small enough that a soft breeze could tumble him away with the autumn leaves. How could such a frail man rouse his partisans and enemies to such passion? His soft voice furnished not the slightest hint of authority.

Yet he somehow struck an imposing figure, sitting exquisitely still in his black silk gown, black gloves, and tight-fitting skullcap. Sharp, birdlike features and a stern expression erupted from the dark garb. The tiny man, reputed to have an enormous intellect, still possessed eyes that promised an alert mind.

My hesitancy allowed another player to enter the scene, a petite black woman who emerged from the house balancing a large tray with tea service. The old man acknowledged her with a faint nod. The woman served the tea with an élan gained from years of experience. She arranged a second cup. Was this meant for the woman of the house or me? The aroma spurred me to action.

As I walked toward the porch, the man's wife reappeared. I stopped—one foot on the first step—waiting for the appropriate moment.

My host glanced at his wife and said to his servant, "Sukey, set breakfast up out here. I don't think we'll have many more mornings to eat outside."

"James, we've already discussed this. Breakfast will be served in the dining room. Sukey, tell Paul to put fresh logs on the fire."

Whirling around, the wife nearly bumped into me. "Oh, good morning, Mr. Witherspoon," she said. "I hope you slept comfortably."

"Yes, very comfortably, thank you."

I turned toward my host. "Good morning, Mr. President."

"Mr. Witherspoon, please sit. Tea tastes especially good on a brisk morning."

I sat opposite the wisp of the once-great man. "You have a wonderful and gracious home. This is my first visit to Virginia, and it's as beautiful as I had imagined."

"You've lived your whole life in New Jersey?"

"I've traveled to New York and New England, but this is my first visit to the South."

"Welcome. You'll find our habits different."

"The South is different, but you're not. I've read everything you've written, and I'm impressed by how much you think like someone from the North."

"I presume you meant that as a compliment?"

"Of course. Your roots are in Virginia, but your thinking and erudition reflect that you were schooled in the North."

The old man sat quietly for a moment. "Have you secured a publisher?"

"High interest. I need only to present a novel view that applies to current politics."

"I hope my views are not novel."

"The views of an actual participant would be novel."

The old man settled back ever so slightly into his chair. "My home has hosted historians, politicians, and other eminent people, but your visit is special. I look fondly back on my days at the College of New Jersey and the Reverend Doctor Witherspoon. I owe a great debt to your grandfather. You should be proud."

These comments from James Madison pleased me more than I would have expected. "Thank you, sir. I struggle to be worthy of his name."

"Where do you wish to start?"

"A difficult question. So little is known. Was it necessary to keep the proceedings secret?"

"Neither nations nor children should be conceived in public."

I was taken aback. "You supported secrecy?"

"It passed unanimously—without debate. The times and circumstances required private deliberation."

"As a historian, I disagree. Secret cabals should not design governments. The Constitutional Convention should have been open."

Madison gave a little laugh. "Jefferson agreed with you. He said that secrecy represented an abominable precedent that could be justified only by ignorance." The sun had fully emerged, and Madison paused to take in the Blue Ridge Mountains, now awash in fall color. When he again made eye contact, he spoke as if there had been no interruption. "Mr. Witherspoon, if the convention had met publicly, it would've stifled debate. Private deliberations allowed the kind of raucous exchanges that illuminate hard choices."

"Why haven't you disclosed the details of the proceedings?"

"Our work should be judged by the outcome, not the process."

"Some would judge the outcome immoral," I blurted.

The next few seconds felt like a minute. "May I ask what novel view you intend to propose to your publisher?"

"An accurate account. You're the last of the founding fathers. You can explain the travesties."

"And what travesties might those be?"

"The victory of property rights over liberty, elitism over representation, and—the worst blasphemy—the endorsement of slavery in our country's most sacred document."

"You're an abolitionist?"

"As are all righteous men."

Madison gave a dismissive shrug. "We were driven to find common ground by need."

"I don't mean to be disrespectful, but the goal should have been to guarantee liberty for everyone, including slaves."

Madison sat quietly, looking at me with an unblinking stare. I could feel the old man taking my measure. "You're young—and perhaps a bit naïve."

He scrunched up in his chair. I unconsciously shifted in my seat as well, stretching my long legs in a new direction. The old man looked as delicate as a ripe dandelion. How could someone so weak intimidate me?

Madison finally said, "What are they teaching young people today? True, it's been nearly fifty years, but how could such important events have become so distorted?"

"Perhaps I've been misinformed. That's why I requested this interview—to get a firsthand account."

"I presume you're aware that I own over a hundred slaves and that your breakfast is even now being prepared by a slave."

"I'm uncomfortable with the situation. Nor do I understand it. You have repeatedly condemned slavery. I can only presume that you had no choice in your lifetime. But change is coming."

"Some adulate change; some abhor it. A few see a degree of change that exists only in their imagination."

I bristled. "I see myself as one who incites change."

"Meaning you're not a tavern abolitionist?"

"I am a revolutionary, as you once were." I took a sloppy sip of tea and wiped my chin. "Excuse me, sir. Of course, you have not grown passive in retirement. You support the expatriation of slaves to Liberia. I simply work for a solution closer to home."

"And what solution might that be?"

"Complete abolition. Unless I misunderstand your writings, you support the same goal."

"You presuppose, young man." Turning slightly to look over my shoulder, Madison said, "Paul, I assume breakfast is ready?"

Paul had walked onto the porch and stood quietly to the side.

"Yes, sir. Mrs. Madison asked me to bring you indoors."

"Of course she did. Very well. Mr. Witherspoon, please precede us. You can assure Mrs. Madison that we are making our interminable way to the dining room."

THE SEAT AT THE head of the table and those on either side had been set at the end near the fire. Mrs. Madison stood behind one chair, so I stood behind the chair opposite. Despite Madison's protestations, I welcomed the warmth from the fire. We kept our places as Paul helped the former president of the United States traverse the length of the room.

As soon as Madison took his seat, Sukey placed a large plate in front of him. The broad expanse of china dwarfed the thin slices of jammed bread accented with a slender wedge of melon. I couldn't help staring at the plate. My long trip had famished me. Surely, more food waited in the kitchen.

Seating herself, Mrs. Madison scooted her chair toward the table, giving me a radiant smile that engaged every feature of her face. In repose, she looked ordinary, but her face when lit up stunned and captivated. I had never before encountered anyone who could shed so many years with a smile.

"James eats little these days," she said. "It doesn't take much to nourish his body. Nourishing his mind, however, is an endless task he still relishes. He's been looking forward to your visit."

Glancing toward the kitchen door, I ironed a linen napkin across my lap with the flat of both hands. "Sir, I must apologize for my comments on the porch. I'm here to learn, not preach. I meant no offense."

"Relax, my boy," Madison said. "Do not fear challenging me. Charge in, question notions, but argue with logic and consistent principles."

Mrs. Madison beamed at me. "James hates sophism, but he lives for sound debate. Your visit has already sparked his mood. Proceed, proceed. No need to apologize or equivocate. James only looks fragile. You'll soon discover the orneriness of a bobcat."

"Dolley exaggerates. A scraggy house cat can challenge the prowess of this weathered creature."

Sukey burst through the door, carrying a large tray. I felt relief at the sight of the hearty meal as she distributed plates and bowls filled with generous portions of porridge, bacon, boiled eggs, biscuits, gravy, and pineapple. The aroma pulled the trigger on my appetite.

"I don't force my habits on my guests," Madison said, looking amused.

Sukey gave me an impish grin and an abbreviated curtsey, and retreated toward the kitchen. Why did I feel that everyone knew my disposition, while I remained baffled as to the temperament of this household?

"Mr. Witherspoon," James Madison said, "there were many hurdles we had to overcome at the Federal Convention—what today people call the Constitutional Convention."

"Mr. President," I interrupted, "shall we save our political discussion until after the meal? I'm sure Mrs. Madison would appreciate lighter conversation."

"Thank you, Mr. Witherspoon," Dolley said. "I never grasped politics, not even after sixteen years in the White House—eight as Jefferson's hostess and eight more with James. A young man such as yourself, with all your schooling, understands these issues so much better than a woman. Perhaps we can talk about the latest European fashions."

"I apologize, madam, but I know little of women's fashions."

James Madison chuckled. "Mr. Witherspoon, let me save you from an embarrassing moment. Dolley enjoys playing the harlequin to humble male conceit. While president, I found few advisors more astute."

"I'm sorry; I didn't mean to denigrate your knowledge of political matters. I was only trying to be polite."

"Of course, Mr. Witherspoon. Your limited perspective isn't entirely your fault."

"Dolley, I believe your egg is getting cold and your mood heated," James Madison said. "Our friend was simply unaware of your interests."

The old man smiled with his eyes as he took a small bite of toast, clearly enjoying the exchange. I felt deflated. I saw my mission, and myself, as more important than merely providing entertainment for an old man.

Madison, apparently done eating, sat back in his chair and watched me devour my breakfast. When Sukey reappeared, he asked for coffee.

"Mr. Witherspoon, we did compromise, but compromise greases the axle of governance."

"One should never compromise principles."

Madison's expression didn't change. "Our goal was to build a functioning republic. We approached collapse. Anarchy was the only other course."

"I find it hard to believe the situation was that dire."

James Madison looked irritated for the first time. "If we had not acted, the Revolution would have been for naught."

"Men died in that Revolution for liberty—liberty that your convention denied to half the citizens of the South."

"Do you mean women?" Dolley asked.

"Women? Well, uh, no. I meant Negroes."

"Negroes aren't citizens," she said.

"They are in the North."

"Women are citizens in the North and the South."

"Women know nothing of politics."

"Slaves do?"

"They can learn."

She leaned back. "I see."

"No. I mean ..."

"Should we free male Negroes and keep their women slaves?"

"Of course not."

"Then what would you have?"

I glanced at James Madison. He seemed to enjoy my predicament. Without thought, I reacted emotionally. "Slavery is an abomination. It has nothing to do with suffrage. A man shouldn't own other human beings."

"Mr. Witherspoon, what are your intentions with this book?" Dolley asked.

Her directness flustered me. "I made that clear in my letter. My intention is to document the founding of our American republic. Many different accounts have circulated, but all are suspect. The rule of secrecy allowed different participants to paint self-glorifying portraits. I want to present a true account."

Madison rubbed his hands, massaging what looked more like huge fleshy walnuts than knuckles. "You don't intend an abolitionist tract?"

Obviously, I wasn't good at deception. "I won't mislead you. I want to expose the deceit that ingrained slavery into our society, but that isn't my sole aim. I sincerely wish to document the founding of our republic."

Dolley gave me one of her radiant smiles. "Do you intend an expansion of the pamphlet you published last spring?"

"You've read it?"

"Of course. Did you imagine Virginia part of the hinterlands?"

"Of course not. It just, well ... the pamphlet sold poorly."

"There are always a few copies around to embarrass a supplicant," Dolley said.

I turned to her husband. "You knew my views, yet you still granted an interview?"

"You seem a sharp, passionate young man. And I owe a debt to your grandfather."

I hesitated and then blurted, "Denying women the right to vote is wrong, but slavery is evil."

"We heard you before," Dolley said.

"But I didn't say it so eloquently."

"A writer should be good with words."

"A writer has the opportunity to rewrite."

"You mean you don't always get it right the first time?" Dolley's smile had turned coy.

I felt embarrassed. These two old people, one quite enfeebled, had made me look foolish.

"The consequences of what you suggest would be catastrophic—then, now, or in your children's lifetime," James Madison said. "I suggest we put aside the issue of slavery for a time. I'll give you an opportunity to examine this institution and to gauge the tenor of our agrarian culture."

Dolley said, "Mr. Witherspoon, you should attempt to understand our way of life before you instruct us on how we ought to live." Now the smile. "Perhaps European fashion would have made a more appropriate breakfast topic."

Her kind face, full of goodwill, erased my embarrassment and created an urge to please rather than irritate. I wondered what would have been the fate of two administrations, absent Dolley's rare gift.

AFTER WE HAD RESETTLED in the sitting room, Dolley asked, "How would you like to start your inquiry?"

I directed my answer to James Madison. "Before my grandfather died, he told me that you took extensive notes during the convention. I'd like to study them."

"No."

Madison's abrupt answer startled me. "May I ask why not?"

"You may ask any questions you like, but you may not have access to my records."

"But that is why I came."

"You requested an interview."

"I thought your notes would prompt my questions."

"They will be published after my death."

"I don't wish to publish them, only to use them to educate myself on the proceedings."

"I shall educate you."

"Your memory—"

The president's firm expression stopped me. After a deep breath, I continued, "Sir, I know delegates engineered compromises that eroded your republican intent. I want to document their obstructionism."

"That's not a question."

Another deep breath. "Why did you compromise?"

"We crafted perilous paths between differing opinions," Madison said, "that allowed us to leave Philadelphia with something to present to an anxious nation. I have no doubt that today we would be under the yoke of a European power if not for the success of the Federal Convention."

"Why did you not include a bill of rights?"

"An error. One I corrected in the First Congress."

"The Bill of Rights does not extend to slaves."

"That would have meant emancipation."

"Justice, and our character as a people, demand that we should consider slaves as human beings, not as mere property. Yet slaves remain in spite of declarations that all men are born equally free."

Dolley's chin lifted. "Those are my husband's words."

"Yes," I answered, keeping my eyes on James Madison.

He glanced down at his folded hands. "My words, not my deeds."

I thought I detected a hint of despondency. "Why did your deeds fall short of your words?"

Madison's eyes closed. "Politicians deal with the practical...the achievable."

"My faith makes no such allowances."

The old man opened his eyes and chuckled. "Roger Sherman used to say that faithfulness is not how one lives, but what one aspires to."

I felt my back stiffen. "I'm appalled to hear you quote Sherman. That man used the Constitution to shackle Negroes."

Madison's eyes lost any hint of melancholy. "Young man, you seem at a loss about how to proceed. I suggest I tell the story as it happened. Then you may judge us against any standards you choose."

"I don't mean to judge."

"Of course you do. We'll start with Roger Sherman."

Part 1

An Assembly of Demigods

1

Tuesday, May 15, 1787

Roger Sherman shook the rain from his heavy cloak.

"Are you meeting someone, sir?"

"Yes, but I don't yet know who."

Sherman ignored the doorman's haughty look and turned his attention to the central hall of the Indian Queen. The bright tavern smelled of wet wool, spilled beer, tobacco, and good food. Knots of men clogging the open spaces boisterously greeted old friends. Cheerful innkeepers swung through the crowd, brandishing tankards of ale and platters of food.

"Can I help, sir?"

Sherman turned to look again at the young doorman.

The Indian Queen was an expensive Philadelphia tavern. The well-built Negro, dressed in a blue embroidered coat, red silk cape, buff waistcoat and breeches, ruffled shirt, and powdered hair, presented an unmistakable message: the poor should continue down Fourth Street to find another tavern, one more suited to their station and budget.

Sherman, sixty-six years old, may have looked out of place in his scuffed brown suit, but he had spent many evenings in similar establishments. The display didn't intimidate him, and he looked forward to a better than average meal. Handing his cloak to the pretentious doorman, Sherman said, "I'm with the Federal Convention. Perhaps you can direct me to some of the other delegates."

"Just to your left, sir. Many of your colleagues have gathered in the Penn Room."

Sherman walked through double doors to a large room arranged with tables covered in turquoise cloth and set with white-and-blue-patterned china. A festive mood filled the room as men carried on animated discussions with their dinner companions. Despite the cheerful appearance, Sherman spied ominous signs in the quieter corners. Beyond the merriment and goodwill, small clusters of powerful men sat quietly scheming. Alliances had already been formed, and he would need to catch up with his opponents.

The United States had won its independence from England four years before, and already the elite plotted to overthrow the government. They believed that the country's loose confederation—sufficient during the imperative of war—had proved inadequate in peacetime. These privileged few wanted a forceful central government, one suited to the empire they intended to rule.

Sherman had arrived today, eager to refresh his intelligence with news, opinions, and tavern gossip. The future of his young nation depended on the outcome of this gathering, and Sherman held few illusions about the task ahead. He feared that this Federal Convention would strive to give unprecedented power to a national government. To protect Connecticut's interests, he had to win delegates to his side.

Sherman spotted James Madison in a far corner. They knew each other from their years together in Congress. Madison's pale, boyish face made him look much younger than his thirty-six years. A small and graceful man, he often appeared dwarfed when standing next to those giants, the tall and stately Gen. Washington or his friend and neighbor, Tom Jefferson. What Madison lacked in physical presence, however, he made up in energy and intellect.

Madison was bright and learned, but Sherman considered him a zealot. He had arrived on May 3, a full eleven days before the scheduled start and well before everyone else. He had prepared for a year, badgered everyone to attend, orchestrated events, and left his imprint everywhere. Sherman believed him capable, but young and naïve in the ways of achieving political consensus.

When Madison briefly caught his eye, Sherman pretended not to notice. He wanted to avoid the Virginians for now. This was a night to gather information and form relationships, not a time to expose his strategy to opponents. Sherman knew Madison had a plan, an alliance, and Gen. Washington on his side. He must break this juggernaut. Connecticut's survival depended on it.

Squeezing his large frame through the packed room, Sherman walked heavily toward a table of South Carolina delegates. Although this key Southern state stood firmly in the Virginia camp, Sherman believed that with patience and skill, he could erode the alliance. His task was to find common ground, but breaking the South Carolina bond with the large states would require care and patience.

"Mr. Butler, may I join you?"

Not surprisingly, Charles Pinckney responded. "Of course. Sit down, sit down." Pinckney scooted his chair aside to make room. "When did you arrive?"

"This afternoon. With the rain and mud, the trip was long and tiring. I'm glad to settle in on hard planks that don't wash side to side like a ship out of trim."

Pinckney didn't look sympathetic. "We came by sea. I'd tell you about it, but the subject fatigues me."

Sherman glanced about the tavern. "Quite a boisterous crowd. Are these delegates? I don't recognize many."

"Most of those noisy gentlemen are members of the Society of the Cincinnati, here for their own convention."

"That explains it." Sherman turned back toward his table companions. "I thought it looked like a gathering of good fellows."

Pinckney sneered. "The officers of the Revolution are still congratulating themselves for thrashing the most powerful nation on earth."

"Surely you don't begrudge our soldiers an occasion to celebrate," Sherman said.

"Soldiers?" Pinckney's tone conveyed disdain. "More like an aristocracy in waiting. Each convinced he single-handedly won the war. Their leader, Gen. Washington, sits over there, regally presiding over the Virginians."

Pinckney—rich, vain, and handsome—was only twenty-nine years old. Despite his upbringing, he did not comport himself as a gentleman. Sherman found him irreverent, aggressive, and, above all, ambitious. Exuding an aristocratic air, Pinckney supported populist and backcountry issues.

"The Presbyterians are here as well," Pinckney continued derisively. "But their pretensions are more ethereal. We must surely have a good convention, with the military class and the clergy to give us guidance."

Sherman had forgotten the Cincinnati would be in Philadelphia. The city had grown large and prosperous, and served as a favorite gathering place for societies, leagues, and conventions. The Society of the Cincinnati was an organization of Revolutionary officers who many feared had their own ideas about how to cut out the decay gripping the nation.

"No wonder Philadelphia has grown expensive," Sherman said. "If the conference goes long, Connecticut may not have authorized sufficient funds."

"Oh, it'll go long—or very short," Pinckney said. "Did you find adequate lodgings?"

"Quite adequate. I can walk to the State House in minutes." Sherman was sure the South Carolinians were quartered far more luxuriously, probably here at the Indian Queen. He decided to turn the conversation in a different direction.

"I visited Dr. Franklin this afternoon and discovered that we are all invited to dine at his home tomorrow afternoon. He promised to open a cask of excellent porter, recently arrived from Europe."

"So you too have made the pilgrimage to the great doctor's home." Pinckney waved dismissively. "So have we all. Sipping tea under his mulberry tree, talking about the great things we've done or intend to do. Chuckling at the old man's witticisms."

Sherman ignored the sarcasm. "How close are we to a quorum?"

"Close with your arrival. Perhaps we can start soon." Pinckney cast his eyes about the table, adding lightly, "I can only wonder at what we'll be starting."

The comment drew subdued laughter. Sherman calculated that they were on their third ale. Unlike Pinckney, he wasn't eager to see the proceedings begin, because he wanted time to talk to delegates before the heat of the convention. Adopting an innocent tone, he said, "We'll build a working government. One that can deliver us from our present disorder."

"What authority do we have?" Pinckney demanded.

"We're sanctioned by Congress," Sherman said.

Pierce Butler shifted in his chair and joined the conversation. "Congress ruled that we may only revise the Articles of Confederation."

Pinckney looked around at his fellow South Carolinians. "That's what we've been debating. Do we have the power to write a new constitution or merely adjust deficiencies in the Articles? Most people believe the latter."

"We have whatever authority we assume," Butler said.

"So we're to be our own masters," Pinckney said. "Those outside our famed little conclave may disagree."

Butler lifted his chin and looked disapprovingly at Pinckney down a long nose that buttressed a massive forehead. An Irishman born to a long line of nobility, Butler scorned wealth as a measure of stature. In his youth, he had served honorably in the British army and later as an officer in the struggle for independence of his adopted country. At forty-three, Butler saw himself as an elder statesman, and Sherman guessed that he disapproved of Pinckney's youthful impudence.

"We must go beyond our charter," Butler said. "Without a sound government, we'll soon be at each other's throats."

Sherman didn't voice his opinion that the Articles could be successfully revised. The innkeeper provided a timely distraction. Sherman ordered ale, soup, and a chicken potpie from the harried-looking man who seemed to be happily calculating the night's receipts as he wove his way back through the crowd.

Turning to Butler, Sherman said, "For eight years we fought the British to win our liberty. Now we risk throwing it all away. Europe watches, ready to pounce when we collapse into warring factions."

Butler looked pleased. "Exactly right. They wait to carve us into pieces."

Sherman always searched for broad areas of agreement before addressing specifics. He had little in common with these men, but despite their differences in temperament, wealth, and pedigree—and unlike the philosophical Virginians—Sherman believed he could deal with South Carolina. These men understood the give-and-take of politics.

Pinckney took a slow sip of ale and said carefully, "Roger, I'm surprised you're prepared to relinquish Connecticut's sovereignty."

"That's the challenge," Sherman said. "How do we increase national authority while retaining state sovereignty?"

"A Gordian knot. Do you believe it can be unraveled?"

"Not with the Virginia Plan."

Pinckney suddenly looked wary. Sherman wondered if he had overstepped. He didn't intend to disclose that he knew about South Carolina's commitment to Madison.

"The Virginia Plan is flawed," Butler interjected, "but it's a starting point. I'd feel more comfortable, however, if Jefferson were with the Virginians."

"I disagree," Pinckney said. "We might need Jefferson's words, but not Jefferson. He'd disparage all but his own schemes."

"Gentlemen, we don't need Jefferson or his elevated prose," Sherman said "Nor do we need rabble-rousers like Patrick Henry or Sam Adams."

"No fear of Henry darkening our chamber," Pinckney sneered. "He spurned his election as a delegate." Pinckney made a show of looking around the room. Then he lifted his nose and sniffed noisily. "He said he smelled a rat."

Butler made a tiny grimace and said, "Patrick fears we'll discard our revolutionary ideals for stability."

"I believe Henry stayed in Virginia so he can throw brickbats at our latticework when we return to seek sanction," Pinckney taunted.

"Just as well," Sherman said. "Our passions must abate so we can build a nation. This job is for realists, not revolutionaries—or philosophers."

"Men such as yourself, Roger?" Pinckney said with an edge.

"I'm here to represent my state. Unlike others, I have no grand scheme."

"Virginia provides desperately needed leadership," Butler said defensively.

"Leadership—or deception?" Sherman asked. "The interests of the large states differ from our respective states."

Butler looked dubious. "Our interests aren't common. The interests of New England and the South are as different as the interests of Russia and Turkey."

Sherman had brought the conversation to where he wanted it. "Perhaps our interests are more common than you suppose." He leaned toward Butler and lowered his voice. "There will be disappointments coming from the large state quarters."

"Surely you're not suggesting an alliance?" Butler asked.

"No, you've made commitments." Sherman shifted his gaze until he caught each man's eye. "Just remember to see me when you feel your vital interests threatened. Connecticut will work with the South on her sensitive issues."

Butler and Pinckney looked intrigued. That was enough for the moment. The innkeeper provided another opportune interruption by bringing Sherman his meal. He eagerly turned his attention to his soup and the inn's famous cornbread.

2

Tuesday, May 15, 1787

A quick motion drew James Madison's attention to the foyer of the Indian Queen. Roger Sherman stood in the entrance, shaking his rain-splattered cloak. Madison watched Sherman with delight and apprehension.

Gen. Washington followed Madison's gaze and remarked, "I see Connecticut sent Sherman."

"Yes," Madison responded. "We're one state closer to a quorum, but he'll fight our plan."

"Without a quorum, we remain idle," Washington said. "Far better to endure a few opponents than to never leave the stable. Our alliance will hold, Jemmy."

Madison feared the general underestimated Sherman. Many did. Sherman was a strange man. His big frame made him one of the few who could look Washington in the eye, but unlike the general, he did not carry himself with even elemental grace. He lacked wealth, dressed plainly, pulled his hair straight back with neither wig nor powder, and hid his humor behind a dour countenance. His big square face, thin lips, dark eyes, and expansive forehead gave the impression of a dullard plodding through a mediocre political career. Madison knew better. Despite his slovenly appearance, Sherman possessed a sharp wit, expansive knowledge, and decades of experience, both in his native Connecticut and on the national level. Madison held no illusions that he could alter Sherman's mission. The small states would fight mindlessly to protect their supposed sovereignty.

It troubled Madison when he saw Sherman sit down with South Carolina. He was a threat Madison would keep his eye on, but Washington was right: bringing Connecticut to the convention was far more important to the upcoming course of events.

Madison returned his attention to his dinner mates. On the other side of the table sat Robert Morris and Gouverneur Morris, both from Pennsylvania, related only by politics. Robert Morris, reputed to be the richest man in the United

States, revered Washington and stayed close to the general, both physically and politically. Gouverneur Morris, a stalwart champion of a strong central government, sat at the end of the table, allowing him to stretch his inflexible wooden leg and girth into the aisle. Thirty-five, talkative, wealthy, and brilliant, Gouverneur Morris usually got his way—in politics, in business, and with women.

Gouverneur Morris had also watched Sherman's entrance. "I wonder what Roger's purpose is with South Carolina?"

Robert Morris swiveled in his seat to look behind him. Watching Sherman squeeze in amongst the South Carolinians, he said, "I don't like this. Sherman likes to stay in the background, negotiating deals out of public sight. He'll do everything in his power to stop us. He's as cunning as the devil. If he suspects you're trying to bamboozle him, you might as well catch an eel by the tail."

"South Carolina will stay with us," Washington said. "Her western settlers are on a pivot, and the touch of a feather will turn them toward the Spanish."

Robert Morris turned back to Washington. "But will she remain steadfast when we address other issues?"

Robert Morris looked exactly like what he was, a wealthy financier: pudgy, with a serene round face well supported by an ample double chin. He exuded the confidence that came from a long line of accomplishments.

Washington took a thoughtful moment. "Connecticut and South Carolina differ in their manners, circumstances, and prejudices. I doubt Roger can find a common interest."

"If a common ground is to be found, he'll find it." Madison put a hand on his knee to quiet a jittery leg. "He's not easily managed." Glancing back toward Sherman, Madison added, "Roger relishes the process, not the outcome. I'm wary of men not guided by principle."

"You're too severe, Jemmy," Washington said. "In my dealings with Sherman, no man has shown a better heart or a clearer head."

"Perhaps," Robert Morris said, "but Sherman is extremely artful in getting his way. That makes him dangerous."

"My good sirs," Gouverneur Morris said jovially, "Connecticut has no more chance of hauling South Carolina to her side than I have of carrying Dr. Franklin to the State House. Sherman is fishing in a droughty pond."

Madison took comfort from Gouverneur Morris's droll assurance, but his unease persisted. He had put so much effort into this plan, worked so hard. He didn't need someone working the back channels to unravel his careful preparations.

The Virginia Plan—his plan—had been Madison's obsession for over a year. He had risked his health, labored to the point of exhaustion, and sacrificed his father's approval to define the essential elements of a new government. Now everything had come together in Philadelphia. He had a plan and he had the votes. Virginia and Pennsylvania represented the solid core of their alliance. Massachusetts and the Southern states assured a majority. South Carolina, as the leader of the Deep South, had to remain firmly tied to their cause.

Madison's greatest achievement sat beside him. When Washington arrived in Philadelphia two days ago, he had been greeted with ceremonial adulation. Three generals, two colonels, and the Light Horse Calvary had escorted him into a city of cheering throngs, exploding cannons, and pealing church bells. The people cherished their Revolutionary hero. Washington's fame was so broad and pure that his mere presence lent credibility and authority to the proceedings. Convincing him to attend had not been easy, but it was a crucial element of Madison's scheme to replace the Articles with a new type of government—one never before seen in world history.

Madison's thoughts brought him back to the issue they had been discussing. "Then we're all agreed. Robert will nominate the general for president of the convention?"

"This seems far too planned and arranged for my taste," Washington said. "Why not let the selection take its own course?"

Robert Morris took the assignment of convincing his reluctant friend. "General, you resisted coming to this convention in fear that it might be a debacle like last year at Annapolis. You decided that the risk to the country exceeded the risk to your reputation. Now that you're here, you must assume the position of leadership to avoid a disastrous outcome."

"Mr. Morris, I do not like to be manipulated."

"General, sir, we have no such—"

"You do, sirs," Washington broke in. "My reputation is far too important to squander on misadventures."

"General, we remain mindful of your reputation," Robert Morris added weakly.

"Mr. Madison and Mr. Jefferson argued for my attendance on the basis that the country was in dire jeopardy, and the convention needed my stature to draw delegates." Washington gave them each a hard stare. "I fulfilled that obligation. Now that you have me, you insist I assume the presidency. What if the vote doesn't go in my favor?"

"I've queried everyone who's arrived," Madison interjected. "I can assure you that you'll be elected overwhelmingly, perhaps unanimously."

"My dear general," Gouverneur Morris said, "your reputation is as safe as a homely maiden's virtue. Do not fear. Jemmy will ne'er squander his greatest asset."

Gouverneur Morris took more liberties with Washington than others dared, but he had learned the limit. He had once wagered that he could slap the general on the back in a hearty greeting but had suffered such a glaring reproach that he never mistook the bounds again.

Washington brooded for a long moment. Eventually, he said, "I agree, but on my terms. I'll preside over the deliberations but take no formal role in the debates. I want strict compliance to parliamentary procedures, and the debates must conform to gentleman's precepts. I'll make my views known, but only to individuals outside the formal gatherings. Is that acceptable?"

"Of course, General," Robert Morris responded for the group.

Washington turned a hard gaze on Madison. "Are you satisfied, Jemmy?"

Madison had urged Jefferson—serving as minister to France—to write letters beseeching Washington to attend the convention. Madison had always intended to convince the general to preside over the assemblage, once the general had committed.

He knew that the people around this table viewed him as their resident scholar, more theologian than practical politician—Jefferson's bright little friend who supplied the rationalization for what they wanted to do. They believed *they* were the experienced national leaders with the stature and temperament to win tough contests. Their attitude didn't distress him. His years in Congress and the Virginia Assembly taught him that his small frame, soft speaking voice, and tendency to argue from history and logic didn't impress seasoned politicians—men more comfortable bartering votes than changing minds. They failed to notice how often he set the stage for their grand appearances.

Madison ignored Washington's rebuff and responded to the general's conditions. "After your election, the convention will appoint a committee to prepare standing rules. George Wythe has agreed to serve, and I'm sure he'll be selected chairman. We can trust our fellow Virginian to follow the general's wishes."

Madison was about to address another sensitive subject, when two impeccably dressed gentlemen interrupted them.

"General, sir, sorry for the intrusion, but we wish to express our delight in seeing you once again lead our nation in this hour of peril."

Washington stood. "Gentlemen, may I introduce Lieutenant Colonel Elijah Vose and Major William Perkins. Both served with distinction in the Continental Army."

Everyone stood. Madison reflexively stepped back when their foul breath accosted him. The soldiers, wearing inane grins, had obviously imbibed well beyond the limit of a gentleman. The little ceremony had an awkward feel as chairs scraped and extended hands tangled, and the two officers gawked when Gouverneur Morris stiffly lurched onto his wooden leg.

"Excuse me, sir, did you lose your leg in service to your country?" Perkins got this out just before a tiny burp punctuated the query.

"Oh, my goodness, no," Morris said. "It embarrasses me to admit this to you fine soldiers, but I lost it jumping from a lady's balcony."

The officers, looking nonplussed, wavered slightly in a vain attempt to maintain erect posture.

With an impish grin, Washington said, "Yes, indeed, and the experience has sharpened his morals. He now works harder to control his illicit impulses."

"My dear general," Morris said, "you argue the point so handsomely that I'm tempted to part with the other leg."

All six men now enjoyed an easy laugh that erased the uncomfortable moment. Madison forced laughter to keep from spoiling the story. Morris had actually lost his leg in a carriage accident, but he savored his reputation as a rake, and this little scene had been played many times before.

"Gentlemen, before we part, I must correct your erroneous notion that I shall lead the Federal Convention," Washington said. "I'm a tired old soldier. We need men with far greater political skills than I to set our government right."

Vose blanched. "Excuse me, sir, but the situation is far too grave for dithering politicians." The man tried to steady his bearing, shuffled half a step, and, after catching himself, comically puffed himself up. "Many fine men have expended their estates, hazarded their lives, and sacrificed their families' needs in the service of our country. Now disorder and anarchy rule. The time has come for decisive action—action dictated by leaders with the will to suppress the rabble."

Washington's expression grew as stern as his voice. "This rabble, as you call them, is composed of our countrymen, who are trying to deal with problems not of their making. Our leaders must see themselves as servants of the people, not disciplinarians."

"Sir, we spent our youth as servants of the people, spilled our blood, and have come to know their miserly and ungrateful nature. Now they defy authority like unruly children," Perkins responded. He added in a rather nasty tone, "The country needs a strong taskmaster, one backed by a loyal army to impose his will."

Madison watched Washington turn crimson. When he spoke, Madison had never heard a colder voice. "May I remind you, a soldier's place is on the battlefield. In peacetime, a warrior may feel discarded, but his blood does not buy him the right to ration his countrymen's liberty. Good night, gentlemen."

Both officers rocked back on their heels. Vose somehow found enough composure to bow and say, "My apologies, General. Impatience prompted our rash comments. We shall leave you to your business."

With that, the two officers squared their shoulders, executed an awkward about-face, and departed with as little staggering as they could muster.

"Did that man threaten an overthrow by the military?" Robert Morris asked.

"I believe so," Gouverneur Morris said. "That young officer sounded as if he meant business."

Washington looked worried but simply said, "Yes, and let's do as the man suggested and return to ours."

3

Tuesday, May 15, 1787

"Land is the only measure of wealth," Pinckney said. "A man must be born to it, marry it, or swindle his way to it."

The Indian Queen's food matched the elegance of its dining room. As Sherman ate, he let the conversation drift to the weather and political gossip, but now Pinckney got himself into an argument with Butler that threatened to become heated.

"A man's birth right is not land, but family name," Butler said.

"A family name has less value than a bean if not propped up by land."

"Do you insult my family?"

"Of course not," Pinckney said. "I was merely trying to explain the fever for western lands."

"I understand the zeal, but land will not make backwoodsmen into gentlemen."

"Perhaps not in the first generation, but land can eventually make a gentleman," Pinckney said. "A gentleman, however, cannot make land—unless he uses his family name to marry it."

Butler looked furious, and Sherman began to feel uncomfortable. Subject to Irish primogeniture laws, which mandated that his father's estate must go to his older brother, Butler had sought his fortune in the British army and the colonies, where he had married the daughter of a rich plantation owner. Now he stood among the landed gentry of South Carolina, still wearing the epaulets of European nobility as if that were the true criterion for a gentleman.

Butler looked ready to stand. "Sir, you tread perilously close to offense— offense that a gentleman would be obliged to answer with honor."

Pinckney laughed uproariously. "Mr. Butler, please, I meant no offense. I myself court a rich man's daughter."

"If I may," Sherman interjected. "Your ideas would be unfamiliar in New England. Must land hold such importance?"

"Ships sink, factories burn," Pinckney said. "Land's permanent. Land conveys noble behavior to one's progeny, while a shipowner's descendents behave like seamen."

"You speak of the landed gentry with reverence," Sherman said. "Yet you champion the backcountry."

Pinckney gave a sideways glance at Butler. "We both own land on the frontier."

"Your plantations far exceed your western holdings," Sherman said.

"In value, not acreage," Butler said in an even tone that showed that he had shed his anger. "You can buy land in the frontier for pennies an acre. Surely you speculate yourself."

"Speculators buy or swindle land from other speculators, Indians, or others with dubious title. No one can unravel the conflicting claims." Sherman arranged his spoon beside his empty bowl. "I don't gamble."

"One day, some men will become incredibly wealthy," Butler said.

"The clever, the shrewd, and the corrupt," Pinckney added derisively.

Sherman suppressed his anger. "I'm more concerned with Connecticut's small landholders. Sheriff's auctions occur every week. Nearly a third of my state's farmers may lose their land."

"The frontier has small farmers as well," Pinckney sniffed, as if that settled the subject.

Sherman could not read Pinckney. The man reveled in playing the ill-mannered cynic but sometimes appeared as aristocratic as Butler. Did he disguise an elitist nature with effrontery, or did he hide behind his rank to subvert his class? Sherman was thankful when the conversation drifted to Philadelphia's notorious late-night amusements.

SHERMAN FINISHED ANOTHER ALE and decided to return to his room. In his youth he could have conversed the night away in noisy taverns, but now he had to husband his energy. He retrieved his cloak and stepped from the Indian Queen into a still night. When the door abruptly closed off the ribald din from the tavern, quiet encircled him. He lumbered slowly back to his boardinghouse.

The rain had mercifully stopped, but the people of Philadelphia remained indoors. Water dripped everywhere, so he moved to the center of the cobbled street, keeping his eyes down to avoid stepping in splattered horse droppings. Sherman marveled at the oil street lamps that threw a warm glow over the wet surfaces. He had read that Philadelphia had imported these globes from London, but he had not appreciated their utility until tonight.

Sherman took the long way back to Mrs. Marshall's house. His friends didn't understand his solitary walks, but he needed them to refresh his mood, test his convictions, forecast opponents' moves, and devise tactics. The muggy air dampened his heavy wool clothing and made it difficult to breathe. He didn't notice.

There was no doubt in his mind that the government must be strengthened. The nation couldn't defend itself nor manage its commerce. He believed that these problems could be rectified with a few simple changes to the Articles. Congress merely lacked the power to enforce its decisions. The states ignored national laws without penalty. He had proposed a set of amendments years ago, but the timing had not been right, the nation not ready. Sherman believed the timing of this convention matched the county's mood, but the Virginians were too ambitious. This plot to gratuitously dispose of the Articles and demolish the country's legitimate government must be stopped.

But he had misgivings. War loomed. Britain and Spain prodded his country's weaknesses. Barbary pirates preyed on American ships in the Mediterranean. Shays's Rebellion in Massachusetts had scared everyone.

Sherman felt heartsick as he watched the states rush toward internecine conflict and possible disintegration. The nation tottered on the brink of dissolution. A fresh approach appealed to many, but another false start might doom their republic. The brutal truth was that a government must govern—and this one did not.

Sherman arrived at his boardinghouse, still puzzling the issues. His landlady, a small, sharp-witted woman, had converted her home to a boardinghouse after the death of her husband. Once a wealthy merchant's home, the now threadbare house was large and comfortable. Startled by the cost of these modest quarters, Sherman had soon discovered that Philadelphia's heady commerce, rather than his landlady's avarice, had dictated the price.

Entering the central hall, he tried to be quiet so as to not disturb the other guests.

"I hope you had an enjoyable evening, Mr. Sherman."

He stopped at the parlor door. "Yes, Mrs. Marshall. Thank you."

She sat comfortably in the room's best chair, knitting something Sherman couldn't identify. "You gentlemen have some serious work ahead of you. How long before you start?"

"A while yet. I think it's safe for you to plan on our boarding with you for many weeks, perhaps the summer."

"Thank you. I'd appreciate any notice you can give about when you might depart. Please let me know if there's anything I can do to make your stay more comfortable."

"I'd appreciate an additional chair in my room."

"If I move the chair from the room reserved for Mr. Ellsworth, would that suffice?" Oliver Ellsworth was another Connecticut delegate, yet to arrive.

"That should be fine." Sherman took half a step into the room. "May I ask a question?"

"Certainly."

"What do you hope will come from our convention?"

"Why ask me?"

"I don't like to decide weighty issues without discussing them with an intelligent woman."

"Do you discuss political matters with your wife?"

"She is my sole confidant."

"Then I suggest you write her a letter. I don't involve myself in politics nor in religion. Today, my house is filled with Presbyterians, Cincinnati, and delegates. Tomorrow will bring others with different affairs."

"I understand."

"There's a *Pennsylvania Journal* on the table. It contains an article on your conference. You may take it to your room to read, if you return it for other guests."

Walking to the table, Sherman said, "I'm curious about what people think, not newspapers."

"What *common* people think? We think about food and shelter. Simple things, things you probably don't understand."

"I understand. I'm not rich. But surely you have other aspirations?"

"When my husband died, his partner took the business. I didn't even receive a share of the profit from the enterprises he'd already started. All I have is this house. I'm not complaining; I'm lucky compared to many widows." Then with a taunting look, she added, "But if you wish to please me, move the capital from New York to Philadelphia."

"I want to please all my countrymen."

"I'm sure you gentlemen will figure it out. You don't need the advice of a mere woman."

She punctuated this last with a return to her knitting that closed the conversation. Sherman took the cue and made his way to his sparsely furnished quarters. As he ascended the stairs, the landing above suddenly went black. Purposely trudging with a heavier step, Sherman made a guttural noise.

A voice floated from the dark. "Excuse me, sir, I thought everyone had retired. Just a moment."

Sherman heard the strike of a tinder pistol. A small light flitted like a firefly, and then a lamp grew a flame to light the landing. Sherman saw shadows dance across an indistinct ebony face as the man bent over to replace the glass chimney. Finished with his task, the man straightened. He seemed to unwind forever and finally stood a full head taller than Sherman's six foot two.

"I'm Howard. I help Mrs. Marshall with the house. I apologize for the inconvenience."

"Not necessary," Sherman said, extending his hand. "I'm Roger Sherman, a delegate to the convention."

"Pleased to meet you," Howard said, apparently surprised by the proffered hand. "May I light the candles in your room?"

"Please. The room is still foreign to me."

Howard was tall and thin, like a slender reed reaching for the sun. Sherman waited in the hall until Howard lit a candle in his room. As a whiff of beeswax reached the doorway, the servant crossed the room and banished dark from another corner. Sherman marveled at how the tall black man moved with such physical assurance.

"Thank you. I appreciate your thoughtfulness."

"Let me know if there's anything else I can do to make your stay more pleasant. I can bring tea to your room in the afternoons."

"I'll keep that in mind."

"Is there anything else this evening?"

"No, thank you, Howard. I'll mention your courtesy to Mrs. Marshall."

"Quite unnecessary. Good night, sir."

Howard departed from the room with no more noise than a cat. Sherman, who had the grace of a pregnant sow, envied Howard's comfort with his tall body. He already liked the man, which made him feel better about his accommodations. His conversation with Mrs. Marshall had disappointed him. He normally related well to people he encountered. Sherman hoped her cooking would make up for her sour temperament.

His room possessed two luxuries he appreciated: a rope bed with a good feather mattress and a stuffed wing chair situated by a window, both well used but serviceable. The only other furnishings were a small writing shelf, a straight-backed chair, and a scuffed-up chest of drawers. Pegs on the wall sufficed to hang his few items of clothing, and when he looked under the bed, he found the requisite chamber pot.

Sherman wasn't impoverished, but he used care with his limited funds. Like many patriots, he had contributed his savings to the Revolutionary cause. He didn't regret his lack of wealth because his wants were few. Honor loomed far larger in his estimation than personal extravagance. He had his religious faith, a large family, and the respect of his countrymen. For over forty years, he had held public office and, in that time, he had learned how to win his way among men with far more wealth and fame.

He hung his cloak on a wall peg and turned the ladder-back chair sideways to the writing shelf so he could cross his long legs. After settling, he pulled the candle closer to cast more light on the newspaper. The editor was positive toward the convention and negative on the nation's state of affairs. The conclusion read, "Upon the event of this great council depends everything that can be essential to the stability of the nation. The future depends on this momentous undertaking." The editor shared his sense of import, but the article presented no unusual viewpoint, nor did it offer any solutions.

He tossed the paper aside. Mrs. Marshall's admonition to write his wife reminded him that his evening remained unfinished. He had married Rebecca three years after his first wife died. He had been forty, while she had just celebrated her twentieth birthday. Sherman couldn't have asked for a better partner, either political or domestic. But Rebecca believed that he had sacrificed enough for his country and needed to stay close to home to rebuild an estate for his family. Although Sherman didn't disagree, Connecticut needed him in Philadelphia, not New Haven. He just hoped this business would go quickly. He didn't have many remaining years to provide for his family.

He extracted writing materials and several sheets of paper from a worn valise. He sat quiet for many minutes. Eventually, he dipped his pen into the inkwell and struck the first words.

Dearest Rebecca,

I have arrived safe, but I do not feel safe. Desperate and able men have gathered for a tense contest that will determine our county's future. There will be no rules, no precedents, no arbitrator. God grant me the wisdom do what is right…

4

Tuesday, May 15, 1787

Madison had felt annoyed ever since the two impolite officers had stumbled out of the Indian Queen. He mentally shook off his irritation, leaned forward, and said, "The Rules Committee must decide whether the proceedings are to be public or private."

"Private," Robert Morris answered instantly.

"I agree," added Washington. "If we're to have any chance of success, we must debate openly, without a gallery, and without the press exciting the people or the Congress."

"Shroud our proceedings in secrecy?" Gouverneur Morris said. "Are we sure it's necessary?"

"Public sentiment is against a strong national government," Madison said. "The delegates need to hear the whole design and debate it without the interference of public passion."

"And our plan will threaten Congress," Robert Morris sniffed.

"Private then," Gouverneur Morris conceded. "Our self-important Congress feels threatened enough. No need to add to their weighty burdens."

Madison expected that many would be stunned at the audacity of their plan. Persuading a majority to support their scheme would take time and seclusion from outside influence.

"Then we're all agreed?" Robert Morris asked.

"Yes." Washington looked at Madison. "Tell Mr. Wythe that the proceedings are to remain secret until we make our final report."

"Of course, sir, but I have a concern. Dr. Franklin always says that three may keep a secret if two are dead."

"Good point, young man," Gouverneur Morris said. "We must put the fear of God into the delegates."

Washington leaned conspiratorially close. "No, gentlemen, not the fear of God—fear of the Society of the Cincinnati."

"Our two visitors?"

"They are but a reminder. As president of the society, I attended early meetings. When I saw the mood, I distanced myself, pleading other obligations. The danger is real, gentlemen. Many of their number believe a military coup d'état offers the only salvation."

"Surely cooler heads will prevail."

"Perhaps, but it would be a grievous error to count on it. Shays was one of their own. His rebellion might spark others, but I believe they'll bide their time as long as I lead the convention."

"You believe that will hold them off?" Gouverneur Morris asked.

Washington spoke in a low voice. "Yes, along with secrecy." Washington met everyone's eyes. "Gentlemen, if they know our path and disapprove, they'll take action."

"This is indeed disquieting. How do we inform the other delegates without causing panic?" Gouverneur Morris said.

"Individually," Madison said. "Each delegate must believe that he is the sole recipient of this privileged and clandestine information. Each must swear to speak naught of it."

"But they will. It will be relayed in hushed tones in taverns and coffee-houses."

"That will further two aims: the election of the general as president and acceptance of secrecy," Madison said.

"Jemmy's right," Washington said. "We can hardly announce the threat in open assembly. Are we all agreed?"

Everyone nodded their heads, but the table assumed a foreboding mood.

"If I may, I have one more issue." Madison shifted uncomfortably in his seat. "Are we sure we want Edmund Randolph to present the Virginia Plan?"

Washington gave Madison a stern look. "Jemmy, we've covered this ground. Randolph has a rightful claim to present the plan. As the governor, he is the senior member of our delegation."

Madison found this statement disingenuous. Randolph held the office of governor, but everyone, from delegate to newspaper vendor, knew that Washington was the real power in the Virginia delegation. Madison held no illusion that Washington would present the plan—his poor delivery made him a reluctant speaker—but Madison had hoped to persuade the general to appoint someone stronger than the weak-willed Randolph to this weighty task.

It wasn't their first time discussing such matters. The seven members of the Virginia delegation had met privately each morning and then joined the Pennsylvanians at three in the afternoon for dinner. There was a difference, however, between building agreement between the two delegations and this confidential discussion with the leaders.

Madison believed his mission both crucial and right. The United States experiment must not fail. He knew, was certain in his heart, that the fifteen resolves in the Virginia Plan encompassed the necessary characteristics for a republic to endure, defend itself, and protect the liberty of its citizens. This mighty objective stoked his ambition and excused his connivance.

This lofty—no, noble—goal required ample cunning to bind the conflicting interests of the states. If Gen. Washington presided, and they carefully directed the committees, then nothing should take them by surprise. There would be setbacks—fierce resistance from some quarters—but momentum and common need would propel events along the desired course. He relaxed and sat back in his chair, confident that the convention could be controlled to his ends.

THEIR BUSINESS SETTLED, THE general and Robert Morris prepared to leave. The owner of the Indian Queen appeared instantly.

Bowing respectfully, he asked, "Gentlemen, is there anything else you desire... another ale, tea and cakes, a plate of cheese? We have excellent cognacs."

"No, no," Morris said. "We're ready to retire. Thank you for your hospitality."

The innkeeper never looked at Morris; instead he aimed a witless grin at Washington. "My pleasure. The general's always welcome at the Indian Queen."

All evening, Madison had found the innkeeper's solicitous behavior irritating. Now he was amused by his inadvertent slight toward the rest of the party. Washington often elicited bumbling adulation.

"Thank you," Washington said, with a regal nod of the head. "We'll be in Philadelphia for a spell, so we'll visit your fine establishment again."

"Yes, the Federal Convention. A noble endeavor. My best wishes."

"And what might those wishes be?" Washington asked.

"My wishes? Oh my. Yes, well, I suppose I... uh... yes... I, uh, wish you gentlemen great success."

When the innkeeper recalled the incident for friends, relatives, and customers, his answer would undoubtedly be eloquent and coherent. He would tell everyone that the great general George Washington had asked for his advice and that he had responded with sage counsel.

Washington betrayed nothing. Looking genuinely interested, he said, "Success comes in many guises. Do you support a strong federal government?"

Now, the innkeeper looked nervous. "Dear General, with deepest respect, I don't think so. I, uh... well, I work hard, all day and well into the night. Please excuse me—sir, I don't mean to be impertinent—but taxes already lighten my purse. A larger government will surely demand more money. I see no benefit."

Washington looked like he was mulling over a new concept. "Taxes are a congenital disease of government. The country, however, suffers from many ills that I believe only a strong federal government can cure."

"Philadelphia seems unaffected by these ills. People prosper, trade flourishes, and our vigorous commerce supports many public works. In time, the rest of the country will follow our lead." Then, with a little stronger voice, the innkeeper added, "Most of our problems emanate from politicians. They already meddle too much."

Madison found the man's newfound tongue intriguing. His purse obviously held greater import than the risk of offending the great hero of the Revolution.

Washington looked contemplative. "You make valid points, sir. I appreciate your forthrightness. Philadelphia, however, is unique in its enviable position. The rest of the nation won't adopt your sound principles as long as state sovereignty reigns uppermost. Your fine city may provide a radiant example, but not a solution."

"Dear General, I believe we can lead the nation far better than New York. Move the nation's capital from that cow pasture to Philadelphia. We deserve no less. Only London has a larger English-speaking population."

Washington bestowed upon the innkeeper a thin smile as he stood to leave. "Thank you, sir, for your views. Balancing the interests of our varied populace will present us with a challenge."

With a slight bow, the innkeeper asked, "Shall I present the bill?"

"Charge it to my quarters, please," Madison said, as he pushed away from the table.

For the first time, the innkeeper turned his attention to someone other than the general. "Of course, sir. James Madison, correct?"

"Yes," Madison said. "I'd be grateful if you itemized the account." Madison nodded to the innkeeper. "Thank you, we had a wonderful evening."

Washington treated everyone with courtesy, despite flaws in opinion or character. He seemed to like everyone he encountered. Madison thought this a splendid attribute for a politician, but it was one he didn't share with the general. As he said good night to his companions, he reminded himself to check the bill carefully.

AFTER THEIR GROUP BROKE up, Madison headed for his room. So many tavern guests had unobtrusively made their way to the exit that the place suddenly seemed to have grown quiet. He knew that some had left to visit one of Philadelphia's notorious bawdy houses, while others may have arranged late-night liaisons with more respectable women. Madison's passions drove him in a different direction.

His apartment was located on the third floor. He bounded up the stairs two at a time. As he reached his landing, an Argand lamp cast a bright glow down the hall. This recent Swiss invention produced ten times the light of a conventional whale oil lamp. Madison made a mental note to buy several for Montpelier and another for Jefferson. This thought reminded him that he wanted to write his friend a letter.

Madison held no doubts. Republics had come and gone throughout history. The challenge was not to forge a republic, but to build one that would endure. The key to a lasting republic was the design. Studying other republics, he had paid special attention to their structure, looking for the flaws that accelerated their demise. The Virginia Plan held the ingredients of a republic for the ages. Now, at long last, it was all about to begin. Thinking in a rush, he had a letter to Jefferson composed in his head by the time he entered his room.

Madison's room was small but pleasing, with an unobstructed view of the Delaware River and the Jersey shore. The furniture included a comfortable bed, a bureau, a writing table with drawers, a large looking glass, stuffed chairs, and two nicely framed oil paintings on the walls. A handsome night cabinet, pushed into a far corner, hid the chamber pot. Today's newspaper and London magazines were splayed across the table.

Shrugging off his coat, he immediately went to the writing table. He spent a minute arranging the ink, the paper, and his thoughts.

The sound of the town crier in the street below disturbed his concentration. "Ten o'clock and weather clear, ten o'clock and weather clear." This Philadelphia tradition irritated him. All night long his sleep would be interrupted on the hour by this rhythmical chant. He hoped time would numb his awareness of the intrusion.

He looked at his ink-stained hand, pen poised to strike the first letter. Madison had never been to Europe, so the idea of communicating to France fascinated him. How he wished he could just talk to Jefferson. The hopes and aspirations they had shared for over a decade were about to come to fruition.

The pen suddenly leaped to life, filling Madison's ears with the familiar and reassuring sound of a quill scratching paper.

Dear Tom,

In a few days, we shall begin at long last to build our republic. If men were angels, no government would be necessary. If angels were to govern men, no controls on government would be necessary...

5

Wednesday, May 16, 1787

"Perhaps I should cease boring you with political matters."

"On the contrary, we need to work together," Paterson said. "Something you've refused to do in the past."

Sherman and William Paterson of New Jersey sat in Mrs. Marshall's parlor. They had met at Sherman's boardinghouse to plot a strategy for the convention.

Sherman tried to look sympathetic. "Our hands are full with the rebellion by our western settlers against Pennsylvania. Times are too tense to engage another state."

New York was using her harbor to extort unreasonable taxes from both Connecticut and New Jersey. When nothing came of New Jersey's request to Congress for redress, New Jersey had quit contributing taxes to the national government and asked Connecticut to join her in an armed offensive against New York. Connecticut had declined.

"Until stopped by force, New York will continue to pillage our treasury."

"The convention can strengthen the government so it can deal with such matters."

"Such talk scares me. Roger, the Virginians advance sedition."

"William, you go too—"

"You aren't suggesting that we withhold criticism of their corrupt scheme?"

"Of course not. You're right to harbor fears, but casting dispersions on their proposal won't be enough."

"We must expose their treachery. Their treason!" Paterson got up and paced the room. "Honor demands that we stop them. Stop the theft of our state sovereignty, stop the theft of our liberty, and stop the theft of our purse."

Sherman glanced toward the door. "William, please lower your voice. Other guests may be within earshot."

Paterson gave Sherman a long stare. The lawyer was forty-one and wore short-cropped hair without a wig unless he was in court. Well-proportioned facial features decorated a small head perched on a stumpy body. His perpetually pinched mouth and disapproving eyes gave people the impression of an earnest clergyman searching for a moral blemish to reprimand. In fact, he was an aggressive prosecutor who preferred much more earthly punishments.

Sherman gestured toward the chair opposite his own. "William, please sit. I agree, we need to stop their plan, but we must proceed with stealth. An enemy forewarned is an enemy forearmed."

Paterson stopped pacing. "I don't believe you see the threat as clearly as I do."

"I see the threat as imminent and frightening, but beating back the Virginians will take more than shouting."

Paterson rested his hands on his ample hips. "What do you propose?"

"We need a plan of our own."

Paterson hesitated, and then the muscles in his face relaxed. "What sort of plan?"

"One that protects our sovereignty."

Paterson sat down. "That'll take time—and allies."

"We must gain time. If Madison is allowed to rush the convention, we're doomed." Sherman spoke as if a new thought had occurred to him. "What about a Committee of the Whole?"

"That would buy us time and force the Virginians to disclose their full scheme." Paterson uncrossed his legs and leaned forward. "Can we get it?"

"I'll petition Gen. Washington."

"He won't help. He leads the Virginians."

"He'll be elected president of the convention and probably leader of the new government. He's already thinking about governing after the new system is approved, and he knows he'll need support from our states." Sherman leaned in conspiratorially, as if confiding to a close friend. "I believe the general will consider arguments that mollify opponents. I'll approach him today."

"New Jersey and Connecticut cannot stand alone."

"Delaware will join us," Sherman said, turning to see who had just entered the parlor.

"May I bring you gentleman tea?" The interruption came from Mrs. Marshall's rangy Negro servant.

"No, thank you, Howard. We must leave soon." Then Sherman impulsively asked, "How long have you worked for Mrs. Marshall?"

"All my life, sir. I first worked for her husband in the shipyard before his death. Now I help Mrs. Marshall with her guests."

"You certainly didn't acquire your deportment in the shipyards. How were you educated?"

"Mr. Marshall took me in when I was twelve. He taught me himself. Each evening he gave me a lesson and encouraged me to learn more on my own."

"Mr. Marshall sounds like a fine man," Sherman said.

Howard flashed a self-deprecating smile. "I suspect he didn't want a big dumb youngster hanging around his dock."

"I'm sure he had grander motives."

Howard stood slightly straighter. "Mr. Marshall was a great man. Many didn't appreciate him because he was a hard taskmaster, but he was fair to those who were loyal and worked hard."

"You're a credit to his character. I'm sorry I didn't have an opportunity to meet him."

"That's a compliment he would have appreciated." Howard bowed his head slightly. "If you gentlemen are content, I have other chores." Looking self-conscious, Howard turned and disappeared into the central hall.

Sherman returned his attention to Paterson, only to find him wearing an expression meant to convey extreme impatience.

"I'm sorry for the interruption," Sherman said. "My curiosity sometimes distracts me from important affairs. We should leave or we'll be late for Dr. Franklin's party."

SHERMAN AND PATERSON LEFT Mrs. Marshall's and walked up Third Street toward Dr. Franklin's house. Sherman marveled at Philadelphia's size and rapid expansion. One of the largest freshwater ports in the world drove the city's prosperity. Philadelphia had been a cultural nucleus since colonial times, but it had grown into the commercial, banking, insurance, and transportation center for the young country.

Construction seemed to burst from every street corner. In late afternoon, when most cities started to quiet down, Philadelphia still rang with hammers and the shouts of men ordering up materials. Elegant carriages squeezed through the streets between wagons carrying lumber, bricks, and goods from around the world. Sherman knew that only darkness would calm the frantic activity.

When they reached Market Street, Paterson touched Sherman's forearm. "I saw you with the South Carolinians. Surely you don't expect to sway their vote?"

Sherman tried to suppress his irritation at having his thoughts interrupted. "Not until events develop further. Our common interests are few, but we each have parochial interests that don't tread on each other's affairs. They can be bartered."

"Don't expect much from South Carolina. Charleston, like New York, extorts an import tax from her neighbors. She'll be unsympathetic to our commercial interests."

Sherman didn't argue the point. Politicians who fixated on a single issue bewildered him. He didn't believe in limiting his options, and he knew that South Carolina could eventually prove useful. His job, however, was not to teach legislative skills but to represent his state.

Market Street was a novelty. Stretching all the way from the docks, a series of narrow stalls ran down the center of the thoroughfare. Tradesmen, merchants, and itinerant vendors peddled every imaginable type of goods in the tiny cubicles. Bustling foot traffic clogged the streets, so experienced Philadelphians directed their horses and carriages along other routes.

In the middle of a block of four-story houses, a stately iron gate marked the entrance to Franklin's hidden courtyard. The gate stood open, but a liveried servant kept the curious at bay. Sherman and Paterson passed unchallenged into an arched alleyway that tunneled through the brick townhouses facing the street's hectic activity. Once they emerged into open air, an odd building stood between them and Franklin's house. The three-story structure had an arched hole in the center that lined up with the passageway they had just walked through. From previous visits, Sherman knew that it was a print shop Franklin had built for his son.

After they passed through the tunnel-like opening, they could see Franklin's handsome home built in the exact center of the busy city block. The groomed gravel walkways, gardens, and manicured grass plots always startled first-time visitors who did not expect an oasis of solitude in the heart of the biggest city in the United States. Sherman saw scattered knots of people in private conversation, but he guided Paterson around to the opposite side of the house, where they found a large crowd gathered under Franklin's famed mulberry tree.

The sound of light laughter came from the circle of people surrounding Franklin. "Everyone seems in a festive mood," Sherman said.

"You'd think we were here to celebrate a wedding, not to annul a nation's faithful compact."

Sherman excused himself and gratefully moved to engage other delegates.

"Have you actually seen a balloon aloft?"

"Oh, yes," said Franklin. "Outside of Paris. Over a hundred thousand people gathered to watch. They nearly rioted during the long preparation, but when it finally lifted, it was magnificent, and the crowd gave a hearty cheer."

Benjamin Franklin sat in his place of honor, surrounded by admirers. Sherman liked and respected Franklin but hadn't seen him in many years. He was saddened to see that he had grown old and trunched in a bulbous body that seemed fixed to the chair. Gout rendered the doctor nearly immobile. A bald pate ringed in white locks above an irreverent grin gave him a mischievous air that belied his plain Quaker dress.

After days of wet gray, the sparkling blue sky had refreshed everyone's spirits and enlivened the conversation. Sherman nodded greetings to several of the delegates, one of whom told him that the discussion had been prompted by someone admiring a balloon brooch worn by Sarah Bache, Franklin's daughter.

Mrs. Bache and her family lived with the doctor, and she served as hostess at his social affairs. She had gained a good share of notoriety during the Revolution by going from door to door to solicit donations. Many men thought the war had confused women and hoped that peace would quickly resettle them into their customary role.

"I wish I could see a real balloon," Mrs. Bache said. "Do you think we'll have them in America?"

"Of course," Franklin said. "England already has balloonists, and we shall have ours, if for no other purpose than to annoy the masters of the British Empire."

"Can anyone ascend with a balloonist?" Madison asked.

Sherman noticed that Madison sat in one of the privileged chairs close by the great doctor.

"Some take passengers. The price is outrageous, but nevertheless it's the rage. You'll not find me, however, venturing into the boundless sky. The thrill of watching is enough for this foolish old man." Franklin wore an impish grin. "How about you, Jemmy, would you fly amongst the birds with these adventurers?"

"Perhaps. I want to see a few flights first ... but I think I might go. I understand weight is crucial, so surely they'd provide me a favorable price. "

Some wag's portrayal of Madison as "no bigger than half a piece of soap," had spread quickly. Sherman thought Madison's self-deprecation clever.

Franklin laughed. "Take care, dear boy. They may mistake you for one of their bags of sand and toss you out."

At this cheerful moment, the crowd parted as if on command. George Washington and Gouverneur Morris broke the outer circle and advanced to greet their host. Both cut a wide swath: the tall, stately Washington by his demeanor and Morris by his wide-swinging wooden leg.

Washington gave a slight bow. "Dr. Franklin, I see you're again moderating merriment and good fellowship."

"We're talking about ballooning. You were a surveyor in your youth. Do you think balloons will allow one surveyor to do the job of twenty?"

As with many aspiring young men, Sherman had also been a surveyor. He had heard about the balloon craze sweeping Europe but had failed to see why they captivated people's attention. The possibility of surveying from the air had never occurred to him—the idea seemed implausible. Still, the question showed him that he had not considered the implications of this new science.

"I'm more concerned with the use of balloons in war," Washington responded.

"That's why the British are so keen to have their own balloonists," Franklin said. "Much inventiveness is prompted by their rivalry with the French. Inventiveness and chicanery. We must keep a wary eye on both. And the Spanish as well. We're but a small, weak child in a world filled with ravenous giants."

"The French are our friends," interjected Mrs. Bache. "Surely with them on our side, we need not fear the British?"

Glancing at Mrs. Bache's Parisian dress, Washington said, "The French will be on our side as long as we oppose the British and buy French goods. We can't assume that we'll align with France forever."

"Unfortunately, the money to purchase foreign goods grows scarce," Franklin said. "Our general justly worries about the defense of our new nation, but we must delay this discussion. We'll have plenty of time to resolve issues once the convention starts. This simple old man foresees a future bright with marvelous innovations, stunning fashions, and liberty unshackled from European intrigue."

"My dear doctor," said Gouverneur Morris, "your views refresh my worrisome soul. Perhaps, when our sessions get stormy, you can use your wit, like your famous lightning rod, to dissipate the negative energy." Morris added with a wink, "Little Jemmy's grand innovation may not rise as easily as one of those celebrated balloons."

SHERMAN FOLLOWED WASHINGTON WHEN he saw the general move away from the crowd.

"General, may I have a private moment?"

"Of course, Mr. Sherman."

They stepped around the corner of Franklin's home to a quiet spot. As Washington faced him, Sherman marveled at his immaculate dress. The buff and blue colors had a hint of the military without looking martial. Washington's shoes glistened with a luster that could only come from fastidious care. Sherman couldn't help but glance at his own scuffed footwear.

"What's on your mind, Roger?"

"As I'm sure you're aware, many of the small states feel uneasy about the plan that Gouverneur Morris alluded to. Perhaps we're unduly apprehensive, but fear is the handmaiden of the unknown."

"I gather you have a specific request?"

"I believe a Committee of the Whole will alleviate anxiety and hold the convention together at its crucial beginning."

"Is there a threat to bolt the convention?"

"I didn't mean to imply that."

Washington only stared in response.

Sherman tried to regain the initiative. "A Committee of the Whole is a standard practice for delicate issues. It would be seen as a sign of fairness and would engender goodwill."

Washington looked thoughtful. Sherman knew he was calculating. A Committee of the Whole, like any committee, could not pass resolutions but only report out recommendations. Declaring the entire assemblage a committee created something like a rehearsal. As issues were debated and voted on, the parliamentary device would expose strategies and the strength of coalitions. A second vote would be required when the Committee of the Whole dissolved and the actual convention reconvened.

A long moment elapsed before Washington spoke. "If I agree to support you in this, will you promise to argue for careful reflection by the hesitant states? More important, and crucial to my support, will you keep Connecticut at the convention?"

Now it was Sherman's turn for silent contemplation. He knew the proposition would carry a price, but he hadn't expected it to be so personal. If he agreed, he would have to represent the small states' views, while arguing for their continued consideration of the plan: a difficult thread to weave.

"You have my word, General."

"Good. Then I will use my feeble influence to get a Committee of the Whole."

Sherman smiled. "I'm sure your feeble influence will be sufficient. You undoubtedly will be president of the convention."

"That's a responsibility I neither seek nor covet. The convention must make its own choice."

"General, this convention needs your leadership to garner the support and energy necessary for our great task. Surely you won't decline?"

Washington turned his back to Sherman and walked two paces. He stood there a second and then spoke without turning around. "Others have made your argument." Another hesitation. "I will not decline, but I'll consent with great reluctance." The general appeared to have a new thought and turned back to face Sherman. "If a draft does ensue, will you encourage the small states to support my candidacy?"

Was this another condition for a Committee of the Whole?

"General, I'd be honored to urge your election to my fellow delegates. I believe it both necessary and richly deserved."

"Thank you, Roger. I appreciate your confidence."

As Washington turned to other guests, Sherman wondered who had got the better of the exchange.

SHERMAN MIGRATED WITH OTHERS toward the dining room. A servant with a deep melodic voice had delivered the call to supper. No one hesitated. The aromas had roused people's appetites, and all the guests were anxious to experience one of Franklin's famed dinners. Book-lined walls, expensive rugs, beautifully crafted furniture, and a perfectly arranged table promised a refined meal. Six uniformed black servants stood silently against the wall as the guests milled around, looking for their name placards.

Sherman took his assigned seat and looked down from his end of the table toward Franklin and his daughter. Americans thought of Benjamin Franklin as a diplomat and philosopher. In Europe, his reputation as a scientist gave him entry into the most exclusive circles. Women found him charming and attentive. In Philadelphia, many admired him for his wealth and business acumen. Most of the delegates, however, didn't take Franklin seriously. They loved his hospitality but grew tired of his anecdotal manner and believed his political skills enfeebled. He had grown old and had been out of the country far too long.

Sherman disagreed. He vowed to watch him carefully.

The guests quieted as the servants disappeared. Once everyone had settled, Franklin tapped his glass, saying, "Welcome, and thank you all. You delight an old man with your presence. This convention is a momentous occasion, one that will challenge us. This afternoon, however, remember that our convention has not yet started, so there is no need to bore ourselves with talk of politics. Enjoy yourself, eat heartily, and freshen old acquaintanceships. We're about to engage in an arduous endeavor. Let us approach it with camaraderie and cheer. I'd now like to offer a small prayer to inaugurate our auspicious undertaking and this distinguished gathering."

At the end of Franklin's short prayer, the servants emerged in pairs, one carrying a large tureen, while the other bore a soup ladle as if it were a scepter. The servants paused just long enough for the rich aroma to waft through the room, and then swiftly dispersed to three points around the table to eloquently ladle a portion of cod chowder to each guest. The table, already set with breads and porter, suddenly became a tangle of reaching arms, clinking glasses, and genial conversation.

After the first course, Franklin again gained everyone's attention. He remained seated but spoke in an engaging manner, as if talking to each guest individually.

"Prior to our next course, I wish to propose a toast." Franklin looked up and down the long table. "I hope great good from our meeting. Failure will strengthen the opinion of some political writers that popular governments cannot support themselves."

Raising his porter, Franklin said in a slightly louder voice, "To our company of delegates, men of character and ability. May they work in harmony and with unerring wisdom to grant us an energetic republican government."

The guests shouted, Hear! Hear! and other affirmative noises from every corner of the room, as they raised their glasses in toast and acknowledgment of their host.

Once again, the six servants reappeared with a flourish, each bearing a platter of oysters. This time they dispersed to six points around the table, bowed slightly in unison, and then extended the platters to guests.

Sherman looked around at his dinner companions. He had been seated with the delegations from New Jersey and Delaware.

George Read, of Delaware, following his gaze, said, "Strange that they seated us together. I'd have thought the Pennsylvanians would have wanted to keep us apart."

"They don't fear us talking to each other; they fear us talking to those who might waver," Sherman said.

"You believe they're plotting the convention?" Read asked.

"Of course," Sherman answered matter-of-factly, his attention on the other end of the table. Talent seemed disproportionately distributed to the large states. Sherman wanted to see who conversed with intimate camaraderie, who inclined their heads with conspiratorial intent, and who seemed argumentative.

Paterson ignored Sherman's obvious distraction. "We cannot allow the large states to dictate the proceedings. We must fight."

"Not the early moves. The Virginians are too well organized. We'd lose." Turning his full frame to face his dinner companions, Sherman explained, "The general will be a fair presiding officer, and his election cannot be stopped in any case. If the rules reported out tilt in their favor, we'll have an opportunity to challenge them or quit a treacherous affair with honor." Sherman looked directly at Paterson. "Most important, we don't have an alternative plan. We must begin working on one immediately."

Paterson's eyes blazed. "We must challenge them immediately. Why wait to write a plan?"

"Because we have no choice," Sherman answered. "The Virginians, and their friends from Pennsylvania, have the votes to control the early days of the convention."

"Then we ought to go home. They can't form a government without us."

"Of course they can," Sherman said. "And without our participation, it will surely match your worst fears."

"Then we'll reject it."

"Connecticut isn't ready to go it alone. The wisest course is for us to concentrate on designing a superior plan—one acceptable to the states and to Congress."

"I don't like passivity," Paterson said. "Do you know what's in their plan?"

"Only the same rumors you've heard. But I know their inclinations and Madison's mind. The plan will be far too ambitious."

Washington interrupted their conversation to offer another toast. "To the good doctor, since no one entertains more respect for your character, none can salute you with more sincerity. Thank you for this enchanting afternoon."

As glasses were again raised, the six servants swept back into the room, bearing huge platters of pork, roasted beef, turkey, and chicken pieces. Each platter had a ring of potatoes, squash, and asparagus surrounding the meats. Even as a provincial New Englander, Sherman knew this opulent display of meat was uniquely American, a way of celebrating their new abundance and escape from European scarcity. He suspected that Franklin served a different meal to his friends visiting from Europe.

Paterson fidgeted beside him and then said angrily, "My instructions won't allow me to participate in any scheme that threatens to dissolve the states." Sherman noted that Paterson's jaw jutted out so far, he could hang a lantern on it. "We cannot sit idle."

Sherman sighed. "For the moment, we must allow the Virginians to believe that they control events. Our initial strategy must be to simply present our views without threat. Meanwhile, we prepare, and then act when we can startle and bewilder their coalition."

Read looked uncomfortable. "This intrigue is beyond my skills and temperament. Delaware needs Dickinson in Philadelphia. I intend to write him this evening and urge him to hurry."

"Excellent," Sherman said. "John can add weight to our side."

John Dickinson was an old friend and political compatriot. Sherman had been disappointed to learn that he hadn't arrived yet and was glad to hear that Read would try to hurry his departure for Philadelphia.

Sherman returned his attention to the other end of the table. He noticed a collective angry gaze from the far side of the room.

6

Wednesday, May 16, 1787

"Mr. Madison?"

Madison had started to merge with the throng moving toward Dr. Franklin's dining room. When he turned, he felt annoyed that the hand on his shoulder belonged to Charles Pinckney. "This isn't an opportune time. We've been called to dinner. It would insult our host to tarry."

"This herd will take forever to file into the house. We have a few moments."

"Can we talk during the meal? I'll be seated next to you."

"This is private."

Remembering Sherman's foray into the South Carolina camp, Madison made a decision. "Let's step out of earshot." While everyone else gravitated toward the house, Madison led Pinckney to a quiet corner in the garden. "What's on your mind, Charles?"

"I've written a proposal for the new government."

"Do you mean improvements to the Virginia Plan?"

"No. I've drawn up an entire system. It has similarities to your plan but diverges in critical areas. I wish to present it to the convention."

Madison realized that the threat to South Carolina's allegiance came from someone other than Sherman. "This is awkward and your timing poor," Madison said. "We must join the other guests."

"A simple 'yes, of course,' takes but a moment."

"My answer cannot be that simple. You have promised to support the Virginia Plan. The introduction of a competing scheme will throw the convention into chaos."

"You refuse to give my plan a hearing?"

"Surely you don't intend to go back on your word?"

"I'm a gentleman," Pinckney said with more strength than Madison would have expected. "You'll have my vote in the initial round, but if we reach a stalemate, I believe my alternative can save us from a debacle."

Madison had spent thousands of hours studying ancient and modern governments, argued their flaws with the greatest minds, designed a faultless system, and artfully secured powerful patrons. Now Pinckney, idle and vainglorious, had jotted a few notes and demanded the stage.

"Mr. Pinckney, I don't control the proceedings, but I assure you that every alteration will be entertained if we reach an impasse. I'll keep your kind offer in mind."

"My offer is not an alteration. It's a unique design based on populist principles."

"In that case, will you make a copy for me? I've made a life's study of governments and am always eager to examine well-conceived innovations."

"Perhaps ... but at a later date."

"The convention will start soon."

"I must polish the finer points."

Madison felt his irritation abate. Pinckney's answer meant that he probably had no plan. "We really must rejoin the party."

"I deserve an answer. Yes or no?"

"I promise you'll receive a hearing if a deadlock ensues. I'm pleased that you've thought ahead. If the need arises, we'll be in your debt."

Lightly gripping Pinckney's elbow, Madison steered him toward the house. He tried to quell his indignation, knowing he would spend the next few hours with Pinckney. He must disguise his shock and consternation.

Madison's previous meals at Franklin's home had been small affairs, and the few guests had been dwarfed by a room designed to seat twenty-four. This recent addition to the house was a combination library-dining room, built after Franklin's return from Paris. The room stretched to over thirty feet and was half as wide. A European marble fireplace interrupted the formation of bookcases along one wall, while busts of great men sprinkled the opposite wall of books. Windows at the north and south ends let in soft afternoon light.

The room exhibited two busts of Franklin next to sculptures of some of the greatest men in history. Most of the delegates probably hadn't noticed the tall clock ticking away just outside the door, uninhibitedly adorned with a portrait of their host.

The long mahogany table was set with fine imported porcelain and silver. A crumb cloth stretched under the entire length of the table to protect the expensive, brightly patterned carpet. The Virginia and Pennsylvania delegations had worked together on the seating. To accommodate the large group, three nut-brown chairs had been interspersed with twenty-four white Windsor chairs.

Franklin, gout ridden, had already been assisted to his chair in the middle of the expansive table. Madison had asked to be seated between Pinckney and

Butler, his intent to keep South Carolina tethered to their commitments. After his garden encounter with Pinckney, Madison thought the cautionary move prescient.

Washington held a place of honor at the head of the table. Alexander Hamilton, representing New York, sat to his immediate left, and Robert Morris to his right. Madison saw that most of the delegates had already taken their seats, but no one seemed to notice his tardy arrival. Everyone was in a merry frame of mind. People enjoyed a feast seasoned with animated discussion. Franklin hosted the event to build camaraderie, temper ill will, and soften inflexible positions. As Madison's sour mood faded, he hoped the celebratory mood would carry over to the State House.

Franklin opened with a few gracious remarks and a prayer. As if cued by a stagehand, six smartly dressed servants entered bearing cod chowder, a Philadelphia tradition. The retinue then proceeded to serve the guests with practiced élan.

Turning to Pinckney, Madison said, "Dr. Franklin sets a fine table."

"Indeed, he does," Pinckney said, sipping from his tankard. "And his porter is as good as promised."

Switching topics abruptly, Madison asked, "What's the mood in South Carolina?"

"Uneasy. Charleston worries about trade, plantation owners fear the cash shortage, and the Spanish and Indians scare the backcountry."

"Sounds dire."

"Everyone has placed an unreasonable amount of hope on this convention. If we fail, we'll face the wrath of our countrymen. Or perhaps our success will incite their fury."

Relieved to be on a more agreeable subject, Madison said, "People want to be delivered from their travails, but they distrust us. We must aim for a government strong enough to address national issues, but retain enough state governance for local concerns."

"Ah, James, ever the philosopher," Pinckney said with a touch of mockery.

"Philosophy can instruct, Charles."

"I search not for purity in principle but for solutions. That's what will please my people. Form matters not to them."

Butler joined the conversation from Madison's other side and seemed to support Pinckney's odd plea for mediocrity. "We must follow the example of Solon. He gave the Athenians not the best government he could devise, but the best they would receive."

For a moment, Madison regretted having asked to be seated between the South Carolinians, but he tucked his irritation away when he remembered that his intent was to measure their mood. To delay a response, Madison dipped his spoon into his soup. He put the half-coated spoon in his mouth and cleaned it with his lips. The taste of the chowder exceeded the promise of the aroma. Eagerly scooping a spoonful, Madison wondered if Butler had endorsed Pinckney's plan—or was the episode a ruse to gain an edge for some other aspiration?

"Mr. Butler, undue caution may render us impotent," Madison said.

"Grand innovations scare people," Butler said, with his Irish accent. "People want order, sound money, and to be free from unwarranted scrutiny of their habits. They don't understand government systems." He looked peeved. "But their representatives do."

"I don't understand your meaning."

"The South Carolina legislature won't sanction a plan that threatens their vital interests."

"Your apprehensions seem newly born," Madison said. "Which interests are under threat?"

"It is not a subject for public discussion," Butler said.

Butler's bitter tone gave Madison a clue to their concern. The conversation drifted to less sensitive subjects until the servants made another grand entrance, each balancing a large platter of oysters on the outstretched palm of his right hand. With a stylish flourish, they gracefully swirled the platters to each guest, as if presenting precious pearls instead of the host body.

Pinckney selected two oysters, each over four inches. Gazing after the neatly uniformed Negro, Pinckney said, "Dr. Franklin dearly loves to instruct. He sweetens his tutelage with anecdotes and humorous stories, but his condescension is nonetheless unmistakable."

Franklin was a known abolitionist. His participation at this month's Pennsylvania Society for Promoting the Abolition of Slavery hadn't gone unnoticed. Madison realized that the skilled and self-assured service by free blacks did convey a message. He mused that his slaves at Montpelier could never put on such a lavish and well-orchestrated ceremony.

All the states had vital interests, and each state must tolerate the others' interests. Madison could see no logical reason why slavery should hinder progress, but emotions, not logic, often ruled politics. This issue must not be allowed to thwart the creation of the world's first durable republic.

"The English and the Spanish are like the two ends of a huge tong, ready to pinch us until we crumble into small bites."

The long meal had reached its final stage, and animated discussion engulfed the length of the table. Alexander Hamilton provoked the conversation at Madison's end. Hamilton, thirty years old, had abundant charm to go with his good looks and lean stature. Women, especially, found his deep blue eyes, auburn hair, and clear skin attractive.

"Shays and his ilk attack from within, but we should be casting an alert eye to the horizon," Robert Morris added.

"No need to look to the horizon," Washington said. "Enough enemies reside in our backyard."

Butler leaned in to gain attention. "The Carolinas and Georgia are deeply troubled by the Spanish on our frontier."

"And England loiters in the Great Lakes region." Hamilton slapped the table. "We must insist that the British comply with the peace treaty and vacate their forts."

"I shall send them a letter forthwith." Washington's rejoinder drew laughter from all sides.

"And if they fail to respond, we must forcibly evict them," Hamilton said, as if Washington had been serious.

"Difficult without an army," Washington said.

Turning to Butler, Hamilton asked, "Did you know that Congress has reduced the army to seven hundred?"

"You must be mistaken," Butler said.

"I visited Secretary Knox's New York headquarters. Three clerks. That's it."

Butler looked at Washington. "How will we defend South Carolina?"

"Not with militia," Washington answered. "And British garrisons within our sovereign territory will eventually lead to another armed conflict."

"Something will break soon," Hamilton huffed. "Either the belligerent British in the North or the crafty Spanish in the South will test our resolve."

Madison wanted to remind South Carolina of their stake in the convention. Turning to Butler, he asked, "How serious is the trouble on your western frontier?"

Butler answered Madison while directing his eyes toward Washington. "If something is not done—and soon—our settlers on the other side of the Appalachians will join the Spanish to protect their families and farms."

From Madison's other side, Pinckney added, "This spring, the Spanish incited Indian raids on the Georgia frontier. Seven families slaughtered."

"The Spanish are testing the pioneers' allegiance to us," Butler said. "Georgia declared martial law. We may not be far behind."

Hamilton now banged the butt of his dinner knife against the table. "We must stop the Spanish before they set the entire frontier ablaze with insurrection."

Madison straightened his napkin and folded his hands in front of him. Brave talk at a dinner party, safely nestled in the heart of a thriving city, didn't impress him. Madison appreciated Hamilton's logical mind, but the man's passion caused him discomfort. Inciting emotions defeated reason. Hamilton's love of bluster would this time, however, serve Madison's purpose. He wanted the delegates to fear a helpless government.

Hamilton shifted to his favorite subject. "The conflict has begun on the field of commerce." Hamilton leaned into a conspiratorial posture. "John Jay has kept me abreast of our trade negotiations in London. He writes that England refuses to lift the embargo on West Indies trade. And the Spanish have already closed the Mississippi to block our western trade. They intend to impoverish us so we cannot raise an army or equip a navy."

When Hamilton spoke, Madison paid attention. During the Revolution, Hamilton had served on Washington's staff and greatly influenced the general's thinking. Or perhaps it was the reverse. Hamilton had a habit of repeating Washington's words, especially in situations in which the general didn't want them directly attributed to him.

"The risk of war is real," Morris said, "but my greater fear is internal rebellion. The mood outside the cities is ugly." Morris looked at Butler. "In the North, farmers dominate state legislatures and get them to pass tender and stay laws that cheat creditors. The states print money like handbills, encouraging slothful behavior and distrust between neighbors."

Madison suppressed a snicker. The richest man in Pennsylvania, perhaps the country, begrudged others a chance to hold on to their small farms. Morris owned huge tracts of western land, and Madison had heard rumors that ethical behavior seldom tempered his speculative fever.

"Are you implying that money is the sole cause of our travails?" Madison asked the two money-obsessed men.

"Money is the root system that supports the tree of liberty," Hamilton answered. "Money is a promise, a commitment. Not good, nor evil."

"You mean debt?" Butler asked.

"No, I speak of money. Money is a promise by the government: if you put it in your purse, everyone will accept it in exchange for goods when you draw it out. The government must keep money whole."

"Just as a debtor must repay," the wealthy Robert Morris added.

Hamilton nodded. "Today, people turn to their state governments to avoid their obligations." Hamilton's voice filled with sarcasm. "The Europeans watch our feeble efforts with glee, anxious to graft our broken pieces onto their empires." Hamilton was building to a climatic moment. "We're not a nation, but mere children playing adult games." Hamilton paused for dramatic effect. "The primary cause of our disorders lies with the small states and the tenacity with which they guard their sovereignty. These intransigent states must not be allowed to destroy our nation."

Everyone turned to glare at the far end of the table. Madison saw that only Sherman took notice.

AS DUSK DARKENED THE large room, most of the dinner guests had left. The banquet was over, but the people next to Washington couldn't leave until the general signaled his readiness to retire. Franklin, with the assistance of his manservant, had moved down the table to join the small group. The stragglers seemed content to smoke their tobacco, sip well-aged brandy, and converse in a relaxed fashion. Pinckney and Butler had turned amiable, their earlier unease dissipated by the meal and drink. Madison hoped they would depart so he could talk openly about their earlier comments, but they also seemed bound by the general's lingering.

Madison found Washington puzzling. Stiff and formal with strangers and in public, he obviously enjoyed being around people. He had heard the general brag that he couldn't remember a meal he had taken alone, or with only Martha. When away from home he dined with his host or a gathering of local dignitaries, or he found a crowded tavern. Mount Vernon's reputation for hospitality provided an endless string of visitors. While commander-in-chief of the Continental Army, he had eaten with his staff officers.

"General, you must voyage to France," Franklin said. "Your name is on the lips of every Parisian. You'll learn what posterity will say of Washington, for a thousand leagues is the same as a thousand years."

"Perhaps you've not noticed that I am otherwise engaged." With a sideways nod at Madison, Washington added, "Our young Jemmy has waylaid me from my preferred inactivity."

"We all had a hand in that," Franklin said.

Washington looked annoyed. "Having brought the ship safely into port, I didn't want to embark on another sea of troubles."

"Our troubles can be managed," Franklin said. "We are an enlightened people. Every man reads and is informed." Franklin took on an expression meant to charm. "But we shouldn't expect our new government to be formed like a game of chess is played. The players of our game are too many, their ideas too different, and their prejudices too strong. Each move will be contested. So, gentlemen," Franklin said with a lilt that signaled the climax of his little parable, "the play is more like backgammon with a box of dice."

"Dr. Franklin, you hearten my soul," Washington said. "I trust my luck with dice far more than my skill at chess."

Everyone laughed at the general's self-deprecating remark.

Hamilton quickly rejoined. "General, I eagerly put my faith in either your luck or your skill. If you can lead us to victory against the mighty British Empire, you can surely handle a few headstrong delegates." The gratuitous flattery caused an awkward moment, but Hamilton seemed unaware.

George Mason joined the conversation. "The Revolution was nothing compared to the business before us. Then, the people were inflamed. Now, we propose to invent a new government through calm reason." Mason ranked with Washington and Jefferson in the Virginia hierarchy. As the sixty-two-year-old patriarch of Gunston Hall, he was one of the richest planters in Virginia. He held an almost religious fervor for reason and individual rights, and had authored the famed Virginia Declaration of Rights. He leaned across the table. "The happiness of unborn millions depends on us."

Madison became excited. "No nation has ever changed its government without war or rebellion. We can set a new course for mankind."

"Most of the world hopes we fail," Mason said.

"The British certainly do," Franklin said. "They don't want our example to incite further rebellion within the empire. The British newspapers exaggerate our disorder and mislead on purpose."

"Perhaps they don't exaggerate as much as you think, Doctor," Pinckney said. "You've been out of the country. Our problems seem difficult to overstate."

"I've had the privilege of observing our European brethren, and I can assure you that we don't hoard the world's woes. Our conditions, desperate though they may seem, are preferable to Europe's troubles. Lofty aims drive our discontent." Again, Franklin struck a whimsical expression. "Everyone can be happy if they maintain a happy disposition; such being necessary even in paradise."

"Ah, so it is merely our dispositions that bring us grief," Pinckney said. "Our reputed difficulties shall disappear as soon as we change our outlook. How simple. We'll merely write a joyful disposition clause into our new constitution."

A flash of irritation crossed Franklin's face, but it was immediately replaced with a bemused smile. "The human condition is never simple, Mr. Pinckney. You cannot legislate how people think. I find humans badly constructed. They are more easily provoked than reconciled, more disposed to do mischief than good, more easily deceived than undeceived, and more impressed with their own self than considerate of others."

Having delivered his disguised reproach, Franklin steered the conversation away from Pinckney's gibe. "I've also observed that man takes more pride in killing than in begetting. Without a blush, they assemble great armies to destroy. Then, when they have killed as many as they can, they exaggerate the number. But men creep into corners or darkness to beget."

Madison laughed. Late evening conversation, once turned to begetting, seldom returned to more serious subjects. Alienating esteemed colleagues never garnered support, nor advanced plans. Also, judging by Butler's look, Pinckney would receive an admonishment from his fellow South Carolinian to restrain his sharp tongue. Madison sat back, ready to enjoy some quick-witted bantering about sexual follies, when Pinckney's voice destroyed his evening.

"Dr. Franklin, do you consider Mr. Madison badly constructed because he owns over a hundred slaves?"

7

Thursday, May 24, 1787

Sherman found the decision hard. Each day he had walked the streets of Phila-delphia, and the same question plagued him. Now he stood with his back to the street as well-dressed people sauntered along the sidewalk behind him. Sherman looked down at his scruffy shoes.

"We can have you measured and fitted in a single day."

Sherman turned to see a boot maker leaning out of his shop door. Sher-man had been staring at a fine set of boots displayed in his window. The wood sign swinging over the door read, "Cordwainer." In Sherman's experience, this pompous term meant that the boots he admired would be expensive.

"My father was a boot maker, and he taught me the trade. These are cer-tainly well-crafted boots."

"Thank you. You have a keen eye for workmanship." Stepping further out into the street, he asked, "Would you care to step in? We have several boots in work. A close inspection by an experienced eye always results in an order."

"That's my fear. My other is that the price is too dear for my purse."

"Our prices are reasonable, when you consider the quality. Cobbled boots don't wear, and they're uncomfortable. Mine will fit expertly and last forever."

"Let's have a look."

In the shop, Sherman saw three apprentices working on different stages of construction. None seemed to take notice of him as the master boot maker led him over to the bench. Oil lamps augmented the large front window to provide the men good light.

The orderliness of the shop impressed Sherman. Tools not in use were neatly hung through holes in a half shelf within easy reach above the bench. Sherman saw tanned leather stacked by color and grade on large shelves along the opposite wall. The floor was clean and nearly free of remnants. An expensive rug lay at the front of the shop, where two sturdy chairs and a table made a comfortable fitting area. The table displayed several pairs of beautifully finished boots.

The scent of the shop recalled his youth. He had grown up above his father's store, and his earliest memory was of the strong smell of leather. The odor permeated the house and his father. He sniffed deep and knew he was going to make a purchase.

"Craftsmanship goes for naught if you don't start with good tanned hide," the boot maker said, as he led Sherman to the orderly shelves of raw material. He pulled out a sample and presented the hide to Sherman as if it were fine lace. "I do all my own buying and deal only with tanners who know their business. You'll not find higher quality anywhere in Philadelphia."

Sherman turned the hide over and felt both sides. "My father also took pride in his skill at selecting the best hides."

"Where're you from?"

"Connecticut. I'm a superior court judge and mayor of New Haven. I represent my state at the Federal Convention."

"You didn't apprentice with your father?" The boot maker had disapproval in his voice.

"Yes, but I was too ambitious. I became a surveyor but soon went into politics, where I've remained ever since."

"Fathers want sons to follow their footsteps. Two of these industrious young men are my sons." With this, the boot maker led him over to the workbench. He picked up a boot and handed it to Sherman. "Look carefully at the stitching. I've trained them well."

"Excellent, but as much as I admire your boots, shoes are what I need at the moment."

Without hesitation, the tradesman picked up a shoe and handed it to Sherman. "Our shoes are worn by the best gentlemen."

Sherman turned the shoe over and examined the sole. "How much?"

The boot maker looked at Sherman's feet, as if calculating. "What style?"

"Simple but made from your finest hide. I don't dress fancy, but I demand well-made shoes." Glancing down, Sherman added, "Unfortunately, their appearance suffers long before their utility."

"Twenty Pennsylvanian dollars or four sovereign crowns."

"You have confirmed my second fear. Do you accept Connecticut shillings?"

The man held up both palms. "They have no value in Pennsylvania."

Sherman drew his purse from his waistcoat. He untied the leather cord, unfolded the flap, and peered inside as if the contents would be a surprise. He couldn't spend four of his six sovereigns. With no hard money, Sherman would feel destitute. "I haven't exchanged my personal funds yet."

"There's a money changer around the corner. He's honest and will give you as good a rate as available in Philadelphia."

Despite the boot maker's endorsement, Sherman wanted to shop around. Experience taught him that money changers' rates fluctuated wildly.

"Thank you, I'll see him, but possibly not until tomorrow. Can we start the measurements in the meantime?"

The boot maker looked thoughtful. "My shoes are custom; they won't fit another." Then with an engaging smile he used to close a sale, he added, "Since you're an esteemed delegate to the Federal Convention, I'll start for a single sovereign. They'll be ready late tomorrow. Of course, delivery requires three additional sovereigns or sixteen Pennsylvania dollars."

"Of course, but if you use paper to calculate, you'll see the remaining tariff is fifteen Pennsylvania dollars."

"My error. I'm sorry, but I would've had the correct figure by the time you arrived tomorrow."

"Very good, let's proceed. May I select my own hide?"

"Of course."

Sherman moved to the racks of tanned hides, thinking that shopkeepers were the same the world over.

A SMALL BELL TINKLED as Sherman pushed the door open. In contrast to the well-lit cordwainer's shop, the dimness of this office signaled the miserly environs of a money changer. A barrier stretched the width of the office, confining him to the foyer. Soon, a short, pudgy man, wearing glasses perched at the end of his nose, stepped from behind a screen.

"May I help you?"

"I'm looking to exchange Connecticut shillings."

"Twelve to one," the money changer said without preamble.

Sherman blanched. After checking two other money changers, Sherman had hoped the one recommended by the boot maker would offer a better rate.

"Such a disappointing exchange will limit my commerce in your fair city."

"There is nothing I can do. Once a month I risk transporting Connecticut money to my New Haven correspondent." He lifted both palms skyward. "I am subject to his avarice."

Sherman calculated that his Philadelphia purchases would cost nearly a third more than back home. The wealthy delegates used English and Spanish coin that carried a premium value. Shopkeepers negotiated splendid deals for the chance of acquiring foreign money. He was sure none of the Virginians had found it necessary to visit this forlorn establishment.

The money changer interpreted Sherman's hesitancy as equivocation. "I know the hardship, but I must heed my own cost and substantial risk. I'll tell you what, if you exchange a hundred and ten shillings, I can give you ten Pennsylvania dollars."

This was the best offer of the day. Sherman noticed that the money changer also sold notions.

"Two hundred and twenty for twenty dollars—if you include fifty sheets of stationery."

"Twenty," countered the money changer.

Sherman hesitated but then carefully counted out the currency.

After Sherman handed over the paper currency, the money changer disappeared behind his screen. Whatever else the convention accomplished, Sherman thought, they must fix the money system. The United States would never be a nation as long as a fair exchange required English or Spanish money.

The money changer quickly returned and counted out sixteen bills and other miscellaneous coins to reach the agreed-upon exchange. Then, picking up a handful of stationery, he deftly separated twenty pages from the stack as if it were paper currency. Sherman had no doubt that the count was exact. He said thank you and escaped to the cheerful people on the street.

MRS. MARSHALL SERVED SUPPER at four in the afternoon. Sherman found her an excellent cook and hated to miss one of her meals, so he picked up his pace. He entered the house, shrugged off his cloak, and immediately entered the room where Mrs. Marshall served meals. Several guests already sat around the large table.

As he circled to an open seat, Mrs. Marshall said, "Mr. Sherman, I'm glad you arrived. I have a courier letter for you from Mr. Paterson."

She picked up an envelope from the sideboard and handed it to him. He took his seat while opening it. After scanning the brief note, he rose and excused himself.

"Oh dear," Mrs. Marshall said. "I hope it isn't bad news."

"Quite the contrary." Sherman smiled. "The full New Jersey delegation has arrived, so the convention can start tomorrow. The note invites me to dine with them at City Tavern. Excuse me, I must hurry."

He walked back into the hall to reclaim his cloak. Mrs. Marshall followed, saying, "I'm happy the convention is taking place. It's sorely needed."

Her comment stopped Sherman. "I thought you weren't sympathetic to our efforts."

"On the contrary, but I don't volunteer opinions. You gentlemen must decide whether we are one nation or thirteen—or perhaps two."

"Two? Do you think more than one nation is workable?"

Mrs. Marshall looked thoughtful and then appeared to make a decision.

"Thirteen means bedlam, one nourishes the seeds of tragedy. I favor two: one slave and another to unite the non-slaveholding states."

"The papers are filled with such counsel, but most writers recommend three nations, with New England and the middle states both nonslave."

"My opinion has not been formed by empty-headed newspaper writers but from watching my guests. Gentlemen from the South treat Howard with haughty disdain, and I know their behavior hides depravity." Patting Sherman on the arm, she smiled and said, "Now hurry along. Pennsylvania's future is safe as long as men like you chart the course."

"I hope your faith isn't misplaced. I'm but a politician after all."

"You are a good man, Mr. Sherman. I have confidence you'll do your best."

Perplexed, Sherman watched her return to her other guests. This was a departure from his previous encounters with Mrs. Marshall. What had changed her mind? Howard must have spoken to her about their conversations. She probably viewed Howard as near family and judged her guests by the way they treated him.

Her ideas appealed to many, but Congress had chartered the convention to repair deficiencies in the Confederation, not to carve the United States into homogeneous realms. He was glad she had decided to express her views, but he would work toward a single, unified nation. Slavery was despicable, but timing was everything in politics. The South couldn't be changed, especially with the power Virginia wielded at this convention. The choice was between dissolution and compromise. Sherman believed that the nation must be held together, or far greater evils would ravage the people of every region.

SHERMAN LEFT MRS. MARSHALL'S and hurried toward the City Tavern, eager because Paterson had refused to discuss substantive issues until his other delegates had arrived. Now they were finally here, giving the convention its requisite seven states. Things would start in earnest tomorrow.

Sherman felt disappointed in his progress since Franklin's party seven days ago. A successful appeal to Washington for a Committee of the Whole represented his sole accomplishment. Sherman hoped that tonight they could hammer out a rough agreement on an alternative plan. New England was still sparsely represented. Even his fellow delegate from Connecticut, Oliver Ellsworth, hadn't arrived yet.

His thoughts turned to Madison. During the past week, Sherman had avoided him. He wanted their first encounter to serve a purpose. Besides, any preliminary conversations would be useless. The Virginians didn't hide their intent because they had the votes, and Madison's political skills would prevent him from accidentally revealing any nuances around their strategy.

Sherman put his thoughts away as he approached the City Tavern, which compared with the Indian Queen in prestige but not in size. The Indian Queen sprawled across several buildings, accommodating many more guests, but more important, its stables could shelter carriages as well as horses, and the outbuildings housed the servants and slaves accompanying rich boarders.

The broad steps of City Tavern led to an elegant central hall with rooms to either side. A bar and coffeehouse occupied the back of the ground floor. When he entered, a doorman directed him to a private room on the second floor.

Sherman knocked and entered to find William Paterson, David Brearley, and Churchill Houston looking morose as they hung over their tankards of ale. These were his allies?

"Gentlemen, welcome to Philadelphia. You have little idea how happy your arrival makes me."

"It's a pleasure to see you again, Roger," Brearley said as he stood to shake hands. "We thought you might not have received our message."

"I returned late to my boardinghouse. I felt entrapped and abandoned, so I assuaged my ill temper with the purchase of a new pair of shoes," Sherman said cheerfully, turning to greet Houston. "Now I regret the extravagance because you've lifted my spirits."

Looking dour, Houston shook Sherman's hand. "I'm glad we have a clever fellow like you on our side. Have you charted a path out of this Virginian quagmire?"

"I see William has been regaling you with the evil doings of our Virginian brethren. Don't despair. They're far too smart for their own good. Political conventions are unpredictable and abound in detours. We'll have ample opportunity to spoil their plans."

"I hope you're right, Roger," Paterson said. His darting eyes refused to remain on any individual for more than a few seconds. "Those praetorian conspirators are drunk with ambition—and they own enough votes to force their will on an unsuspecting populace." Paterson waved his hand to encompass their small gathering. "This feeble group is the last defense against an assault on our liberty."

"Not quite," Sherman said. "Delaware supports us. Our three states against their four is not an insurmountable challenge. We need to turn but one state to gain advantage."

"You make it sound easy, but more states will arrive."

"Yes, but by my estimation, their advantage will remain one state."

"It's unfortunate that Rhode Island has refused to send a delegation," Brearley said. "We could easily deadlock this convention."

Using the popular sobriquet for the state, Sherman said, "We need allies, but we're better off without Rogue Island. She sails the path to anarchy."

Paterson held tight to his melancholy. "The Virginians pose a dire threat to all that I hold dear." Then he asked in a plaintive voice, "What do we do, Roger?"

"Order supper, of course," Sherman answered with a broad smile.

This, at last, drew some laughter from the group. They had remained standing during the exchange and now took seats to the sound of scraping chairs. Brearley rang a bell, which instantly brought a steward.

After ordering, Sherman cheerfully recited his adventures with the boot maker and the money changer. He had fun with the story, exaggerating the money changer's avarice and repugnance. He meant it as a practical example, but Paterson failed to see the parallel. Impatiently, he brought the conversation back to the convention.

"Roger, we must move to business."

"Of course, William. I apologize for the distraction." Sherman scooted his chair toward the table to signal that he was ready to get serious. "I propose we draw up the general terms of a counterproposal to the Virginia Plan."

They spent the next several hours debating the points of their plan. Sherman drew from memory amendments to the Articles that he had advanced several years earlier, but he made sure that everyone else had ample opportunity to include their own ideas. His collegial approach accelerated the planning and generated little disagreement.

Finally, they achieved their limited goal. The outline granted Congress additional powers, levied import duties and stamp taxes, regulated trade, based taxes on free inhabitants instead of property, and provided for state courts to try cases, with appeals to a national judiciary chosen by the executive. If states didn't comply with tax requisitions, then the national government could collect the taxes directly. The executive consisted of more than one person chosen by Congress.

After a review of their night's work, Paterson said, "I feel good for the first time since arriving in this vulgar city. I can support this government, and it should appeal to everyone except the monarchists—and they can be damned to hell."

Houston asked, "When can we present it?"

Sherman bristled at the question. Impatience dashed more good legislation than any other cause. During the course of the evening, he had enjoyed a sumptuous meal, starting with extraordinary truffle soup. He now casually pulled the finale of nuts toward him, pretending deep consideration before answering. He picked up a walnut with his thumb and index finger. He appeared to examine it like a precious stone as he made up his mind.

"We should share our thoughts immediately with Delaware. But we should wait before exposing our strategy to others. Let the Virginians lay out their plan and arouse fear amongst the sensible delegates. That'll be our cue to present our alternative."

"By then it may be too late," Paterson said. "Virginia has six states aligned with her."

"We won't wait until an official vote. We'll start as a Committee of the Whole, so we'll present in committee, but not immediately. In the meantime, we must write it out as a formal resolution, gather support behind closed doors, and discredit their plan."

Paterson didn't look satisfied, so Sherman tried another tack. "William, you must author this plan. Connecticut is neither small nor large. Delaware, New Hampshire, and Maryland distrust us. They fear we might jump to the other side. This must be the New Jersey Plan. Only you can garner the necessary support."

Wearing a thoughtful expression, Paterson asked, "How do you propose we proceed?"

His ruse had worked.

"First, we must present our outline to George Read. Let Delaware adjust the plan around the edges. That'll encourage them to own the design. Maryland and New Hampshire haven't arrived yet, so we'll decide when to bring them in later. As soon as Delaware agrees, you must scribe the resolutions in your hand. Last, we should meet daily to measure events and plot our course."

"Including Delaware?"

Feigning careful consideration, Sherman said, "Yes, I think it is time to solidify our coalition. What do you think?"

"I agree," Paterson said. "We must provide leadership."

"Excellent. Gentlemen, the hour is late for a tired old man. I suggest we meet after tomorrow's opening session. William, what time would you like us to gather?"

"We meet here for supper. I'll invite Read."

"Good idea. I can't remember a finer meal. When tomorrow's session gets deadly dull, I'll remind myself that I will soon be enjoying a superb supper with stalwart companions."

As Sherman washed his face at a basin in his room, he marveled that appeals to vanity worked best with the least capable. No matter. He had won what he wanted at an inconsequential price. The plan they had formulated met his goals. The New Jersey Plan strengthened the national government while preserving the sovereignty of Connecticut.

Sherman went to the writing shelf to tell Rebecca the good news. He hadn't received a response from his last letter, but that wasn't unusual because the round trip took more than a week. She wanted him to complete his business and return home, so she'd be happy to hear that the convention would finally start.

Sherman wrote six pages but omitted mentioning his new shoes. With their limited funds, she wouldn't be sympathetic to his indulgence. Sherman vowed to tighten up on other expenditures. He was grateful that New Jersey had bought his extravagant meal this evening.

As he dressed in his nightshirt, Sherman felt confident about tomorrow's opening session. Madison had made a fatal error. Even if he passed his Virginia Plan, the national Congress and the states would never ratify it. His was an idealist's mistake: purity of principle overriding common and political sense. Sherman's plan remained obedient to the instructions from Congress. Madison's plan dissolved Congress. When the alternatives were laid out to responsible delegates, they would recoil at the attack against their authorizing agency.

Sherman climbed into bed and pulled the comforter tight against the night cold. Snuggled in the soft warmth, he let his weary bones relax. He had earned a good night's sleep.

Suddenly his eyes popped open. James Madison did not make fatal errors.

Part 2

Quorum

8

Thursday, May 24, 1787

Madison tried to pace his breathing to the heaving body beneath him. He wished he could do this as well as other men. He had the timing about right, when a fallen tree in his path made him gasp. He hated jumping a horse.

Damn Robert Morris. It was no accident that Madison sat astride the biggest horse he had ever seen. The beast's back was so broad that Madison's legs were splayed too wide for a comfortable ride. His anger had grown when the livery boy raised the stirrups as high as they would go. Morris had engineered this indignity.

Madison felt more at ease after the huge beast easily bounded over the tree. He searched the narrow trail ahead but saw neither Washington nor Morris. His childhood, no, his life had been plagued by illness, so he had never enjoyed what his father thought of as manly pursuits. Deciding he would never impress his host, he gently tugged on the reins to bring the horse down to a trot. Washington was renowned as possibly the best horseman in the country. It made no sense to speed through unknown woods in an attempt to keep up with him.

Morris had invited Washington, Madison, and Franklin to The Hills, his country estate along the Schuylkill River. Franklin no longer rode, so he had stayed at the mansion to enjoy the clean air, rural sounds, and river view.

Madison took a deep breath. Now that he had slowed the horse to a comfortable pace, he began to enjoy the experience. The woods smelled fresh after the city, and the rhythmic clop of the heavy horse relaxed him. He suddenly felt homesick for Montpelier. Before he could sink into a wistful mood, he turned a corner in the trail and came upon his two companions.

"Mr. Madison, there you are. We were about to circle back to see if you'd had a mishap."

"Quite the contrary, Mr. Morris. This is a fine animal. Quick, obedient, and a good jumper. I slowed the pace after the tree to enjoy this perfect afternoon."

"Glad to hear it. If you're comfortable with Brutus, we'll charge on ahead."

"Brutus and I get along just fine. He told me that he hardly noticed my weight on his sturdy back."

Washington laughed. "He looks a great steed. Robert could have fit out a shelty, but he holds a high regard for your riding ability. Right, Robert?"

"Absolutely. Brutus scares some."

"Really," Madison said as he affectionately patted the horse's neck. "I find him temperate and responsive."

"Well, we'll be off then." Morris turned his thoroughbred horse in a tight circle and spurred it to a full gallop down the trail.

Washington gave Madison a wink. "Enjoy the afternoon, Jemmy." He turned his horse and sped away with the deep seat of an expert horseman.

Madison had never liked Robert Morris, possibly because Morris had never liked him. But now he felt released. He could explore at his own pace, and Washington had let him know that he saw the game Morris had played.

Part of the problem was that Madison failed to understand Morris. He owned land, but he did not honor land like a Southerner. He just bought it and held it long enough to sell for a profit. It made no sense. Land meant standing in the community, a family heritage to be preserved, and an obligation to care for the land and less-well-off neighbors. To a Virginia plantation owner, land meant everything. To a Pennsylvania speculator, land held no value beyond its price.

Madison shrugged off his irritation. After all, they had received word before they left Philadelphia that the full New Jersey delegation had arrived. With this new thought, Madison grew excited. Tomorrow would culminate a year's worth of preparation. It would be a grand day.

He decided that Brutus was a gentle giant with an even temper and a clear-eyed look that hinted of uncommon horse sense. Big and smart. Madison thought of Roger Sherman and dug his heels into Brutus.

"GOOD DELEGATES, PLEASE COME to order. Please come to order." A gavel banged for attention. "Gentlemen, please take your seats."

Madison and Mason stood in a corner of the clamorous chamber. Delegates conversed loudly in the open spaces, while torrential rain pounded the windows, adding a loud, rhythmic din to the male voices. They had been meeting at the State House every day at one o'clock since May 14—the scheduled start of the convention—to see if a quorum had arrived. Because everyone had already heard about New Jersey's arrival, delegates had arrived ahead of time to talk politics, strut their finery, and enjoy the atmosphere of expectancy. The room seethed with anticipation. The day had finally arrived.

Madison turned to Mason. "I've been waiting for this moment for over a year. Let's take our seats."

Madison jostled his way to a center-front table that he had already reserved by distributing his writing materials. He intended to take careful notes of the proceedings and wanted to see and hear everything. Happy delegates interrupted his forward progress by shaking his hand, slapping his shoulder, and offering congratulations. Friend and foe alike seemed intent on thanking him for orchestrating this momentous event.

The green baize tables were arranged in arcs facing the speaker's platform located on the east wall. The white room, with slate-colored wainscoting, received excellent light from twenty-four large pane windows. The square chamber, designed in classic proportions and ornamented with pilasters and tabernacles, radiated dignity. This was a room meant to witness history. The president's chair sat on a low dais behind the very desk where the Declaration of Independence and the Articles of Confederation had been signed. The Continental Congress had met here. Washington had accepted his election as commander in chief of the Continental Army in this room.

Madison reached his table and looked up to see a self-important Robert Morris impatiently waiting for the laggards to settle.

Taking a deep breath and looking about the chamber, Morris said, "Gentlemen, thank you. I'm pleased to announce a quorum." A dramatic pause. "We may proceed."

Cheers rang through the chamber.

"Gentlemen, please. Thank you. Our first order of business is to elect a president." Standing tall upon the short dais, Morris continued, "I'd like to place in nomination a true and selfless patriot, the commander of our victorious Continental Army, a man of unquestioned integrity and honor, the illustrious Gen. George Washington."

Madison found himself instantly on his feet with the other delegates. The applause continued long and spirited, with occasional whoops and cheers. Everyone turned to the sole person who remained seated, George Washington. The general looked genuinely uncomfortable.

The sound hadn't abated, nor had everyone regained their seat before John Rutledge of South Carolina boomed, "I consider it the greatest honor to second the nomination of Gen. George Washington!"

Again, Madison rose, clapping enthusiastically to honor the great hero of the Revolution. And again, Washington sat in embarrassed silence.

As the applause died down, more quickly this time, Morris asked, "Are there any further nominations?"

The room remained still.

Waiting a respectful moment, Morris said, "We have a motion and a second. Will the states please confer, determine your vote, and mark your ballot."

It didn't take long, nor was the vote a surprise. Washington was elected unanimously by the seven states present.

Madison watched Morris escort Washington to the dais. As he had expected, Washington gave a poorly delivered speech. He modestly accepted the honor, thanked the delegates, reminded them that he lacked experience, and hoped that his errors would be excused.

After Major William Jackson of South Carolina was elected secretary, he read their instructions from Congress, a procedure that caused Madison discomfort. The Congress of the United States had authorized a convention of delegates "who shall have been appointed by the several states to meet at Philadelphia, for the sole and express purpose of revising the Articles of Confederation, and reporting to Congress and the several legislatures, such alterations and provisions therein, as shall, when agreed to in Congress, and confirmed by the states, render the federal Constitution adequate to the exigencies of government, and the preservation of the union."

Madison had a copy of the Virginia Plan in front of him. The plan didn't revise the Articles; it replaced them. He didn't intend to present his plan to Congress for agreement or to the states for confirmation. He intended a bloodless coup d'état. Many would be aghast at his effrontery, but making adjustments around the edges of the Articles would never work. Their grand experiment with republicanism would fade into history, remembered as a mishap of foolish aspiration. This plan, however, the one he now fingered possessively, would ensure liberty for the citizens of the United States for countless generations.

Governor Clinton of New York had engineered their restrictive instructions. He ran the state as his personal fiefdom and wanted no interference from a central government. Because Congress convened in his state, Clinton unduly influenced legislation, which extended his power to the national level. New York should have been part of Madison's large state alliance, but Clinton had stacked the delegation with two lackeys to outvote Hamilton. Although New York would fight his proposal, Madison was sure they would never join the small states. New York would remain a maverick and try to position itself on the fulcrum so it could tilt the convention in either direction.

Jackson read the state credentials. Madison knew that even Virginia's credentials allowed only revision of the Articles.

"The state of Georgia by the grace of God, free, sovereign, and independent...."

Thankfully, this was Friday. The weekend would distance the reading of the instructions and credentials from Randolph's presentation of the plan. The convention's vested authority was thin, but at least they were officially sanctioned by Congress. If he could engineer a strong majority, then despite their limited charter, no one would be able to ignore what came out of this convention.

Pinckney suddenly took the floor and made a motion to appoint a committee to draw up rules of order. Wythe, Hamilton, and Pinckney made up the committee, with his fellow Virginian, George Wythe, selected as chairman. When they adjourned until ten o'clock Monday, Madison felt relieved that the first day had held no surprises.

He gathered up his papers, and as he leaned over to pick up his valise, a large shape loomed over him. The first thing he noticed was a handsome pair of new shoes. Looking up, prepared to make some banal comment about the day's proceedings, he saw Roger Sherman of Connecticut.

"Excuse me, James, but I wonder if you'd be kind enough to forward a rule suggestion to Mr. Wythe?"

Madison busied himself shuffling papers. "I'd be pleased to, but I have work I must attend to. It'd be better if you presented your idea directly to Mr. Wythe."

"I agree, but the committee has already charged out of the room. I understand you'll see Mr. Wythe at the Morris house this evening."

Madison head jerked up. Sherman seemed to know everything.

"What's your suggestion?"

"I've been conferring with my colleagues. We believe a rule that any vote can be reconsidered would facilitate deliberations."

Madison slowly stuffed his papers into his valise. "Not unprecedented, but certainly unusual. It could be disruptive."

"I don't see the harm. My colleagues feel strongly that the opportunity to reconsider will quicken debate and soothe disagreement. It's an issue that kindles their passion. I fear early disharmony—perhaps worse."

"That's a vexing statement."

"Unfortunately, the small states aren't organized, nor do they have a leader. Your plan frightens them."

"I see." Madison tucked his case under his arm, preparing to leave. Looking up into Sherman's strangely placid face, he said, "I'll mention your idea to Mr. Wythe."

"Thank you, James. One more item. There's a rumor that the Rules Committee will recommend secrecy. A republican government shouldn't be shrouded from public scrutiny—but I'm sure it's only a false rumor."

Madison hastened out of the chamber.

"GOOD GOD, MAN. MOVE that carriage!"

"Hold your horses, fool!"

Madison stood in the crowded Central Hall, watching the tangle of carriages jockey for position in front of the State House. The unrelenting rain had turned the street into disorder and the coachmen into snarling contestants. The door stood open as the delegates peered over each other to see which carriage had secured a position at the uncovered entrance.

"Do the heavens, my dear Mr. Madison, augur a stormy convention?"

Madison recognized Pinckney's voice at his shoulder. Was he to be haunted by this man? Without turning his head, Madison said, "The weather doesn't foretell, nor can man foretell the weather. Both operate on their own cycle."

"Perhaps you're right, the weather may not foretell, but I predict today's unanimity will disintegrate into the same discord we witness before us."

"Disagreement's inevitable, Mr. Pinckney, but discord sometimes disguises progress. Watch. This mess will sort itself out, and we shall be whisked to our quarters." Turning to look Pinckney in the eye, Madison added, "The convention may suffer some storms, but in the end, we'll deliver to our countrymen a sustainable republican government."

"Hear! Hear! This dismal day needs a dose of optimism. You might be right. A plan might eventually emerge, but who among us can predict its final form?"

"The Virginia Plan provides the framework, and it has sufficient support, especially with South Carolina on our side."

"Don't worry, James, we remain steadfast. But again, things may not proceed in a straight line. If events go awry, my plan may present a more acceptable formula."

Madison had hoped Pinckney had abandoned his plan. "Mr. Pinckney, I'm not so naïve as to believe that the Virginia Plan will pass without a few alterations."

"Perhaps more than a few," Pinckney taunted.

"Liberty depends on the total design. Alterations must be carefully balanced against other elements. I'll fight to pass the Virginia Plan with as few changes as necessary to achieve consensus."

"A grand objective, James, but a question remains: if events go as you expect, how do you propose to get Congress and the states to ratify your plan? You threaten powerful men."

"We shan't seek their permission," Madison said. "There's another authority."

Pinckney's surprised expression pleased Madison.

"And who, may I ask, is this other authority?"

"The people. We'll bypass Congress and the states and go directly to the people."

Pinckney laughed. "Jemmy, I admire your audacity. You are truly a rapscallion mutineer."

Pinckney started the conversation by addressing him as Mr. Madison, shifted to James, and then delivered his jocular reproach using a name reserved for his closest friends. Why did Pinckney do this? Why did it irritate him so? Madison realized that the second question answered the first.

Could history be made with such allies? Did Pinckney take nothing seriously? Was he completely unlearned? Republican theory clearly stated that the people held all political power, and only they could delegate authority to a government. The people were free to change governments at will. They didn't need permission from incumbents.

At that moment, the Indian Queen carriage jostled into position at the foot of the State House steps. Madison took the opportunity to escape Pinckney. Tucking his valise tightly against his chest, Madison dashed to the carriage, arriving before the coachman could climb down and open an umbrella. Trotting in place, head bent against the downpour, Madison fumbled with the carriage door latch. Finally getting it open, he stepped up into the dry interior and collapsed into a seat. Just as he exhaled deeply, Pinckney clambered in behind him.

"This weather makes a warm fire and a brandy seem positively luxurious," Pinckney said with good humor.

Despite himself, Madison laughed in agreement. "Yes, and on such a stormy day, a cozy bed with a willing maiden would be the epitome of decadence."

"A splendid suggestion," said Hamilton as he climbed aboard. "If you gentlemen will excuse me, I won't be getting off with you at the Indian Queen. Jemmy, your bright ideas never cease to amaze me."

The now-crowded coach tittered with amusement. The ribald quip had instantly erased the weather's gloominess and reinstated the exuberance of the Council Chamber.

In his break for the carriage, Madison had forgotten that Pinckney was a fellow guest at the Indian Queen and would follow in his footsteps. But revelry now seemed to be the order, and Pinckney's flippancy fit the mood. Madison quite enjoyed the short carriage ride. Hamilton, true to his word, remained in the carriage but waited to give the coachman directions until they had all departed.

"ABSOLUTELY NOT!" HAMILTON WAS furious. "We cannot accede to this— ever."

"The alternative may be worse," Madison said.

"No! They intend to use this rule to win by attrition. We cannot allow it. Never!"

"What we cannot allow is the shattering of this convention before it has a chance to do its duty." Franklin also looked grim.

"Nothing will come of our work if we concede to unreasonable demands at the outset," Hamilton said.

Franklin leaned toward Hamilton. "Fury doesn't help us resolve this dilemma. It took untold maneuvering to get these men together, and they can disperse as quickly as a flock of disturbed gulls."

"But we cannot acquiesce to a bald threat," Hamilton said.

"Jemmy, was this presented as a threat?" Franklin asked.

"Sherman's too clever to speak directly, but there was no mistaking the meaning. He was offering a trade: secrecy for reconsideration. He said it was beyond his control, but I've seen his work before."

"Delegates bolting isn't our only risk. Congress can withdraw our sanction. Open proceedings might ignite their panic." This came from Robert Morris, in whose parlor they now sat. Morris, known as the Financier of the Revolution, had invited his old friend, Gen. Washington, to stay in his lavish home during the convention. This evening he was hosting a dinner for prominent delegates from Virginia and Pennsylvania.

Hamilton had arrived late, looking slightly disheveled. Entering in a rush, full of apologies, he had given Madison a sly wink. With Hamilton's arrival, they started discussing Sherman's disturbing message as they sipped an excellent French wine from the Morris cellar.

Madison had been thinking. "If I may, we have two issues, and I think the first step is to decide which has greater importance. I believe the issue of secrecy paramount. As long as we hold our coalition, we needn't fear new votes on settled issues."

"I don't know where you're going with this, Jemmy," Hamilton said, "but if you suggest we make concessions, I believe it an error."

"I merely suggest that we analyze the issues based on the greater purpose. Robert's caution is valid. We *must* have closed deliberations."

Franklin suddenly took on a cagey look. "What if George's committee reported out neither rule?"

"My good doctor, we—"

Franklin raised a hand to stop Hamilton. "We can have someone propose a motion for secrecy from the floor and easily get it passed. If Sherman makes a motion to reconsider votes, his weak support will be exposed. Force him out of the corridors and into the chamber where he's less comfortable."

"I don't understand," Morris said. "What does this accomplish? They may still quit the convention. Committee or floor, what is the difference?"

"Appearances, my dear Mr. Morris," Franklin said. "They wish to portray us as unfair to their interests, full of connivance, and in violation of republican principles. They need to justify their mutiny to the people back home. Losing a vote on an arcane parliamentary procedure will not resound with the public." Franklin settled back in his chair. "They'll stay."

"If we back down," Hamilton fumed, "it'll spur them to further fulmination. Ignore Sherman. Appearances are of no consequence."

"Appearances are crucial." Washington had followed the discussion but had remained aloof from the argument until now. "I approve of Ben's course of action. We must avoid a donnybrook on our second day." Washington turned in his seat and bowed toward Franklin. "Thank you for your wisdom, Doctor."

Wythe, silent during the debate, picked up a piece of paper and made a note. The subject was closed.

To Madison, Sherman's strategy was obvious: slow down the proceedings. It was going to be a long summer.

"I need guidance on another matter," Madison said. "Mr. Pinckney has devised a plan of his own, and he wants to present it to the convention."

"What?" Hamilton said. "Are we to lose complete control of this convention?"

"Easy, Alex," Washington said. "What do you know of the design, Jemmy?"

"Nothing. I asked for a copy, but Pinckney made excuses. He's quite adamant and brought it up again this afternoon."

"What commitments did you make?" Hamilton bristled.

"That he may present his plan in the event of a deadlock. Every time he brings it up, I remind him of his commitment to support our plan."

"Hmm," Franklin mused. "If the convention deadlocks, I think your tactic may give weight to Pinckney's proposal. Better to dispose of it immediately. Let him present directly after Randolph. Then we'll refer both plans to committee. We can manage the committee so his grandiose ambitions never resurface."

"I concur," Morris said.

With a twinkle in his eye, Franklin added, "More's been lost in committees than from storms at sea."

"South Carolina's crucial to our alliance," Washington said. "We mustn't slight anyone in this clannish delegation. Give him his platform, but bury the proposal deep in committee."

WASHINGTON SETTLED COMFORTABLY INTO an easy chair. Dinner was over and everyone but Madison had left.

Robert Morris, sitting across from the general said, "You look disturbed, George. What bothers you?"

"I know we're well organized, but it's probable that no plan will be adopted. I fear another dreadful conflict is in our future."

"A year ago we had scant opportunity," Morris said. "Now opportunity sits at our door."

Washington remained despondent. "Perhaps, but I can't help but worry. No morning ever dawned more favorably and no day ever looked more clouded."

Madison knew the general didn't mean the heavy rain outside. Today's opening session had been exuberant and consensual, yet he kept hearing grim premonitions from people within his own bloc of support.

Morris leaned back. "The matter this evening is a bagatelle, easy to overcome."

"I worry about timing. The people may not be ready to retract from error. Evil must be sorely felt before it can be removed."

Madison sat forward. "We mustn't underestimate the people. I assure you, they're ready. People sense misdirection. Daily they feel the dearth of money and its consequences. Entrenched officials are the ones we should fear."

"Many of those entrenched officials reside with us in Philadelphia." Washington took a sip of brandy. "Jemmy, we must present a system the people will accept—all the people, even those from obstinate states. Whoever tries to govern this country must govern all. We're either a united people or thirteen independent sovereignties."

"You know my sentiments, General," Madison said. "The convention may become acrimonious at times, but need will prevail in the end."

Morris bowed his head toward Washington. "And after that fateful event, I'm confident you'll be selected to lead our new government."

"Thank you, but it is far too early to contemplate such events. However, I do have a favor to ask."

"Anything," Morris responded.

"If, in the course of events, we do propose an acceptable system, and I am again selected for leadership, there'll be inevitable accusations of monarchy. I must not be seen as having brewed the ingredients of my own regime. For this reason I'll be reserved in the proceedings ... and I request the same of you."

"Surely people won't attribute my contributions to be at your direction? I have a long and honorable record of public service."

"Robert, I'm staying in your home. We're fast friends. In my silence, people will assume that you're presenting my views. This system must be seen as the judgment of all the states, or I won't be able to govern. If it's thought to be my design, I'll be of no use to the country."

"George, you know I'll honor your request." Then Morris said with a smile, "I assume I'm free to express my opinions in my own home."

"Of course," said Washington, returning the smile.

9

Monday, May 28, 1787

"Convention suffrage?"

"One vote per state."

Sherman threw the answer over his shoulder as he squeezed down the narrow stairs. Oliver Ellsworth, Sherman's fellow delegate from Connecticut, had arrived the night before.

"Gouverneur Morris tried to base suffrage on population, but the Virginians killed the idea," Sherman added. "They were afraid of a small state revolt."

As they entered the dining room, Mrs. Marshall greeted the men. "Good morning, Mr. Sherman, Mr. Ellsworth. Please take a seat, and I'll bring breakfast. Tea or coffee?"

"Coffee, please. It smells wonderful," Sherman said.

"I knew you'd be down soon, so I brewed a fresh pot. Just a moment." She immediately whirled around, departing before Ellsworth could state a preference.

During the war, the British had closed off tea, so it had become a symbol of patriotism to permeate your home with the smell of coffee. Most women burned the beans. Mrs. Marshall had the knack. Whether she was roasting, grinding, or brewing, the hearty aroma always made Sherman crave a cup.

Sherman's relationship with Mrs. Marshall continued to improve, which wasn't a new experience for him. His courtesy, attentive conversation, and oafish ways combined in some haphazard formula that appealed to women in the same way that a big, shaggy dog always finds a caring home.

They took their seats and Mrs. Marshall returned, using a folded towel to carry a coffeepot in one hand and a tin of breakfast puffs in the other. Setting the puffs down, she poured the coffee. From each cup billowed a tiny fog wafting an invigorating aroma. Mrs. Marshall then reached for the cream and placed it directly in front of Sherman.

"There," Mrs. Marshall said. "While I get things together, you just try one of these puffs, Mr. Sherman. The recipe came from a friend in Virginia, and everyone says they're wonderful."

As Sherman took a test sip of the scalding coffee, he noticed that Ellsworth gave Mrs. Marshall a wary look before he said, "I brought a letter from your wife."

"Thank you." Sherman put the sealed envelope in his waistcoat pocket.

Ellsworth's consternation amused him. Mrs. Marshall wasn't unattractive, but at sixty-six, he had other interests on his mind. Sherman never confused a woman's good-hearted attentions with a romantic interest; at least, he hadn't in many years.

Mrs. Marshall smiled. "Mr. Sherman, it seems you have secured the advice you sought from an 'intelligent woman.' I hope between the household news, Mrs. Sherman found time to fulfill her obligations as your political confidant."

Ellsworth looked puzzled. "Political confidant?"

"Mrs. Marshall, please," Sherman said. "You mustn't reveal our late night discourse to Mr. Ellsworth."

When Mrs. Marshall saw Ellsworth's expression, she explained, "I gave Mr. Sherman difficulty one evening." Turning to Sherman, she said, "I apologize. I'm afraid I was not kind."

"No apology needed," Sherman said. "My behavior was brash and inappropriate."

Sherman gave Oliver a reassuring wink just as another guest entered the room. Both men immediately stood.

"Good morning, Reverend," Mrs. Marshall said. "Gentlemen, may I introduce the Reverend Doctor John Witherspoon. The reverend is president of the College of New Jersey. This is Mr. Roger Sherman and Mr. Oliver Ellsworth, delegates to the Federal Convention."

Sherman took a step forward and extended his hand. "It's a great pleasure to see you again, Reverend."

"Mr. Sherman, this is indeed a pleasant surprise," Witherspoon boomed in a voice more appropriate to a classroom. "How grand. Your presence will improve the quality of the evenings."

"You know each other?" Mrs. Marshall asked.

"Oh, they know each other," Ellsworth said. "Neither is inclined to boast, but they both signed the Declaration. You're looking at a couple of genuine revolutionaries."

"Worn and tattered revolutionaries," Sherman said. "What brings you to Philadelphia, Reverend?"

"I'm tutoring two students for the summer. Brothers enrolled at the college. Both equally poor students, burdened with rich parents. Dunderheaded boys forced to feign an interest in scholarship. I fear a long, dreary summer."

This could present difficulties, Sherman thought. "As luck would have it, one of your former students is representing Virginia. Have you had an opportunity to see Mr. Madison?"

"Goodness, no, I arrived just last night. Do you know where he's staying?"

"At the Indian Queen. I'll see him shortly. If you'd like, I can let him know you're in town."

"Please. He was an exceptionally bright student."

"We should adjourn early, perhaps by two o'clock. Will you be here?"

"Yes, yes. I should be returning about that time. I'd consider it a great favor if you would let him know I've boarded at Mrs. Marshall's."

"Of course. James is still a great scholar. He's grown to become the trusted pilot for our noble endeavor."

As they sat down to breakfast, Sherman thought about the possible repercussions of Madison's academic mentor living in the same house as the Connecticut delegation. Would Witherspoon eavesdrop on their conversations? Could he be used to send signals to the other side?

"When did you see Madison last?" Sherman asked.

"Years, but we've traded correspondence. He has an inquisitive mind."

Sherman chewed on a spoonful of oatmeal laced with nuts and raisins. "You must have a half dozen former students at this convention."

"More, I suspect. I look forward to revisiting them all, but Madison possessed a special quality."

"Did he share his plan with you?"

"Goodness, no. Only questions. I'm anxious to hear what he came up with."

"As are we," Sherman said as he vowed to make Witherspoon's presence an opportunity, not a liability.

SHERMAN WENT TO HIS room to read the letter from his wife. What he read between the lines was more important than her words. She had dealt with their fifteen children and household affairs in his absence many times, but obviously things were beginning to overwhelm her.

Rebecca was his second wife. She shared his religious convictions and understood his commitment to civic duty. His first wife had died in 1760, after bearing him seven children. Three years later, he married Rebecca, and Sherman could not imagine a better match. Rebecca was beautiful, shrewd in politics, and always cheerful. Eight more children crowded the boisterous household, and despite several having grown old enough to leave home, the burden on Rebecca remained enormous.

She wanted to know how long he would be away. Too long. This convention would meander for several weeks before he'd be able to measure its duration, but he already knew it would probably run several months.

He decided he needed to write several letters: one to Rebecca, another to his minister, and yet another to a good neighbor. He had to depend on others to keep an eye on his family while he toiled in Philadelphia. Rebecca could handle family and even business affairs, but she needed the kind of encouragement and support that only a husband could provide. Sherman vowed to write to her often.

When his letter was almost complete, he remembered to add a warm salutation from Washington. The general had said nothing, but the small lie would remind her of her proudest moment. Several years ago, Rebecca had visited Roger while he was in Congress, and Washington had invited them to a dinner party. To Rebecca's surprise, the general had escorted her in to dinner and seated her to his immediate left. In an unbelievable breach of etiquette, Mrs. Hancock had complained that she was owed the distinction because of the status of her husband, the governor of Massachusetts. Washington, who disliked the haughty John Hancock, had taken his seat and simply said, "It's my privilege to give my arm to the handsomest woman in the room."

That incident had made Washington a hero in the Sherman household. The general later visited New Haven and called on the family. When he was ready to leave, Sherman's daughter Mehetabel raced to open the door. The general, bowing graciously, said, "You deserve a better office, my dear little lady." Mehetabel curtsied before responding. "Yes, sir, to let you in."

Sherman smiled. He hoped that a greeting from Washington would lift his wife's spirits and give her something to innocently drop into conversations with her friends.

SHERMAN ENTERED THE STATE House Central Hall and looked around for a specific delegate. The Pennsylvania State House was an elegant Georgian building. The Assembly Room stood to the left, through a single door decorated with a shell-and-leaf frieze above the frame. To the right, the architect had used three arches to open the Pennsylvania Supreme Court Chamber to the public. At the back of the Central Hall, a striking Palladian window drew attention to the double-height Stair Hall that gave access to the second floor.

Sherman watched a group of delegates disperse in robust laughter. Obviously, someone had punctuated the end of their conversation with an amusing story. Richard Dobbs Spaight, a young delegate from North Carolina, wore a lingering smile as he walked across the lobby. Sherman moved quickly to intercept Spaight before he became engaged with another group.

"Richard, may I have a moment?"

"Of course, Roger. What's on your mind?"

"The Virginia Plan."

"A bit early to discuss it."

"The plan, yes, but it's not too early to discuss the rules. Do you think the plan will pass intact?"

"Of course not."

"My thinking exactly." Sherman took Spaight's elbow and led him to a quieter corner. "My concern is that we might agree on some aspect of the plan, say, executive term length, before we define the powers of the executive. What may look correct one day might look wrong after several more votes."

"I follow you, Roger, but I don't know where you're going."

"This isn't a single piece of legislation but an entire system. We may need to reconsider prior decisions, especially after we see the distribution of power."

Spaight stiffened. "North Carolina stands firmly with Virginia."

"I'm not suggesting you do otherwise."

"Then what are you suggesting?" A cautionary note suffused Spaight's manner and voice.

"North Carolina has different—sensitive—interests from the Northern states. You must stand fast to your commitments, but you needn't lay yourself bare to their ill-considered compassion."

"We have discussed this among ourselves, but why is Connecticut concerned?"

"We have our own concerns, but one answer serves us both."

"And that is?"

"This proposal isn't without precedent. I suggest…"

SHERMAN HURRIED OUTSIDE TO witness the strange event. Wedged onto the State House steps, his height gave him an unobstructed view over the heads of the other delegates. He quickly spotted the venerable legend, situated like an ancient noble inside a glass-enclosed chair aloft on the shoulders of four strong men. The scene would have had an air of aristocracy if not for the bemused smile on Franklin's face. His wan expression told everyone that no noble, but merely a frail old man, had come to do his duty.

"So, the great doctor makes his entrance. Now that the convicts have hauled his corpulent figure here, we may begin in earnest." This came from Pinckney, standing beside Sherman.

"Careful, Charles, the doctor has powerful friends. Some quite close at hand."

Pinckney gave Sherman a sharp look, but he delivered his answer in an even tone. "Everyone feels the need to caution me." Then after a pause, "Perhaps I should learn to hold my tongue, but I object to the elevation of prominent citizens to demigods. In our republic, all men are created equal."

Were Pinckney's comments heartfelt? Who else had reproached him?

Sherman returned his attention to Franklin. He had heard that the old man intended to use a sedan chair, but the grand arrival had nonetheless startled him. Franklin's gout limited his mobility, so he had imported the chair from France. Although Sherman had heard that even able Parisians used sedan chairs, this was the first he had seen in America.

The rainy weather on Friday had kept Franklin away from their first meeting, but today's bright skies offered no obstacle. The men gently carried their charge up the three steps, down the Central Hall, and into the Assembly Room. Franklin had rented the carriers from the debtors' prison, and they seemed happy for the recess from their boredom.

The delegates had followed the entourage inside. Now they all stood in a circle, three and four deep, as the ill-fated farmers lifted the doctor and carefully placed him in a chair in the first row. A small round of applause accompanied the impromptu ceremony; and then everyone shook Franklin's hand or bowed briefly from the periphery. The delegates broke from the circle, either searching out a seat or breaking into small groups to continue their conversations.

Sherman watched Madison ensconce himself in the same center-front seat as Friday's session. Sherman didn't want his back to the delegates. He had chosen a seat to the rear and side so he could keep a watchful eye on everyone.

Soon Sherman heard the doorkeeper announce, "Gentlemen, the president of the Federal Convention, Gen. George Washington."

The delegates stood as Washington entered from a door to the right at the front of the chamber. The general carried himself with such dignity that as soon as he sat and with no further direction, everyone quietly took a seat. The chamber began to feel crowded. Nine delegates had arrived over the weekend. Confidence had strengthened as the number of represented states grew to eight.

The high windows threw sharp shadows into the chamber, and several men on the periphery had turned their backs to the bright light. Sherman was grateful that the sun had started to bake away the dampness. Heavy wool clothing and a reduced opportunity to bathe had created a ripe, musty odor that hung heavy in the room.

Washington called on Wythe to read the Rules Committee report. Most of the rules were familiar and acceptable. The list didn't include secrecy, nor did it include a right to reconsider prior votes. The Virginians hadn't accepted Sherman's swap.

Most politicians paid scant attention to rules because they were too eager to hear themselves speak. Experience had taught Sherman that rules, wielded with a deft hand, could control proceedings. One of the rules allowed any state to postpone a vote for one day, giving the weaker side an opportunity to marshal additional votes. Sherman guessed the rule was meant to mollify his weak alliance, but he judged it inconsequential.

The Rules Committee had avoided controversy by leaving the real work to be done on the floor, and Sherman didn't believe that any of the rules would raise controversy. He was wrong.

Rufus King, of Massachusetts, immediately asked to speak. Handsome, ambitious, and a fine speaker, the thirty-two-year-old dandy was widely recognized as a rising politician. His political talents were hampered, however, by unattractive bouts of arrogance.

King spoke with the assurance of an exceptionally gifted orator. "Mr. President and honorable delegates, I wish to draw your attention to the rule that votes must be entered in the minutes. Since the early acts of the convention aren't meant to bind the delegates, a record of the votes is dangerous. Changes of opinion will be frequent. We shouldn't furnish handles to our enemies. I move that this rule be stricken."

So, the Virginians wanted a secret meeting with no record of the votes, even for posterity.

Butler, of South Carolina, called for the floor. "Mr. President, it's imperative that we proceed without undue influence from beyond these doors. We must debate, weigh the arguments, adjust our opinions, and finally, after careful deliberation, vote our conscience. To facilitate this lofty aim, I wish to introduce two rules.

"The first is that no member shall be absent from the House without the leave of this assemblage. Congress cannot call members away."

This rule surprised Sherman, but he immediately saw the need. Many of the delegates were members of Congress. In the past, when Congress hadn't liked the course of a conference, they recalled their members to preclude a quorum.

Butler continued, "Another rule is necessary. I propose that no copy of the journal may be taken outside this chamber and that nothing that happens inside this chamber be spoken of outside these walls."

There it was—the dreaded secrecy rule. Madison then asked to speak. His soft voice commanded attention as everyone concentrated to hear his words. Sherman noted that Madison's quick, animated hand movements and unrelenting eye contact also worked to hold his audience.

"We need long debate before we arrive at a uniform opinion. In the meantime, the minds of members may change, and there's much to be gained by proceedings free of public scrutiny."

Turning toward Washington, he continued. "With secret discussions, no man will feel obligated to retain his opinion for the mere appearance of consistency."

Madison had barely taken his seat before his fellow Virginian, George Mason, had secured the floor. "Gentlemen, secrecy is necessary to prevent misrepresentation by our adversaries. We must proceed in private, or we'll exhaust our energies defending preliminary opinions."

The Virginians had expected a vigorous counterargument, so an awkward stillness ensued as Sherman and his allies sat silent.

Richard Dobbs Spaight asked for the floor. "I propose we allow a new vote upon any previous question when a member sees a reasonable cause for reconsideration."

Sherman watched Madison's head spin from Washington's impassive face to look at Franklin. The doctor shrugged faintly as if to say that he had no idea why North Carolina had proposed the rule.

Sherman worked to keep a smile from his face. With a quarter of her population slave, North Carolina feared a runaway convention controlled by the abolitionist North. Sherman used this fear to convince Spaight to support his goal of not finalizing votes until the entire system had been drafted. With this rule, North Carolina could hold prior votes hostage to a final outcome that would protect her slaveholdings.

The first vote of the convention unanimously defeated the motion not to record votes. Sherman was pleased. Open proceedings worked to Connecticut's advantage, but he was willing to barter the issue as long as a complete account became public prior to state ratification.

The rest of the newly introduced rules were referred back to the Rules Committee. This maneuver delayed the vote until the next day, but Sherman foresaw that the two crucial rules would be adopted. The Virginians had the votes to secure secret proceedings and, with North Carolina on his side, he'd have his reconsideration rule. Sherman heard the motion to adjourn with a sense of accomplishment. He had won the first exchange.

SHERMAN DESCENDED THE STATE House steps at a diagonal. Sensing his companion's contemplative mood, Ellsworth kept silent as he walked beside him. After adjournment, Sherman had spent the good part of an hour conversing with the other delegates—nothing substantial, just friendly discussions at the end of a short business day.

Their exit from the State House provided his first moment of private thought. Suddenly Sherman realized that he needed to quicken his pace. He had promised Madison to invite Witherspoon to meet him at the Indian Queen. He had dallied and needed to hurry, or Witherspoon would miss the appointed hour. As he thought about it, he realized he'd been basking in his success. A mistake. His victory had altered the mechanics, not the substance, of the convention. This was no time to slacken. Tomorrow would start the real confrontation.

Ellsworth mistook Sherman's quickened pace to mean that he had finished his musing. Stepping quickly to catch up, he said, "An excellent day; events went exactly as you predicted."

"The rules work to our advantage, but we only won a few delaying tools. They still own the votes. Unless we alter the balance, the convention will be their beast."

"But the stampede has been checked. Besides, I enjoyed the surprise on Madison's face."

Sherman stopped walking and faced Ellsworth. "We've gained their attention, but now the Virginians will be on guard."

Ellsworth took a snuffbox out of his waistcoat, laid an ample portion along his wrist, and raised it to his nose. "The large states sail under a false flag."

He took a long sniff, inhaling every speck.

"Roger, you must force those freebooters to hoist proper colors."

10

Monday, May 28, 1787

"Dr. Witherspoon, what a pleasure to see you." Madison scurried across the Indian Queen foyer, hand extended, to greet his old teacher.

"Please, James, call me John. You're no longer my student."

"Thank you, John. But excuse me if I slip occasionally. Old habits die hard."

"New habits, my dear boy, new habits chase the doldrums away."

"Perhaps, but I cling to old habits like a warm comforter."

"Can we sit somewhere? You can tell me about your habits and exciting new venture."

"Will you be my guest for dinner?"

"Unfortunately not. My benefactor has invited me to dine at his home with my two summer charges. We'll have ample time in the days ahead, but now I'm anxious to hear about your grand scheme of government."

Madison felt Witherspoon's arm around his narrow shoulder as the two men ascended the stairs that led to a sitting room on the second floor. After settling comfortably in two facing wing chairs, Madison ordered tea and cakes from an attentive steward.

"Our proceedings are private," Madison said. "I can't discuss details, but I can tell you that you've influenced the design. Thank you for your letters over the last year."

"I enjoyed the intellectual exchange. Whose philosophy did you follow?"

"You may think this arrogant, but I choose no single guide. I blended Aristotle, Locke, Hume, and Montesquieu with my own reasoning—a unique design."

"Excellent. The student becomes the sage."

"Doctor, I mean John, you're far too generous. I did nothing new; I merely sifted the thoughts of the best minds to mix a new brew."

"Every cook uses the same ingredients. Some prepare indigestible hash, while others concoct dishes that delight the palate. Don't denigrate your feat, young man. I'm confident you're a great cook."

"Thank you. I believe I've designed a system that harnesses man's predilection for wrongdoing."

"Then you've performed a miracle. Man is a bloodstained creature."

"Bloodstained, but capable of noble acts. A sound design can steer him along an elevated course."

"James, that's the function of religion, not government. Don't set your sights too high."

"Government can't make man virtuous, but government can constrain his vices, deny opportunity, and restrain the lust for power."

"No wonder Mr. Sherman spoke so highly of you."

"Roger Sherman? He's positioning himself to lead the opposition. Sherman's an obstructionist."

"Surely you exaggerate. I spoke to him this morning, and he was quite complimentary to you."

"Sherman's a political beast. He tells people what they wish to hear."

"I believe Sherman earnest in his praise."

"I don't trust the man. He has no anchor, no principled underpinnings."

"I've also worked with Roger and have found him a devout Christian and a man of virtuous intentions."

"John, the government must remain secular," Madison said, exasperated.

"You're wrong. The government must not force a particular religion on anyone, but it must never interfere with the free expression of faith." Witherspoon reached out and touched Madison's forearm. "James, a government can never be secular when filled with God-fearing men."

"This is old ground. Our disagreements don't affect the design."

"I shall forgo the argument for the moment," Witherspoon said. "But you must explain your qualms about Sherman. He holds his piety close."

"He holds his fealty to Connecticut closer."

An expression of comprehension came over Witherspoon's face. "I think I understand. Listen, James, Sherman's not a thinker, he's a doer. None better. You want him on your side."

"He'll never join the nationalist cause."

"I hope you're wrong; otherwise you must engage a formidable foe." Witherspoon scrunched up in his seat. "How's your father?"

"Excellent health, thank you."

"And Montpelier?"

"Montpelier prospers."

Witherspoon looked as if he were about to ask another question, then gave a small shrug and said, "I'm glad to hear things are good at home."

When Madison offered no additional information, Witherspoon asked, "Can I address a sensitive subject?"

"Of course. You're a friend."

"What are your intentions about slavery?"

Madison nibbled a piece of cake and followed with a sip of tea. "Slavery cannot become an issue at this convention."

"It must."

"It cannot. It will destroy any chance of agreement."

"James, only you can weave a path out of this evil morass. You're the architect of this new government—and a slaveholder."

"I am not."

"A niggling distinction. You'll inherit slaves."

"You're from the North. You can't grasp the emotions around this issue in my region."

"I can see that slavery corrodes justice." Witherspoon again touched Madison's arm. "James, look inside yourself."

Madison sat for a moment. "I'm helpless."

"I can't accept that. You're one of the smartest men I've ever encountered. Surely you can devise a solution acceptable to your fellow Southerners."

"Southerners aren't the only slaveholders. May I remind you that only Massachusetts has outlawed slavery? Pennsylvania has four thousand slaves, many in Philadelphia. New Jersey—your state—has twelve thousand."

"James that's not fair, you know—"

"It is fair. The South holds no monopoly on this vice."

"Our economy doesn't depend on slavery."

"So why not free yours?" Madison looked away. "Let's change the subject."

"A sinner cannot excuse his depravity by pointing to another sinner. You cannot avoid complicity."

"Ending slavery means sacrificing our republic. Too high a price." Madison tossed a remnant of cake back onto the plate. "And a quixotic quest."

"You must do something," Witherspoon said, with a tranquil earnestness that reflected years of ministering to intractable sinners.

Madison tapped his empty teacup against his front teeth. "There's only one thing I can do. Virginia has outlawed the slave trade. We're the only Southern state to have done so. I can work to extend the prohibition in the new Constitution."

"A start."

"John, I cannot end this evil. The best I can do is to thwart its growth."

"I must trust your political instincts." Witherspoon smiled. "And I'll work to end slavery in New Jersey, so I can be more self-righteous at our next meeting."

Madison laughed at the reverend doctor's self-deprecation. Instead of reminiscing about his college days, they had discussed difficult matters. Better to end on a friendly note. As they parted, Madison realized that he had just negotiated a compromise with a nondelegate. He hesitated a moment and then bolted out the front door, proceeding to Market Street. In two blocks, he reached his destination: Wilcox Apothecary.

"Good afternoon, Mr. Madison. How can I help you?"

"Good day, Mr. Wilcox. Can I have a pennyweight of ginseng mixed with chalk powder and two bottles of Stoughton's?"

"Stomach ailing again?"

"A bottle of balsam of Tolu as well." Madison was grateful that the shop was empty.

"Of course. Take just a moment."

While the chemist busied himself pulling down ceramic pots and measuring jars, Madison wandered over to a wall plastered with broadsides for patent medicines made from plant and animal extracts or metallic derivatives.

"Anything new?"

The chemist kept grinding the pestle against the mortar to mix the ginseng into the chalk. "Keyser's pills, but they're for syphilis."

Madison laughed. "I'll strive to avoid that ailment."

Madison scanned the wall behind the counter. After perusing the tiny drawers interspersed with glass and ceramic pots of every conceivable size, Madison asked, "Anything to quiet bowels?"

The chemist scratched his head. "We've tried everything."

"Wrap my order then. I'm in a hurry."

Madison opened a glass-fronted bookcase and extracted a heavy tome. As he examined the London Dispensatory, he realized that he had learned everything from books. "Which of these dispensatories is the best?"

"Some like Shaw's or Bate's, but I think the one you're holding's superior."

"I'll take it as well."

This request drew a dubious look from Wilcox. "It costs forty dollars. It's for chemists."

Madison handed the shopkeeper the book. "I know."

"Mr. Madison, this will give you a long chalk. Would it be possible to settle at least part of your bill?"

Madison tried to keep his face from showing his reaction. He was going through money fast and that meant he would need to write home. The money always came promptly, but he dreaded the accompanying remonstration to mend his spendthrift ways. He hated being dependent on his father's largesse, but surviving in this expensive city on his miserly remuneration from Congress was impossible. Madison hefted the dispensatory. The book might contain clues to his health problems, so he reached for his purse and handed the chemist four gold sovereigns.

MADISON TUCKED THE LINEN napkin into his breeches and ran his fingers along his waistline to smooth out any gathering. He looked up at the steward and ordered breakfast. "I'll have boiled eggs, ham, and biscuits. And coffee, not tea."

"Yes, sir. Would the gentleman care for a waffle?"

"Yes, thank you. With honey…after the eggs and ham."

"Of course, sir."

Madison scanned the Indian Queen's dining room for an eating companion. He had risen early and encountered no one upon entering. Now he saw Pinckney standing in the doorway.

Madison waved, and Pinckney sauntered over.

"How fortuitous. I was looking for you," Madison said. "Will you join me for breakfast?"

"If we can discuss my plan."

With the flat of an uplifted palm, Madison pointed to the opposite chair. "That's the subject I wish to discuss. But please, let's wait until after coffee."

"So you need a morning lift. I thought you had no vices."

"Morning coffee is one of my minor vices. My major vices I conceal."

"And what might those be?"

"If I tell you, they'll no longer be concealed."

Pinckney's mouth quivered a second, but then he laughed. "You invite my sarcasm—my most debilitating vice." Pinckney shook out his napkin and let it float to his lap.

"Randolph presents today. Are you prepared as well?"

"For what? To present my plan?"

"Yes."

"Today?"

"Directly after Edmund."

Pinckney ignored Madison and caught the eye of a steward. He waved two fingers to summon him to their table. After an inquisition, Pinckney selected a meal with more amendments than a congressional bill and ordered coffee served immediately. The nonplussed steward instantly returned with a silver carafe.

After taking a sip of coffee, Pinckney asked, "Will there be time?"

"There'll be no debate today, just presentation."

"Then I am ready."

"Excellent. We believe a fair hearing requires that both plans be presented together."

"Who's we?"

"I, uh, presented your request to Gen. Washington and a few others. It was received with enthusiasm, and they suggested you follow Edmund."

"When was this?"

"Sometime over the weekend. I've been busy and forgot to see you. My apologies."

"Damn it, James, this is Tuesday. You had ample—"

"Charles, I didn't—"

"Your actions are disingenuous."

"No! I didn't mean to delay. If you're not ready, we'll make other arrangements."

"I'll present *today*." Pinckney stared at Madison. "But I'm not a novice. I recognize political connivance."

Madison met Pinckney's intense glare. "Charles, I know how this looks, but there was no intent to catch you unawares. This is entirely my fault. You were busy with the Rules Committee. I should've searched you out. Please, I feel terrible."

Madison's chagrin was real, but it emanated from underestimating Pinckney. Madison broke eye contact, ceding Pinckney a victory in their little contest.

The steward approached with their meal. Sensing the tension, the steward worked swiftly and departed without a word. With his forearms situated on either side of his meal, Pinckney inspected his breakfast. Deciding that the steward had met his specifications, he lifted a knife and crisply tapped an egg to create a perfect crack one-third of the way down from the top. He lifted the top off in a single motion, deftly swirled the knife around the circumference, and slipped the egg into a small bowl. He replicated the little ceremony with a second egg.

Picking up the salt, he stopped in mid-motion, "James, eat. I shan't stay angry."

"Again, I didn't mean—"

"Stop. But never treat me in this manner again."

"You have my word."

"Now that that's settled, we can enjoy our breakfast. Are there any other plans?"

"No. We'll debate and select a course between the Virginia Plan and the South Carolina Plan."

"The 'Pinckney Plan.' South Carolina isn't tribal like Virginia."

Did ego drive this remark, or had Pinckney been rebuffed by his own delegation? Either way, it was an astonishing statement. The Virginians only appeared unified to foreigners because they hid their dissensions.

Madison picked up a knife and fumbled with his eggs. The rest of the meal proceeded in a bright mood, with Pinckney actually making him laugh at his sardonic portrayal of their fellow delegates. The man was entertaining. He was also a valuable ally and supporter of the republican cause. Madison had mishandled this episode, and he admonished himself not to make the same mistake again.

"GENTLEMEN, OUR PRESENT GOVERNMENT is weak." Edmund Randolph had the attention of the entire chamber. "We cannot control the states' dealings with foreign countries, we cannot field an army, we cannot raise revenue, and we cannot promote commerce."

Now Randolph dropped his voice and spoke with sincerity instead of bombast.

"This is not to denigrate the authors of the Articles. Nothing better could've been obtained at the time. War required compromise, but these accommodations laid an unstable foundation. Now our task is to shore up our republican experiment with a foundation that will support our lofty ideals."

His voice rising again, Randolph announced his transition. "Gentlemen, I'll now describe the fifteen resolves that will build a sustainable government."

Madison looked up from his journal—his private notes, not the official record. The secretary's transcript would be terse, so Madison had decided to keep a complete journal. He could take a break from his note taking because the Virginia resolves sat before him in his own hand. Madison placed the cap on his inkwell.

The day had started with the report from the Rules Committee. The convention quickly approved the report, including secrecy and a right to request a new vote on settled issues. That battle was past.

Randolph had opened with a lengthy description of the crisis in the United States. The delegates wouldn't be here now if they weren't already aware of the problems the nation was facing, but Madison had urged the review to stiffen their will. Franklin had astutely suggested praise for the authors of the Articles of Confederation, because four of them, including Sherman, sat in the chamber.

During the presentation, Washington wore a carefully neutral expression. Madison realized that, with his back to the delegates, he couldn't measure their response. He considered turning around but took his cue from Washington.

Randolph closed his oration to utter silence. Some delegates already knew the plan. Others sat stunned. Washington deftly called on Pinckney to present his proposal. Quickly moving to another subject would soften the blow and preclude debate, which would have only raised anguished protest. Innovations required time to be absorbed.

Madison listened to Pinckney with interest, because their earlier confrontations had aroused his curiosity. He did not, however, remove the cap from his inkwell. Madison felt no need to record the elements of a plan destined for the abyss. Pinckney's plan went beyond republican; it veered toward democratic. The people deserved a voice, but the cacophony of factions destroyed republics. Pinckney's naïveté exposed his lack of research.

Pinckney's eloquent close did rouse polite applause, but Madison knew the proposal went too far to garner support. Good. Pinckney's plan would make the Virginia resolves look cautious by comparison.

The last order of business was to dissolve into a Committee of the Whole. Washington relinquished his chair until the official convention would reconvene. Madison worried that the absence of his stern countenance would lift a restraint from the incendiary members. The informality of the Committee of the Whole could incite combative debate.

With adjournment, Madison stood respectfully with the other delegates as Washington marched out of the chamber. Tomorrow they would unfurl the sails for their great voyage.

"No more dams I'll make for fish;
  Nor fetch in firing
  At requiring
  Nor scrape trenchering, nor wash dish.
  'Ban, 'Ban, Ca—Caliban
  Has a new master, get a new man.
  Freedom, hey-day! Hey-day, freedom! Freedom,
  hey-day, freedom!"
"O brave monster! Lead the way."
Shakespeare's clown scene closed the second act of *The Tempest*. Madison laughed. Gouverneur Morris rolled with merriment. Washington gave a rare uninhibited smile. Hamilton scowled.

"The humor escapes me," Hamilton said. "The Calibans of the world threaten liberty."

"Alex, it is but a play," Washington said.

"With a timely message."

"Alex, my good man, you must learn to relax," Morris said. "Wonderful music, elaborate sets, an intriguing story."

"Mr. Morris, I'll relax when—"

Applause suddenly erupted from the orchestra seats. Madison looked down to see the audience standing with faces uplifted toward their box. Intermission had erupted into a spontaneous demonstration.

Washington stood, stepped toward the rail, and acknowledged the accolade with a series of nods. His response spurred the audience to louder applause, so the general shifted to a more animated wave. With a kind expression, he held up both hands, palms out, to signal that he wished the tribute to end. The clapping gradually subsided as people took their seats or walked up the aisle toward the lobby. Looking relieved, Washington stepped back from the rail and scooted his chair into the recesses of the box.

"The people regale me now, but in the dark moments of the war, I felt abandoned."

"They shift with the tide, while you anchor steadfast on solid shoals," Hamilton said.

"Alex, you make stubbornness sound like a virtue."

"Stubbornness is a virtue when you're in the right. You adhere to principle when the people veer to expediency."

"Fame is merely landing on the side of victory."

Morris laughed. "A fickle populace does follow triumph. May I get you an ale, General?"

"No, I'll venture down on my own."

"Surely not. That audience will turn into a mob," Hamilton said.

"Mr. Hamilton, I'm not a deity." He turned to Morris. "Will you join me, Gouverneur?"

"Of course. I need to stretch my leg," Morris said, giving a sharp rap to his wooden leg.

After the two men had left, Hamilton asked, "What's the theme of the play?"

"Power and usurpation," Madison answered.

"No, it's the folly of democracy."

"I disagree. The play illustrates our need to protect against unshackled demigods."

"The theme is the credulity of the masses. Caliban represents the ignorant that swallow a tyrant's false promises. Democracy is the monster."

"That's but a subplot. Shakespeare means to warn us to guard against the corrupting quest for power."

"Finally, we agree. But the lust for power is not restricted to the elite; the masses also contend. Which is more dangerous?"

"Tell me."

"The masses. You saw the adulation directed toward the general, but given power, they'll choose Stephano, the drunken butler, as their leader."

Madison shrugged. "Stephano would be inept, not evil."

Hamilton made a deprecating noise. "He's already evil. He incites rebellion. Murder. You mean his ineptness would mitigate malfeasance."

"I suppose I do. Competence combined with evil presents a greater danger."

"Jemmy, democracies devour themselves."

Washington and Morris entered the box in a raucous mood. Washington had enjoyed his sojourn into an adoring crowd, and Morris enjoyed everything. Madison suddenly realized that the intermission had gone exceptionally long. Looking toward the stage, he saw a head jerk back after observing the general take his seat. The curtain lifted and the play resumed.

THE FOUR MEN WALKED in pairs down Market Street. Washington and Morris took the lead, while the two disciples followed in their footsteps. Philadelphia spring evenings retained a nip, but it felt good to be outdoors in clean air.

After the play, it had taken more than half an hour to break away from the well-wishers in front of the Opera House. Madison noticed that groups followed on either side of the street, no doubt anxious to discover which tavern the general would choose. Madison had heard that there were one hundred and seventeen taverns in the city. No wonder the theater crowd felt obligated to follow them. The street reverberated good cheer as it echoed the voices of happy people, punctuated by the tap, tap, tapping of Morris's leg.

Madison had enjoyed the play, but he thought it troubling. Life didn't always end on a merry note.

"What's on your mind, Jemmy?"

"Power and usurpation."

"Ha, shall we start our debate anew?" Hamilton asked.

"It is a debate without resolution, like the argument between nature and nurture."

"Yet another theme. We could use Shakespeare at our convention. He knew men's follies."

"Man's follies and nobility. Man can be enlightened."

"All men? I think you napped during part of the play."

"I understand the ambiguity. I believe—I must believe—that man can be channeled for good."

"You're mistaken. Wisdom cannot be shepherded by a system of checks and balances."

Madison turned to look at Hamilton. This last had not been said in his normal confrontational tone. He sounded forlorn. As if conscious of the departure, Hamilton rejoined with a challenge. "Have you deciphered 'this thing of darkness'?"

"The uneducated masses? The ones you believe must be led by an enlightened elite?"

"Quite. You don't turn the tiller over to an idiot."

"Your view is too dark."

"And far too serious, gentlemen," Morris interjected over his shoulder. "Look at the merriment about you. The street is filled with chattering, happy people. Spring is in the air. A new beginning that bodes well for our endeavor. Alex, all is not hopeless."

"Mr. Morris, dear sir, a pint shall alter my dour mood."

"Hear! Hear! Let's find a place to land and get Alex a dose of elixir."

Washington laughed and said, "Just around the corner, gentlemen."

"What impressed you, General?" Madison asked.

"The skill with which the actors commanded attention."

11

Wednesday, May 30, 1787

"This is a coup!" Ellsworth exclaimed.

Sherman and Ellsworth sat in Sherman's room comparing notes on the Virginia Plan. Sherman had meant to spend the previous evening in a study of the proposal, but he had wasted the night trying to extinguish Paterson's temper. Paterson refused to be mollified. Now, with breakfast behind them, they had only a short time to prepare for the day's session.

Sherman shook his head. "The states will never approve this plan."

"I think the fifteenth resolve means they intend to bypass the states."

Sherman slapped his notes against the arm of his chair. "Revolutionaries don't ask permission. This plan's like the Macaroni. Striking in appearance, but so outlandish people will never follow the fashion."

Ellsworth laughed at Sherman's metaphor. The Macaroni were young fops who wore big wigs, little hats, tiny shoes, and quaint two-button coats. The popular Revolutionary song, "Yankee Doodle," had mocked the erstwhile Macaroni. Turning serious, Ellsworth said, "The most worrisome part is that it destroys the equal vote for each state."

Sherman let his papers dangle over the arm of his chair. "The core of this plan is the power of the central government to veto state laws and use force against the states if they refuse to comply." Lifting his notes to get the exact words, he read, "The government can 'call forth the force of the union against any member of the union.'" Sherman snapped the papers at Ellsworth. "They mean to wage war against the states."

Ellsworth picked up his snuffbox, but before opening it, he said, "This plan usurps all state authority."

Sherman spoke almost to himself as he continued to rifle through his notes. "Only 'in all cases to which the states are incompetent.' I presume the Virginians believe themselves the only ones competent." Sherman leaned forward. "Look at the judiciary. It's broader than the Atlantic and, like the ocean, we see only the surface." Sherman tossed his notes to the floor and extended his long legs. After a moment, he said quietly, "Combine an omnipotent judiciary with an absolute executive veto over state laws, and you nullify the states." Sherman slowly shook his head. "The Virginians mean to pitch Connecticut into the ash heap."

"Roger, you're worrying me. You were confident until now."

Sherman used the heels of his hands to rub his eyes. He turned a bloodshot gaze at Ellsworth. "I looked at the Virginians' plot as a challenge to outwit. I've been reminded of the stakes." Sherman took his hands away from his face. "This is political war. The weapons are guile, wit, and force. We have ample quantities of the first two, but the last is in short supply."

"A storm's force can dissipate when it blows too hard too early," Ellsworth offered.

"Don't underestimate a revolutionary cloudburst. It can wash away everything in its path—combatants and bystanders."

'I'm sorry, Roger, but I have a hard time seeing Madison as a world-shaking radical."

"Then you've not grasped the essence of the man."

Ellsworth shrugged. "We don't have much time. What should we do?"

"There's no use scouring these notes any further. We know the peaks and the valleys are of no consequence. Today's debate will reveal the extent of their support." Sherman threw himself out of the chair. "We should leave. I want to arrive at the State House early."

As they entered the State House, Sherman grabbed Ellsworth's elbow. "There's George Read. Go shore up his confidence. Remind him that we're in committee. I'll talk to Paterson."

Ellsworth sped toward Read, while Sherman casually wandered into Paterson's line of sight.

"Roger, may I have a word with you?"

"Of course, William. Let's walk the yard."

The men walked past a sentry and stepped out into the bright sunlight. With the vote to hold the proceedings secret, sentries had arrived in the Central Hall and outside the building. More bothersome, the chamber windows had been nailed shut. The convention had progressed to a serious state. This morning, Sherman noticed that even the cobblestone streets had been layered with sod to quiet the carriages as they passed.

Looking around, Sherman noticed that several groups walked the perimeter of the expansive walled State House yard. It had recently been landscaped with serpentine gravel walkways, grass plots, and hundreds of elm trees and shrubs. The slender trees and tiny shrubs gave the yard a barren appearance.

Buildings were under construction in the two corners bracketing the State

House. To the east, a new county courthouse employed dozens of tradesmen. Along Fifth, set back somewhat from the corner, the American Philosophical Society had laid the foundation for their permanent home. The Society had also positioned an observatory designed by Dr. Franklin in the center of the yard. Sherman had been told that this apparatus mapped the rotation of Venus across the night sky. The Philosophical Society was yet another Franklin enterprise. The man seemed omnipresent in Philadelphia.

Despite the yard's lean appearance, Sherman surmised that it would be a popular respite from the stuffy chamber. Sherman veered right to follow the pattern set by the other delegates. Everyone seemed automatically to move in a counterclockwise direction, and each group kept a respectful distance from the men in front of them.

"Thank you for letting me vent my anger last night."

"That's a friend's obligation," Sherman said.

Paterson rotated his head and flitted his eyes as if fearful of a flanking attack. "I thought I was prepared for their worst, but I was shocked to see how much I underestimated their malice."

"Their plan exceeds my fears as well."

"What are we to do?"

Sherman did not answer at first. After they had taken about six paces, he said, "Our duty is to protect our respective states and Congress. They seek to disband both." After a pause, Sherman added, "I underestimated the importance of secrecy."

"They had the votes. There was nothing we could do."

"You saw the sentries?"

"Yes." As they turned a corner, Paterson looked at Sherman. "Roger, is it treason to remain silent?"

"Let's see today's reaction."

Robert Morris had approached Sherman and told him confidentially about the threat of a military insurrection by the Society of the Cincinnati. Sherman doubted that this intelligence had been shared with Paterson.

"What about our plan?"

"Too early. Pinckney's plan will be entombed in committee. To avoid the same fate, our timing must be perfect."

"I'll accept your leadership on this."

Sherman almost missed a step. Until now, Paterson had been fighting Sherman for the leadership of the small states. Desperation could change a man's outlook. They had by now walked the circumference of the yard, and the clock on the State House wall reminded Sherman that they must reenter the chamber.

Sherman turned to Paterson and clasped his upper arm. "William, don't despair. We've not done badly so far. Political tides ebb unexpectedly. With you on our side, I'm confident we'll prevail."

"Thank you, Roger." Paterson's posture straightened slightly. "I'll do my best to disrupt their merry little march."

ROGER SHERMAN TOOK HIS seat. Randolph again read the Virginia Plan. When he had finished, Sherman felt his body tense—the debate was about to begin. Gouverneur Morris hitched to the front of the chamber. Shifting his weight to his wooden leg, he grabbed both lapels and gazed about the room.

"Gentlemen, I'd make a motion to postpone debate on the plan until we consider the following resolutions.

"One, that a union of the states based on the Articles of Confederation will not accomplish the goals of our meeting.

"Two, that no treaty among the states, as individual sovereignties, can build an adequate government.

"Three, that a national government ought to be established, consisting of a supreme legislative, a supreme executive, and a supreme judiciary."

Sherman scribbled, *They're asking for a vote to overthrow the government*, and passed the note to Ellsworth.

Ellsworth read it with an ashen face.

Morris's motion to postpone consideration of the Virginia Plan received an immediate second. On the call for a vote, Ellsworth turned to Sherman and asked, "Now what?"

Sherman pulled out a piece of paper, tore it in half, and scratched out something. He folded the half-sheet and handed it to Ellsworth, saying, "Wander over and slip this to Read."

Ellsworth got up immediately, not waiting for Sherman to explain the contents of the note.

After a unanimous vote to postpone the Virginia Plan, Sherman sat alert, anxious to discover the sentiment of the chamber. A series of delegates criticized the first proposition. Sherman felt heartened that others believed the Articles could be amended.

Sensing the mood, the Virginia coalition moved to the less controversial third proposition. Sherman could feel the collective relief, but instead of quickly endorsing a three-branch government, debate grew even more raucous over the meaning of the words *national* and *supreme*.

Sherman wondered if he should buy time by letting the debate continue or ask for the floor to center debate on the real issue. Before he could decide, Pinckney gained the floor, appearing to have read Sherman's mind.

"Mr. Randolph, a question hangs over this chamber. If you'd be so kind, sir, would you please provide us with a straightforward answer? Do you intend to abolish the state governments?"

The abrupt question flattened the chamber's rancor. The stunned delegates sat breathless, appalled by the audacious challenge. Randolph looked unsettled as he slowly rose.

"Mr. Pinckney, I shall, of course, give you a straightforward answer. I believe the outline of the proposed system is clear."

As Randolph started to sit, Pinckney leaped to his feet. "That response doesn't answer my question. If you please, Mr. Randolph...do you intend to abolish the state governments?"

"Mr. Pinckney, I apologize if my answer seemed insufficient." Randolph stood beside his table, appeared to ruffle through some papers, and then looked up to say, "I haven't made up my mind. I'm open to any discussion which might throw light on this important subject."

With this, Randolph took his seat and pretended to sort papers again, in the hope that Pinckney would permit his retreat.

Pinckney rose again. "Mr. President, I doubt that Congress authorized a discussion of a system built on principles different from the Articles of Confederation. This collective body has no authority to veer from our instructions."

Without challenging Randolph further, Pinckney sat. The room remained still as everyone waited to see what would next unfold. Morris was recognized again. Sherman knew Morris wouldn't equivocate.

"Gentlemen, please, we're seasoned politicians. There is no need to evade the question. Let's be clear: our proposal is for a supreme government, one with compulsive authority." Morris walked across the front of the chamber, engaging all the delegates. "You may recoil from such a bold statement, but in all of history, there's been but one supreme power and one only."

Morris thumped his wooden leg with the force of a gavel. "Gentlemen, the Articles are based on myth and fable. I propose we begin to address our business with a heady dose of reality. As a supreme government over all the people, our system will act on individuals, not the states. Any intermediary would interfere."

Before he took his seat, Morris said disdainfully, "You now have your straightforward answer."

It was time for Sherman to speak. Standing at his place, he said, "There can be no doubt that Congress must be granted additional powers. The crisis is real. Dissolution threatens. But gentlemen, I implore you, don't squander what may be our sole opportunity to right the situation. If we deviate from our instructions, if we laden our proposals with coercive national powers, if we ignore the spirit of our Revolution, the states will reject our work.

"Shall we lose our sole opportunity due to overzealous ambition? The track we choose in these early days will set the course for the duration. Let's ponder this track with care."

Read moved to postpone debate on the resolution for a supreme national government. Sherman was pleased to hear Pinckney second the motion, but he was displeased to see the motion defeated. The Virginians didn't hesitate to use force, the third political weapon.

Butler immediately called for a vote to approve a supreme national government, signaling apparent discord within the South Carolina delegation, but before Sherman could think it through, the motion passed, with only Connecticut voting nay. It disappointed Sherman that his allies failed to see the significance of the vote.

Filled with victory, the large state alliance went straight to the Virginia Plan's most controversial resolution. With the majority on their side, the Virginians struck hard, intent on vanquishing the opposition.

The secretary read the second resolution. "The rights of suffrage in the national legislature ought to be proportioned to the quotas of contribution, or to the number of free inhabitants."

A long debate ensued within the large state alliance. They vigorously argued over the respective virtues of representation based on taxes or people. Numerous alternate resolutions were proposed. All were postponed.

Sherman spotted the chink in their armor. At first, he thought that they were giddy with their early victory and had charged in an uncoordinated assault, but as the dispute continued, he almost slapped his forehead. This discord within their alliance was not about nuanced words, but a deep chasm within their camp. The resolution would have been precisely worded had they a consensus. Sherman guessed the Pennsylvanians had insisted on the word *free* before *inhabitants*. The slave states had threatened to bolt, so they added an ambiguous reference to tax contributions. He had been wrong this morning: the valleys, as well as the peaks, cast vital signals.

Despite the revelation, Sherman felt annoyance. The large states were debating amongst themselves as if the small states had already been defeated. He bristled at their arrogance. Finally, the large states seemed to agree on an even less precise statement: "that the equal state suffrage established by the Articles of Confederation ought not to prevail in the national legislature, and that an equitable ratio of representation ought to be substituted."

Sherman knew this delayed the argument, but more important, it moved debate from the chamber to a private tavern room. Just before the vote, Read gained the floor.

"Gentlemen, I move to postpone the point. If this motion is passed, Delaware must withdraw. My instructions are clear. We may not assent to any change in suffrage. It will be our unfortunate duty to retire."

Ellsworth's glance told Sherman that he had guessed the contents of the earlier note, and a glare from Washington signaled his sharp disapproval. Sherman hadn't technically gone back on his word. Delaware's instructions were beyond his influence.

A shaken Morris said, "Mr. Read, please weigh the consequences of your action. The secession of a state would raise an alarm throughout the country. It would signal grave discord to people outside. I implore you to reconsider."

Madison gained the floor. "Fellow delegates, the justification for equal state suffrage disappears when a national government is put in place."

Madison continued for several minutes, as if logic could sway George Read's opinion. Then he offered the expedient of a vote on the sense of the members, rather than on the resolution.

"This is a ruse," Read thundered. "If the sense of this assembly is to change state suffrage, I will follow my instructions."

"Mr. Read," Gouverneur Morris said, "I've read the Delaware instructions. I don't believe they require a secession of her deputies."

Read leaped to his feet. "Mr. Morris, it's not up to Pennsylvania to interpret our instructions. The Delaware deputies are quite capable of reading."

Others stood to argue that Delaware's instructions left room for them to remain if they themselves didn't vote for a change in suffrage. When it became obvious that Read refused to budge, the assembly adjourned.

"WILL YOU GENTLEMEN BE needing anything else?"

"No, thank you, Howard." Sherman took a sip of tea and found it to his liking. Howard had expertly coated the bottom of a cup with heavy crème, scraped a generous portion of sugar off a cone, and then poured scalding tea into the cup from a sufficient height to swirl the ingredients together.

"Howard?" Sherman's voice brought the servant back from the central hall and into the parlor.

"Yes, sir."

"Would you inform Mrs. Marshall that we'll not be staying for dinner?"

"She'll be sorely disappointed. The spring vegetables she bought today sent her into a flurry of cooking."

"She's a fine cook, but I'm afraid duty calls."

"You'll miss her famous apple pie."

"Not if you put aside a piece for my breakfast."

Howard gave a broad wink. "I'll arrange it, sir." And he disappeared.

"A capable man," Ellsworth said.

Sherman looked up from his copy of the Virginia Plan. "What?"

"I said Howard is a capable man."

"Yes, he is." Sherman snapped the paper in his hand and went back to reading.

"You're going to use slavery to break the large state coalition, aren't you?"

"I'm trying to find the section of the plan you asked about."

"You'd sacrifice Howard?"

Sherman let the paper fall into his lap. "Howard will be unaffected."

"You know what I mean."

"No plan will leave this convention that doesn't protect slavery. Today, we got a glimpse of the chasm between Pennsylvania and South Carolina. Slavery's the only wedge that can enlarge that gulf."

"No guilt?"

"Let's get back to this plan." Sherman started to read again but then stopped. "Oliver, when this is over, we must work to outlaw slavery in Connecticut."

THE FOUR MEN SAT around a square table. Sherman, Ellsworth, Paterson, and Read had caucused in a private room at the City Tavern.

"Today we taught the insurgents a lesson," Paterson gloated.

"Today was no victory," Sherman said.

"We foiled their plans."

"We merely avoided disaster."

"Everything they proposed was postponed." Paterson patted Read on the back. "They retreated because the smallest state threatened to leave."

"Everything was not postponed. If memory serves me right, the convention passed a resolution to form a supreme national government."

Paterson looked puzzled. "Yes, but a separate legislature, executive, and judiciary are not unique."

"You missed the strategy. The architecture's inconsequential. They wanted to establish our purpose: to build a "supreme national" system. This principle frames everything we do from this point forward."

"Roger, I think you exaggerate the—"

"No, William, I do not. All that remains is the mechanics."

"I'm sorry, Roger, but you've lost me," Read interjected. "Aren't we here to design a stronger national government?"

"Not one that does away with the states. Congress is subservient to the states. Congress is their instrument to achieve common goals. Today, we voted to make the states subservient to the national government."

"You sound alarmist," Read said.

"That's my intent. Think a minute. Congress is enfeebled by lack of funds and must depend on the generosity of the states." Sherman paused. "Gentlemen, money's the crux of today's vote."

Read shook his head. "I don't see the connection."

"A supreme national government can tax our citizens directly—without our permission and without consideration of our needs. Then we'll be the enfeebled party, begging the supreme national government to be generous." Sherman leaned toward Read. "George, how does this differ from being under the thumb of an English monarch?"

Read didn't answer.

"Are we doomed?" Paterson asked.

"We're weakened, not doomed. Form still counts. Our states can thrive if they retain power in the new system."

Sherman bent forward and folded his hands in front of him. "Gentlemen, we're fighting for the survival of our states."

Ellsworth pulled his jeweled snuffbox from his pocket. With a fastidious motion, he extracted a pinch and sniffed it with an abrupt head bob. Then, pulling out a bandana, he carefully wiped his nose. Completing the little ceremony, he looked at his mentor.

"Roger, I beg to differ. We are fighting for the survival of our nation."

12

Thursday, May 31, 1787

"Charles, why?"

"Why what?"

"Don't act innocent. Why'd you challenge Randolph so aggressively?"

"Was I aggressive?"

"You know you were."

Pinckney shrugged. "I tire of the milksop. The real question is, why did you put him in front of the chamber?"

"He's the governor of Virginia," Madison answered, exasperated.

"I was unaware that Virginia was in such a destitute condition."

Madison had been talking to delegates on the sidewalk outside the State House when he spotted Pinckney. "Charles, are you cantankerous by nature or spite?"

"Oh, I should think by nature."

Madison sighed. "What mischief have you planned for today?"

"Mr. Madison, nature's children need not plan. Air and mischief arrive in equal quantities. It's only a matter of plucking the right morsel."

"Damn it, Charles, you must not blaze your own path!"

"Mr. Madison! You startle me. You resort to damnation instead of logic? Please, sir, remember your reputation for control."

Madison blurted, "Gen. Washington was highly displeased with your behavior yesterday."

Pinckney visibly flinched. "So, now we move to intimidation."

"Charles, as a friend, I'm merely passing on a caution."

Pinckney straightened himself. "Very well. I shall make the greatest effort to hold my tongue. I believed I was advancing our cause by pushing the point. Please convey my apologies to the general."

"Will you apologize to Governor Randolph?"

"Now you push the point too far."

Pinckney whirled and entered the State House. Madison watched in befuddlement. He had finally quieted Pinckney's tart tongue, but the man remained a cipher. What was his purpose yesterday?

Madison heard a dull, hard noise reverberate behind him. Clomp, pause, clomp. He turned to see Gouverneur Morris wearing a welcoming grin as he approached the State House.

"Jemmy, my good man, how are you this fine morning?"

"Anxious. And yourself?"

"Ready to take on the world, or at least our small corner."

"Let's hope the world is ready to engage, not postpone."

Morris gave a laugh that jostled his paunch. "Dear Jemmy, relax. Surely, you didn't expect fair weather the entire voyage?"

"A minor squall shouldn't have altered our course. We should've gone forward with the vote. Only Delaware objected."

"Others remained silent because Delaware did their work." Then with a more earnest voice, he added, "Listen, we can pass the resolutions any time we choose, but it would be a mistake to ram our plan down their throats."

"Majorities drive conventions."

"These are proud men. They need to be given voice."

"Voice yes, debate certainly, but threats and extortion?"

"They played their only card." Then with a shrug, "You can't blame them."

Madison started to object, but Morris interrupted. "Tell me, how's Pinckney's mood?"

"Contrite. But I fear it's only temporary."

"No doubt. You can't train a cat, but they do keep the mice at bay."

"I fear Pinckney hunts larger game. Randolph's livid."

"He's only angry because the volley came from his own side."

"Any suggestions?"

"Randolph doesn't know how to tack; he follows the wind. The rest of us must tend the sails. By the way, Washington wishes to speak to you during a break."

"Do you know the subject?"

"Heavens no. The good general forgot to confide in me."

Madison suppressed a twinge of anxiety. "You did a fine job yesterday," he said. "A bit blunt, but it moved us forward."

"Pusillanimous debate sours my stomach. What say, shall we enter the pit?"

"Yes, let's see if Pinckney can keep his claws retracted."

BEFORE MADISON'S INK DRIED, the motion that the legislature should consist of two branches had passed. He quickly scratched out the delegates' comments, using abbreviations and marks. He suddenly realized that he couldn't keep up.

First, someone spoke from over here; then, without pause, someone new started speaking from another area. The exchanges bounced around the room as swiftly as a farmer switched teats on an udder. He decided to capture the proceedings in a quick scribble and rewrite the notes each evening while the events remained fresh.

Sherman had the floor, and the issue was the election of the first branch. "Gentlemen, I strongly urge the election of the national legislature by the state legislatures. Only in this manner will capable and experienced men be chosen. The people should have little to do with government. They are constantly misled."

Sherman stood perfectly straight, left hand balled in a fist, his right hand clutching the wrist of the left. On the rare occasion when his hands moved, the motion was as rigid as starched linen.

Madison appraised his speech as artifice. Connecticut possessed a strong democratic tradition and, among all the states, enjoyed the most republican form of government. Sherman's real objective was to ensure that the states held as much power as possible under the new government.

Elbridge Gerry gained the floor. Although he was from Massachusetts, a member of the large state alliance, Gerry hated the idea of a strong central government. Madison gave thanks that he spoke poorly and digressed into ill-mannered diatribes. Thin-faced, with a sharp, beaklike nose, Gerry always wore a bemused, superior expression that revealed an elitist nature. A nervous head tic exaggerated his birdlike appearance, and he had an odd habit of speaking in bursts, punctuated by unintelligible stammers. Madison didn't worry about Gerry because loyal Massachusetts delegates outnumbered him.

Gerry stuttered a moment and then blurted, "Gentlemen, I heartily agree with our esteemed colleague from Connecticut. The evils we experience flow from an excess of democracy. The masses cannot recognize a good government when it is placed in front of them."

Madison almost chuckled. He wondered if Sherman felt embarrassed to be linked with Gerry's demagoguery.

Gerry went on to vilify the infamous Shays. Most people condemned Shays's farmer revolt, but Madison cherished the Massachusetts insurrection. Without it—and the alarm it raised throughout the nation—these delegates would be snug in their own beds.

Gerry surprised Madison by abruptly shifting his harangue to a personal peeve. "It seems a democratic maxim to starve public servants. The people of Massachusetts always clamor to reduce our salaries." After another stammer, he threw his words like grapeshot. "Honorable men should be properly rewarded for their sacrifice and service. But when the people have voice, they demand that we wallow in the same poverty as an indentured servant tied to a miserly master."

Gerry's head bobbed uncontrollably. "Gentlemen, although I remain sympathetic to the cause, I've learned by experience the danger of the leveling spirit."

As Madison wrote his notes, another part of his mind marveled at the pettiness of some men.

Mason brought reason back to the discussion. "Fellow delegates, we're obligated to protect the rights of every class of citizen. The first branch of the legislature is the repository of our democratic principles. It's true that we have experienced excesses of democracy, but we shouldn't run in the opposite direction. We must design a system that provides for the rights of the lowest, as well as the highest, order of citizens. I urge the election of the first branch directly by the people."

Fervent applause sprinkled the chamber, while others sat with folded hands. The revolutionary spirit waned in many.

Madison was grateful to see James Wilson, from Pennsylvania, point the argument directly at Sherman's undeclared intent. "Gentlemen, we must eliminate interference by state governments. Opposition to national measures comes from the officers of the states, not from the people."

Wilson looked like an owl, bespectacled and always wearing a freshly powdered wig. Many people saw him as pompous, but Madison knew him to be a fervent supporter of a strong national government controlled by the people.

Wilson continued in a condescending manner that gave the impression of a schoolmaster lecturing dull students. "I wish to raise federal authority to a considerable level and, for that reason, it must have popular support. The first branch of the legislature should be elected directly by the people."

Madison set his notes aside to take the floor. "The great fabric of our national government must be stable and durable. This requires a solid foundation of the people, not the shaky pillars of state legislatures." Madison looked directly at Sherman. "I'm an advocate for refining appointments by successive filters, but we can push this device too far. The expedient should be used only in the appointment of the second branch of the legislature, the executive, and the judiciary."

As Madison took his seat, Gerry huffed and strutted to the front of the chamber. Gerry's stutters made it difficult for Madison to record his speech. After an unintelligible mumble, he said, "The common man sees no further than his next meal, and he denies others a place at the table. I don't support giving the people a direct influence on the government."

Gerry sat to astonished whispers. Madison tried to check his prejudice against the merchant class, but Gerry proved strikingly uncultured. The man had built a fortune in commerce, and like many of the newly rich, he lacked basic manners. Madison felt relieved when the assembly moved to a vote.

The popular election of the first branch won six to two. The full Massachusetts delegation buried Gerry. As Madison jotted down the results, two puzzles grabbed his attention: Why had South Carolina voted no—and more perplexing—why had Connecticut divided? Sherman and Ellsworth normally moved as one, and a divided vote was a discarded vote. Madison sneaked a peek at the two men. Sherman wore an impassive expression, but Ellsworth looked disturbed.

The secretary read the fifth resolution of the Virginia Plan. "The second branch of the national legislature ought to be chosen by the first branch from a group that has been nominated by the state legislatures."

Madison was disturbed to see Butler argue against the motion. "This resolution destroys the balance between the states and the national government. The state legislatures must elect the second branch." Butler shifted his weight and looked directly at the governor of Virginia. "I wish to pose a question to Mr. Randolph." After a brief pause for effect, Butler asked, "Please, sir, may we hear your opinion about the number of members in this second branch?"

Flabbergasted, Madison forgot to lift his pen and stained his notes with an expansive blot of ink. Butler had picked up Pinckney's lance. Madison looked straight ahead—he had no desire to see Pinckney's smirk. The thrust aimed at the witless Randolph was meant to penetrate all the way through to him.

Randolph reluctantly struggled to his feet. "When I offered these propositions, I stated my ideas as far as the proposal required."

As Randolph tried to sit, Butler boomed, "Surely, the esteemed governor of Virginia, the leader of his state's government, the protector of its sovereignty, has an opinion on the subject?"

Randolph didn't hide his anger. "The details aren't part of the plan. That's for this assembly to decide."

Randolph tried to regain his composure. Tentatively reaching down, as if to shuffle papers again, he abruptly said, "Uh, if I were to hazard an opinion, I think the number of the second branch ought to be smaller than the first, and uh, yes, small enough to protect against the turbulence of democracy. Some check is needed, and a good senate seems a likely answer."

"Thank you, Mr. Randolph, for sharing your succinct insight and unparalleled wisdom," Butler said as he took his seat.

Madison blanched at the clumsy, capitulating exchange. Each element of the plan must be explained by stressing the harmony of the entire system. Madison realized that Randolph didn't understand what he had presented. He again wished that a better spokesman had been chosen.

Thankfully, Wilson helped the convention move beyond the embarrassing moment, but after a reasoned preamble, he startled Madison with his conclusion. Peering over his glasses, he said, "Gentlemen, I oppose both election by the state legislatures and election by the first branch. The second branch must be independent of both. I strongly urge the popular election of both branches."

The resolution had been crafted to appeal to a broad alliance. The states nominated and then the first branch elected senators from the slate of candidates presented by the states. Butler argued for the election by the states, while Wilson supported election by the people. These two men were supposed to be members of Madison's alliance, yet they attacked a crucial element of the plan from opposite directions. Keeping people in line was proving more difficult than Madison had expected.

The vote, when it came, brought additional surprises. The first, and most devastating, was its defeat, seven against three. Frustrated, Madison scratched, *So the clause was disagreed to & a chasm left in this part of the plan.* He ended the entry with a harsh, oversized exclamation point.

MADISON WALKED THE YARD with Washington. Actually, the general sauntered while Madison's short stride caused him to scurry like a child trying to keep up with an unmindful parent.

"Jemmy, I'd like you to rethink the sixth resolve."

"Excuse me, sir. We all agreed."

"I've changed my mind."

Madison felt alarm. "Deleting the sixth resolve guts the plan."

"Just one section of it."

"Which?"

"The use of force against members of the union."

Surprised, Madison said, "General, with all due respect, you, more than anyone, must understand the need for this provision."

"I understand the frustration that motivated some to include the clause."

"You endorsed it."

"A government cannot make war on its members."

"General, please. You've suffered the defiance of the states. You fought the Revolution with blood while the states ignored your pleas for the barest of necessities."

"I would never have turned my army against a state to collect their levy."

"A single frigate could've easily forced the states to pay."

"Mr. Madison, I would've won the war but lost the point of going to war."

Madison was stunned by the general's sudden intensity. All of this had been arranged in advance. Governments needed money like fire needed wood. An enfeebled Congress had been unable to make the states pay their quota, even when British troops stood ready to kill their sons. After the peace, collecting revenue had become even more difficult.

Madison believed it imperative that the new government should wield enough power to compel payment. And Washington had agreed until now. What changed his mind? Perhaps the threat from the Society of the Cincinnati made him question the use of force. Perhaps Delaware's threat to tear apart the convention made him cautious of proposing too much national power. Perhaps the dissension within their alliance had given him pause.

Madison risked igniting Washington's notorious temper. "General, sir, fairness sometimes requires a government to use force."

"I can't imagine armed action for a concept as vague as fairness."

"If I may, the Articles of Confederation punishes those who do right. Those who pay subsidize the indolent. Force, used judiciously, can right wrongs."

"Find another way."

"No parliamentary trick can substitute for force of arms."

"I'll have no part of a government that can wage war against its citizens. You're a smart lad. Figure something out."

"Of course, sir. I shall think about it."

"Mr. Madison, you may think about it all you want, but you'll withdraw the clause immediately."

"Yes, sir."

AFTER THE RECESS, THE convention began to deal with the powers of the legislature. The first few measures passed without debate, and then the secretary read, "Legislative power in all cases to which the state legislatures are incompetent."

Madison cringed to see Butler take the floor. "I'd like to call on Mr. Randolph to explain his meaning of *incompetent*."

Barely rising, Randolph almost shouted, "I disclaim any intention of granting vague powers to the national legislature. I oppose any inroads on state jurisdictions. My opinion's fixed on the point."

He sat with a stern finality that belied his fear. Could the South Carolina intrigue have no greater purpose than to bully Randolph until he caved? As Madison gained the floor, he wondered if it could be that simple.

"Gentlemen, our deliberations over the last two days have been acrimonious. Delegates have challenged other delegates' honorably held positions." Madison quickstepped across the chamber as he continued to speak. "We must succeed in our noble effort, and I shall not shirk from anything necessary to form a sound republic, one with the authority to provide for the safety, liberty, and happiness of our great nation." He abruptly stopped his rapid pacing and caught the eyes of the delegates. "I plead with you to do the same."

Madison returned to his seat to record the vote. The motion to give power to the national government in all cases where the states were incompetent passed. Again, Connecticut divided. Madison wondered if he could exploit this apparent rift within the Connecticut delegation.

Next, a clause that gave the national legislature power to veto state laws passed without debate.

Late in the day, Madison took the floor to say that, upon reflection, he no longer supported the use of force against a delinquent state. He asked for a postponement of the resolution. Everyone was eager to leave, and postponement passed without dissent. The long session thankfully ended.

MADISON HUNCHED OVER HIS desk to rewrite the day's notes. The task proved more daunting than he had expected. He worried for his health. Always sickly, Madison constantly inventoried his physical condition, fearful that some debilitating illness might get in the way of his mission. He paused to sip his wine and wondered if this private journal would document the founding of a republic or end up as discarded refuse. It could go either way. He refused to entertain the idea of failure, so he bent again to his task.

A soft knock interrupted him. Opening the door, he was surprised to see Randolph. "Edmund, please enter."

"Thank you, James. I'm sorry to bother you, but I need your help."

"Of course, what can I do for you?"

"I want to be relieved of my duties as sponsor of the Virginia Plan. You must assume the mantle. I'm—"

"Please don't let this minor harassment intimidate you."

"Minor? Are you deaf?"

"No, no. I'm sorry. I misspoke. Of course the attacks were not minor. They were—"

"Reprehensible!" Randolph paced the small apartment. "This is your plan. You defend it."

"Edmund, you're already in the forefront. There's no way we can undo the opening sessions."

Randolph took a handkerchief from his pocket and wiped his forehead. "Then you must talk to your friend, Charles Pinckney, and insist that he and his colleagues desist."

"I can't control Charles. And I would hardly call him a friend."

"Then why are you always with him? I see you two scheming together all the time."

Madison laughed. "I wish you could hear our conversations. He may embarrass you in public, but he pillages me in private. No, I cannot appeal to our rogue delegate. He's beyond my reach."

"Whose reach is he within?"

Madison motioned Randolph into a chair. Randolph reluctantly quit pacing and sat down. Madison leaned forward, rested his elbows on his knees, clasped his hands, and held Randolph's eyes.

"Edmund, I believe the South Carolina delegation works in unison. This morning, I upbraided Charles for yesterday's behavior. Today, he quelled his devilish tongue, but Butler adopted his tactics. What do you think they're after?"

For the first time, Randolph looked thoughtful. "It must relate to their slaveholdings."

"My guess as well."

"They back our coalition only to a point. They'll support us until they perceive a threat to their property."

"I believe you're correct. Today, Congress is controlled by the North eight to five, but legislation requires unanimity, so any slaveholding state can block threatening bills. Under our plan, Congress is proportional to population, with no state veto."

Randolph continued to appear thoughtful. "They fear the strength of the North under a new government. That's it. But we're slaveholders and we harbor no such fear."

"What's different between Virginia and the Deep South?" Madison asked.

Randolph paused a minute. "We've outlawed the slave trade. They fear restrictions on the importation of new slaves!"

"Very astute. I've always been impressed by your political instincts. Now that you've deduced the real issue, we should be able to figure out a way to mitigate their fears. I suggest we call a Virginia quorum and use our collective wits to herd South Carolina back into the barn."

"Agreed, as long as I am not a principle in the assault."

"We won't plan an assault. We must find enticing bait to lure them in."

"James, I don't want to be in the foreground." Randolph stood to leave. "My career on stage is at an end."

Madison escorted Randolph to the door and then poured himself a half glass of wine. He uncorked a ceramic jar and poured a generous amount of white powder into the glass. He had heard that some people took medications with water, but his health was far too precarious for that kind of risk. Swirling the wine with his finger, he swallowed it in a single gulp.

He knew what caused his discomfort. He had promised Witherspoon to end the slave trade, but he had just told Randolph that they must assure South Carolina that this convention wouldn't interfere with the trade. Madison poured a splash of wine into the glass and whirled it in tight, fast circles. He discarded the swill into the chamber pot and poured another portion into the glass. This time he filled it to the brim.

13

Saturday, June 2, 1787

Responding to a light knock, Sherman opened the door.

"Come in, Oliver."

"Would you rather talk in the sitting room? We can have tea."

"No, this is private."

"Problem?"

"Let's sit."

Each moved to his customary place, Sherman in the threadbare easy chair and Ellsworth striving to find a comfortable position in a ladder-back chair. Friday's and this morning's sessions had been uneventful, dry and inconclusive discussions of executive powers. As they were leaving the State House, Sherman had asked Ellsworth to visit him in his room after they returned to Mrs. Marshall's.

"Oliver, what's bothering you?"

Ellsworth looked down, then met Sherman's eye. "You mean my votes on Thursday?"

"And Friday."

"The issues yesterday were unimportant."

"It sent signals of disunity in our delegation."

"Are you suggesting that we must be unified in all of our votes?"

"Yes—if we're to influence this convention."

Ellsworth pulled out his German-made snuffbox. This action started an elaborate ritual that would take several minutes. Ellsworth wielded his snuffbox whenever he wanted to stall.

Growing impatient, Sherman said, "Oliver, I'm not suggesting you blindly follow my lead, only that we work together. Explain your position. Perhaps I'm the one in error."

"Roger, you know I respect you." Ellsworth stopped, fidgeted a moment, and then said, "I've modeled my life after you. Normally, I'd never question your judgment."

"But you do now?"

"You obstruct every move. You fight every point. Must we abandon everything we fought for in the Revolution?"

"I don't follow."

"We fought the Revolution so we could control our own destiny, choose our own government. Now everything's falling apart. We must come out of this convention with a strong national government."

"The Virginia Plan?"

"It goes too far. But must we fight every element?"

Sherman settled back in his chair. "Oliver, how do you think legislation is bartered?"

"Must it be bartered?"

"Yes."

"Are there *no* elements we can accept? Shouldn't principles guide us?"

Sherman leaned forward. "Do you accept that we must prepare for some difficult bargaining?"

Ellsworth started to reach for his snuffbox, stopped, then said, "Roger, there's no question that we must negotiate with all our might to protect our interests."

Sherman smiled. "'Negotiate' sounds so civilized, a gentleman's game. Bartering is what we do in the streets. Negotiation means finding common ground between reasonable men. Barter requires owning something that another holds dear. Jefferson negotiates in Paris. We barter in Philadelphia."

"Meaning?"

"We must capture something the Virginians desperately want."

"What?"

"I wish I knew. What are the precious jewels in Madison's plan? We must forage until we discover what holds the highest value for them."

"By contesting every point?"

"At this stage, we shouldn't pursue what we want but seize something the Virginians crave. Later we trade."

Ellsworth reached for his snuffbox. By the time he'd finished, a fine dust had settled about his clothes and person. "In the end, you won't abandon principle?"

"That's my nightly prayer."

"That doesn't sound like a promise."

"It's not." Sherman glanced down and then met Ellsworth's eyes. "I'm sorry, Oliver, but in my long career, I've made some deals I regret, some I loathe."

"Yet you continue to put yourself in situations that totter on the edge of a moral abyss."

"Yes."

"How do you cope?"

"I decided that I don't need to worry about ethics—as long as I continue to worry about ethics."

Ellsworth laughed and then studied his knees. "Roger, I think I understand." Then looking up, he added, "I'm sorry I voted against you."

"No matter. It never hurts to confuse the opposition."

"We should've had this discussion earlier."

"My error." Sherman crossed his legs to signal patience. "Let's get specific. Which principles concern you?"

Sitting straighter, Ellsworth said, "Several." He fingered his snuffbox but didn't pick it up. "You were the one that got me thinking along a different line Wednesday night at the City Tavern. Do you remember the conversation?"

"Of course."

"I supervised Connecticut's war expenditures, and I learned that liberty depends on money."

"Go on."

"Our paramount objective must be to secure a sure source of funds for the national government. The European powers can be held at bay only by a united nation of thirteen states with enough funds to field an army and a navy."

"Agreed."

"But Wednesday night you argued against the national government taxing the people."

"I was appealing to Read and Paterson, not you." Sherman waved dismissively. "You know their biases. But I believe the states must supply the nation's money, or they'll become extraneous."

"My experience says that approach never works."

Now it was Sherman's turn to stall. He went over to a bruised bureau and poured himself a schooner of water from an earthenware pitcher. Returning to his chair, he said, "Oliver, I must accede to your position on this point. You're the one with treasury experience. You went to Yale and Princeton, while I have little formal education. You've been abroad; I've not."

Sherman continued as he settled into the chair. "Let me offer another path. There are many sources of funds. We can reserve specific taxes to the national government and dedicate others to the states. Then each may remain supreme within their realm."

Ellsworth looked thoughtful. "That might work."

"Good. Anything else?"

Ellsworth again started to reach for his snuffbox.

Sherman laughed. "Obviously, yes. Tell me."

"Your comments on democracy angered me."

"That was a device. Well…not entirely. I do have reservations about the wisdom of the people."

"I don't share those reservations."

"You must admit that Shays's Rebellion exemplifies the excesses of democracy?"

"I do not."

Sherman blanched. "Explain."

"You know the situation among our farmers. The country has no money. Hard-working, patriotic farmers can't pay their taxes or buy the most rudimentary implements to till their land. So we throw them in jail and confiscate their property. They have a right to raise up arms."

"*Who* gave them this right?"

"You."

"How? When?"

"You signed the Declaration of Independence. Perhaps you should read it again. It says that man has an inalienable right to rebel against an oppressive government."

"Our government is not oppressive."

Ellsworth snapped his snuffbox hard against his chair. "Many consider physical confinement and loss of livelihood oppressive."

"It's not the government's fault."

"It is."

"We're here to fix that."

"Not at the expense of our republican principles."

Sherman sighed. "The people can be easily duped to follow an anarchist."

"Only when the government gives the anarchist a platform."

"Do you suggest that people are wise when things go well?"

"Yes. Collectively. Some will be foolish, but if we try to guard against the lowest level, we invite rule by the privileged few. We must endure the ignorant to protect the liberty of the majority."

"Your populism may exceed Madison's."

"Virginia is not my model. Connecticut's my model."

Sherman took a sip of water, unclear about how to proceed. Ellsworth was right. Connecticut had a strong republican tradition. Leaning forward, Sherman said, "Oliver, I'm proud to have influenced your political career. I'm even prouder that you've learned to chart your own course. You've given me much to think about."

"Thank you."

Sherman leaned back. "I'll probably not live long enough to measure our success, but you're a young man. You'll hold powerful positions in this new government."

"I may not want to hold a position in the national government."

"That would be our nation's loss."

"I appreciate the compliment, but my loyalty is to Connecticut."

"I understand, but we need to talk about tactics. The political arena doesn't nurture idealism. Rough and ruthless men always emerge to pursue power."

"I have faith that good men will be attracted to a good government."

"Oliver, let me be clear. Politics, disguised by a veneer of civility, is played on the very edge of barbarism."

"I'm not naïve."

"Good. Let's get back to tactics. We must vote together."

"In all cases?"

"Yes."

"What else?"

"I am a horrid speaker. I believe you should present Connecticut's views. I'll speak from time to time, but my talent is to convince in private, not public."

"As we are at the moment."

Sherman chuckled. "Have I succeeded?"

"You've reminded me that our destination requires circuitous detours. I can be a patient and willing passenger." Ellsworth walked to the bureau and poured himself some water. After retaking his seat, he said quietly, "If principle dictates, and my vote won't alter the course you chart, I'd like the freedom to vote my conscience."

"Agreed."

"And speak my mind on occasion?"

"Yes."

"Then tell me how you wish to proceed."

LEAVING HIS ROOM, SHERMAN almost bumped into Witherspoon.

"Good afternoon, Reverend."

"A fine day it is. Do you have time for a stroll?"

"Unfortunately not. I'm rushing to an appointment."

"Oh yes, busy, busy. You have a big challenge."

"I suspect we'll muddle through."

"How's the family?" Witherspoon asked.

"Fine. A little illness, but my church is lending Rebecca a hand. Did you see James?"

"Yes, we had a stimulating conversation. Unfortunately, we resurrected some old disagreements."

"It's a relief to know others disagree."

"Madison sees you as an opponent."

"I was referring to my own allies."

"Do you oppose James?"

Sherman smiled. "Only some of his ideas."

"Allow him to explain. You'll see he makes sense."

"What did you and James argue about?" Sherman asked.

"Slavery."

"A volatile issue."

"What's your position?" Witherspoon asked.

"I'll endeavor to make slavery illegal in Connecticut."

"I meant in the South."

"What's James's position?"

"I asked for yours."

"Reverend, I can't share my positions with you. You're a friend of James Madison."

Howard suddenly emerged from a room he had tidied up.

"Ah, Howard, if I may, how do you feel about slavery?"

Sherman thought Witherspoon's question tactless and inappropriate. Howard couldn't answer such a direct question from a guest.

"My feelings are private," Howard said nonchalantly.

"Then what's your opinion?" Witherspoon refused to be put off.

"First, if I may, sir, what's your opinion?" Howard responded.

"I think slavery is a reprehensible evil."

"You must also believe that God punishes evil."

"I do."

"What's your opinion on violence?" Howard asked.

"Another reprehensible evil."

"Then you must reconcile your reprehensible evils."

Witherspoon started to speak, but Howard interjected, "You must excuse me, sirs, I have chores I must attend to."

Sherman watched Howard's long legs gracefully carry him to the rear staircase, where he quickly disappeared. Turning back to Witherspoon, he was pleased to see him baffled.

"What do you find so amusing, Roger?"

"Riddles. I find riddles amusing."

"I'M GLAD YOU'RE HERE, John. I need your help."

"I wasn't much use today." This morning John Dickinson, of Delaware, had proposed an unsuccessful motion to give the states the power to impeach the executive.

Sherman had arranged to meet Dickinson at the famed botanist John Bartram's garden that had been opened to the public. Dickinson was fifty-five, wealthy, and distinguished looking. Sherman had felt relief when his longtime close friend and colleague had finally arrived a few days previously.

"We'll have another chance."

The elaborate gardens sat west of the city, on the far side of the Schuylkill River. The expanses of arbors, greenhouses, and flowered paths, plus a matchless spring day, had attracted scores of finely turned-out Philadelphians. Children played, couples courted, and families splayed across the lawns. Despite the multitudes, the gardens had a hushed atmosphere, especially after the cacophony of the city. Everyone spoke in private whispers meant only for their companions. Watching the young families, Sherman felt a pang of nostalgia for his own youth. Was this Jefferson's "pursuit of happiness"? It seemed a simple yet powerful idea—people unabashedly enjoying newly bloomed flowers and meticulous pathways without any concern that an oppressive government might intrude into their day.

Sherman and Dickinson strolled in complete privacy. No one noticed the two gentlemen engaged in a quiet dialogue that might shape their future. Sherman reminded himself not to disappoint these people.

"How are Rebecca and the family?"

"She wants me home to put our finances in order."

"Problems?"

"She thinks I'm running out of time."

"Roger, you've done your duty. When this is over, you should turn your attention to more personal matters."

"When this is over."

They both stepped to the side of the gravel path to allow a young arm-in-arm couple to pass. Sherman guessed from their locked gaze that they were betrothed.

"I resent the arrogance of Madison and the other nationalists," Dickinson said as they resumed walking.

"Resentment is a dangerous emotion. We must remain unruffled."

"Surely you feel some anger. We wrote the Articles. Granted, they're flawed, but who gave these interlopers the power to discard our work?"

"Congress sanctioned this convention."

"Sanctioned, yes, but with instructions to amend the Articles," Dickinson said. "They exceed their authority."

"Lately, I've come to believe the Articles' usefulness may be exhausted."

"Why?"

"What type of government do you think best?" Sherman asked.

"You didn't answer my question."

"Gazing about this garden filled with happy and prosperous people, I can almost believe that we've created paradise. But when I look beyond the horizon, the view disturbs me. The Articles may be incapable of saving us from a looming catastrophe."

"Even amended?"

"I desperately want Connecticut's independence secured, but I also want the United States to survive, thrive."

"Which has a higher priority?"

"What type of government do you think best?"

Dickinson gave his old friend a smile. "All right, Roger, I'll let you dodge that one for now."

Dickinson wordlessly pointed in the direction of a massive greenhouse. Both men steered toward the broad entrance. Upon stepping into the greenhouse, Sherman was assaulted by the heavy, damp fragrance of fresh flowers, turned soil, and new spring growth.

Walking down a path walled by head-high exotic plants, Dickinson said, "A limited monarchy is the best government."

"You've never advocated such a system before."

"A limited monarchy was—is—out of the question. Our deplorable heritage under the English crown forbids it. I presumed your question was philosophical, not practical."

"You still surprise me."

"An occasional surprise adds spice to a friendship."

Sherman laughed. "John, don't over season. I've enough to deal with right now."

"Then I'll spare you an elucidation."

"No, you have my interest. Tell me."

"My thoughts are unorthodox." Dickinson, briefly fascinated by a plant, continued. "Ancient republics flourished for a short time and then vanished. Principalities and then monarchies became the order of the world."

Dickinson stopped walking and faced Sherman. "The English happened upon the limited monarchy, a monarch constrained by a parliament with real power. No one laid out a grand scheme as Madison proposes. The limited monarchy functions to the benefit of its citizens. Look at the British Empire. Has there ever been such a prosperous and just nation? Their empire spans the globe. A republic has never delivered such benefits."

The pair turned to continue around the narrow greenhouse path, oblivious of the people who squeezed by in the opposite direction.

"Roger, I think a limited monarchy superior, but I believe we can find a remedy for the republican disease. This is one point in which I find myself in agreement with our little intellectual friend."

"You first startle and now confuse. How do you differ from Madison?"

"In one momentous way. Madison believes he's smart enough to design the perfect system. I have no such conceit. Nor do I believe it plausible that his little highness can accomplish this herculean feat. Madison's self-delusion makes him dangerous."

"But you said you believe we can find a remedy for the republican disease?"

"If we cannot have the English system, then at least we should be clever enough to follow their charted course, a course of gradual evolution. We must allow our system to develop on its own to a more perfect state."

"Then what are we doing here?"

"Amending the worst flaws in the Articles. Grandiose plans bring tragedy. Only fools leap blindly into an abyss," Dickinson asserted.

"Prudence's price is time. I'm not sure we have much to spare."

"That's why I bless the heavens for our luck. The accidental division of this country into thirteen states gives it thirteen chances to happen upon the perfect system. Copying each other's successes speeds our progress."

"Perhaps thirteen chances for chaos."

"No, we're unique! No one in all of history has owned thirteen republican laboratories. And those fools want to throw it away."

"An interesting concept, but I fear we've already exhausted our time for a careful approach," Sherman said.

"I can't accept that. We must strengthen the national government, but we can still preserve powerful state influence, without demolishing every structure already in place." Dickinson shook his head. "The Virginia Plan will wreak havoc. Madison's arrogance is astounding. He's not God. He cannot create a perfect system."

"Perhaps we don't need perfection."

"We need something that works on a practical level, not some philosophically pure form. We must avoid the corrupting influence of too much central power. Only distributing authority to the states can protect liberty and provide laboratories for the evolution of our republics."

"John, I'm stunned. When did you develop this line of reasoning?"

Dickinson smiled. "On the coach trip here."

"Perhaps we should send you to Georgia. Longer ride."

Dickinson laughed. "No, thank you. I hate sharing beds in bug-ridden taverns."

Now it was Sherman's turn to laugh. Small roadside taverns were notorious for doubling up men in a single bed with used linens. Travelers had no voice in where a coach stopped, and the taverns didn't cater to repeat business. Privies tended to be horrid, food barely edible, and cleanliness foreign.

Dickinson turned to Sherman with a broad smile. "As I pondered how to combat the scholarly Virginians, these ideas came to me like a bolt of lightning. Do you like them?"

"Yes. I knew we must protect the sovereignty of our states, but I had no foundation for my conviction. Now we have our own philosophical underpinning."

"The battle lines are drawn: evolution versus revolution."

The men walked in silence. Sherman felt more at peace than at any time since his arrival, but the irony of Ellsworth's lecture on democracy and Dickinson's advocacy for a limited monarchy didn't escape him. Sherman knew Dickinson's cautious bent. His popular newspaper series, *Letters from a Farmer in Pennsylvania*, had excited revolutionary passion, but Dickinson had argued for a nonviolent solution. His Whig loyalties and refusal to sign the Declaration of Independence had cost him his Pennsylvania congressional seat and forced him to relocate to Delaware. After the war started, no one disputed his patriotism. As an enlistee at the Battle of Brandywine, he had personally witnessed the horrors he had warned against.

"How far must we go?" Sherman asked

"Easier to explain how far we must not go. For the national government to be the repository of our collective wisdom, it cannot be placed in a position in which it can dismiss the states. The states must hold some sway over the national government."

"Impeach the executive, elect the legislature, equal sovereignty?"

"Precisely. As I said, the battle lines are drawn."

"Drawn yes, but in battle, lines can shatter with the first shot. We need discipline."

"Roger, you always focus on the tangible, what can be achieved, the obstacles. We've always made a good team. I prepare the battle plan; you command the field."

As they exited the greenhouse, Sherman smiled and put a hand on his old friend's shoulder. Madison and Hamilton walked directly toward them, heads bent in a conspiratorial discussion of their own.

Sherman withdrew his hand and said, "Mr. Madison, Mr. Hamilton, how are you this fine afternoon?"

Checked in midsentence, Madison looked startled. "Mr. Sherman, Mr. Dickinson, what a pleasant surprise."

"It seems everyone needs respite from the chamber's stifling atmosphere." Sherman said.

Hamilton cocked his head arrogantly and said, "The atmosphere could be freshened with a little magnanimity by some of the members."

"Alex, of course, means delegates like Gerry," Madison said.

"I'll exclude present company for the moment," Hamilton said. "These beautiful surroundings shouldn't be desecrated by candor ladled too liberally."

"Of course not," Dickinson interjected. "Only treasonous plotting fits these grand gardens."

"Gentlemen, please," Sherman pleaded. "Let's remain civil. Our intentions are honorable and our positions heartfelt. Let's debate in our commissioned forum."

"Mr. Sherman," Hamilton said, "for you that would be a delightful new habit."

Dickinson bristled. "Then I presume you were regaling Mr. Madison with your latest female conquest."

"How boorish." Hamilton grasped the lapel of his exquisitely tailored coat. "If you must know, I was extolling the virtues of a monarchy. Mr. Madison disagrees, of course, but I still retain the hope that one day I can dissuade him from his absurd faith in commoners."

Madison said lightly, "Alex, you must behave in public. We should use chance encounters to soothe the hard feelings that come naturally from our work, not solidify ill will."

"I agree," Sherman said to Madison, as their two companions glared at each other. "Let's not spoil this gorgeous afternoon with a meaningless quarrel." Giving Dickinson a sly smile, Sherman added, "After a few ales, you and Mr. Hamilton might find yourselves more in tune than in disharmony."

"I apologize," Dickinson said with a slight bow. "Although I doubt Mr. Sherman's last words, it's no reason for rudeness on my part."

Returning the bow in precisely equal measure, Hamilton said, "Apology accepted."

Sherman said quickly, "Mr. Hamilton, I thought it gracious of you to second Dr. Franklin's motion not to pay the executive."

"It was a ridiculous motion, but I wanted to save the doctor embarrassment."

"Very kind of you." Sherman turned to Madison. "And Mr. Madison, I believe we agree that the executive should be a single individual."

"Yes, but as you saw, Randolph opposes it with great earnestness. He believes it must be a council to avoid the appearance of a monarch."

"This hostility toward monarchy raises artificial limits," Hamilton said peevishly.

"Alex, please," Madison said with uncharacteristic sharpness. "We're a republic. We'll remain a republic. No one shares your admiration for a monarchy."

The men faced each other, the acrimony contagious. Hamilton's nickname during the war had been Little Mars. Obviously, his temperament hadn't mellowed in peacetime.

Sherman started to laugh. "Gentlemen, please. Cease." Sherman gave a broad wink to Madison. "I'm encouraged to see your camp as irascible as our own, but the country needs us all."

Madison looked relieved. "Thank you, Roger. It appears I owe Mr. Hamilton an apology as well. I think it best that we move our respective ways."

"Agreed. Gentlemen, please enjoy the remaining afternoon."

The pairs of men started to walk in opposite directions, and then Sherman heard a voice behind him.

"Roger, may I have a moment?"

"Of course, James."

After the two men had separated from their partners, Madison said, "I gather we both suffer trying to keep our respective allies in a corral."

Sherman noticed that Hamilton and Dickinson eyed them suspiciously. "No more than usual in these circumstances."

"Passions run high. This entire enterprise is far too crucial to let emotions overrule reason."

"What do you suggest?"

"We are both reasonable men. Responsible men. We must work together to dampen any undue zeal."

Sherman waited a respectful moment. "Agreed."

"Excellent. Working together, I'm sure we can keep the convention on a sensible course."

"I'm sure we can."

"Good. I feel much more optimistic."

"And I feel less pessimistic."

Madison gave Sherman an odd look and then said, "I was heartened to hear that you promised Washington to keep the small states in assembly."

"James, you have put your best efforts into an innovative system. I disagree with many aspects, but I admire the logic."

"Thank you, Roger. Enjoy the rest of your stroll."

Sherman surprised Madison by extending his hand. Before grasping it, Madison stole a glance behind him. After a hasty waggle, he rejoined Hamilton.

"What was that about?" Dickinson asked after Sherman had rejoined him.

"Mr. James Madison, Esquire, has launched a courtship. He wishes to sway me to the other side."

"The nerve!"

"The brilliance."

14

Monday, June 4, 1787

"We're going too far in this business!"

Keeping his head bent over his notes, Madison peeked up at his friend and fellow Virginian, George Mason. The Virginia delegation seemed to be unraveling. Mason and Randolph feared a powerful executive and supported a council of three men. Arriving late that day, Mason's ire had been raised when he discovered that the convention had approved a single executive in his absence.

The professorial Wilson had solidly argued the case for a single executive by pointing out that all thirteen states had one executive, and that if there were three equal members, they would fight relentlessly for control, and two might never agree. The logic convinced the assembly to approve a single executive.

Mason had started his tirade after Hamilton proposed an absolute veto for the single executive. "Do the gentlemen mean monarchy? Do you believe the people will consent to such an outrage? They'll never consent. Never!"

Due to his gout, Dr. Franklin spoke while seated. "I have experience with an absolute veto in Pennsylvania. The governor constantly used his veto to extort money. When the Indians scalped people in the West, the governor withheld defensive measures until the legislature exempted his estate from taxation. People fought for their lives while he smugly bore no share of the tax to field a militia."

Franklin turned around in his seat to look at the delegates behind him. "We must not vest too much power in the executive. The first man we put at the helm will be a good one, but nobody knows what sort of fellow might follow."

Everyone looked at Washington, who continued to sit impassively after Franklin's allusion to the first man at the helm.

After Sherman said he was against any one man stopping the will of the entire legislature, Madison reluctantly rose to offer a compromise.

"A proper proportion of each branch being allowed to overrule the executive would serve the same purpose as an absolute veto."

The convention gratefully approved an executive veto, with an override by two-thirds of each branch of the legislature. Another emotional issue barely circumvented. Could nothing proceed without bitter debate?

MOST OF THE DELEGATES had already left the chamber when Madison approached a brooding Mason. "George, perhaps you could take a moment and look at my notes from this morning's session."

"To what purpose?"

Madison extended a couple pages toward Mason. "Wilson presented a reasoned case for a single executive. I thought you might like to see his arguments."

Mason made no attempt to accept the notes. "Wilson had his say; I did not."

"I would've talked until you arrived, but I thought you were going to be absent the entire day."

Mason ripped the pages from Madison's hand and quickly scanned the notes. When angry, Mason took on the demeanor of a pouty aristocrat. Although they were longtime allies, Madison often cringed at his friend's overt hostility toward people with different opinions. Mason's arrogant nature repelled men who would otherwise be on his side.

"The points are valid but not convincing."

"If you had been present, the motion would still have passed."

"Do you denigrate my debating skills?"

"I didn't mean that." Madison recovered his pages and put them back in their proper sequence. "Ask for a reconsideration."

"I'll think about it," Mason said in his haughty manner.

"In the future, I'll move to postpone when you're absent."

"I'd expect that of a true colleague."

In an attempt to diminish the quarrel, Madison added, "And you could return the favor. I tend to get carried away. I'd appreciate it if you tugged my coattails when I get too excited."

"Then I recommend you stay by our table and cease scampering around like a squirrel." Mason stood, pulled his coat taut, and tramped out of the chamber.

As Madison gathered up his materials, he felt someone tap his shoulder. The fingers belonged to Gouverneur Morris.

"Jemmy, my good man, may we talk?"

"Of course. At the Indian Queen?"

"No, this won't take long. Let's step into the library."

The two men opened a door to the left of the dais.

"They'll probably name this the Washington Door," Morris chuckled.

Madison understood Morris's reference. When Washington had been nominated as commander in chief of the Continental Army, he had bashfully left the chamber by this door, the same from which he had made his grand entrance on the second day of the convention. Beyond the door was a narrow, dingy library, housed in a temporary lean-to structure scheduled for demolition after the Philosophical Society building was finished. Aside from clerks, hardly anyone except Washington used the door.

The dank room contained two wooden chairs pushed against the wall. Morris pulled a chair out and ungracefully plopped onto the seat, extending his inflexible wooden leg to the side. Madison set his valise on the floor and sat with his legs crossed and his hands clasped in his lap.

"What can I do for you, Gouverneur?"

"I'm disturbed by the lack of discipline in the Virginia delegation."

"If you'll excuse me, I think you might be overreacting. It's natural to have a few disagreements on specific points."

"Dissension within our ranks plays into our opponents' hands," Morris argued.

"A little turbulence is unavoidable."

"It *is* avoidable."

Some aspects of the last few days had disturbed Madison, but he saw no damage. They still plodded ahead. Today they had approved a single executive, worked out a compromise on the veto, and established a supreme judiciary.

"Randolph and Mason stand firmly with us, but you must be tolerant when they voice disagreement," he said. "Even Dr. Franklin argued against an executive veto."

"I'm not talking about Randolph or Mason. I'm talking about you."

"Me?"

"Yes, it's your vacillation I wish to address."

Madison uncrossed his legs and laid his hands on alternate knees. "I'm at a loss."

"Last Thursday, you disagreed with resolution six. Why did you abandon the use of force?"

"Why did you wait until now to discuss it?"

"I just found out that I must leave for a time to settle an estate matter. I wanted to talk to you before I leave in case the resolution reemerges before my return."

"When do you leave?"

"Thursday. Jemmy, why did you abandon our cause?"

Madison shifted once more, this time leaning forward with his elbows resting on his knees, hands folded under his chin. He had to handle this carefully.

"The new government will be granted power from the people and act directly upon the people. The states don't act as an intermediary. The resolution had no purpose in the grand scheme, and it generated resistance."

"That's foolish. The states ignore Congress. You're repeating past mistakes."

"Means other than arms will be strengthened."

"They won't suffice. How can you delude yourself?"

"We'll weaken state sovereignty until it's no longer a factor."

"You don't understand." Morris moved his leg and leaned forward as well. "Power and arms are synonymous. Without force, people defy rulers."

"The people won't defy a government of their own choosing."

"Jemmy, for god's sake, they *choose* the current government."

"A republic doesn't force obedience through arms."

"The government will never use arms against its children, but without the threat, states will continue to ignore higher authority."

"Obedience *must* come freely."

"You believe this?"

"Yes."

"You disappoint me. I was led to believe you had brought the perfect plan to Philadelphia."

"I never claimed divine wisdom. I expected the details to evolve with deliberation, minds changed, improvements made. The flesh of the plan can be transformed as long as the skeletal framework remains intact."

Morris weighed Madison's statements for a moment. "I see a discouraging inflexibility." With that, Morris stood to leave the room. "I hope you don't live to regret this."

Madison sat for a moment, wondering if he had harmed his relationship with Morris. No, other issues would soon emerge to push this one into distant memory. Still, in arguing the case, he had convinced himself that Washington was right. Means other than force had to be designed into the system to make the states comply with federal intentions.

THE NEXT DAY STARTED with the judiciary. Again, the chamber divided into two parts: those who supported a legislative appointment and those who insisted that the executive select the judiciary. In his usual manner, Franklin told an anecdote to relieve the tension.

"Gentlemen, please, the answer to this dilemma is obvious. We must follow Scotland. The Scots are wise and noble—ingenious as well. As I understand their custom, all the lawyers throughout the land select the most prosperous of their profession for judiciary appointment."

Franklin peered over the top of his glasses; his hallmark twinkling eye told his audience that an amusing remark was but a breath away. "This guarantees the selection of the most able jurists—and gets rid of them so the remaining lawyers can divvy up their lucrative practice."

Madison laughed with the rest as he captured the moment in his journal. It occurred to him that his notes flattened the tone of the proceedings. It would be history's task to overlay emotion onto his sterile record.

With their usual predilection to put off difficult issues, the delegates voted to postpone deciding how to select the judiciary. They moved to the most crucial element of Madison's plan: ratification of the new Constitution by conventions appointed by the people.

Sherman presented the opposing argument. "Fellow delegates, this measure is unnecessary. Approval by Congress and the state legislatures is all that's required. There's no need for undue complications."

Madison rebutted. "I beg to differ with my esteemed colleague from Connecticut. This provision is essential. Only the supreme authority of the people can ratify our new Constitution."

Madison caught Sherman's eye. "The Articles are a defective foundation because they're a treaty between sovereign states."

Madison had espoused the small state position. Sherman must wonder where he was going with this argument. "Under the well-established doctrine of treaties, the breach of any one article *by any member* absolves all parties from further obligation. For example," Madison paused and looked directly at Paterson, "New Jersey's refusal to pay their tax is such a breach."

Madison let the point echo around the chamber. "Gentlemen, this convention doesn't pose a threat to the union. The terminal threat to the Articles is buried within itself." Stretching out his arm, Madison slowly waved his hand across the chamber. "Any member can destroy the Articles at will. Is that the authority you wish to ratify our new Constitution? I think not. It's a tottering illusion."

Madison looked around and was pleased to see that he held everyone's attention. "We must submit our Constitution to an unassailable authority, the supreme fountainhead, the strength of our great nation. Gentlemen, we must submit it directly to the people!"

Madison sat to a satisfying burst of applause. Sherman remained stolid, making no effort to recapture the floor. Instead, Gerry spoke. At first, he presented the case that the state legislatures had been picked by the people and were their agents. Their instructions required approval by the states. By emphasizing state approval, Gerry deflected Madison's assault on Congress, a good debate tactic. But then Gerry digressed to another diatribe against commoners.

"Mr. Madison, I cannot fathom your faith in the people. You must have a different breed in Virginia. The people in my part of the world have the wildest ideas. They constantly cry for more and expect others to satisfy their desires." Gerry bobbed his head, stuttered something Madison couldn't catch, and then spit out an intemperate insult. "I'd no more trust the common man than I would an infant."

After Gerry's outburst, the convention recessed to catch its breath and, hopefully, restart on a more positive note. Madison took advantage of the break to catch up with his notes. After he finished, he wandered over to Washington.

"Nice speech, James. Well put," Washington said.

"Thank you, sir, but I fear Gerry's views might be shared by other delegates."

"Not to worry. Every time he talks, we gain converts. Reasonable men don't wish to be associated with his extremism."

Madison glanced at Hamilton, standing alongside the general. Madison guessed he harbored some sympathies with Gerry. "Then let's hope the chamber is filled with reasonable men," Madison said.

"It is. We should put him on stage at every opportunity." Washington waved his hand toward Hamilton. "Alex told me he wants a reconsideration of the absolute veto. I believe the two-thirds rule should prove sufficient. Does it satisfy you, James?"

"It serves the purpose. With the split interests between the North and South, I can't imagine Congress assembling that many votes in both branches."

"See, Alex, it's not a worthy target. No need to expend scarce munitions."

"Very well," Hamilton said, "but I still worry about the legislature running roughshod over the executive."

"Do you now?"

Hamilton gave the slightest bow. "If I may quote our eminent doctor, 'nobody knows what sort of fellow may follow.'"

Washington looked cross. "Nor should anyone make unwarranted assumptions about that first fellow."

AFTER THE RECESS, WILSON lectured the delegates on the flaws of the existing Congress. He pointed out that each state had a veto, so one selfish state could thwart the majority. Then he took the discussion to dangerous ground by saying that he hoped the ratification process allowed a partial union.

Pinckney took the bait. "I thoroughly agree with Mr. Wilson. A majority of states should be free to unite under this new Constitution. As far as I am concerned, the remainder can wither away in their revered sovereignty."

Madison believed the argument for ratification by the people had been won until this impolitic exchange. With tempers inflamed, the only course was yet another postponement. Thanks to Pinckney's tart tongue, today's proceedings had made no progress.

MADISON SAW PINCKNEY STANDING outside the State House, so he started to move in the opposite direction. No. He must confront the man.

"Mr. Pinckney, shall we walk back to the Indian Queen?"

"Together?"

"No, I thought you should walk up Chestnut and I'll use Market Street."

Pinckney looked perplexed. "Should I take you seriously?"

"A smart man wouldn't."

"Does the ever-serious Mr. Madison pretend to make fun of me?"

"The ever-serious Mr. Madison can't pretend."

"You *are* mocking me!"

"No need, Charles. You take care of that yourself. Shall we go?"

"My, what's got into you, James?"

Madison grabbed Pinckney's elbow and guided him down the street. "Your last remarks today were foolish."

"Don't tell me you sympathize with this sovereignty rot."

"Mr. Pinckney, if you were detached to a firing squad, you'd roll up with cannon."

"I prefer the *rapière*," Pinckney said smugly.

"Thrust and retreat?"

"Leaving bewilderment and but a small spot of blood."

"I've noticed blood on my waistcoat from time to time," Madison said, giving Pinckney a sharp look.

"Mere pricks, I'm sure," Pinckney retorted, lengthening his stride. "So you thought I was foolish."

Madison scurried to keep up. "Ratification by the people would've passed if you hadn't insulted the small states."

"Do you suggest that a tiny piece of rudeness can alter the course of debate?"

"Yes, at times."

"How convenient for me."

Madison shook his head. At the State House, he had held the upper hand, but somehow Pinckney had recaptured the advantage. True irreverence couldn't be trammeled. Madison stopped short of the steps leading to the Indian Queen. "If you'll excuse me, I have to pick up something at the apothecary."

"I hope you're not ill."

"No. Something for Montpelier." Madison threw a "good afternoon" over his shoulder as he hastened down the street.

Before he had taken six paces, he heard Pinckney holler, "Mr. Madison, a smart man would take me seriously!"

PINCKNEY OPENED WEDNESDAY'S SESSION with a call to reconsider the election of the first house. He proposed that they be elected by the state legislatures, instead of by the people.

Madison sighed as Gerry endorsed Pinckney's motion. "The worst men get into the legislature. Base men use any tactic, however dirty, to win against men who refuse to stoop to such artifices."

Sherman tried a more rational argument. "Gentlemen, if we intend to abolish the states, then the people ought to elect the legislature. If the states are to continue, then the state legislatures ought to elect the national legislature. This will preserve harmony between the national and state governments."

After a small cough, Sherman continued in his dilatory manner. "The aims of a national government are few and must be strictly defined. I believe they include defense, internal harmony, treaties, and the regulation of commerce. All other matters must be handled by the states."

Madison challenged Sherman's simplistic view. "I'd respectfully like to add to Mr. Sherman's list. A national government must also protect individual rights and dispense steady justice."

Madison made a few more comments on the role of the national government but then could not contain himself. He had to rebut Wilson's and Pinckney's advocacy for a partial union. Without preamble, Madison charged into new terrain. "Gentleman, all societies divide into different sects, factions, and interests. Conflicts grow between the rich and poor, debtors and creditors, landed and commercial interests, this district against that district, followers of this political leader or that political leader, disciples of this religion or that religion.

"When a majority unites by passion or common interest, the minority is in grave danger. What can restrain a majority? Not respect for others, nor conscience. In Greece and Rome, the patricians and plebeians alternately oppressed each other—with equal ferocity. We've seen the mere distinction of color, in our supposed enlightened time, furnish the grounds for the most oppressive dominion ever exercised by man over man."

With this last, startled gasps escaped from various corners of the room. Madison tried to ignore the reaction. His indictment of slavery had been unpremeditated, but now that it had escaped his lips, he couldn't recall it.

"Who imposed these unjust laws? The majority. Debtors defraud creditors. The holders of one type of property throw a heavier tax on other types of property. When a majority has the opportunity, they will always threaten the rights of the minority." Madison shifted his gaze across the sea of delegates. "Make no mistake, in a republic, the majority always has opportunity!"

Madison scurried across the front of the chamber. "The only remedy is to enlarge a nation to include so many interests, so many ideas, so many biases, that none can gain preeminence. We must frame a republic so huge that this ever-present evil is controlled." Madison felt breathless. He marched to his table and paused. Stretching to his full height, he tried to inject command into his soft voice. "For this reason, I resist a partial union of the states."

Madison sat to sparse applause and realized he had veered far afield and delivered an unwelcome sermon. He had previously tried to explain the concept to people. Few grasped it, but years of thought had convinced him of its truth. Republics must be large, the larger the better.

Madison leaned over and whispered to Mason, "You didn't pull my coattails."

"I would've sooner laid a finger on lightning." Then Mason smiled, which told Madison that their quarrel had been forgotten.

Read now burst forth with obviously suppressed emotion. "I've been silent up to now, but I must speak. This chamber displays far too much attachment to the states. The new national government must consolidate them."

Read looked nervous, and Madison thought, with good cause, but the Delaware delegate continued. "The Confederation cannot last! It cannot be amended! If we don't establish a national government on new principles, we must go to ruin.

"Gentlemen, you wrongly suspect that the people object to a strong national government. In truth, their hopes ride on this convention to deliver them from the incompetent state governments. They expect us to save their farms, to protect them from invasion, and to secure their liberty." With an anxious look around, Read blurted his last words before quickly retaking his seat. "I strongly recommend that we proceed posthaste with our duty."

Read had apparently decided to defy the other Delaware delegates and defect from the small state camp. Madison scribbled his notes with growing excitement. Wilson spoke for a moment before Madison grasped the irony of his remarks.

Wilson, head tilted down, glared at the delegates in defiance over the spectacles perched low on his nose. "This nonsense must be challenged. I see no incompatibility between the national and state governments, provided that each stays within its sphere. I vehemently disagree with Mr. Read!" Wilson sat with a firm finality.

The debate showed the weariness of the late afternoon, and a motion to adjourn found quick approval.

MADISON STUFFED HIS PAPERS into his valise a little more aggressively than necessary. Franklin caught his eye as he waved his rented prisoners away.

"An aggravating day, eh, Jemmy?"

"I apologize for showing my disappointment."

"Don't be despondent. We're in committee, a less formal setting. People feel free to speak their minds."

"I noticed."

"But you don't welcome it."

"What bothers me is that everyone is jumping sides. Mason, Butler, and Randolph fight our proposals on the executive. Even you spoke in their support. Pinckney forces a reconsideration of our vote on electing the lower branch. Morris herds me into the library to scold me. Mason is livid because of a supposed affront. Wilson and Pinckney deliver a poorly disguised threat to unite without the small states."

Madison paused and laughed. "All of this would cast me into a pit of despair, except that then Read makes an impassioned speech for our side. Then, astonishingly, Wilson objects to Read's comments. Sherman seems the only predictable man in the chamber. I wonder sometimes if we haven't locked ourselves in a sanitarium."

"Politicians are seldom admired for their healthy mental attitudes."

"Three-quarters of us are lawyers. We're supposed to be logical."

Franklin's laugh joggled his entire body. "Lawyers aren't rational; they rationalize. They tweak and stretch and fondle words until they have transformed sentences into something quite unrecognizable to the simple student of the English language."

"Do I detect the printer's bias for strict composition?"

"And the author's bias for clarity. Perhaps Shakespeare was right in saying we should kill all the lawyers."

"We couldn't assemble a jury of their peers to agree on the sentence."

Franklin gave a hearty laugh, "Quick, my young friend."

Madison beamed with the praise. "I must learn to use witticisms more often. People find me dull."

"Dear Jemmy, we each have our role to play in this little drama. I believe one man can work great change and accomplish great things, if he first forms a good plan, cuts off all amusements that would divert his attention, and makes the execution of the plan his sole business. Our success depends on you."

Madison took a moment to think. Looking about the almost empty chamber, he noticed Franklin's debtors talking animatedly in one corner. They obviously were willing to wait as long as necessary to carry their charge back to his home. He turned to Franklin. "Thank you, sir."

"Something more is bothering you."

"I'm tired."

Franklin raised an eyebrow.

"Well ... I received letters from my parents. They may've set my mood."

"How are they?"

Madison shook his head. "My father again instructed me to protect slavery."

"So you rebelled with an intemperate remark in front of the whole assembly?"

"I suppose I did."

"Don't berate yourself. Someone needed to say it. I'm glad you had the courage."

"Courage or foolhardiness?"

"Some of each, I suspect. How about your mother?"

"She's either sick, recovering from an illness, or detecting symptoms of an oncoming ailment."

"Health can be precarious, especially when you're on constant guard."

"My fear is that I inherited her weak constitution. My father believes we both exaggerate, use ill health as an excuse."

"Do you?"

"A question I ask myself ... at times."

"Well, take care. Get rest. We need you."

"I shall. Thank you." Madison stood to depart.

"What did Morris scold you about?"

Madison sat back down. "My wavering on the use of force against the states."

"That wasn't your call."

"How do you know?"

"The general and I discussed it."

"Morris is leaving the convention for a spell."

"I heard." After a pause, Franklin said, "I'll talk to him before he leaves. He'll present no more trouble. Listen, the give and take of politics is messy at best. The disorder of a republic must be endured. Remember, this is the system you wish to invent."

"I fear for our control."

"Must we control? I take heart in watching people change their minds," Franklin said. "That's the great purpose of deliberating bodies."

"I can accept disagreement for the moment, but before we break our locks of secrecy, we must have solidarity."

Eyes twinkling, Franklin repeated for the hundredth time his now famous repartee delivered after the signing of the Declaration of Independence. "Yes, indeed Jemmy, we must all hang together, or, most assuredly, we'll all hang separately."

15

Thursday, June 7, 1787

"What drove his outburst?" Sherman asked.

"Emotion and necessity." Dickinson hesitated a moment. "Roger, you must understand, Delaware's been a state for only twelve years. For us, survival has a higher priority than sovereignty."

Sherman, Ellsworth, and Dickinson walked three abreast toward the State House. The weather was fair, and a fresh spring day brought people outdoors. Idle shopkeepers stood in doorways, neighbors conversed on corners, and constables tipped their hats to passersby.

Sherman wondered what had transpired in the Delaware caucus. Just a few days ago, Read had threatened to bolt the convention. He had appeared committed to protecting the one vote per state doctrine, but yesterday had reversed himself and all but called for the annihilation of the states.

"John, what instructions did you bring?" The hesitation told Sherman he had guessed right.

"We've been instructed to work for a strong national government. Roger, we're surrounded by powerful and ambitious neighbors. We need a restraining influence on the large states or we're doomed."

"Are you required to record your instructions with the secretary?" Ellsworth asked.

Smart, Sherman thought.

"No. Our instructions aren't from the legislature as a whole, but from prominent members."

Sherman nodded. "That means Delaware's threat to withdraw from the convention can still hover over the chamber. How far must you go?"

"I'm not here to capitulate. We want a strong national government, but one with as much state influence as we can negotiate."

Ellsworth laughed. "Prepare yourself. Roger has already lectured me about negotiations. He believes gentlemen negotiate, but we must barter with brazen marauders.

"Roger, I'm disappointed you have such a low opinion about our esteemed colleagues."

"Oliver engages in hyperbole," Sherman said. "I merely pointed out that to protect our states, we must first plant our pennon on a far hill. Compromise comes after we win territory."

They walked on a few paces, and then Dickinson said, "Delaware's intent shall remain our secret. I promise we'll battle the Virginians as if our life depended on it."

"It does." Sherman kicked a wadded handbill into the street. He realized that his feeble coalition could easily collapse if he didn't come up with a fresh idea.

DICKINSON OPENED THE DAY'S session with a motion that state legislatures appoint the upper house of the legislature, which everyone now called the Senate. Sherman seconded the motion and Gerry took the floor.

"Gentlemen, four modes of appointing the Senate have been proposed.

"First, by the other branch of the legislature,

"Second, by the national executive,

"Third, by the people,

"And, fourth, by the state legislatures."

Gerry rattled these off with fast-moving eyes and comical head bobs. He endorsed election by the state legislatures but digressed into a long and convoluted argument that this method protected commercial interests against landed interests. Sherman nodded at Dickinson to try to salvage the motion.

"Esteemed delegates," Dickinson said, "the Virginia Plan unites thirteen small streams into one great river. Thus, the national government will run in the same direction as the states and possess the same defects. We must design a government like the solar system, where the states are the planets, free to move in their proper orbits."

Dickinson walked over to Wilson and pointed at him with an uplifted palm. "Mr. Wilson wishes to extinguish these planets, forgetting, gentlemen, that those states counterbalance the weight of the sun."

Wilson took the floor in a huff. "I never endorsed extinguishing these so-called planets. Gentlemen, the national government cannot devour the states. On the contrary, the states will devour the national government. The preservation of our liberty demands that the states stay in their proper—and subordinate—orbits."

Wilson walked over and mimicked Dickinson by pointing at him with an uplifted hand. "Perhaps Mr. Dickinson can explain how the great state of Delaware counterbalances the sun."

When Dickinson refused to respond, Madison spoke. "Nothing is more contradictory than to say that the national government will possess the same defects as the states, and in the next breath, say that the states are the proper check on the national government."

Sherman tapped the arm of his chair as he watched Madison return to his table with a smug expression. So far, Sherman's alliance had failed to present a decent argument.

Pinckney spoke next. "The Senate ought to be independent and permanent—appointed by the state legislatures for life."

They'd been debating how to select the Senate, not term length. Now Pinckney had scared the delegates with an aristocratic proposal. Worse, he proceeded to propose dividing the states into three classes according to size, giving the first class three senators, the second two, and the third one. He had switched to suffrage! Pinckney was part of the opposition, but Sherman had hoped that he'd support the small states on this issue. He did. But he bungled it as badly as Sherman's side.

Mason, a trueborn nationalist, surprised Sherman further. "Gentlemen, whatever power we give to the national government, a portion must be left to the states. States must possess some means to defend themselves against oppression by the national government. We've provided for self-defense in every other area. Shall only the states be without a means to protect themselves?"

Someone had finally presented a solid argument, but why had Mason supported a small state proposal? When the vote was tallied, the state legislature appointment of the Senate passed unanimously. Sherman understood.

"No joy in victory?"

"They seek to placate us, but it's not enough."

"The unanimous vote?" Ellsworth asked.

"The vote was arranged. They hope if the states appoint the Senate, we'll accept proportional suffrage in both houses."

The two men sat in Mrs. Marshall's sitting room, drinking tea. Mrs. Marshall entered, bearing a small tray. "Gentlemen, I've brought you some fresh apple fritters."

Sherman sat upright. "Thank you. The aroma's made it difficult to concentrate."

Mrs. Marshall offered the tray to Sherman, bending low to display more cleavage than necessary. "We can't distract you gentlemen from your important work now, can we?"

Sherman kept his eyes on her face and was rewarded with a sly smile. When she offered Ellsworth the tray, minus the deep bow, the two men traded a glance.

Sherman took a bite. "Mrs. Marshall, these are extraordinary. We must keep them a secret, or I won't be able to get a room the next time I'm in your fair city."

"I'll always have a room for you, Mr. Sherman. How long do you think this visit will last?"

"A while. Progress is slow."

"But satisfactory, I hope."

"We may not discuss the proceeding," Ellsworth said quickly.

"Of course. I didn't mean to pry into your business."

Ellsworth broke off a piece of his fritter and, before tossing it in his mouth, said, "We're doing the people's business."

Mrs. Marshall, looking guileless, said, "Then perhaps the people shouldn't be excluded."

Ellsworth nodded. "The press is full of remonstrations."

"I'm not talking about empty-headed newspaper writers, I'm—" Sherman's laughter stopped her midsentence. "And what do you find so amusing, Mr. Sherman?"

"Nothing. Nothing at all." Sherman waved his hand toward Ellsworth. "Please, don't let me stop you. Enlighten the man."

"I speak my own mind," she said, with uplifted chin. "Your proceedings should be public."

"We're not cooking fritters," Ellsworth said.

When Mrs. Marshall looked as if she might reach for a fireplace poker, Sherman found himself laughing uproariously. Mrs. Marshall stood akimbo and glared at the dumbfounded Ellsworth. She waited for a quieter moment and then said, "You may not be cooking fritters, Mr. Ellsworth, but whatever you're brewing smells foul."

Sherman suddenly grew serious. "What've you heard?"

Mrs. Marshall shrugged. "Discord. Your concoction appears to have a tribal flavor."

"Delegates are talking?"

"Not to us, but we see the bickering in tavern corners.

"Good to keep in mind. Thank you."

With an exaggerated curtsey, she said in an overly sweet voice, "Far be it from me to instruct men of such stature." Mrs. Marshall started to leave, but then stopped and looked at each man in turn. "Gentlemen, please remember: we must live off your stew for a long time. Do a proper job."

After she had left, Ellsworth scratched his chin and asked, "Did I miss something?"

"Yes."

"What?"

"The opinion of an intelligent woman."

"Women have no place in politics," Ellsworth said.

"Thank God, or men would be mincemeat."

Ellsworth looked puzzled a moment, shook his head, and then asked, "Was Pinckney proposing a compromise?"

"I doubt it. The Virginians wouldn't entrust Pinckney to carry the mail. I suspect the idea sprang from his own mind. Madison's adamant for proportionality in both houses."

"What do you think of Pinckney's suggestion?"

"It doesn't solve the problem. Do the arithmetic." Sherman washed the last of his fritter down with a sip of tea. "The big states would still dominate."

"It might be better than pure proportionality."

"Too early to surrender."

"Do we go on the offensive?"

"Too early to attack."

Ellsworth looked Sherman in the eye and asked, "What do you intend about Mrs. Marshall?"

"I intend to enjoy her cooking."

FRIDAY'S SESSION STARTED WITH a reconsideration of the veto over state laws. The original rule allowed a veto when state laws violated the Constitution. Pinckney wanted to expand the scope to "negate all state laws the national legislature judged improper."

Madison seconded the motion. "I oppose the use of force, and a veto provides the mildest means available to enforce compliance with national measures."

Gerry, as usual, was angry. "You mean to enslave the states, as you do your Negroes. No overbearing pundit—and there are enough of those around—would have thrown out such a ludicrous idea. We'll never accede to this notion. Never!"

Sherman finally received recognition. "Mr. Madison says the national government must have the power to stop unconstitutional acts by the states." Sherman saw Madison lift his eyes from his notes to look at him. "That resolve already passed. Mr. Pinckney has proposed a broad enlargement. I request he define *improper*, and I further move to postpone until a definition has been supplied."

Wilson responded in an exasperated tone. "It would be impractical to define *improper*. Mr. Sherman should be embarrassed to use such an ordinary delaying tactic."

Pinckney's proposal failed seven to three, and the assembly adjourned in a sour mood. As the delegates departed, Sherman sensed a shift in mood and momentum. The Virginians had suffered their first defeat with their loss of the "improper negative" motion. In politics, victory turned on timing. As Sherman gathered his papers, he wondered if this defeat provided a vital signal. Was it time to counterattack?

PATERSON STARTED SATURDAY'S SESSION by pointing out that with proportional representation in both houses, Virginia would have sixteen votes and Georgia one. "Gentlemen, I'm prepared to give energy and stability to the federal government, but the proposal to destroy state equality is astonishing.

"Mr. Madison insists that New Jersey sacrifice its suffrage. We refuse. What remedy is available?" Paterson's eyes flitted faster than a firefly. "Only one, gentlemen. A map of the United States must be spread out and all the existing boundaries erased. A new partition can then be made into thirteen equal parts. The whole nation must be thrown into hotchpot and equal divisions made. Only then can we have the fair representation that obsesses our dear Mr. Madison."

Titters of laughter sprinkled the assemblage. Sherman grinned at the audacious proposal. Perhaps ridicule might succeed where logic had failed.

Paterson voice grew stern. "The Articles of Confederation are the proper basis for these proceedings. We must keep within its limits or be charged with treason!"

Gasps escaped, but Paterson seemed oblivious. With eyes darting, he continued in a prosecutorial tone. "The people are not easily deceived. Mr. Wilson hints that the large states might confederate among themselves. Let them unite if they please, but they have no right to compel us to unite with them. New Jersey will never confederate under the plan before this committee. She would be swallowed up. I'd rather submit to a monarch, to a despot, even to anarchy, than to such a fate!"

Madison showed obvious frustration. "If the large states possess all the avarice and ambition charged, how secure, may I ask, will the small states be when the national government falls to ruin?"

The parameters of a stalemate were being defined. The small states held off the assault of a more powerful foe by threatening to quit the convention in a public fury. The large states kept them in their seats by raising the specter of chaos and inevitable absorption by the large states.

Wilson charged up the aisle and peered over his spectacles directly at Paterson. "*Mr. Paterson*, you say you cannot accept proportional representation. Are the citizens of New Jersey superior to those of Pennsylvania? Does it require three Pennsylvanians to balance one from New Jersey? If New Jersey refuses to confederate on this plan, then Pennsylvania refuses to confederate on any other!"

Wilson turned to the assembly at large and spat, "If New Jersey refuses to part with her precious sovereignty, then it's futile to continue."

Men shouted objections, chairs scraped as some stood and others turned to their compatriots, and knots of men suddenly gathered at the back of the chamber for impromptu caucuses. The chairman gaveled to no use, until someone finally shouted a motion to adjourn. A second came equally as loud, and the men stopped clamoring long enough to vote. Upon adjournment, everyone immediately vacated the chamber, destined for various taverns where they could talk in private. Sherman was shocked at how quickly the chamber took on the feel of a crypt.

THE MEN SAT AROUND the table with grim faces. Sherman, Ellsworth, Paterson, Dickinson, and Luther Martin met in a private room at the City Tavern. Martin had arrived from Maryland that morning. Although renowned as a skillful litigator, Martin's slovenly nature, verbose speaking style, and fondness for drink offended Sherman. Despite his distaste, Sherman had inducted Martin into their group. His alliance now included Connecticut, New Jersey, Delaware, and Maryland. New York often voted with them, but for selfish reasons.

"It's time to decide what we can accept," Sherman said.

"To what purpose?" Paterson asked.

"To define the limits of compromise," Sherman responded.

"Again, to what purpose? Wilson said it all: further exertion is futile. We should quit. This convention will imprison us."

"The convention has far to go before it seals our fate. We can still manage affairs. The alternative is dire."

"How dire?" Ellsworth asked.

"Civil war, perhaps, but I suspect the Society of the Cincinnati will thrust an emperor into power first."

A few knowing glances darted around the room.

Martin poured himself another brandy, the third in less than half an hour. "If today's an indication, this is a waste of my time." He threw the brandy down in a single swallow. "I left a lucrative practice to listen to idiots."

Dickinson's face pinched in distaste. "I beg your pardon, Luther, but we all left gainful endeavors to come here. You trot into town and—"

"And bring us much needed expertise in political affairs," Sherman interjected. "How do you suggest we gain the upper hand?"

"Against the haughty Virginians?"

"And their allies."

"Well," Martin said, "it shan't be easy, but I'd like nothing better than to scatter the Virginians back to their precious plantations. First, I'd..."

Martin droned on with no new ideas. He talked endlessly, washing down hastily gnawed bread with huge swallows of brandy. Within minutes, he had sprinkled bits of bread all over his protruding belly. Sherman decided he must win his cases by exhausting his opponents.

Tired of waiting for an opportune break, Sherman interrupted. "Mr. Martin, I'm enthralled by your ideas, but if you'll excuse me, I'd like to discuss what we can accept before we figure out how to get it."

"Splendid idea, Roger," Dickinson said. "Do you have a suggestion?"

"A proposition," Sherman said, as he refilled Martin's brandy. "Suppose we allow the lower house to be proportional but succeed in getting one vote per state in the Senate. Can we accept that?"

"No!" Paterson said.

"Think a minute, William. The Senate will be more powerful, the state legislatures elect its members, and senators enjoy a longer term. Doesn't this provide sufficient protection?"

Martin spewed a belch before saying, "You'll never get it."

"What if we did?"

"Then we'd support the new government," Dickinson said.

"Damned if *we* would!" Paterson shouted. "If we surrender, we'll be condemned for sedition and cowardice."

"William, if the states control the Senate, we'll remain secure," Ellsworth argued.

"Secure?" Martin boomed. "What about sovereignty?"

"Sovereignty follows might," Sherman said, irritated. "Can Maryland defend herself against enemies here and abroad?"

"We can take care of the supercilious Virginians," Paterson said, but he looked ready to fight the men in this room. "They mean to gobble us up, and this convention is rigged to follow their wind."

Sherman held up the flat of his hand. "Rigging can be altered. Remember, the big states lost the improper veto clause yesterday. They suffered defeat, yet we wail and whine. None of us expected an easy fight. Your states selected you because of your character and will to prevail."

Martin roiled in laughter. "Perhaps the latter, my friend, perhaps the latter."

Despite his crudeness, Sherman appreciated Martin's churlish diversion.

Paterson ignored Martin. "What about my plan? Why won't you let me present it? Why must we accept theirs?"

Sherman marveled at Paterson's use of the personal pronoun. "John, I'm not suggesting we accept their plan. I'm asking us to define what we can accept at a minimum, where the limits are. You'll present your plan, but as a counter-weight."

"The New Jersey Plan is solid—and within our instructions. Why can't we have it?"

"Because we don't have the votes," Sherman said with firm finality.

The two men stared at each other. Paterson's challenge to his leadership had to be addressed, but not today. His immediate concern was how to achieve a consensus that included New Jersey. Sherman was wondering how to move Paterson, when Martin surprised him.

"As I understand it, the convention has already determined that the state legislatures will elect the Senate?"

"Correct."

"Hmm ... the lower house will be proportional, elected by the people. If the Senate has one vote per state, and the states elect senators, then I can probably sell the new government to Maryland. If the remaining components make sense, of course."

Sherman turned a questioning look to Paterson. Paterson scowled and folded his arms in front of him. "I want something closer to my plan."

"And you can have it if you win over delegates." Sherman gave Paterson a moment to grasp the futility. "We're trying to define the minimum we can accept."

Paterson glanced at Martin and then gave a longer, harder look at Dickinson. Finally, his face muscles slackened, and he unwound his arms, laying both palms flat on the table. "All right, Roger. I don't like it, but I'll go along. With Martin's caveat. All the other components must make sense."

"Then we're all agreed." Sherman didn't wait for equivocation. "I'll propose the compromise on Monday."

"You don't suppose they'll buy it?" Ellsworth asked.

"Not on Monday, probably not next week, but they will."

SHERMAN ENTERED MRS. MARSHALL'S house, weary from a long session and a seemingly longer caucus. On their return walk, Ellsworth had been effusive in his praise for how Sherman had handled their contentious group. Ellsworth seemed energized; Sherman wanted to go to bed.

"Mr. Sherman, what an opportune arrival. May we talk a few minutes?" The voice belonged to Witherspoon.

"If we keep it short, Reverend. I'm in need of a feathered mattress."

"If you don't mind, Roger, I'll retire and let you two gentlemen while away the night." Sherman watched Ellsworth ascend the stairs, wearing a devious grin.

"I have a bottle of brandy in the sitting room," Witherspoon said.

"Then by all means, let's join it."

After Sherman and Witherspoon had settled and chitchatted for a few minutes, Sherman said, "I'm afraid I'm very tired, Reverend. What's on your mind?"

"I think you should talk privately with James."

"Why?"

"He needs your help. I know how deft you are in political matters. Young James needs a seasoned hand to guide him."

"He has Washington, Franklin, and a bevy of Virginians. He doesn't need my counsel."

"He doesn't need your opposition."

"We have different aims."

"You have the same aim, only different means."

"Nothing can be accomplished by our meeting."

"Nothing can be harmed by your meeting."

"Reverend, we both share an affection for James, but I cannot accede to his plans."

"Politics tend to become uncivil. A chat early on can open a door before it's bolted tight. Perhaps a compromise only the two of you could engineer could save the nation."

"James won't compromise his precious plan."

"Nor, I hear, will you sacrifice Connecticut's sovereignty."

"You hear wrong. Connecticut does not have the military might to claim sovereignty. I'm here to protect Connecticut from being swept into oblivion."

"You believe the proud Virginians will sacrifice their state?"

"They think they'll run the new government."

"You're more headstrong than I expected."

"Headstrong, yes; shortsighted, no." Sherman pushed himself up. "I'll see James."

"You're a shrewd man." Witherspoon stood to signal that he had achieved his aim. "A dialogue between the two of you is in the country's interest."

"Reverend, I'll not slip Connecticut over to the large state side."

"I never imagined that you would."

"Good night, Reverend."

"Yes, a good night."

Part 3

Deadlock

16

Sunday, June 10, 1787

Sunday mornings found Philadelphia's streets full of people strolling to church. The two men mixed with the parade but were destined for different churches. Steeples and tavern signs were the most visible emblems of town life, and thirty churches stood within a few blocks of State House. While in Philadelphia, Sherman worshipped at the Old Pine Street Church, a Presbyterian denomination. Madison, along with most of the Virginians, attended the Anglican Christ Church on Second Street.

Dressed in a black suit, Madison strolled with his hands clasped behind his back. Sherman trudged alongside, his fists buried deep in the pockets of his sturdy brown coat. Sherman withdrew a hand and pointed toward the Walnut Street Prison.

"Government must have a better purpose than to build prisons for debtors."

Sherman and Madison watched the prisoners use poles to extend their hats out to passing churchgoers. A few quickly dropped a few coins in the proffered hats, but most walked briskly along toward their destination. Although the prisoners accepted donations with jocular good wishes, they seemed to take greater delight in throwing insults at those who ignored them.

"It looks cruel," Madison said, "but the sanctity of contracts must be upheld."

"Many believe government shares the blame."

"Nevertheless, government must protect property."

"Shouldn't a *good* government do more?"

"A *good* government should be impartial when it protects property."

"If the aim of government is so elementary, why did you make it a life's study?"

"It took a life's study for me to discover that it was so elementary."

"Are you serious?"

"Quite." Madison smiled. "But I entertain a broad view of property."

"How broad?"

"Nations engage in war to protect or acquire property—territory. Governments must protect property from larceny and theft. If a man owns no land, commerce, or trade, he still owns his liberty, and liberty is the most precious property of all."

"In my experience, governments are more inclined to threaten liberty than to protect it."

"Exactly. Tyrants shamelessly demand tribute and obedience; while republics show a predilection toward embezzlement—slowly snatching liberty when attention is distracted. History records an uninterrupted stream of states that deny liberty, confiscate property, or enable some to swindle others."

"A gloomy outlook."

"That's why I'm so passionate about a sound design. In a republic, the majority rules, so the majority can steal from those with fewer votes, be they rich or from another region, commercial class, or religious faith. Democracies have always been turbulent and short-lived, with violent deaths. Theologians believe that by granting equal rights, they can equalize possessions, opinions, and passions. They're wrong. Historically, democracies threatened liberty and property rights."

"You believe your plan corrects this tendency?"

"The Virginia Plan balances power and checks the erosive tendencies of republics." Madison gave a shrug and added, "But I'm accused of being too philosophical. Forgive me. How's the mood in your camp?"

"We'll be present Monday."

"Fairly noncommittal."

"On the contrary, attendance was not a given."

"I see."

"We must compromise on proportionality."

"We must not."

"James, we're at a stalemate. One side must give."

"We already have. The states may elect the Senate."

"Not enough. Tomorrow I'll propose a single vote per state in the Senate."

"And I'll oppose it."

"We can't proceed until this issue is resolved."

"Then you must accept proportional suffrage. Fairness dictates it. The states will continue to exist because of our vast territory, not because of an intrinsic right to govern."

"My group doesn't share your view."

"Obviously. Your doggedness has kept us from moving forward. We must become a single nation—a single nation with its power derived directly from the people."

"We'll insist on a single vote in the Senate."

"You'll lose. And isolated, you'll have no choice but to join us."

"James, please keep that smug attitude."

Madison whipped his head around. Sherman did not make contentious statements. "You believe you can win?"

"I believe politics, not philosophy, will prevail."

"Votes prevail."

"That's what I said."

MADISON, HAMILTON, RANDOLPH, AND Pinckney stood in a corner of Franklin's serene courtyard. Washington and Franklin had asked for a few moments alone after church to converse in private, and the four men had given them some distance. Madison feared that the two leaders had invited this group over to Franklin's home to gain agreement on a compromise.

"The whole thing may collapse: the convention, the nation, our independence. How can I explain to the people back home?"

"Mr. Randolph, I'm sure your exquisitely honed political skills will shield you from the slightest blame for this debacle." Pinckney spoke so smoothly that Randolph looked unsure whether to take offense.

He decided to ignore the comment. "The small states ruin every opportunity."

"We must ignore the little deeds of little politicians," Hamilton said.

"Which little politicians are those?" Pinckney teased.

"Paterson, for one," Randolph huffed.

"Yes, of course, those little politicians." Pinckney looked straight at Randolph with an impish grin.

Randolph gave Pinckney a disconcerted glance and turned to Madison. "Mr. Madison, must we tolerate this obstructionism?"

"Yes, Mr. Madison, can we not abandon our traveling companions and leave them to the bears, the Indians, and the European powers?" Pinckney showed far too much delight in tormenting Randolph.

"I'd like nothing better than to unite only those states committed to republican principles, but others disagree." With this, Madison nodded toward the two men bent in whispered conversation under the famed mulberry tree.

Madison rolled forward on his toes and arched his back. His back ached from bending over his desk, and stretching felt good. As he settled back on his heels, Madison worried that he might be coming down with some illness.

"We must avoid a partial union, or we'll see the same evils which have scourged the old world," Hamilton said.

"Which evils?" Pinckney asked. Madison noticed that his voice had lost the derisive tone he used with Randolph.

"War. Vicinity dictates a country's natural enemies. Only a fool believes separate nations wouldn't be fighting frequent wars."

"Surely war can be avoided," Randolph protested.

"War is natural and the threat of war devours liberty." Hamilton's voice took on a forlorn note. "The most powerful influence on a nation's conduct is safety. People sacrifice freedom to feel safe."

"Americans don't rely on government for safety," Madison said.

"One day, they may. Autocrats slyly build anxiety and fear, and then offer up government to protect people from these shadowy threats. Each submission erodes liberty."

"You paint a bleak future," Pinckney said.

"No bleaker than Europe—and no healthier."

"I can't believe—"

"Gentlemen," Madison interrupted, "the general is signaling us to come over."

The four men immediately approached. Three additional chairs faced the two seated men, so Madison waved the others into the chairs and gratefully remained standing.

"Good afternoon, General, Doctor," Madison said. "I hope this morning's service was enlightening."

Washington smiled. "On the contrary, Jemmy, I left completely befuddled."

"Were you visiting another church again?"

"The Dutch Reformed Church." Washington made a habit of attending different services to "broaden his viewpoint," but Madison believed he wanted to spread his presence to as many voters as possible. "Gentlemen, don't look so distressed. I'm in no danger of becoming a proselyte. The sermon was delivered in Dutch, so I didn't understand a single word."

Franklin laughed while everyone else politely smiled.

"Religions are like a man traveling in foggy weather," Franklin said. "A man sees those at a distance wrapped in fog, but near him all appears clear. In truth, he's shrouded in fog as well. A clever man strives to see things from another's vantage point."

"I believe you've cleared up a mystery," Pinckney said. "I believe some in our party stand fast in a deep haze."

Randolph went crimson. "Mr. Pinckney, that's enough. I don't need—"

"Gentlemen." This single word from Washington put a contrite expression on everyone's face.

"Dear Mr. Pinckney," Franklin said in a conciliatory tone, "you amuse only yourself. Let's not spoil this fine afternoon."

"My apologies. I referred to our opponents at the convention, not to anyone present."

"Very well," Washington said. "Mr. Madison, we seem to be at an impasse. Do you have any suggestions?"

Madison shook his head. "The small states hold progress hostage to their petty ambitions."

Hamilton looked smug. "Ambition, avarice, and personal animosity operate on those who support, as well those who oppose, the right side of a question."

Washington ignored Hamilton. "How do we break the deadlock?"

"By remaining steadfast," Madison offered.

"That seems insufficient. The small states may retire. Noisily, I'm sure."

"They'll remain."

"Speculation?"

"No, I'm sure."

"How?"

Madison paused. He felt uncomfortable revealing a confidence in front of so many. Deciding, he said, "I spoke with Sherman this morning—privately."

"I understand." Washington looked at each man. "No one's to mention this." Everyone nodded. "The situation may not be as dire as I had feared. But we must move forward. The doctor has a compromise he has graciously offered to present tomorrow."

Madison tensed. "Sir, you don't propose that we sacrifice proportional representation?"

"Not exactly," Franklin said. "I'll propose equal representation based on equal contribution in taxes."

Madison hesitated, not sure how to raise objections to a revered legend. "Equal contributions will bankrupt the small states. Can you explain your scheme?"

"I could, but you shan't understand it."

"Excuse me, sir—and I don't mean to be presumptuous—but if I can't understand it, how will the delegates understand it?"

"I'm a befuddled old man. I often say unfathomable things."

"Not in my presence."

"Kind of you, but untrue." Then with his trademark twinkle, Franklin said, "James, my dear boy, sometimes a fire must be smothered, not doused."

The doctor was right, Madison didn't understand. But since people he trusted had concocted the scheme, he decided not to pursue the issue. He'd wait for events to unfold.

SHERMAN OPENED MONDAY MORNING with a proposal for one vote per state in the Senate, but then he threw in a surprise. He said membership in the first branch should be based on the number of free inhabitants. It was said in passing, but everyone heard it. Madison thought this devilish. Sherman had spotted the crevice in their alliance and had adroitly exploited it.

An energized buzz filled the chamber. The big state delegates conferred angrily or sat sour faced. Obviously, tempers hadn't cooled under the influence of Sunday services. The endless seesaw of political maneuvering had filed emotions raw, and Madison worried that the chamber was ready to erupt. With relief, he saw Franklin take the floor. Perhaps the doctor had concocted a formula that would extricate them from this mire.

Franklin spoke in an engaging and friendly manner. "It has given me great pleasure to observe that until proportionality, our debates were in good humor. We were sent here to deliberate, not fight. Bold declarations neither enlighten nor convince. Heated debate on one side begets hot responses from the other. I originally hoped that every delegate would consider himself a representative of the United States, rather than as an agent of his particular state. Unfortunately, this is not the case.

"Gentlemen, when England and Scotland united, the Scot patriots cried that England would swallow tiny Scotland. After they finally agreed to unite, the Scots were given only forty members in the Commons and sixteen in the House of Lords. A great inferiority!"

With a gentle smile and the timing of a thespian, Franklin concluded his story. "But when the Duke of Argyle came to government, he put so many Scots into civil posts that Jonah swallowed the whale."

Madison laughed with the rest of the delegates. In a simple yet eloquent way, Franklin had once again dissipated the passion in the chamber. He was not done, however. Madison noticed that he held many more pages of prepared remarks.

"To this day, Parliament hasn't injured Scotland. Nor should the small states fear injury from an energized central government."

Franklin explained that under the single vote per state rule, seven small states could override the majority of people in the six large states. "Gentlemen, the large states naturally resist having their property controlled by the smaller, just as the small states harbor the same fear of the larger. We need a just solution to this dilemma."

Franklin presented a long and convoluted proposal that based representation on tax contributions. The complexities strained Madison's ability to capture the essence of the scheme. When the doctor finished, Madison wondered if Franklin meant this compromise to be taken seriously, or if he merely wanted to talk until he had diffused tempers. Whatever the case, the delegates ignored his ideas and returned to the question of representation in the legislature.

Pinckney quickly moved to clarify suffrage in the lower house with new wording: "in proportion to the whole number of white citizens of every age, sex, and, condition, including those bound to servitude, and three-fifths of all other persons not included in the foregoing description, except Indians not paying taxes."

This motion countered Sherman's attempt to split the large Northern states and the slaveholding South. When Wilson seconded, Pennsylvania joined South Carolina in sending a message that slavery couldn't be used to rend their alliance.

Grabbing the floor, Gerry took a belligerent stance, fists firmly planted on each hip. "I'm just an ill-informed man from a small wayward state. Could someone familiar with your strange customs please enlighten me? I seek an answer to a simple question. Are blacks people or property?"

Gerry's eyes flitted around the chamber, but no one volunteered to "enlighten" him. "Gentlemen, property should not be the standard for representation. The government doesn't represent land, buildings, and poultry. It represents people. Why should blacks—which are unquestionably property in the South—be counted, in whole or in part? This makes no sense. If we count slaves, then what's the proper count for cows, horses, and hogs?

"May I make a humble suggestion? If you desire additional representation, free your slaves. We of the simple North will then gladly count each black as a full person."

Gerry sat to a stunned audience. Gentlemen used euphemisms to speak about sensitive issues. Gerry charged in with no subtlety and little regard for propriety. Without further debate, the large states passed the Pinckney amendment. Lower house representation would be based on whites and a three-fifth count of slaves.

Sherman immediately again moved that the second branch should have one vote per state. "*Everything* depends on this. The smaller states will never agree to any plan that doesn't include equal suffrage in the Senate."

Everything, Madison knew, meant continued attendance.

Sherman's motion went down to defeat, six to five. Close, but the big state alliance held. New York had sided with the small states because Hamilton had been outvoted by his two fellow delegates. Governor Clinton's stacked delegation had again made Hamilton superfluous.

Hamilton's motion that suffrage in the Senate be the same as in the first branch passed with the same alignment of states.

Madison recorded the vote with a huge sigh of relief. Finally, this contentious issue had been put behind them. If his alliance could pass these resolutions in the Committee of the Whole, they could pass them when the convention reconvened. Sherman had cleverly tried to use slavery to divide and conquer, but the large states had worked out the three-fifths rule beforehand.

This was no small victory. The states were now diminished, and the national government could rule. The big Northern states had representation based on their larger populations. The price had been a partial count of slaves that gave the South additional representation. This devilish deal achieved a supreme national government based on a close approximation of equal representation.

As the delegates began to rise after adjournment, Washington stood and demanded attention with a simple, "Gentlemen."

Everyone held still or sat back down.

"I'm sorry to report that one of our members has been neglectful."

Those who remained standing quickly retook their seats.

"So neglectful that he dropped a copy of our proceedings outside this chamber." Washington looked around with a stern countenance. "By luck, it was picked up and delivered to me this morning. I entreat you to be more careful, lest our transactions get into the newspapers."

Madison shivered. Early revelation, especially of today's victory, would ignite angry opposition.

Washington held the papers high above his head. "I don't know whose paper this is but let him who owns it take it." With that, he flung the paper onto the desk with a sharp slap. Washington picked up his tricorn, firmly snugged it on his head, and stormed down the central aisle and out the door.

Madison watched several delegates shyly approach the desk and peek at the papers. Each showed obvious relief as they turned to leave without picking up the notes. Madison knew they weren't his. His care in handling his own journal exceeded the protection of his purse.

By the time he had organized his materials, the chamber room had almost emptied. Curiosity drew him to the notes. Shock gripped him. He recognized the handwriting. He whirled around to find Robert Morris still in his seat. Washington's friend just sat there and gave Madison a sly wink. Working to keep his composure, Madison returned to his table to pick up his valise. As he walked out of the chamber, Madison thought that if the Philadelphia Shakespearian Company ever needed another member, he knew where they could find an accomplished thespian.

As MADISON EXITED THE State House, he saw that Franklin's charges had set his sedan chair down on the sidewalk so he could talk with Washington. Neither seemed as happy as they should be. Eager to hear about the little charade at the end of the session, Madison walked over to the two men.

Bowing slightly, Madison said, "Doctor, I want to thank you for your speech. It went far to dampen emotion."

Franklin lifted his head to look the standing Madison in the eye. "Mr. Madison, we have made an immoral pact. This slave issue will hamper ratification."

Madison was taken aback. "Doctor, we had no choice."

Franklin paused. "Perhaps not, but that doesn't mean I have to like it." He looked at each of the slaveholders in turn. "Words pale next to action. I'm afraid this rubs badly against my beliefs."

Franklin looked sad as he laboriously shifted his gout-ridden body. "I'm not deluded, gentlemen. I'm quite aware I've been a party to this arrangement. It weighs heavy on me."

With a beckoning wave to his prisoners, Franklin said, "You are both honorable and worked for the best we could achieve, but I believe we'll rue this day."

As the prisoners lifted the sedan chair, Franklin added, "Please excuse me, but I wish to return to my courtyard sanctuary and take tea in private."

17

Wednesday, June 13, 1787

Sherman watched the sturdy-looking young man enter the coffeehouse. Abraham Baldwin quickly made his way to Sherman's table.

"Good afternoon, Abe," Sherman said with enthusiasm. "Thank you for joining me."

Baldwin clasped Sherman's upper arm with his left hand as he eagerly shook with his right. "Anytime, anytime. But thank you for picking an out-of-the-way establishment. Can't have my fellow delegates thinking I'm consorting with the opposition."

"We certainly can't have that. Besides, I'm not scheming. I just want to talk to an old friend."

"Ha, that's a hoot."

"I'd never use a friend to advance a personal agenda."

"Balderdash!"

"Abe?" Sherman said with arms splayed wide.

"My God, man, don't tell me you've gone flaccid with old age. I've been looking forward to some titillating intrigue."

"Maybe we'll get to something later, but first tell me, how's life treating you in Georgia?"

Both men conveyed the eagerness of old friends wanting to catch up with each other. Sherman had picked a coffeehouse in the commercial district at the corner of Market and Front streets, far from the political neighborhood around the State House. Philadelphia had a problem with beggars, pickpockets, and drunks, so Sherman was pretty confident that other delegates would avoid this rough neighborhood. Besides, this coffeehouse catered to sea captains who wanted privacy to negotiate their next cargo.

After ordering, Baldwin said, "Georgia's backcountry couldn't fit me better."

"You were never comfortable in the city."

"New Haven's a burg compared to Philadelphia. I may never get this city stench off me. The Wilkes County bumpkins may throw me to the Creeks on my return."

"How goes it with the Creeks?"

"Bad. The Spanish provide them with arms and sanctuary in Florida. We're too spread out to protect ourselves from their raids."

"So to buy security, you joined the nationalist cause?"

"You do have a scheme. Tell me. I won't help, but I surely do enjoy a good conspiracy."

"Abe, what ever caused you to see me as a blackguard?"

"Years of observation."

The two men smiled at each other, relaxed in the camaraderie of old warriors. Baldwin, born and raised in Connecticut, had moved to Georgia just three years ago and quickly established himself in the state's political circles. Before he left, Sherman and Baldwin had been fast friends. It helped that both held uninhibited political ambitions.

Baldwin, only thirty-three, had had a varied career. When Sherman held the post of Yale University treasurer, Baldwin had been a student and tutor. Later, he became the minister for the school. About the time Baldwin graduated, Sherman had been awarded an honorary masters degree for his service and contributions to Yale. In those prewar days, Baldwin had also kept a running account at a store Sherman owned that catered to Yale students and faculty. Baldwin, born to a blacksmith, and Sherman, the son of a boot maker, found they had much in common.

After serving as a chaplain in the Continental Army, Baldwin was offered a professorship in divinity at Yale. He declined the offer, attended law school, and established himself as an attorney in New Haven. Baldwin dabbled in politics, entered the ministry, tried academia, practiced law, but never found his niche. A brisk outdoor man, with little patience for polite society, Baldwin finally decided it was place, not profession, that disquieted him. Sherman was happy to see his friend content in rural Georgia.

"Roger, I'm glad you lead the opposition. Your judgment will keep the convention from going too far astray."

"I'm having trouble keeping the small states tethered."

"You mean the threat to withdraw is real?"

"And imminent."

"Damn, that'll bring ruin." Baldwin gave Sherman a hard look. "Why, you ol' scoundrel, it appears our reminiscing's over. What's bouncing around in that head of yours?"

"We need a compromise on suffrage in the Senate. My people will acquiesce to the Virginia Plan only if they have an equal voice in at least one house."

"Roger, I can't sway Georgia. Even if I vote with you—which I won't—I'm only one vote amongst four. None of the other Georgia delegates will accept your compromise."

"Why won't you vote with me?"

"I'm a Georgian now."

"I see." Sherman signaled for another cup of coffee.

Baldwin laughed. "You don't give up, do you? You ordered more coffee so you can continue to cajole me. You nefarious old rascal, I'll never yield. Never."

Sherman grinned. "But you'll listen?"

"Blather away."

"Why do you find an equal vote in the Senate so reprehensible?"

"I don't. In fact, I believe it's in Georgia's interest. We're sparsely populated and will be disadvantaged by suffrage based solely on population." Baldwin swung around to sit sideways with his legs crossed. "Roger, understand this, my delegation has sworn allegiance to Virginia."

Sherman tried his most engaging smile. "Abe, this is politics. Allegiances last but a fortnight."

"My backcountrymen distrust a strong national government, so I need the appearance of unity with seaboard Georgians. I can't go against the rest of my delegation."

"What would convince the other Georgia delegates to support a single vote in the Senate?"

"So, it's games you want to play. All right, I'll tell you. Your gambit on slavery won't work. Compared to the other Southern states, Georgia isn't as dependent on slaveholdings—and my district has an even lower ratio of slaves."

"What will work?"

"You're asking how you can buy their votes?"

"What do they fear? Assuaging fear costs less than feeding appetites."

"You fiend. You never cease to astound me." Baldwin uncrossed his legs and faced Sherman directly. "Remember, we speak hypothetically. Georgia claims vast tracts of land to the west, all the way to the Mississippi. The greatest fear in my state is that a national government will take this land away from Georgia and carve it into new, independent states. This isn't just hubris. Huge fortunes are at stake."

"Does this concern you personally?"

"It concerns Wilkes County—and prominent people along the seaboard."

"Thank you, Abe. You've given me something to work with."

"I've given you nothing. I'm serious, Roger. No deal, no assurances, no staked-out common ground. We leave as we entered—good friends who just happen to be on the opposite sides of a peevish political dilemma."

"I understand," Sherman said.

Baldwin grinned like a privateer that had just caught sight of a Spanish galleon. "I must admit, my friend; I can't wait to see what you do with this bit of flotsam."

"WE'VE BEEN TROUNCED." PATERSON looked downtrodden.

Sherman kept his voice light. "We're in committee and we need only one more state."

"Which state do you propose to seduce?" Paterson asked. "They're fitted tighter than a dovetailed chest of drawers."

"William, it's time for you to present your plan," Sherman said.

"I'm not ready."

"What?"

"I'm not ready."

"William, we've passed the Virginia Plan. You must present now."

On Tuesday and today, the convention had whipped through the rest of the Virginia Plan. With the suffrage issue behind them, no one had any more fight. This morning, after approving nineteen resolves, four more than originally proposed, the Committee of the Whole officially reported out the plan.

"Roger, you were the one who told me to seek advice from Delaware and Maryland. Martin drives me crazy."

"How much time do you need?"

"Maybe Friday."

Sherman gave an exasperated sigh. "I don't want to expend political points asking for a delay."

"You control Martin then. I'm done with this charade."

Sherman stopped short. "You're right. I apologize. I gave you an impossible task. We'll just have to seek more time."

"Do you think they'll consider my plan?"

"When the delegates see it, we'll win converts. Sanity will once again prevail in the chamber."

Sherman didn't believe a word he said.

"GENERAL, MAY I SPEAK to you?"

"Mr. Sherman, just the man I was looking for. Let's talk."

Both had just arrived at the State House for Thursday's session. Sherman followed Washington to the tower Stair Hall and up to the landing midway to the second floor. The landing was the architectural masterpiece of the building. Its Ionic pilasters were capped with bellflower pendants. A cornice framed a high Palladian window that looked down to the yard below.

"Why were you looking for me, General?"

"I wanted to check the mood of the small states. The campaign can be wrapped up quickly with your support."

"With all due respect, I don't believe things can be wrapped up quickly."

Washington gave Sherman an unrelenting stare. "Why not?"

"Paterson has worked tirelessly on a plan with the other small states. They insist on presenting it."

"The committee already reported out a plan. One, if memory serves, that was vigorously debated. The will of the Committee of the Whole has been determined."

"The assembly hasn't had an opportunity to see this plan."

"Why've you delayed in bringing it forward?"

"The small states came unprepared. It had to be hashed out in the scant time between sessions. Maryland arrived late."

"Who's behind this plan?" Washington demanded.

Did Washington mean which states or which men? Sherman, tall enough to maintain level eye contact, suddenly felt in want of stature. "New Jersey, Delaware, Maryland, and Connecticut. Possibly New York."

"You support this infamy?"

"Yes, sir." Sherman paused. "But honest disagreement is not infamy."

"It's at least foolish. The country disintegrates, and you quibble over peccadilloes."

Washington walked over to the Gothic laced window. He looked down at the yard for a long period, then squared his shoulders and returned to where Sherman stood. "Mr. Sherman, we must come out of this convention with a plan for a new government. It's imperative. What must I do to secure your cooperation?"

"Sir, you have my cooperation."

"But you don't support the plan duly voted for by the committee."

"No, sir, I do not."

"Why not!"

"It will trample Connecticut."

"My god, man, can you not see? Are things so different in Connecticut?"

"No, sir. The situation in Connecticut is dire."

"Then why can't you support this plan?"

"Because it's sedition!"

Washington looked ready to explode. Sherman braced himself, but instead, the general turned and walked back to gaze out the window again. After a longer recess, he slowly turned to face Sherman. "We disagree… obviously." Washington turned his full frame toward Sherman but stayed at the window casing. He spoke softly. "Roger, presently we're weak at home and a disgrace abroad. I believe state governments cause our disorder. They go to incredible length to guard their power." Washington took a step closer. "Your refusal to yield will destroy this great country."

"General, I believe every word you just said, except the last sentence. If not for my efforts, this convention would already be dead."

Washington slowly closed the space between the two men; then, surprisingly, he put his hand on Sherman's shoulder. "I believe you. Now what must we do to save our country?"

"Allow Paterson to present his plan. It won't pass, but an idea or two weaved into the Virginia Plan might win the united support we need."

"I'll instruct Gorham to give Paterson the floor."

"Thank you. He'll be ready tomorrow."

"Why not today?"

"I need time to counsel him. His ire must be harnessed."

With exasperation, Washington said, "Very well. I'll support a recess."

Washington removed his hand and made a motion to leave.

"Sir, if I may."

"Yes."

"We want the same goal, but we serve different constituents. You have my commitment to work for a sound national government, but I must continue to present my views."

"Roger, I insist on your vote to get us out of committee."

"If I say yes, what am I committing to?"

"When we vote out the final recommendation of the Committee of the Whole, I want you to vote with the will of the chamber."

"ALL RIGHT, WILLIAM, EXPLAIN it to us again."

They all grouped around the table where Mrs. Marshall served meals. After being granted a one-day recess, the small state leaders had rushed to the boardinghouse to go over Paterson's plan one more time.

The room had a comfortable feel. The bright yellow wainscoting complemented the pastoral wallpaper highlighted with traces of yellow. The massive sideboard along one wall, created by the English furniture maker Thomas Chippendale, must have been Mrs. Marshall's prized possession and displayed her willow-patterned china and sparkling silver service. The seafaring paintings around the room paid tribute to her deceased merchant husband.

Paterson cleared his throat. "The first resolve quotes our instructions from Congress to remind the delegates of our limited authority."

"I don't need a reminder to see we've verged off course," Martin said.

"Let's hold the criticism and allow William to move through this quickly," Sherman said. "We're out of time."

Paterson read through the plan with no further interruptions. The laws of Congress were supreme and bound the states. Congress had the authority to apply duties on import and provide penalties for noncompliance. The state courts interpreted laws, with appeals to the national judiciary. Taxes were levied based on the formula used by the Virginia Plan for representation. The national government could use force to collect unpaid taxes or to enforce laws, but only after an unspecified number of states concurred. The executive consisted of more than one person and could be impeached by a majority of state executives. The state executives collectively appointed federal officers and a supreme tribunal of judges, and controlled the military. The supreme tribunal held the power to impeach all federal officers except the executive.

Since this was a revision of the Articles, then by omission, each state continued to have one vote. There were other details, but basically, this version was more refined than the plan they had outlined three weeks ago. They used language from the Virginia Plan, including "three-fifths of all other persons," to determine taxes as a ploy. If slaves justified increased representation, then slaves could determine taxes.

Sherman still believed that Congress would accept this plan, but he had been convinced during the debates that they must go further. What should he do?

"Does everyone agree?" Sherman asked.

He visually worked his way around the table, getting a nod or short affirmative answer from everyone. Everyone except Luther Martin, who sat to his immediate left.

"Luther, how do you vote?"

"I presume you don't wish me to pontificate?" Martin asked.

"Brevity makes a man appear smarter," Sherman answered.

With an uplifted eyebrow, Martin voted. "Aye."

Sherman smiled. "You must want to appear a genius."

This caused genuine laughter. Relief that they had all agreed heightened the levity. Sherman decided not to voice his reservations.

"William, how long to scribe a clean copy?" Sherman asked.

"Two, three hours."

"Before you start, we have one last issue. Who pays for copies?" After a long silence, Sherman added, "You must all want to appear smart."

Now the mood verged on dizzy euphoria. Sherman regretted the quip; he needed to deal with this issue seriously. "William, can you buy the copies?"

"No." Paterson assumed a helpless expression. "We've written for more funds. Our delegation—"

"This is the New Jersey Plan," Sherman interrupted.

"Yes, but—"

"But what?"

"We have no money."

Sherman looked around at the other men. No one volunteered.

"Very well, Connecticut will fund the copies. On one condition: there are sure to be additional expenses, so each of you must write your legislatures for additional funds."

After Sherman received a commitment from everyone to write their legislatures, the group broke to allow Paterson time to scribe an original. As the delegates left, Ellsworth approached Sherman.

"How can Connecticut pay? We've consumed our allowance."

"I'll buy the copies. It's not a big expense; it just irks me that everyone pleads poverty after they entertain each other in taverns with public money."

"The price of leadership?"

"The price of leadership."

"Roger, I apologize, but I no longer like this plan."

"Don't apologize; neither do I." Sherman liked Ellsworth's look of surprise. He probably had expected a rebuff.

"Well, uh, may I propose amendments from the floor?"

"Yes." Still more surprise on Ellsworth's face.

"Roger, what's our position?"

"Neither plan fits the country's needs, but a system that falls between them might work."

"What about the Virginia Plan with equal vote in the Senate?"

"What do you think?"

"I can support such a system."

"We need more, but the rest will fall after suffrage."

"And you have a plan?"

"I'm working on one."

"THAT WAS A QUICK meeting."

"Things move fast now."

Howard had come to freshen up the room when he saw the men leave. Sherman had a thought. "Howard, are you familiar with copiers?"

"Not personally, but boarders seemed pleased with Williamson's."

"Reasonably priced?"

"I've never heard a complaint."

"Where are they located?"

"On Chestnut, between Seventh and Eighth, not far from the State House."

"Thank you."

"Anything else I can do for you?"

"Yes, do you know where Robert Morris lives?"

"Of course, on the corner of Market and Sixth. It's the grandest home in Philadelphia."

"I need a letter delivered."

"My pleasure, sir."

"Thank you. I'll bring it down in a minute."

Sherman climbed the stairs to his room to write letters. He decided to write Rebecca first. Her last correspondence conveyed a forlorn tone. She continued to worry about money and the children's health, and she had been particularly upset by the theft of an heirloom silver tankard. The loss also upset Sherman, but he wanted to make light of it to ease her mind. When he got to that part of the letter, he wrote, "How much trouble and anxiety is saved. We shall no longer be troubled to put it away so carefully every night."

He tried to assuage her other concerns but knew that only his return would make her happy. The convention would go long or badly. He could only hope for a long enough recess to visit New Haven. He tucked that goal in the back of his mind as he turned to the other letter he needed to write.

The letter to Washington required care. Sherman wanted to be brief and explicit, much more difficult than being verbose and vague. He sat at his writing shelf thinking that his little note would probably take as long to compose as Paterson would need to scribe the entire New Jersey Plan.

After several false starts, marked by the balled-up stationery strewn at his feet, Sherman finally found the right tone.

Your Excellency,

Thank you for your precious time this morning. You have my cooperation within the limits of my obligations.

This convention must report out a sound system of government that strengthens the national system. I believe it will. Compromises will be struck and a consensus built.

However, if Congress fights our work, all will be lost. I believe that a confidential dialogue with key congressional members may avert disaster. If I may, I recommend sending an emissary to New York to act as an arbitrator between the two bodies.

This individual must enjoy your highest trust. I suggest Mr. Hamilton. No one would doubt that he spoke for the leadership of the Federal Convention and his vote is wasted in any case.

With sincerest regards,
Roger Sherman

Sherman wondered how this letter would be received. The advice was sound, but Washington would suspect that Sherman had a private scheme in mind. He didn't—only an inkling of a plan—but it depended upon a communication channel to Congress. Sherman could set one up, but the channel had to be tied directly to the power at this convention. His idea depended on Virginia's endorsement, so they might as well control the emissary. Sherman hoped Washington would sense the need and that his trust in Hamilton would override his reservations. Governor Clinton had stacked his New York delegation with cronies who would fight a strong federal government, so the loss of Hamilton's vote posed no additional risk.

Sherman read the note several more times. He resisted the temptation to add to it. The more he wrote, the more suspicion he would raise. Washington would take the bait because he knew Sherman had his own contacts in Congress. The Hamilton suggestion was the masterstroke. He was a member of Congress, lived in New York, spoke for Washington, and possessed a genius for finance.

Sherman heard a light knock on the door.

"Come in."

"Mr. Sherman, this package arrived for you."

"Thank you, Howard. Can you take this letter to Mr. Morris's home right away?"

"Of course, sir."

Howard turned to leave, then immediately whirled. "This letter is addressed to Gen. George Washington."

"He's staying with Mr. Morris."

"Should I insist on hand delivery?"

"I shouldn't think that necessary."

Howard looked disappointed. "I just thought I might meet the great man."

Sherman smiled, remembering his own meeting this morning with "the great man." "I'm sorry, Howard, I don't know what I was thinking. You're quite right. This is highly important, and I want you to insist on hand delivering it to the general."

"Thank you, Mr. Sherman."

SHERMAN CLIMBED THE NARROW staircase. The package Howard had delivered had held Paterson's original of the New Jersey Plan, and Sherman had left immediately to have copies made. By the time he arrived, it was already after three in the afternoon. Williamson's occupied the second floor of a new brick building sandwiched between other buildings under construction.

Sherman entered through a door marked with a brass plaque that read "Williamson Secretary & Copyist." About a dozen men sat facing the two walls, each intently bent over his desk with quill in hand. Three large tables ran down the center of the room dividing the men. Obsessively neat stacks of papers lay across the tables, each held in position by a brass paperweight positioned at the exact midpoint of the top page. An intensely groomed man approached him immediately.

"May I help you?"

"I hope so. I have an emergency."

"We've never had one of those before," the man said with a self-confident grin.

"I have twelve pages, and I need ten copies by tomorrow morning."

"The Federal Convention?"

"How did you guess?"

"Ten copies, plus the original, meet the needs of eleven states."

"This must be handled with strict confidentiality. Our proceedings are secret."

"As I've been reminded repeatedly. My firm does work for the Pennsylvania legislature and all the prominent attorneys in Philadelphia. Not a word has ever been whispered outside that door." With a voice that brooked no haggling, the man added, "The fee is two sovereign crowns."

"How many Pennsylvania dollars?"

"Emergencies dictate sovereign crowns."

Sherman sighed and reached for his purse.

18

Saturday, June 16, 1787

Madison read the note he had written in his journal.

The members from Cont., N.Y., N. J, DEL. and perhaps Mister Martin from Maryland, made common cause on different principles and had concocted the New Jersey plan. The eagerness displayed from these different motives produced serious anxiety for the result of the Convention.

The previous evening, he had been too disturbed to organize his notes. Following breakfast, he hurried back to his room to rewrite his record of the prior day's proceedings, adding this rare personal observation. Madison lifted his pen to strike the comment and then laid it back down. He might change it later, prior to publication, but for now he'd leave it.

Why had Washington insisted on giving Paterson an opportunity to present? This only delayed matters. Madison believed their six to five margin would hold, but they'd have to endure endless hours of arguments. Old ground covered again. The New Jersey Plan made lilliputian improvements to the Articles, improvements so restrained that they didn't merit consideration. Yet, here they were, ready to debate a plan that would throw the country into ruin.

Madison jostled the new pages and laid them neatly on top of a substantial stack of stationery. He stared for a moment at the pile of paper that comprised his diary of the proceedings. Would the journal tell the story of calamity or godsend? How high would the stack grow? Madison let his eyes wander to the ceiling. No, he smiled, surely the convention couldn't last that long.

Madison packed his valise with a fresh supply of stationery, a blotter, his silver penknife, and two quills. He always knew that getting his plan adopted would be difficult. Republics represented the rarest form of government, and trying to combine thirteen existing republics added unimaginable complexity. He needed patience and perseverance, spiced with a healthy dose of connivance, to assemble a United States of America.

His mood improved as he trotted down the stairs. Then as he turned a corner, he nearly bumped into Pinckney.

"Mr. Madison, can we walk together?"

"It'll be a pleasure."

"You seem bright this morning. With the interference from all these vicious little gnats, I presumed you'd be swathed in gloom.

"Mr. Pinckney, one must learn to ignore gnats. Nothing's to be done with them."

"You can kill them."

"Not all of them. Better to continue to your destination with all due haste."

"Excuse me, but I believe we've been thrown back to our starting point."

"A brief detour. We'll be back on course in a day or two."

"We have three plans. You really believe a few days will extricate us from this bog of schemes?"

His query pulled Madison up short. Pinckney's plan was never reported out of committee. "The will of the delegates has been determined. The New Jersey Plan won't require lengthy deliberations. It's a weak patchwork."

"And my plan?"

"It's already been considered."

"And dismissed without debate. You smothered it."

"I did not. It was your obligation to draw support to your side. Has your state endorsed it?"

"You promised that if the convention deadlocked, I'd get a full hearing. We're heading for a cul-de-sac."

"You had a full hearing and, if memory serves, no one stood to second your proposal."

"Perhaps converts now teeter in my direction. The days ahead will be bloody, and my plan may provide the only—"

"Mr. Pinckney, why do you persist in this penny-farthing?"

"Mr. Madison, why do you resist democracy?"

"A sound government must protect itself from the mob."

"People turn into a mob only when aroused."

"Then they're easily aroused."

Madison realized their pace had quickened with their words. He stopped and faced Pinckney. "Charles, we differ only in degree. I want safeguards; you advocate unfettered experimentation. Republics of your concoction decay faster than a ripe peach."

"You think yourself the only expert. I demand another opportunity to present my plan."

"Demand?"

"I am a South Carolina delegate to the Federal Convention. I have as much right as you to propose a new system."

Resenting Pinckney's smug expression, Madison said, "I'll see what I can do."

The two men resumed their walk in silence. After a few minutes, Pinckney said, "I'm sorry to be brash, but I believe in my proposal. It's not just ego."

"I said I'd see what I could do."

"The people can be trusted."

"They have shown otherwise."

"Only on occasion and only temporarily."

"It takes but one occasion to destroy a republic."

Pinckney stopped at the base of the State House steps and put his hand on Madison's shoulder. "James, I'm sincere in my faith in the people. Don't misjudge me by my scoffing airs."

"I don't doubt your sincerity; I doubt the validity of your plan."

Pinckney smiled, not his typical smirk but an expression of friendly embrace. "In that case, I'll endeavor to argue with more persuasive fervor." Patting Madison's shoulder, he said, "I believe it's time for us to enter the fray."

With that, the two men climbed the three steps and entered the State House.

John Lansing, a New York Clinton lackey, began the session. He attacked the convention's authority and claimed the people would never approve the Virginia Plan. Concluding his harangue, he said, "Randolph's plan absorbs all power except for the tiniest local matters. New York cannot and will not support it!"

Governor Clinton ran the most corrupt government in the nation and shamelessly used his delegation to guard his interests. New York City was the center of government and a hotbed for western land speculation. The two were intertwined, and the governor bribed legislators with participation in his elaborate deals. Clinton was an astute politician and had the foresight to see that a new government might move the capital away from his fondling hands.

Paterson followed. "I've already given my sentiments on Randolph's plan and will avoid repetition."

Madison noticed with irritation that both Lansing and Paterson referred to it as Randolph's plan. Following the approving vote earlier in the week, Madison believed it rightfully should be called the Federal Convention Plan.

Paterson continued, "The New Jersey Plan remains faithful to our instructions and the sentiments of the people. If the confederacy is mortally flawed, let's return to Congress and ask for larger powers, not assume them. If proportional representation is so right, then why do we vote here with one vote per state?"

Wilson, normally reserved, jumped up and nearly shouted, "The larger states conceded the point, not because it was right, but because it was the only way to gather the states into this chamber."

"Are you now at liberty to take it back?" Paterson shouted back. "This convention doesn't have the authority to change equal sovereignty."

Wilson compared the two plans as if he were presenting a lesson.

"In the Virginia Plan, there are two branches in the legislature. In the New Jersey Plan, a single house.

"The people provide the base for one. State legislatures pillar the other.

"Proportional representation in one. Equal state suffrage in the other.

"A single executive heads one. A plurality in the other.

"In the one, the national legislature makes laws in all cases to which the states are incompetent. In the other, Congress has limited authority.

"In one, a veto of state laws. In the other, no veto.

"In one, the executive can be removed by impeachment and conviction. In the other, the executives are removable by a majority of the state executives.

"Revision of the laws provided for in one. No such check in the other.

"Finally, ratification by the people versus ratification by the states."

Wilson stood a moment to let the comparison hang in the chamber.

"Gentlemen, this comparison speaks for itself. The plan of New Jersey vests executive power in a plurality, a grievous error. Three men will fight until one becomes the master. In the triumvirates of Rome, first Caesar, then Augustus, witnessed this truth. The kings of Sparta and the consuls of Rome prove the factious consequences of dividing the executive.

"I also wish to address this absurd notion that we lack authority. Gentlemen, we are authorized to conclude nothing—but are at liberty to propose anything.

"As for the sentiments of the people, how are we to know? We commonly mistake those in our circle for the general voice. Why should a national government be unpopular? Has it less dignity? Will citizens enjoy less liberty? Will becoming a citizen of the United States debase a citizen of Delaware?

"Gentlemen, place the plans on a scale. The New Jersey Plan is light as air."

Enthusiastic applause burst from the large state tables, while the small state proponents sat with frozen expressions.

Mason challenged Paterson directly. "Explain to me, Mr. Paterson, will the militia march from state to state to collect taxes?" Mason turned to the entire assembly. "Not even despots decree death to punish tax delinquents. And make no mistake, the bayonet does not discriminate between the innocent and the guilty."

Mason sat to the same distribution of applause, and then Madison cringed to see Pinckney gain the floor.

"The whole comes to this: give New Jersey an equal vote, and she'll forget her scruples. Withhold an equal vote, and she'll sacrifice our great nation." Pinckney stared directly at Paterson. "I can't imagine greater selfishness."

Edmund Randolph looked nervous but evidently felt the need to defend the Randolph plan. "Some accuse us of treason, but it would be treason to not propose what is necessary to save our nation. There're seasons when we must dispense with caution and the present moment is favorable—and the last available."

As the meeting adjourned, Madison thought the session had gone better than expected. Except for Pinckney's insults, debate had been mostly polite. As he gathered up his things, Robert Morris came over and whispered, "Please join us at my home, immediately."

Before Madison looked up, Morris had passed on to greet another delegate. Madison knew *immediately* meant without a stop at the Indian Queen to lighten his load and freshen up. Whatever was being schemed, he was grateful to be included.

Dickinson wandered over next. "Mr. Madison, I presume you see the consequence of pushing things too far."

"I fear the consequences of not pushing things far enough."

"If we can't come to a mutual understanding, we'll be stuck in this stuffy chamber all summer." Dickinson looked over to the sealed windows and then at Madison. "I'd rather be home."

"As would I."

"Mr. Madison, please understand, some small state members support a strong national government."

"Then it should be easy for you to vote against the New Jersey Plan."

"We'd sooner submit to a foreign power than be deprived of equal suffrage in both houses of the legislature. You must yield on at least one house."

"Republican principles dictate proportional representation."

"No one dictates to this convention."

"A poor choice of words, but my meaning was clear. You have no principled justification for equal votes."

"Our survival provides justification enough."

"No one threatens your survival. I tire of all this talk about the big states wanting to devour you." Madison rapped his knuckles against the table. "Mr. Dickinson, I'd appreciate it if you would arrest your suspicions."

"We'll check our paranoia when we see our views respected. You ramrod this convention. Your deeds feed our fears."

"Paterson was given an opportunity to present his plan. Respect doesn't mean capitulation."

"Your stubbornness astounds me."

"You utter my exact words."

The two men stared at each other, all civility discarded. Finally, Dickinson whirled and marched out of the chamber. The formal debate had lacked emotion, but Madison saw that rage simmered below the surface. Why couldn't they see reason? Sound principles demanded proportional representation, but logic persuaded no one. Everyone stood in the exact spot in which they had arrived.

MADISON KNOCKED ON THE door of the Morris home. A servant led him to the parlor used by men when they retreated after a meal. Morris, Washington, and Franklin sat in the comfortable room smoking pipes and sipping port.

Following recent discoveries and excavations abroad, the room had been decorated in the Herculaneum- and Pompeii-inspired neoclassical style. The yellow wallpaper employed a Doric column pattern, and a geometric rug in indigo covered the wide-plank floor. Charles Willson Peale and John Singleton Copley portraits flanked a fireplace carved with Greek relief figures. Expensive European furniture accented the room, and a cane daybed imported from China rested against one wall.

"Come in, come in," Morris said. "We've been waiting for you."

"I'm sorry for the delay. Dickinson held me up."

"What'd he want?"

"Unconditional surrender."

"Our boys were feeling their oats today. Never mind, we have some plans of our own."

Madison poured a glass of port from a sideboard. As he took a wing chair, a garish new painting over the mantle startled him. The colors were bright pastels, with frothy lines, curlicues, and vivid flowers. The contrast with the room's classical formality made it look out of place.

"You have a new painting," Madison said.

"Do you like it?"

"I've never seen anything like it."

"It's in the French rococo style. A fashion popular before neoclassical, but it appeals to my prurient spirit. This one is by François Boucher."

"Quite interesting."

Morris laughed uproariously. "Quite tactful, Jemmy. Tell me, what do you really think?"

"To tell the truth, it looks feminine."

"Ha, right you are. The general shares your opinion."

"Then may I ask why you display it in the parlor?"

"Because it's scandalous, my boy. You're supposed to read sexual innuendo into the symbolism. The garlands of flowers, baskets, and hats represent the female anatomy. The flute, of course, symbolizes something quite the opposite. No. We can't have that out in front of the ladies."

"The imagery escapes me."

"Because you don't see with a Frenchman's eyes," Franklin said. "That young damsel is luring those two men into an amorous fling. Perhaps together."

"Together?"

"Indeed," Franklin chuckled.

"I've never heard of such a thing. You must be mistaken."

"No, the good doctor knows the French intimately. This dandy erotic piece cost me a large sum."

"Money poorly spent. I believe the artist merely painted an idyllic peasant picnic."

"You must stretch your imagination."

"It refuses to stretch that far."

Everyone laughed, including Washington. Madison felt uncomfortable with the conversation, so he asked a question to change the subject.

"Will Hamilton join us?"

"No. You'll see why in a moment," Washington said.

"Jemmy, we're in a quandary," Franklin said. "We must build broader support for the convention's plan."

Madison became wary. Was Washington ready to compromise?

"If five states repudiate the convention's work, ratification will fail," Washington said

"You'd sacrifice proportionality?" Madison asked.

"Nothing's decided," Morris answered.

"But you have a scenario you wish to discuss." Madison felt the seed of his apprehension grow.

"More like a finesse," Washington said. "Do you understand the need for a broad consensus?"

"I know we must seduce some small states to support the plan. My guess is at least three to gain credibility. Without that, we'll surely suffer disharmony, possibly war. I also know that logic and reason have gotten us nowhere."

"You do understand. What you don't know is that New Hampshire may send a delegation."

Madison froze. New Hampshire's attendance boded disaster. The six large states would be pitted against five small states, plus possibly New York. Gover-

nor Clinton could control the convention by causing a deadlock, then demanding an enormous price to switch over to the large state side.

"Rhode Island?"

"Thankfully, no," Morris said.

"Are you sure?"

"I have sources," Morris said. "The Rhode Island legislature is so corrupt, it's
easy to buy information. If need be, I can buy obstruction."

"Jemmy, we have to negotiate a middle ground," Washington said. "But a
choice halfway between the two plans looks appalling. We need a third plan."

"Not Pinckney's?"

"Oh, goodness no," Franklin said, "I'd forgotten about that one."

"He hasn't," Madison said. "He demanded to present it again, just this
morning."

"It is on the wrong side of the Virginia Plan," Franklin said. "We need something on the other side."

"The other side?"

"A limited monarchy," Franklin said with his twinkle.

"A monarchy? That would be discarded with contempt."

"We need something that makes our plan look prudent," Franklin said.

"Who would propose such a thing?" The silence of the three men answered
the question. "Does Alex know?"

Washington said, "We'll have dinner together."

"He may refuse."

"He'd never refuse me."

"There are risks," Madison said.

"Yes, horrible risks," Washington said in mock terror. "I could be made
king."

"Seriously, people might assume that he speaks in your behalf."

"I shall punish him for broaching the subject."

"How?"

"All part of the ruse," Franklin said. "We want Alex in New York to keep an
eye on Clinton and, if necessary, to act as an emissary to Congress."

"Excellent. Clinton must be watched," Madison said. "Who came up with
that idea?"

"Not important," Washington said with a dismissive air. "I trust Alex, and the
need for an emissary may arise. In any case, Yates and Lansing outvote him."

"How can we get leverage on Clinton?"

"Whatever leverage exists lies in the western lands," Morris said. "Greed
consumes the man."

"When will Alex present his proposal?"

"Monday," Washington said. "I'll instruct him to make it long and exhausting."

"May I suggest yet another complexity?" Madison asked.

"That's why you're here, my boy," Franklin said.

"Rufus King has been silent to this point. Although he votes with us, he's highly suspicious of a strong central government."

"If he's won over, how do you propose to use him?" Morris asked.

"King is a great speaker. We need a strong orator that can appeal to emotion."

"My dear boy," said Franklin, "so quick to abandon your precious logic?"

Madison smiled. "I'm ready to try anything."

"What do you suggest?" Washington asked.

"Alex and Rufus are friends. Hamilton can be very persuasive when he sets his mind to it. Give Alex the assignment to win Rufus over, and then we can propel him on stage."

"Excellent," Washington said. "Anything else?"

"What about Pinckney?"

"We'll have to give him voice again," Washington said. "The question is, when?"

"Delay him," Franklin suggested. "Too many cooks spoil the pot."

"Agreed. Tell him we'll schedule him Monday after next," Washington instructed.

"Very well," Madison said.

"Did you enjoy your port?" Morris asked.

Madison looked at the glass sitting on the side table. He had never touched it. He picked it up by the stem and took an appreciative sip. "Excellent. I'll have to come by more often."

"A bright lad like yourself is always welcome," Morris said with a smile. "You enliven conversation and stimulate the intrigue."

"We do seem to be in the thick of it."

19

Monday, June 18, 1787

Sherman caught Baldwin's eye and motioned with his head toward the door. Sherman rose and walked across the back of the chamber, out the door, and past the ever-present sentry. He waited under one of the three arches leading to the Judicial Chamber. A trial was in full progress, with about twenty people in the chamber. Three red-robed judges peered down from the bench at the defendant standing in a cagelike dock in the middle of the room. Lawyers garbed in black robes hovered around paper-strewn tables, and a jury sat inside a paneled partition. After a few minutes observing the trial, Sherman guessed that the unlucky defendant would soon spend a few years in the debtors' prison behind the State House yard.

Baldwin escaped from the chamber and softly closed the door behind him. The rules required their attendance, but delegates discreetly entered and exited the chamber continuously.

Baldwin wandered over to the arch and stood beside Sherman. After a few moments, he asked, "Did you call me out to observe this trial?"

Sherman said, "I thought you might need to use the privy."

"That's what I like about you, Roger, always considerate."

"Always that. Let's go."

Sherman turned and walked toward the rear exit that led to the yard. The men turned left toward the privy strategically placed about forty feet behind the east wing. Both men entered the two-holer and unbuttoned.

"Is this your idea of a private meeting?" Baldwin asked.

"Something's up. This makes no sense."

"Surprises you, does it, Roger? I can understand at your age."

"I'm talking about the convention."

"So we *are* having a meeting."

Sherman couldn't help but laugh. "Come on, button up and we'll take a walk." They proceeded through the arcade, nodded at another sentry, and walked into the street.

"Hamilton recites the entire history of Western civilization," Sherman said. "Two hours, and he hasn't broached his plan."

"A stall?"

"To what purpose?"

"To bore us into submission?"

"If that's their intent, I'll set Luther Martin on them," Sherman said with a smile.

Baldwin threw his hands up. "Please, I relent! I'll do anything that would stop that torture."

"Seriously, this lecture has a purpose. What do you think?"

"Hum, his plan, once he gets around to it, will support a far stronger central government than anything presented to date. As for the verbosity, I do think they mean to wear down the opposition."

"I believe you're right on both counts. They mean to lay out an extreme plan that makes theirs look reasonable."

"And your reaction?" Baldwin asked.

"Silence."

"Silence?"

"They want to draw us into a debate on Hamilton's plan. Discussion will lend it legitimacy."

"And the Virginia Plan becomes the rational middle ground?"

"Exactly. No matter how they provoke us, we'll not rise to the challenge. We'll ignore it. I'll tell New Jersey; you inform Maryland."

"Roger, that's presumptuous. I may play truant with you, but I'm a Georgia delegate."

Baldwin's response gave Sherman a start. He had unconsciously signaled his friend to leave the chamber with him because they'd been compatriots in New Haven and often thrashed out political puzzles together. "Sorry, my error. I was trying to accommodate your fondness for intrigue."

"You devil. Very well, I'll inform the cantankerous Luther Martin."

Sherman felt relief. "Do you think the other New York delegates support Hamilton?"

"They want to tar and feather the scoundrel and then bludgeon him until his arrogance withers."

Sherman feigned shock. "All that in the City of Brotherly Love."

"They're New York simpletons, unschooled in the piety of Philadelphia."

"First Martin, now our esteemed delegates from New York." Sherman shook his head in mock alarm. "Must you disparage all my allies?"

"That's why I prefer my side. I comport with full-grown men."

Sherman looked at Baldwin. "Then why do you meet with me?"

"I want to see if David can slay Goliath."

"A severe wound might be sufficient."

"New Yorkers believe politics is a mortal contest," Baldwin said.

"I prefer to beguile."

"So, are we walking all the way to the Delaware River, or do we return to hear Hamilton's plan?"

Sherman stopped. They had walked nearly six blocks from the State House. Carriages, horses, and wagons choked the street, chattering people surrounded them, and he became conscious of the banging and clatter of construction. As Sherman shook his head in wonderment, he caught the first whiff of a dank rot that hovered around the harbor side. The city vibrated with unrestrained energy, but Sherman had been oblivious to all.

"I suppose we should return," Sherman said, reversing direction. "There may yet be surprises."

"Early adjournment?"

"No. I'm afraid our friends may have cooked up a more complex plot."

"Impossible. Who could be so fiendish?"

"Dr. Franklin, for one. Anyone who can pry money and arms out of the French deserves to be watched closely."

"He seems harmless."

"An act, my friend, an act. He's a confidant of Robert Morris and Gen. Washington. The richest man in the country and the most popular man in the country."

"Washington and Morris have remained silent."

"Only in the chamber. Hamilton would never have joined this brawl without the general's permission."

"Goliath looks more forbidding with each step we take toward the State House."

SHERMAN WAS MAKING HIS way along the back of the chamber when Hamilton's words caught his attention.

"Gentlemen, I'm unfriendly to both the New Jersey Plan and the Virginia Plan. Both deliver mere pork with different sauces. Neither considers the amazing turbulence of the democratic spirit. When a popular passion seizes people, it spreads like wildfire. In every society, there'll be a division of people into the few and the many. Give all power to the many and they oppress the few. Give all power to the few and they oppress the many. We're now watching uncontrolled passion destroy this great country. The union is dissolving—in truth, it has already dissolved."

Hamilton stared intently at his audience. "Gentlemen, let me assure you, the evils which breed in the states will cure the people of their fondness for democracy."

Sherman found his seat and pulled Ellsworth's notes over for a quick scan. It seemed that Hamilton had lectured on the Amphictyonic Council, the German Confederacy, Swiss cantons, Roman emperors, and every modern European state. Sherman pushed the notes back to Ellsworth and wrote a short directive to not challenge Hamilton. He stood, casually stretched, and walked over to drop the note in front of Paterson. Sherman saw Baldwin follow his example with Martin.

Returning to his table, Sherman saw that Hamilton had let his notes drop to his side. "Gentlemen, I see no reason to keep the states. They're not necessary for commerce, revenue, or agriculture. Avarice, ambition, and corruption will continue as long as they exist."

Hamilton raised his notes, took a minute to find his place, and continued. "The British system is the best in the world. The House of Lords is a noble institution. Having nothing to gain from change—and owning great property—the lords form a permanent barrier against pernicious passions, whether advocated by the crown or the commons.

"You might ask, can a government based on the British model be republican? Yes—if all the officials are appointed by the people."

Sherman didn't normally take notes. He believed the distraction caused him to miss nuances and the larger canvas, but in this instance, he pulled a piece of paper forward and scribbled a summary of the Hamilton plan. As Hamilton presented an emotional appeal for support, Sherman reviewed the design. The concept was bold, and, as suggested beforehand, similar to the British system. The executive, judiciary, and Senate held power for life, unless they did something so outlandish as to be impeached.

Hamilton finished his exhortation to sparse applause that quickly tapered off to a deathly silence. After an embarrassing interval, someone made a motion to adjourn, which raised an appreciative second and unanimous concurrence.

SHERMAN STUFFED HIS MEAGER notes into a battered valise and walked with Ellsworth across the back of the chamber toward the door. "Let's meet for a short discussion. My room?"

"Certainly, unless you're open to a different venue."

Sherman stopped before reaching the chamber door. "Where?"

"An adventure. We won't leave the State House and it's private."

"Lead on," Sherman said, his uplifted palm pointed toward the door.

"First, let's drop our valises back at the table so we won't have to lug them."

"You're taking me to the tower."

"You've been there before?"

"Oliver, with all the time I've spent in this building, do you think I never ventured up the tower?" At Ellsworth's crestfallen look, Sherman quickly added, "But it's a splendid idea. I haven't been up this trip and it's a glorious day."

With Ellsworth's excitement rekindled, the two men disposed of their cases and headed toward the tower Stair Hall. As they reached the Palladian window landing, Sherman found it ironic that he and Washington had discussed right here the issues he needed to explain to Ellsworth.

They continued across the landing and climbed to the second floor. The two floors of the State House had differing layouts. The grand Central Hall divided the first floor into two equal chambers, one for the Pennsylvania supreme court and another for the assembly. The assembly was in recess, so the convention used this room for its sessions. The second floor was arranged with three unequally sized rooms. The Stair Hall opened onto the Long Gallery, which extended the entire width of the front of the building. The gallery, which was used for banquets, balls, and public events, gave access to the Governor's Council Chamber and a large committee room.

The tower sat at the rear of the building and extended upward an additional three stories. At the third-floor level, they encountered an unfinished room used for storage. From this point, the staircase lost its formal appearance and became a rough-hewn narrow access to the belfry. As they neared the top, Sherman's labored breathing reminded him that he was no longer a young man. Ellsworth threw open the door to the observation deck, and fresh air chased a musty smell back into the recesses below.

Sherman ducked his head and passed through a miniature door to the tiny deck that circumvented the tower just below the bell. A finely carved banister provided a convenient handhold that helped Sherman control his fear of falling.

"Spectacular," Sherman said.

"You can see forever. I can't wait to go up in a balloon."

"You and Madison."

Ellsworth looked puzzled but evidently decided not to pursue the matter. "Roger, if the days stay nice, you'll have a tough time keeping me in that stuffy chamber."

"Then I'll make a motion for inclement weather."

"I'll not second."

Sherman laughed. "Take me on the tour."

"Yes, sir, but I insist on a halfpence."

"With pleasure. This is the best bargain I've encountered in all of Philadelphia."

The terrace was so narrow that the two men had to sidestep single file. They could see the entire city. As they moved to the left, Sherman spotted Mrs. Marshall's house. Along the Delaware River frontage, countless ship masts serrated the horizon, and Sherman could see the roof of the coffeehouse where he had met Baldwin. The city had expanded from the river, so buildings clogged most of the space between the water's edge and the State House. As they continued to circle, they looked directly down on Franklin's courtyard. Further to the left, beyond the Robert Morris house, trees began to dominate the scattered structures to the north and west.

As they returned to their starting point and looked over the yard, Sherman said, "Oliver, Connecticut must vote for the Virginia Plan in committee."

"You'll get no argument from me."

Sherman tested the strength of the handrail. "Our vote was the price of presenting the New Jersey Plan."

"You made the trade in advance? To whom?"

"Gen. Washington."

"I see." Ellsworth flicked a bird dropping off the banister rail. "Actually, I don't see. What did we gain from such a trade?"

"We got to present our views and argue our points, and we retained the leadership of the small states."

Ellsworth looked annoyed. "You mean, you retained leadership of the small states?"

"We work together."

"Evidently not all the time."

Sherman winced. "Oliver, I didn't know what price would be demanded, or I would have consulted you. Presenting the plan was important. Now we can incorporate some of our ideas into the final design."

"Not if we don't garner more votes. The convention alignment seems fixed."

"Nothing in politics is fixed."

Ellsworth raised an eyebrow. "Who're you seducing?"

"The South. I need to break one state free."

"Georgia? Baldwin?"

"You scare me, Oliver. You're beginning to think ahead of me."

"Not likely. How far along are you?"

"Preliminary stage. The problem is the other Georgia delegates. They'll never come over."

"Convince them to go home."

"I'm inclined to send them north."

"New York?"

"Precisely. Haven't figured how, but I'm working on it."

"They're congressmen. You'll need something so narrow that the other congressional members won't feel the need to return."

"Now you're really scaring me."

Ellsworth flicked another bird dropping. "How can I help?"

"First, let's climb down from this crow's nest. Intrigue should be garnished with ale."

WHEN A NEW DAY brought continued silence on Hamilton's proposal, the debate returned to the New Jersey Plan. Sherman felt comfortable that they had successfully parried the gambit.

Madison spoke first. "Gentlemen, the New Jersey Plan calls for election of the national legislature by the state legislatures. In Connecticut, the people, not the legislature, chose their present congressmen." Madison turned and looked directly at Sherman. "Does Connecticut wish to snatch away a right already awarded to her citizens?"

Sherman worked to keep his face impassive. Madison knew how to skewer a weakness and hoist it up for all to see. Sherman also caught an "I told you so" glance from Ellsworth.

Madison walked to the New Jersey table. "Our task is to build a new government," He pointed at Paterson. "One to replace the confederacy that New Jersey destroyed."

Sherman had to smile. The little man spoke with a gentle voice, but his words echoed with a resounding boom. Madison sent ill-conceived positions flying like a well-placed mortar shot scattered undisciplined soldiers.

With surprising swiftness, a resolution to postpone the New Jersey Plan had been moved and seconded. Sherman found himself in a quandary. Did this vote represent a test of his promise to support the Virginia Plan? Sherman decided that it did. The resolve to postpone passed, with only New York and New Jersey voting against it.

Rufus King then moved to report out the Virginia Plan. For all intents and purposes, this vote declared the position of the Committee of the Whole. The Virginia Plan won the vote with only New York, New Jersey, and Delaware voting nay. Although he noticed a quizzical look from Dickinson, Sherman felt a surge of relief. He had fulfilled his obligation to Washington and rid himself of the obligation to support a flawed plan. He was now free to focus all his attention on his grand compromise.

Hamilton gained the floor. He voiced agreement with the Virginia Plan and claimed he had been misunderstood the day before. Sherman felt sorry for him. He had been used in a ruse that hadn't worked. The Virginia Plan had been approved by raw force, not finesse, and Hamilton had harmed his reputation to no purpose. Sherman didn't doubt that Hamilton believed in the system he proposed, but as an astute politician, he would've kept his beliefs to himself if not prodded by someone.

The regular convention would start the following morning. The large states had won, but the small states would never accept the plan as reported out. Something had to break the stalemate. With the business of the Committee of the Whole concluded, Sherman expected adjournment. Instead, King walked to the short dais and stepped up.

"Gentlemen, I hope tomorrow we can focus on real issues. We seem to be stuck on the illusion of state sovereignty."

King was a handsome and engaging young man, reputed to be an excellent orator. "State sovereignty is a myth, and our progress depends on facing this fiction honestly." After a perfectly timed pause, King continued, "Do the states possess the peculiar features of sovereignty? They do not."

King stepped from the dais and walked down between the delegates. "They're defenseless, for they cannot raise troops or equip vessels for war. The states divested themselves of sovereignty when they joined the Confederation. I doubt the practicality of annihilating the states, but much of their remaining power must be taken from them. If a 'union of the states' has the right to establish a confederation, it also has the right to consolidate a nation."

Martin leaped to his feet and shouted for the floor. Rufus King didn't appear to be finished, but he gave Martin an eloquent bow to signal his willingness to relinquish the floor.

"Gentlemen," Martin sputtered in controlled fury, "the separation from Great Britain placed the thirteen colonies in a state of equality. They remain in that state to this time. They entered into the Confederation on equal footing, and we meet now to amend the Confederation on equal footing. I'll never accede to a plan that would introduce an inequality that would lay ten states at the mercy of Virginia, Massachusetts, and Pennsylvania." Martin sat with a finality that reinforced his resolve.

The chamber grew still. Hamilton asked to speak. "I don't believe the states were ever independent of each other. Read our Declaration of Independence. You'll find it a joint declaration."

Martin demanded to speak again. With exasperation, Hamilton gave him a nod. "Mr. Hamilton, I've read the Declaration of Independence. Have you, sir? It declares the founding of these united States, with the word *united* spelled lowercase. Not a mistake, I assure you." Martin sat with a heavy plop that scraped his chair across the hardwood planks and filled the chamber with a shrill rasp.

Hamilton strove to look indifferent. "The fears of the small states are over-wrought. The three largest states are separated by distance and interest."

As Sherman listened to Hamilton, he realized that the meeting had not ad-journed, because the big states were too excited to call it a day. Their victory caused them to impulsively start the debate that really should have opened the next day's session. Sherman thought this foolish. Hamilton and his little friend Madison seemed to believe that a bit of logic sprinkled in the direction of the small states might seep into their simple minds, and all would be well on the morrow.

They were wrong. The small states would not be soothed by sham reassur-ances and sloppy rationalizations. This battle for political power would turn on votes—votes cast because of heartfelt conviction, cajoling, or brutal barters.

20

Wednesday, June 20, 1787

Madison's pen stopped. Ellsworth started the day by proposing an alteration to the first clause of the Virginia Plan. His revision read, "that the government of the United States ought to consist of a supreme legislative, executive and judiciary."

The change seemed small, but the implications were immense; it replaced "national" with "United States." Was this a signal? Connecticut had voted in committee for the Virginia Plan, and now they had moved to strengthen the first resolve of the Plan. Madison smiled. Connecticut had joined the large state alliance. There could be no other explanation for them endorsing a supreme "United States" government.

Midmorning sunlight beamed through the high windows to brighten the far reaches of the chamber. Madison looked around and saw a number of knowing nods and relieved faces. It looked like emotion had finally been spent, and they could get working on the great task that had beckoned them to Philadelphia.

Ellsworth went on to warn that irresolute conventions of the people might tear down their work instead of ratifying it. Madison noticed with relief that Ellsworth presented his position with logic, not peevish partisanship. Reason had once more enveloped the chamber.

Connecticut had come to accept that a constitution would emerge from this convention, and they had begun to worry about ratification. They were wrong to resist assemblies of the people, but he could maneuver this last turn in their conversion.

"You look pleased."

"Sentiment rushes toward the Virginia Plan."

"With alterations."

"Minor only, minor only. We'll hold the basic structure intact."

Madison and Pinckney had left the chamber and were walking back to the Indian Queen. Pinckney stopped short and looked quizzically at Madison. "Do you consider one vote per state in the Senate a minor adjustment?"

"We can overcome that."

As they started walking again, Pinckney said softly, "James, I'd never presume to advise you, but it's clear that the continued cooperation of Connecticut depends on this compromise."

"They'll continue to move in our direction. Last week, they obstinately supported an entirely different plan."

"And this week, you appear the obstinate one."

"A republic must be based on proportional representation." Madison quickened his step. "They'll yield."

"You're mistaken."

Madison smiled. "Not this time. Sherman controls Connecticut, and I can control Mr. Sherman."

"You're worse than mistaken; you're a fool!"

It was Madison's turn to pull up short. "Do you presume to lecture me?"

"Lecturing a fool is a waste of words."

"Mr. Pinckney, in our scheme, there's no place for the states. Ours will be a government of the people, not of the states."

"You must let go of your zealotry."

"I am not a zealot. These are republican principles, and basic principles cannot be compromised."

Pinckney looked glum. "Then I fear this convention shall come to naught. You risk everything for petty dogma."

"Petty dogma? Are you completely ignorant of the great thinkers?"

"Your great thinkers wrote from cloistered quarters. We—on the other hand—reside in the barbed world of political interests. Government is power. You must agree to share that power with the states or risk going home with nothing."

"I'll go home to celebrate a grand republic based on proportionality in both houses of the legislature. It's within reach."

Pinckney's expression turned bleak, and his voice took on a despondent tone. "James, you *are* a fool. Perhaps a dangerous one."

"You throw a label that fits your shoulders."

"Please listen. You believe in separation of power. Can't you see that the states provide a natural defense against an unbridled national government? An extension of your own principles?"

"The states are rife with corruption."

"The states are rife with democracy."

"Democracy must be structured, controlled, and channeled."

"You're hopeless."

"No—I'm full of hope."

The two men again glared at each other. Finally, Pinckney said, "Please excuse me, I forgot a previous engagement." With that, he whirled and marched off in the opposite direction.

THURSDAY'S SESSION BEGAN WITH Connecticut again insisting on an equal vote in the Senate.

Madison maintained a blank expression as he gained the floor. "In Connecticut, townships are incorporated, with limitations imposed by the state. Has Connecticut usurped local authority? No. Nor, sirs, should you fear the central government's usurpation of state authority."

Madison knew he had hit the mark when he saw Sherman play the stoic, but he winced when Hamilton added that the states might dwindle into nothing, so the government design shouldn't depend on their existence. Madison wished Hamilton could restrain himself from tweaking the noses of his opponents.

When no one cared to parry Hamilton's taunt, Madison's leg jiggled with excitement as he glimpsed complete victory.

The next item, term length in the lower house, shouldn't have been controversial. The Virginia Plan called for three years, but instead of quick concurrence, they debated for hours on whether it ought to be one, two, or three. Madison pointed out that it would be expensive for members to travel back and forth for elections. Sherman immediately rejoined that representatives should return home to mix with the people, or they'd acquire the habits of the nation's capital. The sentiment in the chamber shifted endlessly, but eventually they voted for two years as the natural compromise and called it a day.

MADISON SPRANG FROM THE carriage he had rented. Normally, he walked the two blocks between the Indian Queen and Robert Morris's home, but he was dressed in his best finery, and a formal invitation dictated a formal entrance. Morris had invited Philadelphia society, as well as selected delegates, to a grand ball at his home.

The previous sessions had remained tepid. They debated pay for the lower house and whether a representative could also hold a state office. Both subjects had been concluded to Madison's satisfaction. Everyone was in an excellent mood, so Morris couldn't have picked a better time for a party.

Madison straightened his jacket, looked around, and took note of several groups of men who had spilled out of the corner house to sip from glasses, smoke pipes, and laugh in congenial conversation. Two very proper servants stood sentry on the stoop. As Madison entered the house, he realized why some people had gathered on the sidewalk. The house boomed with riotous gaiety, men and women clogged the central hall, and lively music competed with flirtatious bantering.

Madison squeezed through the crowd toward the music. He danced poorly, but he enjoyed watching other couples whirl with élan and grace. The large front parlor had been stripped of furniture, and a four-piece ensemble played beautifully in one corner. Madison took possession of an open space along one wall and admired the six couples that danced effortlessly in the center of the room.

The most prominent was Washington. He smoothly waltzed Eliza Powell in stately turns that made the other dancers look stiff and awkward. Everyone watched the couple, but Madison thought the vivacious and pretty Eliza Powell would command attention even if she were burdened with an awkward partner. Married to the wealthy mayor of Philadelphia, her reputation as the city's leading socialite was tainted by whispers of alleged infidelities. Madison thought her an engaging coquette, but he suspected that jealousy triggered the gossip.

"He's danced with her six times."

"Good evening, Mr. Mason. I didn't notice you standing there."

"You couldn't take your eyes off *Mrs.* Powell."

"Nor can anyone else. She's striking."

"Our general will start tongues wagging if he continues to monopolize her favors."

"He loves to dance. Hours from now, he'll still be twirling around the floor."

"He has the stamina of a horse, but he should take care to entertain all the ladies. Let's get some punch."

Madison enjoyed watching the dancers but followed Mason anyway. To the slight Madison, the room across the hall presented a sea of shoulders. People chatted amiably in clusters, blocking access to the refreshments. Madison trailed Mason's back as he impolitely shoved his way through the guests. Reaching the steward, Mason asked, "What do you have to drink this evening?"

"What would you like?"

"Red wine."

"Of course, sir."

"I'll have the same," Madison added.

The steward turned to a sideboard arrayed with fancifully shaped bottles and decanters. On the shelves above, crystal stemware reflected sparks from the uneven chandelier light. The steward, moving with practiced ease, grabbed two glasses by the stems with the splayed figures of a single hand and set them down on the sideboard without the slightest clink. He then presented a wine bottle, holding the neck with one hand as he cradled the body in the palm of the other.

"A claret from the Bordeaux region of France. A fine red that I highly recommend."

Mason responded with a perfunctory flipping of his fingers that said forget the theatrics and pour. After they had secured their wine, Madison again scurried behind as Mason rudely pushed his way out of the room. Madison was disappointed when, after reaching the central hall, Mason turned left, toward the back of the house. He had hoped to reenter the parlor to watch the dancing, but he could not ignore the powerful Virginian. Mason continued out the back door and walked away from the boisterous party until he found a quiet spot toward the rear of the large corner lot. Nothing advertised Morris's wealth more than his elaborate outbuildings. The yard included a hothouse, an icehouse, and a twelve-horse stable, all immaculately maintained.

They turned and looked back at the gaily lit house. The evening was pleasant, a bit warm and muggy, but a slight breeze felt refreshing. The ensemble's notes wafted through the open windows to give the garden an aura of enchantment. Madison felt a rare serene moment until Mason trounced his mood.

"God, I hate Philadelphia. I grow weary of the showy etiquette and pretentious nonsense so fashionable in this city."

The remark surprised Madison. He liked Philadelphia and intended to enjoy the evening. "Their habits are different from Virginia's," Madison said neutrally.

"Different and boorish. It's not worth the effort to learn how to conform to their silly fashion and formalities. Their narcissism deserves disdain."

Madison thought this hypocritical coming from the owner of Gunston Hall, one of the richest plantations in Virginia. Madison had always appreciated Mason's commitment to reason, but he looked anew at the man and saw a prissy, self-satisfied aristocrat that loathed people who didn't comport themselves as he thought proper. He also showed little patience with people too ignorant to immediately accept his learned and enlightened opinions. Despite his off-putting haughtiness, Mason held strong republican convictions. He was an especially strong proponent of the natural rights of man and personal liberty, having personally crafted the much-copied Virginia Declaration of Rights.

Madison took a sip of the excellent wine. "George, if I may be so bold, you seem out of sorts this evening."

Mason looked directly at Madison. "We're on the wrong path."

"The wrong path? This has been an exceptional week. Great progress. What displeases you?"

"The deification of our grand hero of the Revolution." Mason gestured toward the house with his wineglass. "This convention means to anoint him."

"Don't you support him?"

"My support does not require me to condone a coronation."

"No one suggests that."

"Mr. Hamilton?"

"Alex gets carried away. His devotion sometimes skews his otherwise sound judgment, but he sways no one."

"The general sways delegates without their conscious knowledge. They design an unrestrained executive, assuming his personal restraint will safeguard our republic." Mason took a forceful swig of wine. "Very shortsighted."

Madison looked down and shuffle-kicked a small rock back into a flower bed. Had Mason seen something he had missed? After a moment, he said, "George, your concern is valid, but premature. We haven't defined the powers of the various branches. Checks and balances will overwhelm any individual."

"You approved a single executive when I was out of chamber." The tone was accusatory.

Madison understood. Mason still wanted an executive that comprised three men. He suspected Mason craved executive office but judged his opportunity slight if the office were restricted to a single individual. Harboring no such ambitions himself, Madison had missed how lust for office could bias a delegate's opinion.

"The debate was sound and I believe the decision right."

"I'll never agree to entrust the rights of the people to a single magistrate."

"The rights of the people will be entrusted to a system, not one man. Do you distrust the general?" Madison challenged.

"Washington's a man, not a saint," Mason snapped, but quickly added in a softer tone, "I trust him more than others, but we must think in term of generations, not years. Adulation seldom charts a wise course."

"Do you suggest I'm blinded by adulation?"

"You? No, my young friend, you're blinded by a greater vice, the ambition to invent the perfect republic."

"Guilty. And unrepentant."

"There's dirty work ahead. Crafty and powerful men will tempt you to settle for half a loaf. Don't let ambition for your precious plan grind your principles to dust."

Madison decided that he wasn't enjoying this conversation. He had looked forward to this party and had no intention of wasting the evening with a bitter old man. "George, I'm going to refill my glass and join the gaiety inside. We'll talk when there're fewer distractions."

Madison quickly turned and walked away as fast as good manners would permit. At the intersection of two garden paths, a giggling young woman banged into him with such force that she nearly knocked him down. Instinctively, he grabbed her shoulders with both hands as they spun a half circle to keep their balance. As they steadied, Madison stood inches from a pretty face lit with laughter. Embarrassed, he realized that she had a firm grip on his forearms.

"Excuse me, sir. I beg your pardon."

Madison could find no words, at least, no words he could utter. The young girl's frisky blue eyes and sweet face had instantly enchanted him. She let go of his arms and stood there expectantly. He realized he still held her shoulders and lifted his hands as if he had placed them on a hot griddle.

"Excuse me," he said with a slight bow. "My obvious clumsiness."

"Not at all. I was looking behind me as I ran. Please excuse my unladylike behavior."

"No need to apologize. This was my first dance of the evening."

The young woman rewarded him with a crackling smile that lit up every feature of her face. "You're a gentleman. Thank you."

With another giggle, she whirled and continued down the garden at a more dignified pace. As she retreated, Madison could not take his eyes off her backside, which she swung with a subtle rhythm that must have been for his benefit.

As Madison turned to enter the house, he spotted Hamilton on the rear stoop wearing an impish grin. "My, my, the shy little Madison makes a play for a married woman. A child, no less. You should leave such nonsense to us seasoned rakes."

Madison felt a blush. "I had no such intention. She crashed into me."

"The engagement held less import than the disengagement." Hamilton gave a good-hearted laugh. "Stealing wonton glances at a woman's behind will taint your stellar reputation."

Madison climbed the first step and glanced back. She was gone. "I couldn't help myself. Married, you say?"

"Dolley Payne Todd is her name, and she was running away from her playful husband. You must step into the house and hunt legal game."

"Nothing will compare. The brief encounter has spoiled me."

Hamilton clasped Madison's shoulder and pulled him toward the house. "Come. There're lots of ladies eager to meet a wealthy gentleman. Fate has someone picked out for you."

"Alex, I must trust in fate, for my charms seduce no one."

"You underestimate the seductive power of money."

Madison couldn't help but laugh as he bounced back into the house, eager to rejoin the party. But the image of the bright young girl lingered, titillating him. It was a moment he would not soon forget.

21

Sunday, June 24, 1787

"No way to make it simple?" Ellsworth looked worried.

"I'm open to suggestions," Sherman said. "But sometimes politics just gets complicated."

"Simplicity is highly overrated," Dickinson huffed.

Sherman had arranged to met Ellsworth and Dickinson in his room after church. He wanted to test his plan with his closest friends, away from adversaries or the curious.

"Can we coordinate events in both Philadelphia and New York?" Ellsworth asked.

"Others can."

Ellsworth went for his snuff, a sure sign of his unease. Sherman sipped his tea and waited.

Finally Ellsworth said, "I hope you don't intend to appeal to Washington's greed."

"No," Sherman responded immediately. "It wouldn't work, nor is it necessary."

Dickinson said, "Anyone who approached him with something that looked like a bribe would find himself on the receiving end of a cane."

Ellsworth continued to look worried. "Robert Morris owns huge expanses of western lands, and Franklin and Washington also have interests in the frontier. A deal of this sort increases the value of their holdings. They might misconstrue your intent."

Ellsworth had touched on Sherman's biggest concern. "Prudent advice. I haven't felt the cane since my father died."

"Must you use Washington?" Ellsworth asked. "The price'll be dear."

"No one else can control both delegations."

"Our side isn't without influence in Congress," Ellsworth said.

"Perhaps I've missed something. Have we captured this convention?"

"Of course not. The Virginians hold the reins."

"And only a Virginian can take us down a different path."

Ellsworth shook his head. "I feel like we're conspiring with the opposition."

Dickinson reached over and patted Ellsworth's forearm. "Trust those instincts, my boy, for that's exactly what our devious friend proposes."

Ellsworth looked soulful as he slowly fingered his snuffbox. "I didn't anticipate building a great republic with something so seedy."

Dickinson wore a sly expression. "It may look untidy, but if you watch the early brushstrokes of an artist, his work looks puzzling and unattractive. Later—and from a distance—you see symmetry and beauty. Those apparent random colors eventually become a work of art."

"My error," Ellsworth said with a taint of sarcasm. "I forgot we're artists, laying down dark hues that'll one day blossom into a beautiful pastoral scene."

Dickinson gave Ellsworth another pat on the arm. "You do eventually catch on."

Ignoring his snuff, Ellsworth turned to Sherman. "Have you considered approaching someone other than the general?"

"Washington's the only choice. Mason's too arrogant, Randolph's a weather vane, and Madison's a purist. Washington can ram a constitution through this convention, but he knows it'll never get ratified without support from a few small states. He sees this clearly—one of the few." Sherman hefted the teapot and felt that it was empty. "Besides, Washington carries enough clout to pull this off."

"Why would he conspire with us?" Ellsworth asked.

"Washington can put the preliminaries in place, but I hold the lynchpin. When I lay it out, he'll see we must work together."

Ellsworth went for his snuff and took an inordinate amount of time with his little ritual. "Roger, wait a few more days. You said we need only one state to shift to our side. Surely, we can find another way."

"The morality bothers you?"

Ellsworth answered Sherman with silence.

"John?"

"It's a nasty piece of business." Dickinson hesitated. "Sometimes, if you stall, problems disappear; passions abate. Other times, if you dawdle, you lose opportunity. Why do you want to move now?"

"Hamilton is about to leave for New York. He must carry instructions from the general."

Dickinson spun his empty teacup in a chipped saucer. After a few distracted seconds, he looked up, and Sherman was surprised to see compassion in his eyes. "Roger, how do you feel about this?"

Sherman felt a pang of melancholy. Working out the mechanics had mercifully seized his mind for the last few days. Sherman didn't tend toward introspection, but he had wrestled with these issues on many solitary walks. In the end, he couldn't reconcile his proposal with his religious beliefs. The money side bothered him, but he could live with the consequences. It was the slavery side that struck deep, far too deep to slough off with little excuses.

Was he too determined to make a deal, any deal? Would he sacrifice any principle? Roger believed himself an honest man. An honest man must first and foremost be honest with himself. His plan didn't sanction slavery, but it used the South's need to protect this institution as a means to protect Connecticut. The convention would never endorse a government that didn't tolerate slavery, but he couldn't use this as a rationalization. He had decided to do wrong—to sacrifice the freedom of thirty-five percent of the population in the South to get a workable federal government.

Perhaps sacrifice was too strong a word. Negroes were already in bondage, and nothing that happened in Philadelphia in the summer of 1787 would change their condition. Every state except Massachusetts allowed slaves. A less honest man might tell himself that bargaining with something the other side already controlled was clever, not evil. Sherman knew better. As soon as he struck his deal, he would be sucked into the morass of slavery.

Sherman heard a quiet knock at the door. "Come in."

Howard opened the door enough to stick his head in and asked, "Would you gentlemen care for more tea? Mrs. Marshall has baked fresh scones."

"Thank you, Howard. You're very thoughtful. A fresh pot of tea sounds good, and I never turn down Mrs. Marshall's cooking."

"I'll return in about ten minutes. Sorry to interrupt."

The three men sat silent until Howard withdrew his head and closed the door with a barely audible click.

Dickinson caught Sherman's eye. "Are we cutting a pact with the devil?"

Sherman glanced at the closed door, then returned to meet Dickinson's eyes, "No, John, but his surrogates fill our dance card."

SHERMAN ENTERED THE CHAMBER and immediately felt suffocated by the humid atmosphere. Summer had come early this year, and the morning temperature was unusually warm. He glanced toward the closed windows and wished they could be opened to allow some unspoiled air into the chamber. As he took his seat, Sherman feared that both the heat and tempers would worsen in the days ahead.

At the opening of every session, he made a habit of looking around to observe the members' moods, to see if he could spot any knowing glances between delegates who had conspired into the night, or perhaps catch a hard glare between men who had gone to bed angry. Pinckney started speaking before Sherman completed his scrutiny of the room, and he found himself drawn into a skillful exhibition of eloquence and energy.

Sherman got his work done by craft and perseverance. How much more could he have accomplished with Pinckney's good looks and easy grace? Despite the clammy heat, Pinckney appeared cool and unaffected. He moved with poise, spoke with authority, and projected confidence. Sherman tugged at his moist wool pants and felt envious of the linen attire favored by Southerners.

"Gentlemen, we must remember that we're unique. Compared to other countries, there are few distinctions of rank and fortune. Every freeman has the same rights, honors, and privileges."

In private conversation, Pinckney enjoyed irritating people, but he knew how to deliver a speech and command a chamber's attention. Although he often wasted his talent to make small points, today he seemed to have a larger sense of purpose.

"Equality will continue in our new country because we reward industry. Almost every member of our society enjoys an equal opportunity to achieve wealth or rise to high office. Gentlemen, it would be a mistake to design a government meant for a different people."

Pinckney modulated his voice in a pleasing rhythm that seemed natural to those reared in the Southern aristocracy. Sherman knew his Yankee twang grated on the ears of the gentlemen from the South.

"Our situation is distinct from the people of Greece or Rome. Can Solon's orders work in the United States? Do the military habits of Sparta resemble our habits? Are the distinctions of patrician and plebeian known among us? Were the Helvetica or Belgic confederacies, or the Germanic Empire, similar to us? No—they're all different."

Pinckney's reminder of his own classical education was aimed at the scribbling little man in the front row. Madison sat at his usual place, his quill pen moving in smooth swirls, interrupted by unconscious detours to the inkwell. Sherman wondered what Madison intended to do with his precious notes.

"The constitution of Great Britain may be the best in existence, but Parliament is a creature of chance. The monarch needed money, and the nobility wouldn't permit taxation unless they were given a voice, so they blended the Commons with the Lords to form Parliament."

As Pinckney said this, he raised his hands in front of him at equal height, right palm up and the left palm down. "Since that time, nobility have been a part of Parliament, but their power has diminished, as the power of the Commons increased." With this he lowered his left hand and raised his right palm upward. Sherman grew jealous. He never used appropriate gestures to accent important points. In fact, he seldom used gestures at all.

"The United States will never accept nobility, and this country contains few men wealthy enough to pose a dangerous influence. Perhaps there aren't one hundred such men on this continent."

Sherman thought that at least thirty of those with "dangerous influence" sat in this chamber. The thirty-first stood before them.

"Can this situation change?" Pinckney asked. "From what cause? The landed? That interest is too divided. Moneyed interest? If that happened, it would be the first time nobility sprang from merchants."

This last was said with such disdain that no one could mistake Pinckney's contempt for the merchant class. Sherman stole a glance at Gerry and spotted annoyance.

"Fellow delegates, we're here to form a government for the people of the United States. We're a vast new country, capable of extending the blessings of liberty to all its citizens—capable even of making them happy.

"What kind of government suits us best?" Pinckney then stepped to his desk and picked up his notes.

After what Sherman considered an excellent preamble, Pinckney proceeded for the second time to present his plan of government. Unfortunately, the high interest shown for his opening remarks didn't extend to the populist theme of his plan. Sherman detected no converts. He noticed that even Madison had put down his quill and folded his hands on the table, a clear sign that he didn't intend to record Pinckney's plan. Sherman was pleased that the tiff between Madison and Pinckney hadn't been squelched. Personal rivalries often presented a mallet to break opposing coalitions into manageable pieces.

"If no better plan is proposed, I move for the adoption of this one."

With this weak close, Pinckney walked over and plopped a copy of his plan on the table in front of Madison. Madison kept his hands folded and studiously appeared indifferent to the document.

"An excellent scheme; I highly endorse it," Robert Morris said.

Washington gave Morris a cautionary glance. "I'll consider it overnight and speak to you before the opening of tomorrow's session."

Strange, but Sherman felt more comfortable with Washington's equivocation than with the unqualified endorsement from Morris. Both had speculated in western lands, but Washington dabbled, while Morris had committed a huge portion of his vast fortune. The general's measured response made Sherman feel better. If Washington came to embrace the plan, it meant he too had decided that the objective justified whatever expedients might be necessary.

"Of course, sir. I expected nothing more," Sherman said.

"On the contrary, your expectations astound me."

Washington's crisp reproach surprised Sherman. The three men sat in the parlor of the Morris home. Sherman wanted to meet with Washington alone, but the general had insisted that Morris be present. Sherman assumed that Washington had an inkling of the visit's purpose and wanted a witness.

"I'm sorry, Your Excellency, but I can't think of another way to move us beyond this impasse."

"Mr. Sherman, you're a religious man, yet you barter with slavery."

Sherman was taken aback by Washington's indignation about the slavery side of the proposition instead of the western lands. When Sherman heard himself speak, he sounded defensive. "Only with the greatest reluctance, sir."

"The greatest reluctance would have aborted your proposal."

"There are unsavory aspects of this plan but nothing unique. I only pulled the strands together. This convention won't put restrictions on slavery, in any case."

Washington looked sad. "Mr. Sherman, there's not a man living who wishes more than I for the gradual abolition of slavery. Slaveholders with such sympathies must rely on New Englanders to trigger change. You disappoint me."

"I apologize, General. I wouldn't have approached you except under duress."

"What duress?" Washington seemed incredulous.

"Bald-faced insistence that I accept a government that threatens Connecticut's existence."

Washington took a long moment. "If you'll excuse us, we'll consider your proposal. Good night, Mr. Sherman."

SHERMAN WAS DISAPPOINTED THAT the next day's session started with no word from Washington. In fact, the general didn't arrive until just before the gavel fell.

Today's debate was on the term length for senators. Madison spoke first.

"In framing a system for the ages, we shouldn't forget the changes which the ages will produce. An increase of population will increase the demands for a more equal distribution of wealth. Inequalities exist because they're the unavoidable result of liberty. In time, the indigent may outnumber those who own property. With equal suffrage, power will slide into the hands of the former. A leveling spirit has appeared enough to warn of future danger.

"How should this danger be guarded against? How is the danger of any coalition to oppress a minority to be guarded against? By a senate respectful of property. Thus, the term of office should be long, at least seven years."

Sherman disagreed. "Gentlemen, frequent elections ensure good behavior. In Connecticut, elections are frequent, yet we have experienced great stability for more than one hundred and thirty years. I agree with Mr. Madison on the need for steady wisdom, but four or six years will suffice."

Hamilton made a sharp response. "Mr. Sherman forgets that the first branch of the legislature is designed to guard poorer citizens. Of late, mobs have intimidated the states. Fear of rebellion prevents responsible fiscal measures." Hamilton walked between the tables and approached Sherman. "Mr. Sherman, is Connecticut so stable that you'd dare impose a new tax?"

Sherman thought Hamilton had a point. The Connecticut legislature had shown extreme caution of late, but he wouldn't give weight to the charge by responding. Despite Madison and Hamilton's best efforts, Sherman's proposal passed six to four. The Senate would have a six-year term with one-third going out biennially.

"WASHINGTON AVOIDING YOU?"

"The only possible conclusion."

Sherman walked along the river docks with Dickinson. Even if someone wanted to eavesdrop, the clamor of the waterfront made it impossible. Sherman counted eleven ships being loaded or unloaded by noisy stevedores. They stepped between two rows of barrels to get out of the way of a crate swinging off a crosstree. As the load descended, six stevedores surrounded the crate, their arms held up to grab an edge. The men tried to ease contact with the wharf, but the load hit the planks with enough force to give rise to a jarring mixture of notes. Someone was going to be the proud owner of a new pianoforte.

"Are these barrels coming or going?" Sherman asked as he looked at the rows of stacked barrels.

Dickinson gave them a quick glance. "They're staged to be loaded. Cod."

"Who decides all these trades?" Sherman asked. "Goods come, goods go, and nobody coordinates a thing."

"The invisible hand. That's what Adam Smith calls it in *The Wealth of Nations*."

"I read it last year and found it boring. I tend toward practical matters."

"Like money?"

"Like money."

"Money controls trade between nations. My father-in-law insists that unless we establish a sound money system, we'll be at the mercy of the great powers."

Sherman waved his hand. "How is this trade negotiated?"

"Mostly barter, which puts us at a disadvantage."

Sherman walked a few paces and then said, "Before we can address trade issues, we need a strong national government."

"And Washington hasn't responded?"

"No, but Hamilton hasn't left either."

"He was supposed to leave days ago."

"As long as he remains, I believe Washington's still considering my proposal."

"What's your next move?"

"When you're in the majority, vote; when you're in the minority, talk."

"You're going to talk?"

"Not me."

"Who?" Dickinson asked with trepidation.

Sherman laughed. "Not you. Luther Martin."

Dickinson slapped Sherman on the back. "You heartless scoundrel. May God have mercy on your soul."

EVEN SHERMAN REGRETTED ASKING Martin to speak. The man talked for over two days and said nothing coherent. When he mercifully exhausted himself on Thursday, Madison felt compelled to answer with a long sermon of his own. The chamber was clammy, crowded, and filled with rancid hot air.

It appeared they'd be allowed to exit, when Franklin gained recognition. "After five weeks, we've made scant progress. This assembly is unable to recognize truth when presented. How has this happened? Why have we not thought of humbly applying to the Father to illuminate our understandings?

"During the war with Great Britain, we prayed daily in this room, and our prayers were graciously answered. Have we forgotten that powerful friend? Do we imagine that we no longer need his assistance?

"If a sparrow can't fall without his notice, can we raise an empire without his aid? If we don't seek his guidance, governments will only be created by chance, war, or conquest.

"I move that clergy-led prayers be held in this assembly every morning."

Sherman wanted to bless the old man for his wisdom and seconded the motion.

Hamilton quelled an immediate vote. "At this late date, such a resolution will signal distress." Hamilton made a flip gesture. "Besides, I don't believe we need foreign aid."

Randolph suggested a special sermon on the Fourth of July, which was approved. Then Madison moved to adjourn. Sherman was surprised that the adjournment passed—a silent veto of Franklin's motion.

22

Friday, June 29, 1787

"Two long days of unbearable speechifying. Tortured mercilessly in an airless oven. I surrender! The small states may have their way with me."

"Alex, this isn't funny."

"But it is. I nearly bowled over in laughter when Luther said he was too exhausted to finish and asked to continue on Thursday."

"I was mortified," Madison said.

"Dear Jemmy, it was your horrified expression which prompted my amusement."

"I failed to see the humor."

"Don't take things so seriously. You've lost too much hair for such a young man."

Hamilton's reference to his receding hairline didn't lighten Madison's mood. As the two men walked to the State House, Madison wondered why Hamilton had thrown in a personal slight.

"His speech was a delaying tactic," Madison said, as evenly as he could.

"And how did you respond—with a long sermon of your own."

"His challenge had to be answered."

"No, it didn't. No one took his ranting seriously. You added vinegar to an already disagreeable drink."

Madison seethed for a minute. After he settled down, he realized that Hamilton was right—he should have ignored Martin's rambling diatribe. His loud and relentless condemnation of the Virginia Plan had so infuriated Madison that he felt compelled to respond. "You're right, I should've left him to wallow in his own brew."

"Play by your rules, not theirs."

Madison looked at Hamilton. "Alex, I wish you didn't have to leave."

"If the last two days are any indication, I'm glad to be free of Philadelphia." Hamilton grinned brazenly. "Besides, there are some gentlewomen in New York that rely on my visitations."

"When do you leave?"

"Tomorrow."

"Who will I confide in?"

"Let me think. Yes, I shall designate Charles Pinckney as my surrogate."

"Mr. Hamilton, another remark like that and I'll call for your carriage myself."

"Jemmy, you'd be wise to take Charles into your confidence. He can do little good, but he can do enormous harm. Hold him close."

MADISON ENTERED THE STATE House and immediately dreaded the long day ahead. The oppressive heat was now accompanied by huge black flies. As he arranged his writing materials, he tried to chase the persistent pests away from his sweaty eyes. His mood did not improve when Ellsworth reproposed equal state suffrage in the Senate.

After being recognized, Madison jumped up and quick-stepped to the back of the chamber. "Please ponder the consequences of demanding concessions that will break the confederacy into pieces." Madison tapped the Connecticut table with his fingertips. "I beg you, sirs, renounce this principle of equal state suffrage. It will infect our Constitution with a mortal illness."

Madison whirled and walked back to his table. Just before sitting, he looked back at the Connecticut table. "Gentlemen, relent, or your countrymen will never forgive you."

Hamilton slowly unwound to his full height, which seemed taller than his five foot seven. As Madison picked up his quill, his friend gave him a mischievous wink. "The small states say we ask them to renounce their liberty." Hamilton paused and then filled the chamber with a booming voice. "This is a contest for power, not liberty."

Hamilton's bombast had gained the attention of every man in the room. He pointed at the Delaware table and declared, "Delaware, with forty thousand souls, will lose power to Pennsylvania, with four hundred thousand. But will a person in Delaware be less free than a citizen of Pennsylvania? Of course not." Hamilton stared at Paterson. "Some of you pretend to protect liberty, but your real aim is to protect your illusion of power. An illusion, because if you don't give it up freely—here, now—it shall be taken from you by force."

Madison felt the men in the chamber stiffen as Hamilton continued. "Make no mistake, if dissolution occurs, Europe will pounce. It's a miracle that we can sit here, engaged in tranquil deliberation."

He placed a hand on the rear of his chair, and just before he sat, he said, with the kind of disdain only he could muster, "Only a madman would trust in further miracles."

Gerry stammered a few beats and then controlled himself of everything but an odd tic that caused his head to bob to no discernible beat. "I regret that instead of coming here like a band of brothers, we see our role as negotiators. I am from a proud state, but I consider myself a citizen of the United States."

Gerry continued arguing reasonably but then concluded, "Gentlemen, I think we should remember that if we don't agree on something, few of us will be appointed to Congress."

Madison sighed. Gerry had abruptly degraded everything he had said with a selfish plea.

Next, Ellsworth defended his proposal. "Proportional representation in the first branch protects the large states against the small. An equality of voice in the second branch protects the small states against the large. Nature has given self-defense to the smallest insect. Can't we do the same? We must compromise or our meeting will be for naught. I'm not a halfway man, yet I prefer doing half the good we can, than to do no good at all."

Madison felt dejected as he gathered up his things. His journal would show no progress today, only whining and exhortations to do something, anything.

MADISON AND HAMILTON SAT in comfortable chairs in front of a dead fireplace. The Indian Queen harbored its own cloud of flies that added annoyance to the sticky heat. Philadelphia hired boys to scoop up horse droppings, but the summer fly problem grew worse as the days grew hotter.

Madison made a constant motion with a fan. "Alex, why are you leaving? You saw today's proceedings. We need you."

"We must try a different tack."

"What're you talking about? What's your mission in New York?"

"I've been sworn to secrecy, but all the levers of power don't reside in Philadelphia."

"Your comments brought sense to the debate. Votes follow logic."

"Don't delude yourself. Votes follow power—power and money."

"What deal are you sent to barter?"

"I've said too much already. Please don't force me to be rude."

Madison sat and contemplated. Only the general could authorize a scheme that required Hamilton to be in New York. What plot had he hatched? Who was privy? Why hadn't he been informed? Madison became irritated. They'd decided that their young and idealistic philosopher was not mature enough to be taken into their confidence. The general had formulated a deal that included Congress—a deal that possibly exceeded the bounds of propriety. Was it necessary? Not yet. The large states could control the convention only if they had the will. Madison threw down a swallow of Madeira and vowed to get to the bottom of these dealings.

DESPITE MADISON'S AND HAMILTON'S exhortations the previous day, Ellsworth continued to insist that each state have an equal vote in the second branch.

Wilson removed his spectacles and looked directly at the delegates. "If there is a compromise, it won't come from the large states. Shall one-quarter of the United States withdraw from the union, or shall three-quarters of the population abandon their rights?" Wilson let an uncharacteristic edge creep into his voice. "If these defiant little states refuse to join us, then separation it shall be."

Madison watched Ellsworth display uncharacteristic emotion as he answered Wilson's attack. "The danger of the big states combining is not imaginary. Suppose three free ports are to be established. Wouldn't an alliance be formed to favor Boston, Philadelphia, and some port in Chesapeake?"

Ellsworth absentmindedly reached into his waistcoat, pulled out his snuffbox, looked down at it, and stuffed it back in his pocket. He looked as if he wanted to add something but then glared at Wilson as he returned to his seat.

Madison rose to offer a rebuttal, but his frustration with the stupidity of the entire debate caused him to utter the unspeakable. "Gentlemen, let's be honest. Our differences don't lie between the large and small states. Our divisions result from whether we own slaves or do not own slaves. If defensive powers are to be given, they ought to go to slaveholding states."

Madison sat to stunned silence. As he reached for his quill to note his own remarks, he realized he had stumbled badly.

As the embarrassed silence extended, Franklin tried to relieve the tension by moving the debate away from slavery. "Opinions turn on two points. With proportional representation, the small states claim their liberty is at risk. With equal state votes, the large states fear their property is at risk. When a broad table is to be made and the edges of the planks don't fit, the carpenter takes a little from both planks to make a perfect fit. In like manner, both sides must part with some of their demands in order to achieve other accommodations."

Madison seethed as Franklin presented some complex and convoluted proposal that the doctor intended as wadding to cushion Madison's faux pas. He knew he had overstepped the unspoken bounds of propriety, but if they were to move the convention forward, they needed to address the real issues instead of false dilemmas. They argued endlessly over state power, but everyone squeezed their eyes tight against the greatest danger to the new nation. Slavery held a scythe above the delegates' heads that could slice their best intentions to bloody pieces.

When King spoke, he looked directly at Sherman. "I'm astonished, sir, that when a fair government is within reach, you renounce the blessing because of an idealistic attachment to your state."

As King sat, Paterson stood unrecognized and nearly shouted, "The large states must believe we're blind! The South is so puffed up with her wealth and Negroes that evenhanded treatment is out of the question." Paterson swatted a fly away with enough force to stun it, had he had the luck to connect. "There is no middle way. Look at the votes. They've been cast by interest, ambition, and the desire for power."

Paterson's face grew red as a ripe tomato. "Give ambition opportunity and it will abuse it. The whole history of mankind proves it." Paterson threw his hand through the air. Madison wondered if he meant to shoo another fly or take a swat at the large states. "The small states can never agree to the Virginia Plan because the small states will end in ruin, and if we're to be ruined, I'd rather let a foreign power take us by the hand."

Madison looked at Washington. Why didn't he silence this tirade? Paterson had not been recognized, and his deportment violated their rules. The general's withering look was wasted on Paterson's back, but he made no move toward his gavel.

Paterson blustered on. "The little states have been told, with a dictatorial air, that this is our last chance to build a good government. The large states dare not dissolve this Confederation. If they do, the small ones will find a foreign ally, one with honor and good faith."

Madison grew increasingly alarmed. Could no one stop this man?

"Let me be clear," Paterson said, in his prosecutorial voice. "It's treason to annihilate our duly established government. Treason!"

He stood arms akimbo. "Gentlemen, I do not trust you!"

Paterson finally walked over to his seat, but before sitting he spat, "The sword may decide this controversy."

King started to respond with patience. "Sir, I didn't speak in dictatorial language." Despite what looked like a gallant attempt, King lost his own composure. Shaking his head, he turned to the general assembly but pointed at Paterson. "This intemperance has marked Mr. Paterson himself. I wasn't the one to speak with a rage previously unheard in this chamber. I wasn't the one to say I was ready to abandon our common country and court the protection of some foreign hand."

King turned to face Paterson directly. "I'm grieved that such a thought entered into Mr. Paterson's head. I'm stunned he allowed it to escape his lips. I, sir, would never court protection from a foreign power. Never! Mr. Paterson, there's no excuse that justifies your insults."

When King sat down, the chamber grew breathlessly silent. Finally, someone behind Madison softly moved for adjournment. The second came in a voice just above a whisper. After the vote, Madison sat still and felt, rather than saw, the delegates file quietly out of the room. He soon sat alone, looking down at his laborious and all-embracing journal. Was this the end?

MADISON WALKED WITH HIS normal rapid pace toward the Indian Queen. He had felt miserable when he left the State House, and his mood had not improved with the chance to move around and breathe air that others had not exhaled.

"The Virginia Plan is a festering corpse."

Madison turned to see his nemesis. "Mr. Pinckney, we need only to vote to revive the plan."

"A deep coma then?"

"We've merely had a three-day detour."

"So the Virginia Plan is divine. It shall be resurrected after three days. Please excuse my ignorance."

"Charles, I need your help."

Pinckney put a hand on Madison's shoulder and stopped his progress. "James, you ask for my help?"

"I and the republic. Give me your advice. How do we break this deadlock?"

Pinckney began to stroll toward their inn. "Why not give in to equal suffrage in the Senate? I agree the real issue is not small versus large states. A cooler Senate can protect our slaveholdings."

Madison grew wary. "Equality in the Senate is a bad solution."

"You must admit that our frontier grows faster than the Northwest. The next states will be in the South."

"You've talked with Sherman."

"I talk to all the delegates."

"But your allegiance is with the South, not New England."

"My allegiance is to South Carolina."

"Don't conspire with Sherman. Deal with me first. I can be accommodating."

"Your newfound broadmindedness is welcome—but perhaps too late."

"What do you mean?"

"Actions have already been put in motion."

"What actions?"

"I'm afraid you must learn this from someone other than me."

Madison fumed. Pinckney knew. He must learn what was going on, or his credibility with the other delegates, and Pinckney in particular, would be destroyed. No, it was already shattered.

THE NEXT DAY, MADISON skipped down the church steps after Sunday services. He wanted to catch Gouverneur Morris, who had returned from his personal trip.

"Mr. Morris, may I have a word?"

Morris halted his own awkward descent and gave Madison a hearty smile. "Of course, my dear boy. Come along, but you must slow your pace to my hobbled gait."

"Neither an absent leg nor a dreadful convention has crushed your spirit. How do you remain so cheerful?"

"With pigheadedness. I refuse to let other people's fulminations disrupt my life. This morning's sermon only convinced me to remain an unrepentant rogue."

"Mr. Morris, do you know what's going on?"

"Something, my dear boy, something. I'm on my way to Robert Morris's home to find out exactly what."

"You don't know?"

"I believe our dear general and the doctor have hatched a plan, but I know not what."

"May I join you? This private scheming has me troubled."

"Of course. We'll beseech our compatriots to confess their sins."

Madison's spirits soared. If Gouverneur Morris didn't know, then his own ignorance felt more comfortable. Besides, even the general couldn't ignore two senior delegates. He'd soon know the worst.

THE TWO MEN WERE led into the parlor to find a dejected Morris and Washington. Robert slouched in a wing chair, staring at the cold fireplace, while Washington sat on the other side of the room, writing a letter. Madison could sense that they hadn't been talking.

"Gentlemen, please come in," Morris said.

The general barely acknowledged their entrance.

Gouverneur Morris opened the conversation. "Sorry to disturb, but we want to talk about the convention."

"Do you bring news?" Robert Morris asked.

"We came seeking information," Madison said.

"What kind of information?"

"Why was Hamilton dispatched to New York?" Madison asked.

Madison sensed an abrupt movement from where Washington sat writing his letter. "Mr. Hamilton is on personal business for me," the general said. The hard tone signaled that no further inquiry would be entertained.

"Emotion runs high," Madison said. "The delegates are obstinate and—"

"Indeed!"

Everyone sat silently, waiting for Washington to elaborate. Finally, he said, "More than a few delegates have threatened to go home. Each minute, I sit in fear that news will arrive that the convention has dissolved. The current crisis cannot be exaggerated."

"I agree," Madison ventured. "I hope Hamilton's trip means you've crafted a solution. May I ask his mission?"

"You may not."

Madison fought for control. "General, I deserve to be taken into your confidence."

"His mission doesn't fit into your neat plan," Washington said with more than a little sarcasm.

"You believe I caused this crisis?"

"Your insistence on perfection has not helped matters."

"I'm trying to avoid the sins of the past."

Washington turned around in his chair and looked at the three men on the other side of the room. "I'm concerned with the sins of the present." He turned back to his letter and muttered, "And the parishioners do not repent."

Gouverneur Morris and Madison exchanged a quick glance, but Morris offered no support. Evidently, the general's fulminations could dampen his spirit.

Madison decided he had to proceed, even if alone. "General, I know how disappointed you are, but—"

"No, Jemmy, you do *not*."

"Please, excuse me, sir, but—"

This time Washington cut him off with an uplifted finger because a servant had entered. "General, sir, Roger Sherman requests to see you," the servant said.

Washington paused a long second and then said, "Show him to another room and ask him to wait."

Washington sat for several minutes before slowly rising. "If you'll excuse me, gentlemen." He looked down at the letter he had been writing. With a slight shrug, he walked over and handed it to Madison. "Here, Jemmy, you may read my correspondence while I talk to my guest."

Madison quickly scanned the letter, hoping to find out what this was all about. Instead he got a glimpse into the general's heart.

Everybody expects something from this convention; but what will be the final result? I am persuaded that the primary cause of our disorder lies in the different state governments and the tenacity with which they grip power. Independent sovereignty is ardently contended for, whilst separate interests refuse to yield to a more enlarged scale of politics. Disrespect for a general government renders this great country weak at home and disgraceful abroad.

I have no more ardent wish than to know what kind of government is best for us. No doubt there will be diversity on this important subject and it is necessary to hear all the arguments. To please all is impossible and to attempt it would be in vain. The only way is to form a government as good as we can and then trust the good sense of the people to carry it into effect.

23

Sunday, July 1, 1787

Sherman hastily stood when he heard the door open. Washington turned his back to Sherman, sliding the pocket doors together until they met with a light clap. "Mr. Paterson is your charge." Washington turned to glare at Sherman.

"I apologize for his intemperate remarks."

"Intemperate?" The general looked tired and dejected. "That man may have destroyed my country."

Sherman didn't know how to respond, so he simply asked, "Has Alex left?"

"Mr. Sherman, I thought if I acquiesced to your intrigue, we could salvage this convention."

"General, with all due respect, you did more than acquiesce. The design is now as much yours as mine."

"Can you not control your people?"

"My people know nothing of our doings."

"Only a weak commander gains allegiance by disclosing private discussions with his superior."

"You're correct; that was a poor excuse." Sherman noticed that no tea had been offered, so he went directly back to his question. "Sir, did Alex leave?"

Washington glowered a moment, then simply said, "Yesterday."

"I believe we must proceed as if nothing untoward has happened."

"You do, do you? Well, I disagree."

"General, the plan can still work. Hamilton's on his way. Give it a chance."

"We shall, but we won't pretend nothing *untoward* has happened." Washington stretched to his full height. "Mr. Sherman, I expect you to proceed immediately to Mr. Paterson and upbraid that firebrand to within an inch of his life. Another outburst like that, and I'll personally ride to Trenton and get the man disbarred. You have vital tasks in this intrigue—do not misstep. Last, I'll hold you to your promise to keep the small states at this convention. Good day."

With that, Washington marched toward the doors, flung them aside, whirled around in the central hall, and snapped them together like a clap of thunder.

"It had to be said."

Sherman shook his head. "No, William, it did not."

"Especially not in such harsh words," Dickinson added.

Sherman, Ellsworth, Dickinson, and Paterson sat in a private room at the City Tavern. Sherman had arranged the meeting immediately after his truncated appointment with Washington.

Ellsworth snapped his snuffbox against the table. "You went overboard."

"I told the truth. Damn their so-called Southern manners."

"You said you'd find a foreign ally and that the sword would decide this controversy." Dickinson's voice conveyed contempt. "You went far beyond violating Southern manners."

Paterson leaped to his feet and shoved the chair away with so much force that it tipped over and clattered across the floor. "The bastards plot treason!" Paterson spat.

Sherman strained to remain calm. "William, sit down. Get control of yourself."

"Treason, control? Those words don't go together."

Sherman took a deep breath. "William, it's not treason to replace a government that's already lifeless."

"Our Revolution is not dead!"

"I'm talking about the Confederation. Our ideals can survive if we rekindle the flame, but you threaten to douse the few remaining embers."

"The Virginians, not I, threaten hearth and home."

"Sit. You're too excited. Sometimes a frontal assault isn't the best way."

"Brave men face villains squarely. They don't—"

"William, I'm trying to be patient, but you push too hard."

"I'll push even harder. I'll not rest until—"

"You leave only rubble?" Sherman inserted a quiet pause, then said in a conciliatory tone, "William, please sit. Let's talk sensibly."

"Roger, do not placate me. I'm not in the mood."

Sherman flew out of his chair, walked around the table in two quick strides, picked Paterson's chair off the floor, and slammed it down square on all four legs. "William, you wear your mood with far too much pride. Now sit!"

Paterson stood a moment and then sat without a murmur.

Everyone sat in silence, eyes averted, as they studied their hands or seemed to find something unexpected in their tankard. Sherman realized that this rare exhibit of temper had caught them by surprise. So be it. He took a deep breath and tried to regain his composure. "William, in a week or so, I could have broken this convention open. Now, you may have wrecked my plans—and your career."

"What are you talking about?"

"I've been instructed to flog you into submission—or else. Powerful forces want you disbarred." Sherman retook his seat and spoke quietly. "William, they can do it."

After a moment of silence, Sherman saw the defiance in Paterson's face before he heard the words. "I'll apologize or do whatever else is necessary." Paterson's eyes swept those of everyone in the room. "But I want you to know, Roger, I'll humiliate myself only to stay in the fight."

Sherman didn't think this fulfilled Washington's directive, but their elaborate plan required New Jersey's vote. He poured Madeira into Paterson's half-filled glass. "I think that wise, William." Sherman set the bottle down. "Can you give me a week—no more attacks?"

Paterson looked at his refilled glass and then met Sherman's eyes. "I'll hold my tongue for one week. After that, I must do my duty."

Sherman lifted his glass and raised it in a salute. "Excellent. Could I have gotten a fortnight?"

Paterson returned the gesture, but before taking a sip, he said, "Roger, you know my tongue could never remain tied for that long."

The laughter told Sherman that they had circumvented the matter for the time being. He could only hope that events in the next few days would relegate this episode to distant memory.

SHERMAN LEFT THE CITY Tavern to rendezvous with Baldwin. When he stepped into the glare, he wondered if nature had decided to punish the guilty with insufferable heat. He walked slowly to keep from perspiring too much, but before he got halfway to the wharf area, he was so sticky that he resumed his normal pace. He told himself that if he had hired a carriage, he'd still feel like a lathered horse.

He had selected the same out-of-the-way coffeehouse where he had clandestinely met with Baldwin several weeks ago. When Sherman entered the commercial district tavern, he saw that his friend had already arrived. He felt relief walking into the dark recesses and quickly dropped his valise and shrugged off his coat. A great advantage of a place by the docks was that no one paid attention to the gentlemen's code requiring a man to have a coat on in public.

"You ol' reprobate, how'd you pull this off?"

Sherman slid into the tall hardwood booth. "And good morning to you."

"Oh, pleasantries is it? You make me trudge to this workingman's tavern for chitchat?"

"I picked this place because I thought you'd feel at home with the clientele."

"I do." Baldwin waved his arm around. "These are honest seafaring men. They have a lot in common with my Wilkes County constituents: hardworking, unpretentious, and eager to be left alone." With a nod in Sherman's direction, Baldwin added, "You, on the other hand, sully the place. For our next meeting, I'll locate a pirate's den."

"Mr. Baldwin, what in the world has you so worked up?"

"Why did Pierce and Few board a coach for New York?"

"Perhaps we should talk about that."

"Indeed, we should. Two of my state's delegation just up and grab a coach to New York like a plague had suddenly hit Philadelphia."

"They're members of Congress, returning to do their duty."

"Don't play innocent. They left with William Blount."

"Blount's also a congressman."

"Blount's a crook!"

"Tsk, tsk, Mr. Baldwin, you mustn't defame the honorable delegate from North Carolina."

"Roger, that man defames himself. He lies, steals, and cheats. He's obsessed by money. How can you use such a man?"

"When you use money as bait, you catch the greedy."

"Pierce and Few are honest men. Why're they sharing a coach with the only member of this convention I would decline to dine with?"

"Perhaps they're not as judgmental as you."

"Roger, quit being evasive."

"Abe, we're old friends. I merely—"

"I'm looking for a new friend."

"With four Georgia delegates, your vote—"

"You assume I'd vote with you. That's amazingly presumptuous."

"Abe, we need your vote to hold this convention together. I had to reduce the number of Georgia delegates to make your vote count."

"So you took it upon yourself to alter the sovereign state of Georgia's delegation to the Federal Convention. Roger, at times you're aggressively insolent."

Sherman gave a dismissive shrug. "Nobody's perfect. If you're through twaddling, would you like to hear the plan?"

Baldwin looked Sherman in the eye for a long moment. "If you'll quit being oblique, I'll listen. But it had better be good. I'm still angry."

"I'll explain everything because I need your vote." Sherman settled back into the recesses of the bench seat. "The North controls Congress, eight states to five, but fifteen members are here, so there's no quorum. When Blount, Few, and Pierce arrive in New York, there'll be a quorum, and the South will hold a temporary majority."

"Too bad Congress has no power."

"Congress isn't completely powerless. Jay is negotiating a trade bill in Europe, and the North is giving away navigation rights on the Mississippi to get access to Caribbean trade."

"Damn." Baldwin thought that through. "A Southern majority can reverse Jay's instructions."

"Exactly. Your charming state claims all land west to the Mississippi, so Pierce and Few saw an opportunity to safeguard your state's interests."

Baldwin leaned toward Sherman. "Blount?"

"With no way to reach the sea, the value of his western lands will collapse. A treaty consistent with Jay's instructions would be sweet for the North, a threat to Georgia, but a catastrophe for our ever-enterprising Mr. Blount. He's bought vast tracts along the Mississippi."

"Swindled, you mean. That man wouldn't pay a fair price for his mother's funeral."

"Mr. Baldwin, you must pray for tolerance. The weak depend on the forbearance of others."

"I shall make a note of it." Baldwin sat back and laced his fingers around his cup. "No wonder Blount took off like a spooked mare." Looking into Sherman's eyes, he asked, "Roger, why do you care about our western lands?"

"I used the issue to lure your colleagues away. What I need is for you to hold a potent vote."

"Houstoun will counterbalance my vote."

"I only need Georgia to split."

"Negate Georgia's vote? You've convinced another state to swing your way?"

"A deadlock serves my purpose."

"There's more, isn't there?"

"There's always more."

Baldwin leaned forward. "You rascal, what else have you cooked up?"

"Nothing has been sealed, but have you heard of Manasseh Cutler?"

"My God, you have made a pact with the devil."

Sherman smiled. "The devil may not covet as much land."

"The devil has clear title to his domain."

Cutler represented the Society of the Cincinnati in front of Congress. The Northern chapters of the society, through Cutler, had petitioned Congress for land grants in lieu of back pay. So far, Congress had stalled. Rumors circulated that Congress and certain powerful New York politicians wanted a share of any land grant before they would approve the deal.

Sherman leaned conspiratorially close. "Abe, the nation needs revenue to pay off the war debt. In the next few weeks, Congress will get off its hindquarters.

They'll establish a governing authority for the Northwest Territory and award two massive land grants."

"And how does that serve the South?"

"In a minute. The Ohio Company is controlled by the Society of the Cincinnati. They'll get one and a half million acres. They'll pay an immediate five hundred thousand dollars and another five hundred in the future. That's about sixty-seven cents an acre. In a side deal, the Scioto Company gets five million acres. Same price."

"Whoa! Who controls Scioto?"

"I can only say that it includes many powerful men. The Ohio deal couldn't have been done without tying the two speculations together."

"Clinton holds the reins in New York," Baldwin mused. "He must be up to his neck in this. Every influential member of Congress must hold a piece of Scioto."

"Draw your own conclusion," Sherman said. "I'd never suggest that Clinton or our sniffy Congress could be seduced by a rigged investment."

"What do we get from Congress?"

"Congress won't challenge the convention's authority. They'll pass our work on to the states for ratification without raising too much ruckus."

"And the South?"

"The Northwest Ordinance will restrict the number of new states from fifteen to five."

"That's only valuable if you get an equal vote in the Senate—ten senators instead of thirty." A servant approached their table, but Baldwin waved him away. "Surely that's not enough?"

"Fugitive slaves can be pursued across state lines."

Baldwin thought about that piece of news. "The right to chase runaway slaves is vital, especially on the frontier. Damn clever."

"The legislation also reduces the population requirement for new states. Since the South populates its frontier faster, they'll heavily influence the Senate for decades."

"What does the North get?"

"We get equal suffrage in the Senate, protection against squatters in our western lands, and slavery is prohibited in the Northwest Territory."

"You clever rogue. When you stoop to debauchery, you don't dither."

"I do my best."

"And all this somehow fits with equality in the Senate?"

"More directly than you might imagine. Each man's price got piled on top of all the previous barters. It's like a river: the course shifts as new floodwaters join and try to dominate the main current."

"You got full measure for your pieces of silver." Baldwin sat for a moment and then released one of his wicked smiles. "What do I get for my vote?"

"My undying friendship?"

"Already in my possession. What else?"

"Abe, I need your vote. The country needs your vote, and it will put you in good stead with the gentry in Savannah. Besides, you said equal suffrage is good for Georgia."

"Others disagree." Baldwin leaned forward, serious again. "Roger, we're talking about the corruption of our vestal Congress. This must be the largest land deal in history. No king would be so generous."

"It's scandalous, but we believe it's the only way to salvage this mess."

"Who's 'we'?"

"I'm sworn to secrecy."

Baldwin thought a moment before saying, "A plot of this magnitude must include Washington, and only Robert Morris could broker a land deal this size."

Sherman sat silent.

When it became obvious that Sherman was not going to answer, Baldwin regained the twinkle in his eye. "Save the convention, parcel out the Northwest Territory, mollify the Cincinnati, and pay off our revolutionary war debt. Roger, you've been busy."

"You forgot to mention killing the Jay treaty, reducing the number of Northern states, lowering the population requirement for new states, and allowing the pursuit of fugitive slaves."

Baldwin let his weight fall against the wing-backed bench. "My, my, such squalid deeds to launch such a romantic vision."

"I merely find things that tempt men to do what I want."

"Any more pieces?"

"I've made personal assurances to support the South in later deliberations."

"Slavery? Is your great compromise worth such a price?"

Sherman ignored the question. "Abe, I need your support."

"Indeed you do. I'm the lynchpin of the entire deal."

"What do you want?"

Without hesitation, Baldwin said, "How about your undying friendship?" Baldwin reached across the table, and Sherman immediately grasped his friend's hand in a poignant shake. "Roger, you're gifted. It's a treat to watch you work."

Sherman laughed. "Thanks, Abe. I owe you."

"The whole country owes me. Thank God, I'm a man of small wants."

"You alone preserved your integrity. Not a small want."

With a blush, Baldwin raised his coffee in mock salute. "Then, to the greater glory of the American Empire."

Sherman returned the gesture but altered the toast, "To God, family, and our countrymen."

Baldwin took a sip and then said, "For the first time in weeks, I'm beginning to believe we'll make something of this splintered land. Congratulations, you ol' rascal"

Sherman grinned. "Keep your eyes open. Tomorrow is going to be an interesting day."

As SHERMAN ENTERED THE State House chamber the next morning, he felt less troubled than at any time since his thorny compromise had tugged at his conscience. Baldwin's open-minded support and good-natured ribbing lightened his unease and made him feel better about his draggletail conduct. Still, he had worries. He had presented this hydra-headed deal as if a compact had been struck. In truth, time would either tie things together or blow his plan to every point on the compass.

Moving briskly, Sherman settled into his customary seat in the back of the chamber. The first order of business was the vote on Ellsworth's motion for equal suffrage in the Senate.

Sherman watched the delegates as the secretary announced the vote. Connecticut, New York, New Jersey, and Delaware voted aye. Maryland was a swing state that usually split on votes that were important to Sherman. Daniel of St. Thomas Jenifer—a close friend of Washington—normally voted to cancel out Luther Martin's vote for the small state side. Today, the aristocratic Jenifer was inexplicably absent. With the rare opportunity to control the Maryland vote, Martin threw his state behind equal suffrage in the Senate.

Sherman had five of the eleven votes.

The two large Northern states Pennsylvania and Massachusetts voted no. Then Virginia, North Carolina, and South Carolina held fast and voted no.

Madison had five of the eleven votes.

The secretary read the votes geographically, from north to south. Georgia was last. The delegates sat relaxed because no one anticipated any change in the Georgia vote and assumed a six to five defeat of equal suffrage in the Senate.

The secretary hesitated and then read in a startled voice, "Georgia divided."

Sherman felt the entire chamber go taut. Georgia had never previously broken with the Deep South. William Houstoun had voted no, and Abe had cast his vote, along with a conspiratorial glance, to Sherman. The convention was deadlocked.

Sherman took pleasure in seeing Madison's head swing left and right as he tried to spot an explanation on someone's face. Sherman followed Madison's sudden shift of attention to the back of the chamber, where the door made a soft but purposeful thud as it swung wide enough to bounce against the wall. Backlit by the great Palladian window in the Central Hall, the patrician Daniel of St. Thomas Jenifer stood on the threshold. After a theatrical pause, he sauntered into the chamber with a bearing, pace, and smile that said his tardiness was no accident.

Sherman marveled at Washington's political instincts. Both had a hand in dispatching Pierce, Few, and Blount to New York. As agreed on Sunday, Sherman had delivered Baldwin, and Washington had convinced Jenifer to let Martin control the Maryland vote. He realized how blind he was to the imagery of power. The staging of Jenifer's entrance, only moments after the shattering vote, sent the unmistakable signal that the general himself had orchestrated events, and that fighting the altered course meant fighting the most powerful political figure in the country.

Sherman looked at Washington, who sat as impassively as ever on the low dais. Not a clue could be read from his emotionless face. Jenifer took his seat and adjusted his coat with a gallant flip of the tails. As he turned his gaze to the front, Sherman realized that the chamber had been still during Jenifer's entrance—stage center, as it were.

Rufus King leaped to his feet. "Mr. President, it's obvious that Mr. Jenifer has been unavoidably detained. I respectfully request a new vote on the motion."

Washington gave a sharp rap with his gavel and said in an unusually loud voice, "Denied. The rules do not provide for a second vote on the same day. We shall proceed with other business."

No one stirred until Washington averted his gaze and moved his left forearm from the top of the table to his lap. Charles Pinckney then cleared his throat and asked for the floor.

Pinckney gave the barest of bows to Washington. "Gentlemen, I consent to the motion. Beyond the issue of large and small states, there's a distinction between Northern and Southern interests. For example, North Carolina, South Carolina, and Georgia have an interest in rice and indigo, which the North might sacrifice to achieve their own commercial aims.

"How can powerful states be prevented from controlling the government?" With a whirl that put him directly in front of Madison, Pinckney answered his own question. "By allowing the weak states a stronger vote in the second branch."

Pinckney turned away from Madison and directed his attention to the delegates. "This is our last chance. Nothing prevents a general collapse except this convention. I can't exaggerate the consequences if we dissolve this meeting. I propose a committee consisting of one member from each state be appointed to devise a resolution to this stalemate."

Sherman's admiration for Washington continued to grow. The idea of using a committee to work around the deadlock had been agreed to in advance. After they had decided on the committee membership, Washington said he would talk to a few delegates and convey to them a script for their parts. Charles Pinckney had never been mentioned as a coconspirator, but his recruitment was a masterstroke. Having played a small part, Pinckney could be gracefully blended into the new alliance.

Sherman stood to reinforce the committee idea. "We're now at a full stop, and nobody wants to break up without doing something. I believe a committee will hit on some expedient."

Gouverneur Morris agreed. "I think a committee is advisable, but the committee should also review the mode of appointing senators and their term. The executive must appoint senators, and senators must serve for life. If we change our laws, nobody will trust us, so we must avoid a change in laws by avoiding a change of men. The rich always strive to enslave the rest, so safety depends on keeping the rich together in the Senate and watching them from every side."

Sherman gave a sideways glance at Ellsworth. This had not been scripted. Morris had veered badly off course. At least, Sherman hoped Washington didn't endorse an aristocratic senate appointed by the executive for life.

Morris, as was his habit, banged his wooden leg on the floor to draw attention to his words. "Demagogues must be bribed, and a Senate seat for life is a grand enticement."

Morris took his seat to scattered applause. Hamilton had also strongly endorsed the House of Lords model. Perhaps keeping the rich penned up provided greater protection than allowing them to mingle among commoners disguised in democratic garb.

Madison overcame his shock at the torrent of surprises and regained his voice. "Please, sirs, a committee rarely produces anything but delay. Any scheme a committee might propose can as easily be proposed in this chamber." Madison walked over to his table and leaned into the chamber on splayed fingertips. "Gentlemen, this committee will be controlled by one vote per state. This is the very principle I've been fighting against."

After that brittle note, a motion to establish a committee passed nine to two. Everyone in the chamber understood that Washington was eager to find a compromise. The next step was crucial to their plans. Sherman and Washington had conspired to load the committee with delegates sympathetic to the small state position, or at least not rigid in support of an unaltered Virginia Plan.

The election of committee members went smoothly. Ellsworth from Connecticut, Paterson from New Jersey, Gunning Bedford from Delaware, and Yates from New York championed the small state cause. Baldwin represented Georgia, and Daniel of St. Thomas Jenifer bowed out gracefully to let Luther Martin represent Maryland. Instead of the unbendable James Wilson, the affable Franklin represented Pennsylvania. Instead of the purist James Madison, the reasonable George Mason represented Virginia. Within the Massachusetts delegation, Nathaniel Gorham and Rufus King normally outvoted the hot-tempered Gerry, but Gerry would represent his state this time. Rutledge, a strong advocate for state rights, would sit for South Carolina and William Davie, an ardent champion of the South, represented North Carolina.

The die had been cast.

Everyone in the chamber saw the tidal change. Every committeeman had an interest in retaining some level of state authority over the central government. This group could be trusted to craft a compromise that used the states as a check against the tyranny of concentrated power.

Sherman made a motion to adjourn until Thursday, the fifth of July. "Gentlemen, this will give the committee time to do its work, and it will provide us with a recess to celebrate the anniversary of our independence."

The motion was quickly seconded and passed, but prior to people departing, Robert Morris asked for attention. "Gentlemen, I know you're anxious to leave, but if I could have a moment. I'd like to invite everyone to dine at the Indian Queen at three o'clock this afternoon. Please, everyone join us. We'll start the celebration of our independence and refresh our spirit."

When Morris finished, every man in the room seemed to simultaneously funnel out the door. The unnatural absence of conversation told Sherman that everyone wanted to get away to converse in private with close associates. This indeed had been an eventful day.

SHERMAN AND ELLSWORTH ENTERED the large private room on the second floor of the Indian Queen to find it full. The mood was grimmer than Sherman had expected. Delegates milled around, drinking and talking in hushed tones. He spotted Madison in a corner, talking to Franklin. He couldn't hear what they were saying, but the movement of their bodies told him that they weren't exchanging idle banter. When Madison became animated, Franklin placed a fatherly hand on his shoulder to calm him.

The group dinner had been Washington's idea, another example of how the general thought through the imagery of the moment. He wanted these men together where he could measure their reaction, cajole, and, when necessary, offer enticements. Sherman watched him move about the room, engaging one group after another. Sherman decided he had a similar duty. He dispatched Ellsworth to talk to the small state delegates, while he approached Pinckney.

"Good afternoon, Charles. Thank you for recommending a committee."

"Mr. Sherman, the maestro himself."

"I'm merely a simple delegate from Connecticut."

"And I'm courteous and reverential."

"Charles, you can be difficult at times, but you're always engaging. By the way, Rutledge was a good choice for the committee."

"John's my relative," Pinckney said with a dismissive air. "What else have you adults cooked up?"

"Sorry, Charles, but your sarcasm escapes me."

"You know quite well what I mean. You, Washington, and Franklin treat the rest of us like children. You elders send us to bed early so you can play illicit games."

"You sound angry."

"The Virginia Plan has been gutted without the slightest consideration of my plan. There's a plot to keep me out of the foreground."

"Didn't the general ask you to propose the committee?"

"His Royal Highness neglected to tell me about the intrigue that made the committee possible. I don't like to be used."

"Then you must get out of politics."

Pinckney laughed. "Roger, you're one of the few who don't lose your balance when someone violates accepted norms."

"Does it work? These brash assaults?"

"Quite often. More frequently with Southerners, I'm afraid."

"Why do you think that is?"

"Why do I suspect you're doing research for future intrigues?"

Now Sherman laughed. "My interest is genuine. I fail to understand Southern culture."

"We're more insular, I suppose. And less religious. We impose more social structure to make up for fewer spiritual rules."

"How sad. Religion guides the soul."

"As it has in your political machinations?"

This barb caught Sherman unawares, so a moment passed before he said, "Faithfulness is not how one lives, but what one aspires to."

"Convenient."

"Not very."

"Ah, yes, the Calvinist guilt. I'm sure you are a better man because you feel bad about your misdeeds."

"It does hold extreme excesses in check."

"It's comforting to know that you didn't go to excess this time."

"Charles, your sarcasm could be dismissed if you didn't touch on the truth so often. Mercifully, it appears we're ready to eat. Shall we find a seat?"

Sherman and Pinckney chose seats together at one of the four long tables. As was his habit, Sherman kept a watch on the room as he talked to Pinckney. The mood continued to be one of restraint. The delegates had buried their ill will for the moment, but the tottering convention had sanded nerves crimson.

Franklin and Madison seemed to hold the most interesting exchange. Sherman felt a pang of sympathy for Madison. He had worked hard, and his plan remained more intact than Pinckney had alluded to in his fit of jealousy. The basic structure held, and there would have been no convention without his obsessive dedication to a stronger central government. The intense little man deserved the gratitude of all the delegates. Madison's only failing was his strict adherence to principle. While he strove for perfection, the real world muddled through with good enough.

Madison had too much to contribute to become disenchanted, and the nation needed the balance of his philosophical perspective. Sherman decided the time had come to work with Madison.

Part 4

Shifting Alliances

24

Monday, July 2, 1787

"You know why you weren't taken into our confidence."

"I deserved an opportunity to express my opinion."

"You would've fought every element."

Madison cringed. Washington's statement did not invite argument. The two men walked the State House yard in the waning light of evening. They were very much alone. The block-size square seemed unnaturally still and separate from the city life just beyond the walls.

When the Indian Queen dinner had ended, the delegates had scattered to talk in private. Washington, no doubt prompted by Franklin, had asked Madison to take a walk with him. It surprised Madison to discover that Washington liked the yard when he could have it to himself. Madison didn't see the general as someone who appreciated solitude. He wondered if his perception was wrong. As a young man, Washington had spent long periods alone on the frontier with only his thoughts. Later, as a Revolutionary commander, he lived isolated from interpersonal relationships. Nowadays, Washington surrounded himself with people, but perhaps this habit was meant to compensate for years of loneliness.

Coming back to the subject at hand, Madison said, "General, I understand the hard realities of politics."

Washington, in a rare display of physical closeness, put a hand on Madison's forearm. "Jemmy, you're an exceptional student of government forms, but you must learn the delicate art of political timing before you can weave your ideas into history."

"General, sir, with all due respect, you may have been precipitous."

"The convention shattered on Saturday. Were you not there?"

"Tempers flared, but our coalition could have held."

Washington lifted his hand from Madison's arm. "Damn it, Jemmy, equal state suffrage in one house doesn't negate the republican form. If we break into pieces, we'll be like Europe. We need one nation unified under a single government."

"During the war, you suffered under the impotency of the Confederacy. Surely, you learned that a weak Congress can't protect the nation."

"I don't appreciate being told what lessons I learned commanding the Continental Army."

"My apologies. I didn't mean to instruct Your Excellency."

"Now you're being insolent."

"I'm sorry, sir. An inappropriate lapse." Madison had regretted the "Excellency" as soon as it left his lips. Washington warranted the title, but using it in that context had been a dangerous taunt. He was not handling the conversation well. Or perhaps Washington was handling it exceptionally well.

They had completed two circuits around the yard and were next to the privy. Madison excused himself, more to gain time than to relieve himself. Washington had summarized the arrangement with Congress with little prompting. Madison admired the symmetry of the deal but despised the sacrifice of principle. He also felt sad. The ease with which Congress could be corrupted reinforced his reservations about democracy. Protections, checks, and offsetting power centers must be built into the system to secure the country from human vice. Madison finished his business and, as he stepped back into the twilight, vowed to continue fighting for a proportional Senate.

When he emerged, Washington immediately started walking again. After a few paces, he said, "Congress is the pivot on which the government turns, but we must create a real government first. We need to rely on our national character to amend our errors."

"I don't believe we should abandon this opportunity to build a sound system."

"Strive for perfection, or achieve what's possible? The choice requires wisdom."

This stopped Madison. To argue further, then, was to question the general's wisdom. He contemplated. Washington would make a fine first executive. He had mastered the art of political persuasion and knew how to pin an opponent with a subtlety that didn't offend. No wonder he won his way so often, yet maintained so many friendships.

Madison looked up Washington's tall frame and caught his eyes. "General, sir, although in time I may need to yield, at the moment, I feel I must continue to fight for a proportional Senate."

"Jemmy, don't let proportionality become your sine qua non. Timely withdrawals often lead to later victory."

"Sir, there may not be a later engagement."

Instead of a stern reproach, Washington smiled and then said, "Very well, contained passion has a habit of exploding unexpectedly."

Washington had cut deep. Madison took pride in expunging passion for logic. But Washington's reluctant permission to continue fighting was the most he could win, so he answered with a simple, "Thank you, sir."

BOOM! BOOM! BOOM!

The cannon fire hurt Madison's ears and teared his eyes as concussions pounded his body. Sulfuric mephitis scratched his throat, and the rotten egg odor made him queasy. The thirteen reports ended, but before Madison could draw a grateful and tranquil breath, the artillery brigade started another round. After three consecutive resounding salutes of thirteen cannon shots, Madison felt exhausted.

He had been jostling for a position from which to see the Independence Day celebration when the cannon fire assaulted his senses. The State House Commons throbbed with people keyed up with rum and excitement. The crowd churned on the periphery of the Commons, while the Society of the Cincinnati, the City Calvary, the Light Infantry, and a battalion of militia vied for attention in the center of the swirling people. Each military formation, spruced up in their finest regalia, stood eager to demonstrate their parade skills. The units waited, as did Madison, for the artillery to finish their noisy salute.

Philadelphia, as the site of the signing of the Declaration of Independence, took pride in holding the rowdiest Fourth of July gala in the nation. Festivities would go from dawn until deep into the night. The city echoed with public celebrations, ringing bells, and martial music. Every church would conduct special devotionals, and all 117 taverns would compete for revelers with loud entertainment. The formal celebrations had started early in the morning, with city officials, aspiring orators, and preachers making the customary thirteen toasts.

Fascinated by the inebriated throng, Madison failed to notice Pinckney walk up beside him.

"Perhaps we should dramatically increase the size of any new state."

Madison said, "Thank God, we will. Fewer states in the Northwest Territory may save us from drunken mobs. Imagine twenty toasts —we'd have to stretch our celebration to the fifth."

Pinckney looked surprised that Madison had caught the allusion. Madison would have been embarrassed if Washington hadn't told him about that part of the arrangement with Congress. By acting blasé about Pinckney's remark, he'd stopped what would have been a series of snide comments designed to show off privileged knowledge.

"Did they finally agree the number of states in the Northwest Territory?" Pinckney asked to verify that Madison knew the particulars of the deal.

"Only five states." Without turning, Madison noticed Pinckney's slight shrug. Good, Madison thought, he knows we are on equal footing.

Pinckney complained, "This whole exhibition seems excessive. Everyone acts as if independence were an end in itself. We're independent, but we're adrift without a sextant."

"These people have no—"

Before Madison could finish his point, a huge, flushed man, dressed in a suit that struggled to cover his overhanging belly, started yelling in his ear. "Gentlemen, lift your drinks. Let us rejoice in the year of our lord one thousand seven hundred and eighty-seven and the year of our independence, the twelfth!"

The city had distributed kegs of grog at each corner of the Commons and, despite the early hour, many toasts had already made the crowd boisterous. A loud cheer erupted, and those experienced enough to bring their own tankards threw down another swallow of the watered-down rum.

The chubby man's next words added hot embers to Madison's heartache. "People, another toast to the grand Federal Convention—may they form a constitution for an eternal republic"

Pinckney said, "These people are too simple to discern a republic from a public privy."

"Charles, you're too cynical. The people can be fooled for a time, but Americans won't allow a tyrant to steal their liberty."

Pinckney grunted with disgust. "No, they'll sell their liberty for free grog."

"Let's move into the State House," Madison said abruptly. Madison feared that someone might overhear in the close crowd, even though Pinckney spoke nearly in his ear. If someone picked up his voice, his words could be reported in a newspaper or spread by tavern gossip. Madison turned and entered the State House so Pinckney would be obliged to follow. The guards, standing on either side of the door, recognized them as delegates and allowed them to enter.

Madison saw delegates gathered in the Central Hall between the Judicial Chamber and the Assembly Room. Most were deep in conversation, ignoring the events outside. Madison threw a glance at the windows in the Judicial Chamber and saw that other delegates and city dignitaries blocked them.

Without looking into the Assembly Room, where they regularly met, Madison said, "Let's go upstairs."

He sprang up the Great Hall staircase, sprinted past the Palladian window at the half-story landing, and continued up to the Long Gallery that extended the entire length of the building. As expected, men with enough influence to gain access to the State House blocked these windows as well. At the east end of the hall, Madison spotted James Wilson.

"Charles, can you excuse me? I need to talk to Mr. Wilson."

"But of course, go, speak to your last faithful brother-in-arms."

"Do you no longer support our cause?"

"I'm a realist. You get what you can."

"How do you know where the line that cannot be crossed is drawn?"

"Not easy. You must lose all to know for certain. Anytime you stop short of full failure, you may have been six inches or six feet from that gossamer boundary." Pinckney looked in both directions down the Long Gallery. Evidently not seeing anyone of interest, he said, "Go confer with Mr. Wilson. I prefer to mix with the plebian throng instead of witnessing their merriment from behind a shield of glass."

Before Madison felt the stab of the insult, Pinckney had reversed course and bounded down the staircase. As Madison approached Wilson, he watched the pudgy man peer with disapproval over the top of his reading glasses. Had this visage prompted Pinckney's cutting remark?

"Mr. Wilson, how are you on this fine anniversary of our independence?"

Wilson directed his scowl toward Madison. "Good morning, Mr. Madison. I take it from your greeting that you believe declaring something makes it true. What a simple view of life."

"Nothing in life seems simple to me anymore, but your reference escapes me."

"We declared our independence on July 4, 1776." Wilson turned his condescending gaze on Madison. "If memory serves me right, we fought seven bloody years and spent our progeny's birth right to actually become independent. Saying it was so did not make it so."

"The people need their celebrations and their symbols," Madison said. "What raised your ire?"

"What raised my ire?" Wilson parroted. "What tiny annoyances have fouled my normally cheery mood? Let's see. Drunken imbeciles cheering banalities espoused by minor functionaries. An ignorant citizenry oblivious to our imminent demise. A convention eager to propose a sham republic. Yes, it's possible these things have soured my mood." Wilson turned back to the window. "If not those things, then perhaps a pompous military strutting around the Commons makes me fear rule by the sword."

"I believe our army and militia have earned this day in the sun."

"Our soldiers, yes, but I fear the Society of the Cincinnati."

"Washington can control them."

Wilson didn't respond, so Madison looked through the window. He saw the Light Infantry prepare to execute a *feu de joie*, Madison's favorite parade maneuver. The soldiers stood in a dressed line and readied their rifles. The first man on the right snapped the rifle tight into his shoulder and fired into the air.

Each man, from right to left, quickly copied the movement and fired so fast, it sounded like one continuous shot instead of twenty. Madison loved the symmetry of the rifle reports and the practiced precision of the movements. Today, the Light Infantry executed the difficult maneuver flawlessly.

Without turning, Wilson said, "At the conclusion of these ceremonies, the Cincinnati will march us to the Reformed Calvinist Church for a special sermon. As president of the society, Washington will lead the procession." Wilson shook his head. "The radicals want to put unrestrained power into the hands of one of their own. Can the great general resist the siren song?"

"I've no doubt that he can and will," Madison said.

Looking away from the window, Wilson asked, "How can you be sure?"

"He's working hard to put together a government through the auspices of this convention. He wants the proposal for a new government to come from us, not the Cincinnati. I don't agree with the course he's charted, but his intent is honorable. He'll not succumb to the Cincinnati."

"Even if you're right, other dangers lurk."

"Agreed."

"Where are you?"

"I stepped over to ask you the same question," Madison said.

"I'll fight to my last breath for a true republic. I'll fight for representation based on population—in both houses. I'll fight to reduce the influence of the states. *I've* not moved." Wilson struck a pompous pose and asked, "Have you?"

"No. And it cost me dearly."

"Good. Then we shall continue to work together."

"It will be my honor," Madison said. The pair spent a few minutes watching the parade movements. Madison said, "They've packed the committee."

"Did you know Ellsworth conveniently came down sick? Sherman has taken his place."

"This whole thing has Sherman's imprint."

"More than Sherman's. Elements of this scheme could not have happened without Virginia's Gen. Washington."

"Nor without Pennsylvania's Franklin."

"Touché. They must be working together." Wilson looked even more dejected than when Madison had first approached him. "How do we fight them?"

"Pinckney tells me logic doesn't win political battles. Power wins."

"Pinckney's another turncoat. We must hold the remaining South, Pennsylvania, and Massachusetts." Wilson lost his affected look of superiority. "Have we lost already?"

Madison had absorbed Wilson's melancholy, but he vowed to remain firm and fight this awful mistake. The delegates in the Long Gallery started to migrate downstairs. Madison gestured in their direction. "It looks like we're preparing to march."

"I understand we'll hear a sermon by James Campbell, some aspiring young reverend." Wilson started to move in the direction of the stairs. "It'd be a shame not to be blessed by his untainted wisdom."

On June 28, Franklin had made a motion for a special sermon on the Fourth of July. A simple sermon had exploded into an orchestrated procession from the State House to the Sassafras Street church, led in grand martial style by the Society of the Cincinnati.

When Madison and Wilson emerged from the State House, the Cincinnati had formed in the street, with Washington in the lead. Madison felt the rat-tat-tat beat of the fife and drum unit that stood immediately behind Washington. Looking behind the ramrod columns of military officers of the Revolution, Madison saw the delegates looking ill at ease and disorganized. "Shall we join the jumbled mess?" Madison asked lightly. "It appears our fellow delegates have brought the disorder of the chamber into the street."

They joined the throng and soon found themselves unconsciously walking somewhat to the beat of the drums. When they arrived at the church, the Cincinnati stood politely aside as the delegates filed through the double doors and took the honorary front pews. Madison turned in his seat and watched the officers take the remaining seats or find standing room in the back. Every available space had been filled. Settling forward, Madison was startled to see a very young man climb the circular steps to the elevated pulpit. The immature reverend looked relaxed and at ease, as if he preached to a packed house of illustrious dignitaries every Sunday.

The man gazed over the congregation until everyone grew silent. When he spoke, his surprisingly robust voice easily carried his words to the far corners of the meetinghouse. "Gentlemen of the Federal Convention, welcome. I'm gratified that you've come to seek God's guidance in your unprecedented and formidable commission." Then with a self-deprecating smile, he added in a light tone, "We all need a little help now and then. Shall we pray?"

After a brief, eloquent prayer, the Reverend James Campbell looked over his congregation and spoke in a commanding voice.

"Gentlemen, your country looks to you with anxious expectations on your decisions. She rests confident that the men who cut the cords of foreign tyranny are also capable of framing a government that will embrace all of our interests. This is our chance for a new beginning. The illustrious Federal Convention should not rely upon the state constitutions, for they were made on the spur of the occasion, with a bayonet at our breast, and cannot reflect a perfect republic."

Madison sat upright. Perhaps he and Wilson had another ally. He couldn't have agreed more with the reverend's first words. The state constitutions were a poor model for a general government, and the expediency of war had caused many states to forego many of the principles of a true republic.

"A plan acceptable to the people must remain faithful to the principles of our present government and the American character."

These words deflated Madison's hopes. Was the reverend suggesting that the convention must remain faithful to the Articles of Confederation?

"Any proposition to add kingly power to our federal system should be regarded as treason."

This sharp statement might be a warning against a strong central government or, more literally, against enthroning an emperor.

"Is the science of government so difficult that we don't have men among us capable of unfolding its mysteries and binding the states together by mutual interests and obligations? No! God will not abandon us after shepherding us to freedom. I already see the fabric of a free and vigorous government rising out of the wisdom of the Federal Convention."

Madison decided that the reverend had no particular form of government in mind, only a heartfelt desire to preserve liberty. His reference to the science of government appealed to Madison. He believed that government was something that could be deciphered by analyzing ancient and modern systems. Madison knew he had designed a republic that could protect liberty and endure for generations, but now powerful forces threatened to gut his plan. This was wrong. The national government must represent freemen, not the self-righteous states.

If the young reverend's intent was to inspire the delegates to rise to the occasion and hold fast to their principles, he had succeeded with at least one in the congregation.

25

Thursday, July 5, 1787

Sherman charged into the room and circled his sweat-soaked collar with a finger to get air to his neck. He had rushed to a meeting with Ellsworth, Paterson, and Dickinson at the City Tavern.

"Where've you been?" Ellsworth asked.

"My apologies. The Reverend Witherspoon tied me up."

"What did he want?"

"He believes I should be more tolerant of Madison's positions."

"The man should mind his own business," Paterson said.

"Government is everyone's business."

"Not at the moment," Paterson said. "Did Madison violate our oath of secrecy?"

"Witherspoon seems aware only that there's discord."

"That's still a violation," Paterson yelled. "It should be reported to Gen. Washington."

"To what purpose?"

"To quiet the man." Paterson slapped the table. "That little cat's-paw ought to be taught a lesson."

"William, I'll hear no more of this. As soon as we breach this wall, we'll need Madison. Opponents are temporary; enemies last a lifetime."

"We need to be at the State House in a little over an hour," Dickinson interjected.

"Thank you, John," Sherman said. "First, the committee will propose a senate with one vote per state."

"We won," William Paterson said with a self-satisfied air.

"Not completely. All money bills must originate in the lower house, and the Senate cannot make amendments."

"That's outrageous!"

"William, please," Sherman pleaded. "We gave up the least possible."

"Does this money bill issue matter?" Ellsworth asked.

"Inconsequential, but important. Inconsequential because the Senate won't pass a bill they don't like, so the two houses will have to negotiate behind the scene."

"Then why's it important?" Dickinson asked.

"Because Franklin proposed it."

"That old fogy," Paterson said. "Why pay that cockeyed storyteller any mind?"

"William, you must adjust your attitude. Your negativism exhausts me."

"I'll adjust my attitude after the plan is adjusted."

"That's backward. You can't get your back up every time you don't get your way. When you throw ill-timed insults, it sets us back."

"That old man's opinion's not important."

"He's an astute politician—and tightly tied to Washington."

Looking like he wanted to protest, Paterson merely asked, "What's his rationale?"

"Equal suffrage in the Senate could allow the small states to spend large state money. By requiring appropriations to be initiated in the lower house, the large states can protect themselves against our supposed avarice."

"That's an empty fear. They can keep their money."

Sherman sighed. "If the doctor believes it's a lever, he'll convince others."

Ellsworth interrupted. "Do you think we should accept this?"

Sherman felt relieved to answer a question from someone other than Paterson. "We must. The proof is that we barely got the doubtful members to acquiesce."

"I don't like concessions," Paterson said.

"Then find another profession," Sherman snapped. As he wiped his neck with a handkerchief, Sherman sensed that his patience was about to crack like an eggshell struck with a knife.

"I refuse to sit idle while my country is taken over by Virginia tyrants."

"William, let's step outside a minute."

"I see no need."

"I insist," Sherman said with force. Paterson looked like he might make a scene, but instead, he stood and walked out the door. Sherman followed him into the hall. They walked in stony silence down the stairs and out the back door into a sun so bright, it blurred the sharp edges of buildings. As they stepped into the herb garden, Sherman said, "William, you're hurting our cause. If you continue to fight my leadership, I'll exclude you from our deliberations."

Paterson looked stunned. "I can't believe what I just heard. We've worked together from the beginning."

"And we'll work to the end, but only if you accept my leadership."

"I represent New Jersey."

"You represent disaster. For me, the convention, and the country."

"Friends don't talk to each other like this."

"Friends talk to each other exactly like this."

Paterson turned and walked a few steps toward the back of the lot. When he turned around, Paterson asked, "You believe I'm a stumbling block?"

"William, you're a great pile of rubble strewn across the landscape."

"I fight for principle."

"Your powder's wet and your shot's out of round."

Paterson gave Sherman a puzzled look and then took a few more steps into the yard. When he turned, he seemed more contrite. "Why are you doing this to me?"

"You let emotion addle your brilliant mind."

"You think my anger unjustified?"

Sherman shrugged. "Emotion doesn't help. We need to be coldly detached."

"And under your leadership?"

"Yes."

"Give me a reason."

"Because I've established inroads into the opposition, and I can orchestrate the necessary moves." Sherman closed one step toward Paterson. "I insist on a firm commitment."

"Or you'll expel me?"

"Yes."

"You don't give a man much room."

"I've given you too much room."

Paterson stood about ten feet from Sherman. He looked down a moment and then raised a proud head to Sherman. "May I have one condition?"

"What?"

"If the threat to New Jersey becomes imminent, I can withdraw my pledge?"

"If you agree to let me know in advance. No surprise mutiny."

"I can live with that."

"Then we have a deal?"

Paterson walked over to where Sherman had remained rooted. Sherman felt relief as he used both hands to grasp Paterson's outstretched hand. After an enthusiastic shake, Sherman said with a disarming smile, "William, you're one ornery son of a bitch. Thankfully, you're our son of a bitch."

"And you're a cold bastard. Thankfully, you're on our side."

With that, Sherman broke into laughter and clasped Paterson around the shoulders, giving him a brotherly hug that was returned, with the addition of a few slaps on his shoulder. "Come on. Let's rejoin our little party of patriots."

As they entered the private room, Sherman threw his arm around Paterson and said, "Great idea, William. If you don't mind, I'll claim it as my own."

Sherman saw the look of gratitude in Paterson's eyes as he said, "By all means."

"Sorry for the interruption," Sherman said. "Now where were we?"

"Close to having to leave for the State House," Dickinson said.

"Yes, well … does anyone have a question?"

"What's our plan for today?"

"We'll let the heat dissipate."

GERRY OPENED THE SESSION by reading their report. Sherman crossed his legs and immediately uncrossed them. His wool pants felt sticky, causing him to glance jealously at Pinckney, looking fresh in his linen suit.

"The committee submits the following report to be considered only in total. In the first branch, each state shall be allowed one member for every forty thousand inhabitants, and each state not containing that number shall be allowed one member.

"Second, all bills for appropriating money shall originate in the first branch, and shall not be altered by the second branch.

"Third, in the second branch, each state shall have an equal vote."

Gorham asked why the propositions had to be adopted as a package. Gerry bobbed his head and muttered to himself before saying, "If all the elements aren't adopted together, committee members may withdraw their support."

"The committee exceeded its authority," Wilson barked. "We're not obligated to accept or reject the report in total. I move to divide the resolutions for separate votes."

Madison spoke with more emotion than Sherman had ever heard from the diminutive scholar. "The origination of money bills in the lower house is meaningless. If the small states believe this a concession, they're wrong! If both branches must say yes, it is of little consequence which says yes first." In a rare display, Madison raised his voice. "All my objections against an equal voice in the Senate stand!"

Sherman marveled at Madison's quick mind. He had skewered the meaningless concession in his first breath.

Madison bounced across the front of the chamber. "It's fruitless to purchase immediate accord in exchange for everlasting discord." As was his habit, Madison stopped his pacing in front of his table to signal that he was about to conclude his remarks. "Gentlemen, the small states won't court foreign powers as

Mr. Paterson threatened. They'll make noise for a time, but they won't defy sound republican principles."

Gouverneur Morris gained the floor and thumped his wooden leg around before beginning. "This report is fatally flawed. The whole aspect is wrong! The states were originally nothing but colonial corporations. Upon the Declaration of Independence, governments were formed. The small states took advantage of the moment and demanded equality." The usually amiable Morris glared at the delegates. "As proposed, the Senate will undermine the general government. Germany proves my point. The Germans share a common language, common law, common manners, and common interests, yet their local jurisdictions destroy every tie. The case was the same in the Grecian states. As we speak, the United Netherlands is torn into factions. Do you wish the same here?"

Morris stomped his leg with the force of a gavel. "Good God, sirs, is it possible we so delude ourselves? Who can say whether he himself, much less his children, will next year inhabit this state or that state? This country must unite. If persuasion does not unite it, the sword will."

Morris directed his glare at Paterson. "What part foreign powers might take in a conflict, I cannot say. Mr. Paterson has thrown this threat at us." Turning to the full assembly, Morris softened his tone. "Gentlemen, I came here as a citizen of America. Are we here to bargain for our states? No. We're here to build a nation."

Paterson signaled that he wanted to defend himself. "Gentleman, I've been misunderstood. I didn't mean that New Jersey would court foreign powers. I only meant that foreign nations might use the abandoned states to apply pressure to the states that do unite. Lastly, I must ask some allowance for my profession. Heated exchanges are natural for prosecuting attorneys. If I may so humbly suggest, an apology is also due from Gouverneur Morris for his statement that the sword would force the small states to unite."

Sherman accepted Paterson's comments as an attempt to live up to his pledge on Sunday, but it was a far reach to interpret his words as an apology. He didn't believe Morris would feel obliged to follow suit.

Mason spoke in a sensible, matter-of-fact voice. "Despite objections, the report is preferable to different sides appealing to the world for armed support." A touch of melancholy crept into Mason's final words, making them personal and heartfelt. "It's highly inconvenient for me to remain absent from my private affairs, but I promise to bury my bones in this city rather than see my country dissolve. We must yield on some point for the sake of accommodation."

Gouverneur Morris refused to relent and attacked the report from yet another direction. "Property is the main purpose of society. People renounce absolute liberty for the sake of property." Morris paused a few beats. "Gentlemen, if property is the main object of government, then property ought to influence government. In addition to the number of inhabitants, property ought to be taken into account when determining representation.

"If you'll allow me an additional point—" Morris glanced toward Washington, then returned his attention to the delegates in front of him. "I also fear new states. The rule of representation ought to secure the Atlantic states a permanent majority in the national councils. Some might say this is unjust, but the western settlers will know the conditions in advance."

Wilson adjusted his glasses and stood for a long moment to collect his thoughts. "Gentleman, if the interior country should acquire population, then it has the right to govern, whether we like it or not. The same jealousy just displayed in this chamber misled Great Britain. And what were the consequences? Separation. We will suffer the same results if we pursue a self-serving policy."

Mason, someone Sherman admired for always being reasonable, supported the self-important Wilson. "When the western states are made part of the union, they must be admitted on an equal footing. It's impossible to rig the sails of our nationhood in a way that favors those in this room. At least, not without restricting the horizons of our empire."

Mason had offered the alternatives: build an expansive empire or crowd together along the Atlantic. The western territories could be made into colonies and ruled as the British had ruled the American colonies, but the irony of that solution escaped no one. Sherman gave Mason a friendly nod as he jostled his way toward the exit after a long day.

SHERMAN DIDN'T BOTHER TO knock on the door but walked directly behind the house to the mulberry tree. As expected, Franklin sat in his overstuffed chair, enjoying the waning light with a hot cup of tea.

"Good evening, Mr. Sherman. Would you care for tea or something stronger?"

"Thank you, Doctor. Coffee, if it wouldn't be too much trouble."

Franklin picked up a bell, but before he could ring it, his manservant appeared as if by magic. "Service for two, sir?"

"Thank you, John, but could you brew a cup of coffee for our guest? Fresh tea for me. And could you bring some of those little cakes? I'll feel guilty eating before dinner, but at my age, a little guilt keeps life from becoming flat and tasteless."

"Of course, sir. I'll bring the cranberry ones. They're especially wicked."

"Good man. When I die, I shall take you with me."

"With greatest respect, sir, I have reached a hobbled age myself. I no longer travel."

"More's the pity," Franklin said with a devious grin. "I don't know what I'll do in the hereafter without you."

"Tell earthy stories, I suppose," John said with his own disarming smile.

As the servant disappeared into the house, Franklin said, "John's been with me for years. A good friend, actually."

"Doctor, I can't imagine anyone not becoming your friend after getting to know you."

"You must talk to John Adams," Franklin said with a twinkle. "Anyway, what did you think of today's session?"

"Frustrating. The course has been set, but some still fight the wind."

"You mean you've won and you're miffed others don't surrender."

Sherman felt his back stiffen. "Thank you, Doctor. I mustn't become complacent."

"Nor presumptuous. We worked with you, but we did so under duress. We're friends, not political allies. Even if we share the same goal, our armies are not at each other's disposal."

"Point accepted, Doctor. What did you think about today's session?"

"Something came up we didn't expect. Important delegates will fight the report unless we give them one more concession."

"What do they want?"

"A different committee to define proportionality in the lower house. This time they chose the membership."

"I see." Sherman sat for a moment and for the first time envied Ellsworth's ruse with his snuffbox. "This looks like a strategy to divide and conquer."

"I thought that at first. Get one of the three elements of the report separated and dispatched to a committee of alligators. But after much conversation, I believe they merely want to influence the proportionality rules."

"How?" Sherman asked.

"Some property consideration. I didn't expect you to object since they seek to define the branch not ruled by the states."

"It could change the balance. Destroy Madison's well-thought-out scheme."

"I thought you already did that."

"Once the states are protected, I believe the rest of Madison's plan sound."

"How tolerant of you," Franklin said with an edge. "Let's return to the point. Will you support another committee assigned to work out the lower house proportionality?"

"I won't fight it."

"Will you vote for it?"

Sherman made a show of looking around. "Tea and coffee would be a helpful diversion."

"John will be along in a moment."

Sherman settled back and smiled at the wily old man. "Yes, sir, Connecticut will vote for recommitment."

"Excellent. A small price. You get the Senate and they get the first branch. Ah, here's John now."

Had Sherman missed a subtle signal, or had the two worked together so long that an overt gesture was unneeded? John used both hands to hold a silver tray arrayed with service pieces. After setting the tray down, John poured coffee and held the crème aloft with a questioning glance. Sherman nodded and watched John turn the black coffee to the tempting shade of morning toast. Franklin leaned forward and lifted a porcelain dish that held a cranberry cake encrusted with brown sugar.

"Try one. They're delicious and so light they won't spoil your dinner."

"With pleasure, Doctor," Sherman said, as he lifted his cup in salute. "I always like to sweeten bitter moments."

On Friday morning, Gouverneur Morris proposed that the first element of the committee report be recommitted. King then went into matters that made Sherman wince. "The United States owns the Northwest Territory. Congress has made a compact with the settlers that as soon as the number in any state equals that of the smallest of the original thirteen states, it may claim admission into the union. Gentlemen, Delaware contains thirty-five thousand souls. Fifteen new votes may be added to the Senate, with fewer inhabitants than are represented by a single Pennsylvania vote."

Sherman thought this was too close to their covert negotiations with Congress. Someone had talked and triggered the delegates to consider the ramifications of a rash of new western states. Sherman understood what was going on. The western states could add population faster than wealth. If the South and their allies could get property into the equation, the new states wouldn't pose a threat for many years. Sherman wondered what Madison thought about his side violating his precious principles.

When they voted, Sherman lived up to his promise, and Connecticut joined six other states to pass the recommitment. The new committee membership reversed the bias of the prior committee. The members included Gouverneur Morris, Edmund Randolph, Rufus King, Nathaniel Gorham, and John Rutledge. All five men were on a mission to fend off the power of new states. Sherman marveled at how resolving one aspect of the government just raised another issue. He made a mental note to write Connecticut for more money. The summer had just begun.

Once the first clause had been sent to committee, Wilson and Mason proposed that they move directly to representation in the Senate. The gambit to bypass the money clause irked Sherman. Franklin saw the threat as well. He immediately said that Senate representation could not be debated by itself. The doctor abandoned his normally congenial manner to say quite strongly, "I refuse to vote for the propositions separately. I'll vote only on the whole report."

Mason, with exaggerated innocence, said, "Dear sir, I agree with your point and kindly suggest that the rest of the report be sent to the recently appointed committee. That way, all three propositions can be considered together."

Sherman bristled. They wanted to ride roughshod over his work with a committee of their own. Madison then interjected some of his maddening logic. He said that if the other two propositions were irrevocably connected to the one just sent to committee, they should all be sent to committee. If they weren't connected, then the remaining two propositions could be debated in any sequence. Despite the parliamentary maneuvers, Sherman's group forced the debate to the money clause.

Gouverneur Morris started. "All laws take money out of people's pockets. I've waited patiently to hear the good effects of the money bill restriction, but I've heard none."

Adjusting his spectacles with thumb and forefinger, Franklin spoke directly to Morris. "Public revenue bestows power to the people authorized to spend it. Money matters must be restricted to the immediate representatives of the people." Then, with a twinkling smile and dismissive wave of the hand, he said, "As to the danger that might arise from Senate backroom shenanigans, it can be easily gotten around by declaring that there will be no Senate."

These sharp remarks from the convention's most senior delegate led to an immediate vote on the money clause. If Sherman lost, the carefully crafted committee report would be gutted like a luckless mackerel pulled onto a Gloucester boat. Sherman exhaled a long slow breath when the convention voted five to three to keep the clause in the report. Three divided states signaled that their report had straddled that fine line where a proposal passes, but nobody goes away happy.

SHERMAN STEPPED INTO THE glare of the midafternoon sun and squinted until he could throw his left hand up to shade his eyes. As he descended the few steps leading to the broad sidewalk in front of the State House, Sherman recognized the soft, eager voice of Madison.

"May Mr. Wilson and I join you?"

"If we can find a piece of shade, I'd be delighted."

"Let's cross the street. We can stand under one of the trees next to the Coach and Horses."

"Please," Sherman said with an underhanded wave of the hand, "lead the way before this sun bakes me dark as a sailor."

Wilson looked miserable. With droplets of perspiration leaking from beneath his powdered wig, he said, "Yes, let's get out of this blasted sun."

The three men navigated the perilous crossing, somehow avoiding the carriages, wagons, horsemen, and hand-pulled carts. Madison led the way around the inn's guests who had cordoned off a piece of grass for lawn bowling. From the boisterous taunting of their opponents, it was obvious that the bowlers had drunk and wagered enough to make the game interesting. When they reached the shade of a tree, the pudgy Wilson was wheezing like he had just sprinted the State House yard. Despite his flushed face, heaving chest, and glistening brow, Wilson was still able to throw a disdainful glance back at the commoners, who bowled with more exuberance than skill. "Those ruffians have no idea of the seriousness of our work."

Madison pointed to a rough-hewn bench sitting under a tree further behind the inn. "Let's sit over there in the shade."

Wilson said, "You two go, and I'll see if I can convince some wench at this inferior inn to bring us cold lemonade."

"James doesn't suffer the heat well," Madison said.

"I noticed," Sherman said evenly.

Madison gave Sherman an appraising glance. Evidently detecting no mockery, Madison said, "We're not making progress."

"On the contrary, we've made excellent progress. You must allow other ideas to be woven into your design." Since Madison looked unyielding, Sherman tried logic. "With an equal vote in the Senate, a majority of states, as well as a majority of the people, will support public measures."

Madison disappointed Sherman by ignoring his comment. "Mr. Sherman, I've come to see you because you've directed this sad series of events. Can't we come to some accommodation that stops this endless bickering over representation?"

Before Sherman could respond, Wilson waddled over in a way that suggested he had developed a heat rash between his legs. "I'm promised that we'll soon be sipping a cool lemonade, but I'm not optimistic. The man looked brutish and in want of base intellect."

"I've just broached the subject with Mr. Sherman," Madison said.

Wilson gave a hopeful look at Sherman. "What say you? Is there no way out of this mire you've sucked us into?"

"We've already waded onto solid ground," Sherman said. "The committee report is a firm foundation for moving forward."

"The committee report is unjust, reprehensible, and engineered to the advantage of the small states," Wilson fumed. "If you think—"

Madison quickly jumped in. "Mr. Sherman, please excuse Mr. Wilson's anger. He had such high hopes for this convention. Now he sees everything at risk."

"Mr. Madison, do not apologize for me. I don't regret my comments."

"Perhaps you should just explain what you find objectionable," Sherman said.

"The domination of the most powerful arm of the government by the states," Wilson exploded. "Damn you and damn your blind loyalty to your precious Connecticut!"

"Please, we're not here to hurl insults," Madison said, his soft voice commanding more attention than a shout.

"What are you here for?" Sherman asked.

Madison answered, "You must surrender part of your state's autonomy."

"We already have. We insist on influence in only one legislative house in a government of three branches."

"That's enough to destroy the Federation."

"You believe the states need no protection?"

"From what threat?"

Sherman could not control his frustration. "I'll assume from Mr. Wilson's remarks that we're to speak our mind without reservation." Sherman shifted his gaze from Wilson to Madison. "Gentleman, you're hypocrites. You say the small states need no protection, yet your saintly cohorts argue for permanent supremacy for your states over the future western states." Sherman stood to leave. "Good day, gentlemen. You may see me again when you apply your precious principles to all Americans, both present and future."

As Sherman walked away, he overheard Madison mutter, "Damn Gouverneur Morris."

26

Saturday, July 7, 1787

Madison knocked on the door a third time. He guessed the owner was upstairs, but the heavy brass knocker should have reverberated all the way to his sanctuary on the third floor. Finally, he heard a noise, and the door opened to reveal a middle-aged man in an immaculate white smock.

"Yes."

"Good afternoon, Mr. Peale. I'm here to see Gen. Washington."

"See him another time." The man started to close the door.

"He told me to come at this appointed hour."

Peale hung his head around the partially closed door. "Then he was in error. I don't allow visitors at a sitting."

"Please check with the general."

"No."

"I'm sorry, but I must insist."

The man gave Madison a nasty look and then said, "Wait," before he slammed the door.

He would wait. When Washington set an appointment, he meant it to be met promptly. Charles Willson Peale's crabby nature didn't surprise Madison, because he had also sat for the celebrated portraitist. He turned to look down Chestnut Street toward the State House. The convention on Saturday morning had rehashed the same old arguments on both sides of the Senate suffrage issue. Madison tapped his foot. His alliance was unraveling. Only Virginia, Pennsylvania, and South Carolina remained firm. It had been a disappointing day, but Madison hoped that some states might switch back when emotion abated and reason reasserted itself.

The door reopened and Peale said, "Come."

Madison followed Peale up a dark, narrow staircase that creaked with every step.

"I visited your museum last Tuesday, Mr. Peale. Very impressive."

"My exhibit is public, my studio private."

"I apologize."

As Madison approached the stair landing, his nostrils flared from a stench of turpentine and linseed oil. A wave of nausea reminded him why, despite pleas from his father, he had avoided another sitting. The brightness of the studio always startled Madison. Whitewashed walls reflected the natural light that glared from several casement windows. In the middle of the room, a white linen cloth hung behind a shaft of light that fell from an overhead lightwell. Washington, sitting ramrod straight in a close-fitting wig, was dressed in his famed blue and buff uniform with three gold stars on each shoulder. The light beam that spilled from the glass-covered opening in the ceiling brought to mind the image of a saint awash in radiance.

Without comment, Peale moved to his work area and picked up a brush to test how much it had dried and stiffened. The canvas showed a sketched composition dominated by an oval destined to represent Washington's face. Everything but the artist's palette looked neat and ordered. Madison saw evidence of the meticulous nature that inspired Peale to collect and catalog an elaborate collection he exhibited at his museum near the State House. Differently sized brushes lay in orderly rows, and animal bladders filled with paint were arrayed with such precision that Peale could select one without looking. "My portraits cannot carry a chain of expressions," Peale said. "Keep your conversation brief."

"I'll strive to maintain my stoic reputation," Washington answered.

"General, sir, with all due respect, in the future, please do not schedule a meeting during one of my sittings."

"I shan't answer for fear my expression might change."

Madison suppressed a grin as he sat in a ladder-back chair against the wall.

"Why did you ask for an appointment, Jemmy?" Washington asked without turning his head.

"Sir, I'll get to the point," Madison said. "The convention provides only the punctuation for issues. The maneuvering occurs outside chamber doors."

"We've had this discussion. You'll no longer be excluded from our schemes."

"Thank you, but I have another request. I want to be assigned to committees."

Washington swiveled to look at Madison. A frustrated "Damn," escaped Peale's lips. "Jemmy, you've been excluded from committees to protect your health."

"I feel fit at the moment. I want to serve wherever I can be of benefit."

"You work incessantly."

"This opportunity will not come again."

"Yes, but——"

"I've complained in the past, but I can manage a committee assignment."

"And your journal?"

"I can manage."

Washington returned to his pose. "This is good news. You can add reason and balance to our committee work. Thank you."

Madison took the cue and stood to depart. "I apologize for the interruption, Mr. Peale."

"Please excuse my rudeness," Peale said midstroke. "I look forward to a commission to paint your portrait again. Perhaps later this summer?"

"I'll make a point of it. Good day, gentlemen."

ON MONDAY, GOUVERNEUR MORRIS delivered the committee's report. Washington sat on the short dais in full military regalia. Madison wondered if some of the delegates thought Washington intended to amplify his authority to encourage decorum. Most of them probably didn't know that after adjournment, the general planned to walk across the street for another sitting at Peale's studio.

Morris looked nervous. "Gentlemen, we've concluded that the first branch should comprise fifty-six members." He listed each state's allocation, and Madison instantly saw that the committee had skewed the numbers to the advantage of the South: thirty-one representatives for the nonslave states and twenty-five votes for the South. Not a majority, but certainly beyond what their population warranted. They could check legislation with only minimal support from the North.

"Secondly, if new states are created, the legislature shall possess the authority to regulate the number of representatives based on wealth and inhabitants."

Sherman stood, clasped his hands in front of his waistcoat, and spoke without a trace of enmity. Madison studied him. The man was driven by passion, yet he displayed less emotion than a worn-out harlot. "Could someone please explain how the committee settled on the numbers? They don't appear to correspond to any criteria discussed in this chamber."

Gorham tried to explain. "We used the number of whites and blacks, with some regard to property." Appearing uncomfortable, he soldiered on. "There were objections to membership based purely on population, because the legislature would grow very large, and western states might one day outvote our Atlantic states."

Paterson took the floor, and Madison braced for an angry onslaught. Instead, Paterson gave a terse response. "I considered the rules too vague." As he started to take his seat, he calmly declared, "New Jersey will resist the report." But before his posterior actually touched the seat, he bolted upright again.

"May I ask a simple question? In the sovereign state of Virginia, does a man hold a vote for each of his slaves? Or even for three-fifths of his slaves?" Paterson glared around the chamber. "No, gentlemen, he does not! We use representatives because it's impossible to gather all the people. But if such a meeting occurred in Virginia, would slaves attend? They would not! You don't allow Negroes representation in your own states, so why should we allow them to be represented in the general government?"

As he sat down, Paterson threw out a final challenge. "Please excuse my befuddlement, but could someone please explain the underlying principle to me?"

While Madison scratched out Paterson's outburst, Sherman moved that the report should be referred to yet another committee, one with a member from each state. Madison felt divided; his loyalty to the South conflicted with his foremost principle of proportional representation. This was where Sherman's obsession with equal suffrage in the Senate had driven them: dueling committees to apportion the other house. Principles once violated bred corruption.

Gouverneur Morris interrupted his thoughts. "The report is little more than a guess. I second the motion." Madison didn't know the inner workings of the committee, but if Morris could defect so easily, it must have been acrimonious. The assembly quickly passed the motion for a new committee, with only two nays. The new committee members included himself, Roger Sherman, Gouverneur Morris, Rufus King, Pierce Butler, and six other capable delegates. As the meeting adjourned, Madison realized that Washington had already kept his promise, but he had never imagined that another committee would be formed so soon.

As he stood to leave, Sherman caught his eye and gave him one of his quirky smiles. The meaning escaped him until he realized that this would be the first time in nearly two months that the two adversaries would work together. It was about time.

THE ONLY WAY TO reach the two small chambers facing the back of the building was through doors that opened from the Long Gallery. The governor of Pennsylvania occupied the room to the left, so Madison turned right and walked the ten paces to the Committee Chamber door.

Most of the eleven members sat around four tables that had been pushed together to form a large work area. Madison took an empty seat next to Gouverneur Morris, who looked agitated.

"Good afternoon, Gouverneur."

"We shall see."

"You sound unhappy."

"This business may never end."

"It must. I hate snow." This brought some tense laughter from around the table.

"Damn it, if you had stood by your committee's work, we'd be closer," Butler said.

Morris chose not to reply, so Madison spread out his papers and arranged his inkpot and quills. Soon all eleven members were present, and Butler said testily, "Let's get to work."

Sherman made a guttural noise and said, "I propose Gouverneur Morris chair the committee."

"Why?" Butler demanded.

"Because he was on the prior committee, and he can guide us around the shoals."

"That committee failed," Butler protested.

"I decline," Morris said, obviously peeved. "If you think someone from the prior committee can provide guidance, I nominate Mr. King."

Nobody spoke. Some looked around the table; others pretended to consult their papers. The mood frightened Madison. The muggy room didn't help, but at least on the second floor, they could open the windows to catch whatever faint breeze wafted above the hot streets. Nailing the windows shut in the Assembly Room seemed excessive when a few sentries could have kept eavesdroppers away from the building.

Finally, Sherman said, "I think Mr. King is a fine choice, and I second the nomination." Rufus King voiced no objection and quickly won the dubious honor.

Before King could set the order of business, Butler grabbed everyone's attention. "The South insists on security for her Negroes. They won't be taken from us."

"No one threatens that," Sherman said.

"Some gentlemen have a very good mind to do just that."

"Mr. Butler," Sherman said, "we all have special interests that warrant protection."

"The strength of America swells faster in the South," Butler exclaimed.

"Meaning?"

"This committee should award the South a larger proportion of representatives."

"You demand equality?" Morris asked, incredulous.

"I demand protection for my property."

Gouverneur Morris pushed his inkwell away, as if finished for the day. "This business has led me into a deep gloom. A division has been manufactured between the North and South, and the distinction is groundless."

"Groundless!" Butler grew red in the face. "We sit in the North. Go sit in the South and judge if it's groundless."

"Whether groundless or genuine, you persist in it. You'll not relent until you gain a majority in the public councils. You want—"

"We *demand* protection for our property."

"Now you demand protection for your peculiar objects; soon you'll demand war with Spain, which would threaten our commercial interests."

"Spain must be thrown from our frontier!"

"Damn you, sir, I'll vote for that vicious principle of equality in the Senate just to defend myself against your tyranny."

"Our tyranny? Good God, man, you've taken leave of your senses."

"I've come to my senses. Either this distinction between North and South is fictitious or real." Morris rose from his chair. "If real, we should take leave of each other."

"Gentlemen, please," Madison said. "First, we fight small against large, now South against North. The tactics remain the same: angry ultimatums, pleas to the emotions, threats to secede. We must return to reason. Both houses must be based on inhabitants."

"Then where's my security?" demanded Butler.

"And where's mine?" demanded Morris, thumping his wooden leg against the wood floor.

Everyone fell silent. Madison looked at Sherman, who wore the innocent expression of a fresh-scrubbed boy at his first day of school. Madison felt infuriated. "Gentlemen, please," he pleaded. "Let's assume for the moment that the protection you seek can be delivered by the Senate. Additional infractions shouldn't be imposed on the lower house."

"We voted to proportion the lower house based on the number of freemen, with slaves counted as three-fifths," Sherman said. "I suggest we proceed on that basis."

Butler looked as if a thought had just struck him. "Do you mean to count your blacks as full inhabitants?"

"All freemen should receive a full count," Sherman said in a surprisingly strong voice.

"Let's not pursue that issue," King interjected. "It's far too inconsequential."

"I agree," Madison said. "If we must argue, let's argue about something that matters."

Everyone looked warily at each other, but no one pushed to argue about the status of free blacks. Madison finally suggested a break, and everyone filed out of the room without comment.

"THERE'S SAFETY IN NUMBERS," Madison said with exasperation.

"There's confusion in numbers," Sherman said offhandedly, as he struggled with some long division.

The committee had cajoled, bartered, and negotiated until they had something they were willing to submit to the full assembly. Madison felt relief that the men in the room had put away their grievances for a few hours to concentrate on their task, using mechanics instead of emotion. Surprisingly, his strongest ally until now had been Sherman. They had settled on a ratio between North and South that was identical with that of the committee of five, except that they had shifted the weight from the Deep South to the perimeter states of Virginia and Maryland. So many representatives allocated to the South could not be justified, even if slaves were counted with the three-fifths rule, but North Carolina, South Carolina, and Georgia insisted on a disproportionate share of representatives. Shifting numbers around within the South was the most they would tolerate without threatening to leave the convention.

The Northern members acquiesced because Virginia had outlawed the slave trade, and Maryland usually voted with the North on commercial matters. The Southern states had acquiesced because of a further promise that would not be disclosed to the rest of the assembly until after the report had been approved.

Madison should have known that Sherman's newfound cooperative nature was too good to last. "Numbers cannot confuse; they're absolute."

Sherman looked up from his reckoning to display a streak of ink across his nose, "What are we talking about?"

"A larger legislature. One hundred and thirty. You must admit that it's more difficult to corrupt a majority in a large house. It's base arithmetic."

"Sixty-five is sufficient," Sherman said matter-of-factly as he went back to his calculations. "Doubling the number is too expensive. It's base arithmetic."

Madison found Sherman exasperating. He looked around for support, but he could see that the other committee members were exhausted and ready to return to their quarters. Pushing the issue further would be an error.

"All right," Madison said.

"Excellent," King said, showing more energy that he had in hours. "I move to adjourn."

TUESDAY SAW THE DELEGATES quibble over the committee report. All day they argued over the number of representatives assigned to each state. Several votes were taken to change the count for this state or that, but every one failed. Finally, unable to alter the allocation, the convention voted nine to two to accept the committee report as submitted.

Madison traded a nod with Sherman as they left the State House.

RANDOLPH OPENED WEDNESDAY'S SESSION with a proposal to require a periodic census to reassign representatives by state. This was the promised proposition that got the Deep South to agree to shifting representatives away from them to their brethren in Virginia and Maryland.

Mason provided the rationale. "A revision from time to time according to some standard is essential. Today, the North has a right to a majority, but possibly not in the future. Those with power do not release it. If the Southern states increase their population faster than the North, they may complain for generations without redress."

Pierce Butler then arrogantly violated their agreement. "I insist that blacks count equal with whites and therefore move that the word *three-fifths* be struck."

Mason leaped back up, speaking angrily. "I cannot agree to the motion, despite its being favorable to Virginia. It's wrong and..." Mason paused and then nearly yelled. "I don't regard Negroes as equal to freemen!"

When Butler declined to argue that blacks were equal to whites, his motion faded as quickly as a snuffed candle.

Sherman supported a census. "At first, I thought we should leave the matter to the legislature, but I've been convinced that the method of revising representation must be clearly stated within the Constitution."

Gouverneur Morris spoke, and Madison discovered that his fear of the West had deep roots. "If the West gets power, they'll ruin the Atlantic states. Let the representatives set their own membership. Surely, those who come after us can judge the present better than we can judge the future."

Gorham countered, "If we're perplexed, how can we expect a biased legislature to settle on a standard? This convention must set the rule."

Madison put logic back into the disjointed discourse. "The South fears a Northern majority, while the North fears a western majority. To reconcile the inconsistency, it would be necessary to imagine that points of a compass determine human character.

"When commerce is free, labor moves until competition destroys inequalities. For this reason, people swarm to less populous places—from Europe to America, from the Atlantic states to the western frontier. People go where land is cheap and labor dear. Since land has no value without labor, it seems clear that population is a sufficient measure of wealth and should be the sole basis for representation."

The vote to count slaves in the proportion of three-fifths failed six to four, with Connecticut voting aye. Rutledge exploded. "Some gentlemen wish to deprive the South of any representation for their blacks. If the North means to exclude them altogether, this business is at an end."

King showed unusual vehemence when he said, "If the South threatens to separate now, does anyone doubt that in the future she'll do the same? During the coming years, there'll be no time when she'll not say, do us justice or we'll separate."

The session ended on this sour note.

MADISON FOUND GOUVERNEUR MORRIS in the parlor of his home, reading a newspaper. The room displayed geometric patterns in bright yellow, sky blue, and watermelon red in both the carpet and the wallpaper. Madison felt as if he had stepped into a cheery spring day brought indoors.

"Gouverneur, I appreciate your time."

"I wish I could manufacture a twenty-five-hour day."

"While you're at it, please construct an eight-day week."

"Jefferson called us an assembly of demigods, but evidently God withheld the power to alter time from his diminutive cousins."

"And for good reason. If we held the power, the convention would change time at every whisper of the wind."

"True words, my boy. What's on your mind?"

"How old are you?"

"You came to determine my age?"

"I apologize, but everyone calls me 'my boy.' I'm small, but if I'm not mistaken, I'm older than you."

"No offense, Jemmy. I just meant to be friendly." Morris folded the paper and dropped it on the floor beside his chair. "I'm thirty-five, by the way."

"And I thirty-six."

"I thought you much younger."

Madison made a dismissive wave with his hand. "I came to talk about your unreasonable stand on the western territories. New states must be admitted on an equal basis."

"The South believes population will migrate to the sunnier climes, but they're wrong. Once Congress passes the Northwest Ordinance, the Ohio territories will explode with settlers. You said today that people go where land is cheap, but they want clear title. That's what this law will accomplish."

Madison hesitated. "You think the Ohio Valley will be ready for statehood soon?"

"Probably faster than we can finish this interminable convention."

Madison laughed. "I've made better progress with mud up to my axle."

"Listen, this scheme to resolve the Ohio territories will change the course of the country."

"New states must be admitted on an equal basis."

Morris leaned in. "You should spend time on the frontier. They're not Americans. In point of fact, they don't even speak English."

"We'll make them Americans. Just as our forefathers became American. Several delegates at this convention are foreign-born."

"You're an idealist."

Madison started to grow angry. "You won't budge?"

"I'll give it some thought."

"If you come around to my way of thinking, you may call me whatever you want."

"Then I won't remain completely immovable, or I'll have to call you Mr. Madison."

PINCKNEY OPENED THURSDAY'S SESSION with a new gambit. "South Carolina exported £600,000 sterling last year—all from slave labor. Will she be represented in proportion to this amount? No. Then she shouldn't be taxed on it. The Constitution must prohibit export taxes."

Madison's head jerked up. The South had evidently caucused and decided to insist that the Constitution prohibit export taxes. How much more could they demand?

Ellsworth responded by resurrecting the three-fifths rule with an added caveat that taxation would also be subject to the three-fifths rule. Butler seconded the motion. This told Madison that Connecticut and South Carolina worked together. Was there no end to these side deals?

The convention voted on representation in the lower house, and the committee recommendation passed. The clause provided for a census within six years and every ten years thereafter, and the census would count whites and three-fifths of blacks for the purpose of taxation and representation. While Madison had visited Morris to broker a better deal for new states, others had placed the final seal on the slavery conundrum. Madison suddenly realized that he had unconsciously avoided the subject. Now that he thought about it, he was content that others had wrangled out a solution.

By the time Madison caught up with his notes, he sat alone in the chamber. He looked around the stately room and wondered what the nation would think of their work in a hundred years. Would they understand the contradictions they had struggled to navigate? Would they understand their moment in time?

As he gathered up his materials, Madison knew that the kind of republic he wanted to build would never fathom the blemishes that had disfigured its birth.

27

Friday, July 13, 1787

Sherman stopped short of the tavern steps. When he looked up the street, he spotted Baldwin walking in his direction. Baldwin was the only person in this city that Sherman felt comfortable enough with to completely drop his guard and relax. After all the tense meetings at this very same establishment, he looked forward to simply enjoying their excellent food without politics on the menu.

"Roger, this is a grand alteration to our normal meeting place. Are the docks no longer good enough for you?"

"No further need for secrecy. Since the vote, everyone knows we're in league."

"Yes, I've felt the heat." Baldwin put his arm on Sherman's shoulder as they climbed the steps. "I appreciate your buying me a fine supper."

"I assumed you were buying."

"The obligation belongs to the debtor."

"I believe the duty rests with the supplicant."

"I asked for nothing."

"You begged for relief from your boorish delegation."

"If I'm to pay for our entertainment, then we must return to our former haunts."

"Since neither of us is rich or generously supplied by our states, I propose we split the cost of the evening."

"You ol' skinflint, is there nothing you won't barter?"

"Nothing … except possibly my wife. That I must think about."

"Think hard. Rebecca's the only valuable thing you possess."

"Let's go in. After a long winter, I crave fresh vegetables."

"You can have green things. I smell roast beef."

Sherman and Baldwin were shown to an elegant table set with willow-pattern china on an indigo blue tablecloth. A card at each place setting listed the night's offerings.

"Since I'm going to pay only half, I suggest we order a bottle of French wine," Baldwin said.

"Do we have something to celebrate?"

"Not today's session. I was bored into a stupor."

"We argued the fate of the empire."

"Raw wilderness is more like it. If rocks and trees don't keep a good man from making a go of it, then savages will take a turn at dashing a man's dreams."

A servant came to take their order. "What can I get you gentlemen?"

"Are the vegetables fresh?" Sherman asked.

"Yes, sir. Arrived by ship from Savannah this morning."

Sherman traded a smile with Baldwin. "It looks like we have an opportunity to support Georgia commerce."

Baldwin laughed. "I'll have the roast beef, a heavy portion. And a big stack of cornbread."

"And you, sir?"

"The same, only for me a heavy portion of vegetables."

"And to drink?"

"I'll let my young friend order; he's partial to French wine."

The servant inclined his head toward Baldwin. "We've received glowing reports on a new Bordeaux."

"That'll be fine," he said.

"May I bring you gentlemen water?"

"Where do you get it?" Baldwin asked.

"From far up the Schuylkill River. We bring it in daily and chill it."

"By all means." After the servant left, Baldwin turned to Sherman. "Now I know how the rich live. Fresh cold water brought in daily. I'll bet they even wash the goblets."

"Yes, with tainted well water."

"You scoundrel, don't spoil my evening."

"You may already have spoiled mine. You never asked the price of the wine."

"The wine's my treat. I just received a generous allowance from Georgia."

"I wish I could say the same. I write to no response."

"Our respective states know our worth."

"Jesting aside, I need money or I'll soon take food off my family's table."

"Then we must finish our business. Besides, I tire of being jailed up with a bunch of windbags in a sizzling oven." Baldwin started rocking his spoon with his middle finger, slapping the stem against his wrist. "Someone should explain to those rambling fools that you can't use the same kindling over and over."

"They think we're stupid. They believe if they explain things one more time, we might finally grasp the point. They fail to recognize that we understand but disagree."

"Blind bastards. I sometimes want to march to the front of the chamber, shake that prudish Wilson, and tell him that I don't need to hear any more of his sanctimonious preaching."

"In that case, I'm glad you were bored into a stupor. Safer for us all."

Baldwin stopped his nervous twitch with the spoon. "Roger, when will I get to go home?"

"The same question Rebecca asks me."

"Problems?"

"I have fifteen children, four still at home, the youngest two ill. I'm almost insolvent. In a fit of patriotism, I invested all my savings in worthless Connecticut bonds." Sherman looked into his friend's eyes. "Abe, Rebecca's a saint, not a martyr. She wants me home to put things in order."

"Can you blame her?"

Sherman tried the trick with the spoon but had no rhythm. "I must complete this business. It may be all I bequeath to my children."

Sherman thought a minute. "These things have their own rhythm." Roger picked up the spoon and showed it to Baldwin. "I'm a clumsy man. That's the real reason I'm not a boot maker." Sherman laughed. "Probably would have punched an awl through my palm. I don't have physical grace, but I possess a keen sense for the rhythm of politics." Sherman put the spoon down. "I have sad news for you. It will be some time before you get to go home."

"If we can get past the legislature, the rest should fall easily."

"We haven't sealed our bargain with New York." Sherman leaned across the table. "Hamilton returned last night. He brought someone with him—Manasseh Cutler."

"Cutler? That's good news, right?"

"One would presume so. He would not have made the trip from New York if he hadn't taken the bait."

"Then why can't we get this damn thing over with?"

"I'll push tomorrow morning for a vote on the entire legislative proposal, but that still leaves the executive and the judiciary."

Baldwin nodded and then said, "Any scuttlebutt on Cutler?"

"None I've heard. I presume he's meeting with Washington and Franklin."

"They've not taken you into their confidence?"

Sherman picked up the spoon and distractedly held it aloft, as if fascinated by his upside down image reflected on its shiny surface. "They want to come to an understanding amongst themselves first."

"Roger, I'm willing to struggle through new issues, but I fatigue at rehashing the same old ground. We backwoodsmen like the direct route. Chop down the trees, roll the boulders out of the way, and plow a future filled with plenty."

"First you must survey the landscape."

"And kill the Indians."

"Or bribe them to go elsewhere."

ON SATURDAY, SHERMAN TRIED to force a comprehensive vote. "I move that we consider the legislature on the whole: equality in the Senate, the money bill privilege, and the lower house proportionality. It is a conciliatory plan, and a great deal of time has been spent on it. If we alter any part now, we will have to go over the ground again."

Gerry surprised Sherman with an unusual proposal. "In the interest of progress, I offer an additional compromise. I propose that each state have two senators and that each vote independently."

Sherman sat straighter. This was an idea he could embrace. Give away something that has the appearance of substance, but in fact, changes nothing. He believed that the states could control their representatives.

King threw in another surprise. "In order to tie the states' allegiance to the new government, I propose that all state debts be absorbed by the national government, making one aggregate debt of about seventy million dollars."

Sherman guessed this suggestion came from Hamilton. It made sense, and his Connecticut bonds might again have value. He made a mental note to put this in a letter to Rebecca. It would lighten her concern if she thought he could do more in this chamber than at home to improve their financial future. After some additional squabbling, he was disappointed to see them adjourn without voting on any of the day's proposals.

SHERMAN CIRCLED FRANKLIN'S HOUSE to the rear courtyard and saw Hamilton sitting with the doctor. "Good afternoon, Doctor. Am I early?"

"Oh goodness, no. The others are scheduled to arrive in a half hour. I thought the three of us should talk privately first."

"Always a pleasure," Sherman said as he warily sat in a chair facing Franklin.

"Roger, the deal is struck." Franklin inclined his head toward Hamilton and added, "Alex has handled the negotiations to this point, but Cutler wants to hear from the leader of the opposition."

Without bidding, John brought Sherman coffee service. After the little ceremony, Sherman asked, "Doctor, if I may ask, do you have qualms about this?"

Franklin's normally good-humored countenance grew serious. "Every night. Yourself?"

"Every waking moment."

"It's late to bring up reservations."

"I'd suggest another approach, but I'm empty."

"Then we're of the same mind."

Hamilton shooed away a fly with a nonchalant flick. "Our contemptible Congress would never move solely due to an enlightened regard for the country."

Franklin gave Hamilton a pat on the forearm. "Alex, you never fail to offer a slice of gloom to temper my natural goodwill."

"We all have a role to play in this little drama."

"Indeed we do. But we're here to discuss Mr. Sherman's role."

Sherman set down his coffee. "That's why you called me here before the others arrived?"

"There are things we need to discuss." Franklin's eyes conveyed not a hint of their typical mirth. "Roger, I want your assurance that you'll add no new conditions."

"You fear I came to negotiate?"

"Cutler wants to get your measure. The general doesn't want you to view this as an opportunity to gain additional concessions."

"That's disappointing. I was going to ask for a two-horse buggy."

Franklin threw a sideways glace at Hamilton. "I apologize if I offended you."

"No need to apologize; we're engaged in politics." Sherman leaned back, crossed his legs, and tried for a relaxed pose. "You have my assurance."

"Excellent. I shall convey your assurance to Gen. Washington."

"More politics?"

"Yes, indeed. It's a pleasure working with a professional."

"What's the timing?"

"Congress will pass an ordinance in a week or so. We'll have to do our part in a session shortly thereafter. In the meantime, we'll pass your committee's full recommendation on Monday."

"Thank you."

"Roger, Virginia and Pennsylvania won't vote for the resolution. We have large delegations, and not everyone has been taken into our confidence."

"The committee report should still pass with six or seven votes."

"Five to four." Franklin spoke with finality. "Massachusetts will split, and the New York delegation will be conveniently absent. The price of Clinton's acquiescence."

"And you worry about new concessions from me?"

"Clinton doesn't want footprints."

"He wants more."

"We'll handle him." Franklin signaled closure on the subject by taking a huge bite of teacake that would occupy his mouth for a long moment.

There had to be more to this story. Governor Clinton had the most to lose from a strong central government. Persistent rumors hinted that he sought complete independence for New York. Sherman was certain Clinton was working dual strategies: tentative support for the union, while keeping his options open to strike out on his own.

"Anything not discussed previously?" Sherman asked Hamilton.

Hamilton looked at Franklin and received a nod. "Full concurrence required some sweetener. Gen. Arthur St. Clair, president of Congress, will be appointed governor of the Northwest Territory, and Colonel William Duer used his pivotal position in Treasury to become another sprocket in our wheel of intrigue."

"How?"

Hamilton placed both elbows on his knees and rested his chin against his folded hands. "Duer will loan the Ohio Company the money to finance the first payment, and in return he will be given a major interest in the companion Scioto Company. Both companies will be awarded their grants simultaneously. Congress will have previously set up a territorial government."

Sherman kept quiet for a moment. He expected personal accommodations and guessed that Hamilton had only disclosed the breaking water of this conspiratorial sea. Sherman knew St. Clair and Duer, and believed them capable, but seldom constrained by ethical norms. St. Clair brandished political power like a whip, and Duer alternately competed or partnered with Robert Morris for financial primacy. Manasseh Cutler looked wholesome in comparison.

"Your thoughts?" Franklin asked.

Sherman switched eye contact from Hamilton to the worldly old man. "Doctor, when you wade into a swamp, you encounter nasty creatures. One must find a way to survive them in order to get to the other side."

"May I say again that it's a pleasure working with a professional." Franklin offered an appreciative expression that said more than his words. Turning in the direction of the house, Franklin called, "Ah, Mr. Cutler, Mr. Gerry, welcome." Manasseh Cutler and Elbridge Gerry had emerged from the side of the house. Gerry, a representative from Cutler's state of Massachusetts, served as his guide. Sherman was surprised to see that Cutler was a small man who looked more like a bookkeeper than a land speculator.

Without rising from his seat, Franklin said, "Mr. Cutler, may I introduce Roger Sherman, a delegate from Connecticut."

"Good afternoon," Sherman said, as he rose and approached the two men with an extended hand.

Cutler shook with more strength than Sherman had expected. "Mr. Sherman, a pleasure."

Franklin made a grand wave, indicating that his guests should take a seat. "Among his many talents, Mr. Cutler is a scientist and a member of my little club, the American Philosophical Society."

Gerry took a seat and crossed his long legs at the thighs. "Mr. Cutler has been a lawyer, a physician, and a minister, as well as a scientist. His new career is land speculator."

Cutler bristled at Gerry's impolitic introduction. "If I may beg your pardon, I have no interest in speculation. I intend to build a new community of freemen, a civil society, absent the dishonesty, villainy, and extreme ignorance rampant here. Our first town, which we shall name Marietta, will be nestled along the Ohio River, and it will be built on pristine land with no wrong habits or rubbish to remove."

"Excuse me," Gerry said with his chronic head bob, "but it appears you may add dreamer to your curriculum vitae."

"A dreamer doesn't make things happen. I do."

Sherman shifted his posture slightly toward Cutler. "How was your trip?"

"Fascinating. Mr. Hamilton—"

"The Cincinnati extorted a price far beyond their contribution." Gerry refused to relent.

Cutler swung his head toward Gerry. "The Cincinnati received their just due. Others extorted tribute. Our selfless soldiers deserve the opportunity to build a family farm. Land renders a man secure against a bungling government."

The irascible Gerry had taken the conversation close to a flash point. This would not serve their purpose. Sherman threw a glance at Franklin and saw an uncharacteristic scowl. Before speaking, Franklin instantly manufactured a cheery expression. "Gentlemen, it does no good to damn the ingredients of a meal. We must consume it anyway. Mr. Cutler, you were saying your trip was enjoyable."

"Mr. Hamilton makes a captivating travel partner. Full of irregular opinions delivered with singular wit."

Franklin feigned shock. "Eight hours in a coach with Alex. You must be exhausted."

"I am, but not from the trip. I'm staying at the Indian Queen and conversed the night away with many of your delegates. I didn't retire until half past one and then rose early to breakfast at Mr. Gerry's. He then graciously took me on a tour of Philadelphia."

Grateful to have diverted the conversation to an innocuous subject, Sherman asked, "What parts of the city have you seen?"

"After a well-prepared breakfast with the delightful Mrs. Gerry, we visited the Peale Museum and the State House, and walked the streets. Tomorrow Mr. Hamilton has promised to take me to the botanical gardens of John Bartram."

Sherman saw Hamilton and Franklin trade knowing glances. The "delightful Mrs. Gerry" was seventeen years old and strikingly pretty. She presented a sharp contrast to her odd-looking husband, who appeared far older than his forty-three years.

"What're your impressions of the city?" Hamilton asked.

"With my interest in science, I was much pleased with the Peale exhibit, and I'm anxious to see the botanical gardens. The city bustles and throbs with people in a hurry to go God knows where. You must watch yourself when you cross a street, or you'll be squashed flat as yesterday's horse droppings."

"Yes, yes," Franklin said. "Look both ways and step with care. But whatever you do, don't venture across Race Street."

"My goodness, where's that?" Cutler asked.

"Actually it's Sassafras Street," Hamilton explained. "Notorious for young gallants racing their horses against all comers. They must maim one or two careless gawkers each day." The easy laughter erased the earlier tension, and Sherman hoped that Gerry would refrain from tossing a rude brickbat into the conversation.

Gerry seemed to read Sherman's mind and decided to engage in the light banter. "Mr. Cutler, what did you think of the State House?"

"I found the State House a noble building. Quite a fine example of Georgian architecture. I was disappointed to see the sentries stationed within and without."

"A fine building. The pride of our city," Franklin said, ignoring the reference to the guards. "Did you see the construction behind the State House on Fifth Street?"

"Yes, Mr. Gerry pointed it out and told me that it was to be our new home for the American Philosophical Society."

"Since your dues helped build the site, you must return as my guest when it's finished."

"I'd be delighted. I'll bring notes on the flora and fauna of the Ohio Valley."

"Excellent," Franklin said. "It would be a grand addition to our library. Ah, here's John. Would you gentlemen care for refreshment?"

Everyone agreed to chilled lemonade. John had started toward the house when Dr. Franklin politely interrupted his progress. "John, before you get the lemonade, could you bring out my specimen?"

"Of course, sir," John said without asking for clarification.

"Mr. Cutler, I have a very interesting specimen to show you. Something I'm sure you've never seen before."

"Good. I was afraid I'd be suffocated in boring political talk."

"We may get to that, but first I want to show off."

"I've seen almost everything."

"Do you like snakes?"

"I've cataloged every known species."

John returned holding a quart jar with both hands. As he approached, Sherman could see something coiled in a clear liquid. He would rather John had brought the lemonade. Franklin accepted the jar like it was a precious porcelain vase. John bowed quickly and, without a word, returned to the house to fetch their refreshments.

"Have you seen anything like this?" Franklin asked as he handed the jar to Cutler.

Cutler wore a bemused expression as he examined the garden-variety snake. Then he exclaimed, "Oh, my God!"

"Yes, an unusual specimen. A freak of nature."

Sherman craned his neck to get a better look but saw nothing unusual. Then he noticed something odd. "Does that snake have two heads?"

"Yes, two heads, one body," Franklin said with great pride.

Cutler turned the jar, peering hard. "Is this a trick?"

"No, it's as real as you having two feet."

"Will you sell it?" Cutler asked.

"I'm sorry, but it gives me too much pleasure."

"I'll pay a generous price."

"This oddity is priceless," Franklin said with a chuckle. "Poor dumb creature. It probably never knew whether it was coming or going."

"Perhaps not so dumb," Sherman said. "Two heads means two brains. Perhaps that jar holds a towering intellect among the community of snakes."

"Now that's a thought." Franklin laughed. "Two brains and nothing to do but slither about."

"Would two brains enlighten or confuse?" Hamilton asked.

"Confuse, I'm sure," Franklin said. "What if the snake approached a branch, and one head decided to go to one side, and the other started in the opposite direction? The ensuing bewilderment parallels our own convention. One faction demands—"

"Excuse me, sir," Hamilton interrupted, "I apologize, but I wish to remind you about our oath of secrecy."

"Of course, Mr. Hamilton. Thank you for saving a befuddled old man an embarrassing moment."

Sherman thought the admonishment unnecessary. Franklin was hardly befuddled, and his example was probably going in an innocent direction. Besides, Cutler seemed to be oblivious to the exchange, his attention focused on the jar. "I'll give you twenty sovereigns for the specimen."

Sherman sat back, interested to see how the great diplomat would handle this churlish proposition without damaging their delicate negotiations.

"Mr. Cutler, that's a fine offer. You tempt me, but unfortunately the specimen is already designated for my daughter in my will. I'm afraid she has her hat set for it. As much as I appreciate your generous proposal, I must live out my remaining days dependent on my daughter's good nature."

After a pause, Cutler said, "I can make the offer more generous."

"Oh my goodness, you embarrass me. But I'll keep it in mind. Perhaps one day my daughter may tire of it. So you intend to catalog the Ohio Valley?"

"It depends on our little pact. I look forward to new terrain."

Sherman saw the opening. "I'm sure everything will proceed along the lines that have been discussed."

"You're aware of the intricacies?"

"I am."

"And you're confident?"

"I am."

Cutler smiled and then said, "It's a shame I must hurry back to New York to snip a few loose ends."

Sherman wanted to probe further but knew better. He looked at Franklin and received the slightest of nods. The business portion of this meeting was over.

On Monday, July 16, Sherman's compromise passed just as Franklin had promised. No debate. No delaying tactics. Sherman suppressed a smile. He had won. Everything. The states would have an equal voice in the Senate. The lower house would be proportioned to the numbers his second committee had recommended. A census would be required every ten years to determine representation. The number of representatives must be adjusted to the census of inhabitants, with the three-fifths rule for "all others." New states would be admitted on an equal basis. Direct taxation would be tied to representation. Money bills originated in the lower house, and the Senate could not alter appropriations.

The impasse had been breached.

Sherman sighed. He scribbled out a note to Ellsworth that simply said, "We won!" Ellsworth turned from the page with a huge smile and started to extend his hand. Sherman gave a tiny shake of his head to ward off an unseemly celebration and turned his eyes forward to reinforce the message. Gloating would not be productive.

In short order, several mechanical resolves from the Virginia Plan passed in quick succession. Sherman felt the relief and renewed energy in the chamber.

Randolph didn't share the sense of relief. "The vote this morning embarrassed this assembly. I see no reason to discuss the subject further and move for adjournment so the large states can consult on this sad crisis." Randolph started to return to his table but stopped and looked directly at Paterson. "I suggest the small states deliberate on a means to conciliate."

Paterson could not contain his anger. "There will be no further conciliation from the smaller states. I agree with Mr. Randolph. It's high time to adjourn. I also believe that the rule of secrecy ought to be rescinded so we can consult with our constituents." Paterson slapped his notes against the table. "If Mr. Randolph will revise the form of his motion for an adjournment sine die, I'll second it with all my heart."

Sherman winced at Paterson's angry rejoinder. Adjournment sine die meant an adjournment with no specified day to reconvene—in effect, a permanent suspension of the convention.

Pinckney quickly asked, "Did Mr. Randolph mean an adjournment sine die? I wish him to know that if I go home, I'll not return to this ... place."

Randolph responded in his equivocal manner. "I never entertained an adjournment sine die. I merely recommended an adjournment until tomorrow. The large states need to decide on appropriate actions."

John Rutledge muttered in a voice strong enough to be heard throughout the chamber, "All that remains is for the large states to decide whether they capitulate."

Further progress seemed impossible, so the assembly voted to adjourn for the day. The room quickly bunched up into noisy clusters of men expressing their joy or anger. Sherman walked over and stood with his back to the northwest corner of the chamber, and soon all the small state delegates surrounded him in a tight, boisterous semicircle. Sherman held up both hands, palms out, to quiet their jabbering.

A quick exodus for the door signaled that the large states had arranged their meeting place. Sherman looked over the heads of his contingent and said, "The large states will meet at the Indian Queen. We'll go to the City Tavern."

"When?"

"Now." Sherman broke through the circle and walked to the exit. He didn't look to see if his troupe followed.

28

Tuesday, July 17, 1787

Madison alone remained seated. He shook his head, and the word *pandemonium* sprang to mind. The big state delegations had met yesterday, to no avail, and then quickly broke into tribes of angry men. They had decided to try again in the State House chamber prior to today's session, but heated exchanges had accomplished nothing. Now the delegates stood in different parts of the room quarreling, their arms flailing, looks stern, voices a touch too loud. Madison despaired. The convention would either dissolve or recommend a fatally flawed system. Which would it be?

"Gentlemen, please! Gather round!" Gouverneur Morris boomed over the noise. "This bickering resolves nothing. We must agree on a course of action."

Madison stood to reinforce Morris's plea. Gradually, the delegates gathered in a tight circle.

"To what use?" Wilson demanded.

"We'll accomplish nothing in splintered groups," Morris said. "Capitulate to their extortion or unite on our own: that's the decision before us."

"We discarded uniting on our own last night," Hamilton said in exasperation.

"Why weren't you here for yesterday's vote?" Wilson demanded.

"Not important," Hamilton said.

"The hell it isn't!" Wilson barked.

"Clinton pulled Yates and Lansing back to New York. I don't have the authority to cast the New York vote by myself," Hamilton said. "Can we proceed to something relevant?"

"I don't agree that we discarded any options last night," Randolph put in.

"Strong political forces won't abide a partial union," Hamilton said.

"Where's Washington?" Mason demanded.

"He doesn't share our uncertainty," Hamilton answered.

"Then he should elucidate his certainty for us," Mason said with uncharacteristic anger.

"One man cannot dictate the design of our government," Wilson said

"The rules allow reconsideration," Madison interjected. "Perhaps we should move forward until a more opportune time."

"Surrender?"

"Withdraw—for the moment," Madison suggested.

"We're approaching this backwards," Gouverneur Morris said. "We're defining the structure and then the powers. We should define the powers and then design a system to administer those powers." Thumping around on his wooden leg, he added in disgust, "After yesterday's vote, bias will infect questions concerning the powers of the three branches."

"We can't start over," Wilson said.

"We can," Randolph cried. "Let's quit this convention."

"And when will we get together again. Next summer?" Madison asked. "We must act now."

Some delegates had drifted into chairs, while others remained standing. Madison didn't like the mood. The delegates wavered between fatalism and belligerence. Even Mason had abandoned reason. Madison noticed Sherman and Dickinson wander into the chamber and take a seat near the back. Damn. They should have met in a private room.

"If you think we can alter the plan later you're mistaken." Mason seemed oblivious to their new visitors. "The little states will never relent. Ever!"

Wilson looked as if he had come to some internal reconciliation. "Perhaps state equality in only one house isn't so bad."

"I can't believe my ears!" Randolph screamed. "What have we been fighting for?"

"A republic." Wilson's voice carried a note of hopefulness. "Perhaps we've been too focused on past mistakes."

A sudden stillness gripped the men. A few shuffled in indecision, while others gradually rose to their feet.

"What are we going to do?" Mason asked quietly.

After another long silence, Madison said, "Let's see where the day takes us."

No one offered another option, so the caucus decided to take a short break prior to the start of the regular session. Madison left immediately to beat the others to the privy. He wanted to spend any spare time making notes, not standing in line. As he passed Sherman and Dickinson, heads bent together in muted whispers, he knew that they had overheard nothing that would give them pause. Madison reached the privy first and quickly unbuttoned his trousers. As he started to urinate, he heard the door open behind him.

"We must defrock the Senate."

Without turning, Madison said, "You think we can push forward?"

Wilson positioned himself at the station next to Madison. "I saw you bolt and realized you had the right priority." He sighed with relief. "Too much tea this morning."

"The Senate?"

"Let's move to fresh air."

Madison opened the door and stepped into a crowd of about twenty delegates. The eager shuffled in line, while the long-suffering hovered in drifting conversation and tobacco smoke.

"Let's wander into the yard," Wilson suggested.

After they had walked a few paces, Madison said, "You seem calmer."

"Resigned."

"You believe we can still devise a good system?" Madison asked.

"Adequate."

"How?"

"We must shift power from the legislature to the executive and judiciary."

"A stronger executive scares people."

"Legislative tyranny inflicts the same pain as a despot."

Madison feared an overreaction would tilt unwisely in favor of the executive. "The legislature must hold dominion over lawmaking."

"Adjustments can be made."

"Where?" Madison asked.

"Appointments, revisionary power, selection of the executive. Other nuances will surface."

"You no longer support the Virginia Plan?"

"The Virginia Plan has been violated. You can't restore a maidenhead."

"An errant loss of virginity doesn't compel licentious behavior."

Wilson gave Madison a condescending look over the top of his glasses. "A path once chosen leads in a single direction."

Madison glanced toward the State House. "Everyone has reentered. We need to go."

"Very well. But think. It's your strongest skill."

"Let's see where the day takes us."

MADISON OPENED THE REGULAR session with a series of arguments in support of a veto over state laws. He stopped his customary pacing to conclude, "Gentlemen, the power to veto improper state laws is the mildest way to preserve harmony."

After some additional discussion, Madison was disappointed to see that the power to revise state laws failed three to seven. Martin then magnanimously offered a sound alternative. "Legislative acts of the United States shall be the supreme law and the several states shall be bound by these laws." Madison was pleased to see this alternative agreed to with no objection. It didn't give a clear veto of state laws, but it allowed the national legislature to override state laws. With the legislative powers issue resolved, the debate shifted to the method of electing the executive.

Gouverneur Morris remained edgy. "I'm against an executive chosen by the national legislature. If the legislature can appoint and impeach him, he'll be their lackey. Election by the legislature can only result in intrigue similar to the election of a pope by a conclave of cardinals. I move to strike out 'national legislature' and insert 'citizens of the United States.'"

Mason continued to argue for the national legislature to pick the executive. Madison put down his quill. Mason plied the waters he knew, oblivious to the fact that the rest of the fleet had changed course. Madison believed Mason had not yet grasped the irreversibility of Senate suffrage. Beyond being a sound republican principle, election of the executive by the people truncated Senate power.

"Gentlemen," Madison said, "it's essential that legislative, executive, and judicial powers remain separate and independent. Judges are not appointed by the legislature because they might pander to the legislature, whose laws they interpret. Likewise, if the legislature appoints the executive, it infringes on the execution of laws."

Madison was disappointed to see election by the people overwhelmingly defeated by nine to one. Martin then proposed that electors, appointed by state legislatures, should choose the executive. Madison appreciated Martin's new-found pliancy, but that motion failed as well. Another vote reconfirmed the Virginia Plan's proposal that the executive should "be chosen by the national legislature."

Sherman surprised Madison by proposing to strike the clause that prohibited the executive from a second term. Madison was wary of Sherman and felt uncomfortable when he made unexpected moves. Sherman was like a crafty chess master who inexplicably moved a peripheral pawn. The wise opponent paused until he figured out the endgame.

Gouverneur Morris charged ahead, undeterred by this left-handed move. "I agree. An executive who can't seek office again will make hay while the sun shines."

Sherman's motion passed, and the delegates called it a day.

He had chosen to take a walk instead of immediately returning to the Indian Queen. Madison examined his feelings. Wilson told him to think, but his emotions were what puzzled him. He felt devastated that Sherman had won equality in the Senate, but the new sense of progress elated him. Perhaps he had been too strident. Wilson had a valid point, if not taken to an extreme. Something might still be made of this hodgepodge if powers were shifted to the executive and judiciary. Fear of a monarch had restricted using the executive to hold the legislature in check, but perhaps a settled structure permitted a fresh look at balancing power between the branches. He had to examine everything anew. Securing the popular election of the executive was a prerequisite. He decided to fight for this deviation from the Virginia Plan.

Madison considered Sherman's strategy. The man thought several steps ahead and apparently had figured out that the opposition would strive to shift power to the executive from the legislature. So he pushed for multiple terms. Sherman intended to use fear of a monarch as a defense. An executive with too much power could ensure his reelection by the ruthless use of favors and patronage.

Looking ahead, Madison saw a noisy crowd and an image that tested his sense of reality. A two-story building appeared to be casually strolling down the street. He quickened his pace to investigate the aberration. He discovered that a house undeniably traveled down the center of the city street, but ten strapping horses dragged the uprooted structure. The crowd of spectators had hidden a crude frame with huge wooden wheels that freed the house from its normally moored state. Somehow the house had been hoisted onto this contraption, and the horses, escorted by six whip-wielding men, were rolling the house to a new lot, where it presumably would behave itself and stay put.

Madison spotted Pinckney and sidled over to him. "Good afternoon, Charles."

"A good afternoon would be ten degrees cooler."

"The heat seems relentless."

"Like our bickering."

"Have you ever seen anything like this?"

"I never imagined anyone would be stupid enough to move a house."

"Damn clever, I think."

"Clever? All this trouble to save a clapboard eyesore."

"It still has utility."

"So do the Articles. Yet you don't hesitate to tear them down to build afresh."

"This is a solid house, not a cobbled expedient. It can still provide service."

"For someone beyond Seventh Street, I would hazard."

"Don't they deserve a place to live?"

Pinckney expression showed disdain. "You propose that *they* should elect our chief executive?"

"I do."

"Foolish." Pinckney looked at Madison. "Tell me, where do your loyalties lie?"

"I beg pardon."

"To the big states or to the slaveholding states?"

"To a republican system."

"You're evading the question."

"I don't understand the question."

"James, you lost the big state battle. It's time to show your loyalty to the South, your home—and your way of life."

"You want me to defend slavery?"

"I want you to shed your hypocrisy."

"You say that without your normal droll note."

"I'm quite serious."

"Then I'm quite offended."

"Be that as it may, you must come to your senses. Without slaves, Montpelier would go under. Your countrymen insist on your allegiance."

"Insist? My family's plantation depends on slaves, but that doesn't obligate me to protect an institution I abhor."

"Slavery has been around since the beginning of mankind."

"You want me to speak out for slavery?"

"Deeds trump words. You live well off the labor of slaves. Preaching abolition will not bestow absolution."

"Good day, Mr. Pinckney."

Madison whirled and hurried away. What had riled Charles? He had never assaulted him that way, at least not with a mean spirit. Fear. The South smelled a threat to slavery. The Northwest? Cutler's deal struck terror into the slaveholding states, but the South got a good piece of the bargain, and equality in the Senate provided a sturdy bulwark. Something else. Revisionary power? They feared the power to negate state laws. He had spoken out in support of revisionary power that very day.

Madison slowed his angry pace. His intent was to control the unruly state legislatures that issued paper money, extracted tribute from neighboring states, and caused all sorts of mischief. His target had been the North, but his grapeshot could easily splatter the South. Having figured out the cause of Pinckney's anger quieted his intellect but did not ease his emotional torment. The charge of hypocrisy hurt. Montpelier did depend on slavery. He lived a rich and comfortable life, so comfortable that he could dedicate his life to scholarship and government systems.

Indeed, "Deeds trump words." What could he do? Nothing. At least nothing while his father was alive. What would he do when he inherited Montpelier? His heart thumped and he felt faint. Madison hurried his pace. He needed shade, a cool drink, and time to catch up on his notes. Yes, he had to scribe the day's session, and he owed Jefferson a letter. He would find time to think about this later.

WEDNESDAY MORNING STARTED WITH the judiciary. The Virginia Plan called for appointment by the Senate. With the Senate safely in state hands, the small states now supported the Virginia Plan, while the big states wanted executive appointment. Gouverneur Morris's fear of bias had already surfaced. Delegates shifted positions like a gusty wind whipping around a courtyard, and Madison feared that the sundry details could keep them here for many more weeks.

Mason started with a reasonable point. "The mode of appointing judges should depend on the mode of executive impeachment. If the judges form a tribunal for impeachment, then the executive cannot appoint them."

Dickinson jumped in with a rare display of emotion. "Talk about impeachment is nonsense. It'll be near impossible to punish an executive for misdeeds."

Madison wanted to press their goal to weaken the Senate, so he offered the first compromise that popped into his head: judges appointed by the executive had to be approved by two-thirds of the Senate.

Sherman surprised Madison by speaking in support of the compromise, but the vote was postponed until the next day.

The debate moved to the guarantee of a republican government for each state. It should have been simple, but some objected that it might preclude the use of force to put down rebellions. Madison lamented that Shays's Rebellion skewed the debate away from sound principles.

Wilson proposed a compromise that everyone accepted: "a republican form of government shall be guaranteed to each state and that each state shall be protected against foreign and domestic violence." Wilson's wording permitted the national government to put down insurrections and override tyranny imposed at the state level. The convention used this high point to adjourn on a positive note.

"JEMMY, QUICK, JUMP IN the coach." Gouverneur Morris sat in a hired coach, propping the door open with his wooden leg.

"Where're you going?"

"Sassafras Street. The general commandeered a thoroughbred from Robert Morris and intends to race any devil-may-care with a fat purse."

Madison hopped into the coach and squeezed between five other delegates. He looked across at Hamilton. "What's the general thinking?"

"He's thinking fun," Hamilton said. "Horse racing and gambling are two of his favorite pastimes."

Gouverneur Morris chuckled. "And I'll enjoy pocketing some dupe's coin."

Everyone shared a laugh except Madison. "The appeal escapes me."

"Jemmy, my boy," Morris said. "Racing's a basic impulse of the human species. Since the beginning of time, if it moves, someone wants to race it. Whether it's on foot, on hoof, or on wheels, people enjoy contests of speed. Especially our dear general."

Hamilton slapped the roof of the carriage and yelled, "Faster, driver! A quarter doubloon if you get us there in five minutes!"

Madison heard the crack of a whip and the scream of a pedestrian as the coach lurched forward and bounded along the cobblestones at breathtaking speed. Madison grabbed a leather strap hanging from the roof and held on for dear life. Their destination was the northern edge of the city. The official name, Sassafras Street, had been supplanted by the nickname Race Street due to the rowdy pastime that had claimed the dirt road.

In less than five minutes, the coach came to a slow roll. Hamilton stuck his head out and said, "Word's out. The street's clogged with foot and carriage traffic. Let's walk."

The men tumbled from the coach, and Hamilton made good his promise to the driver. The streets were packed with people in a frenzied gay mood, all moving north in a hurry. Madison and his friends joined the throng and eventually elbowed their way onto Race Street. At first, it looked like bedlam, but once they squeezed by the ruffians, the street peddlers, and the merely curious, they spotted Washington astride a mount about a block ahead.

By moving to the center of the street, they were able to walk quickly toward their leader. For once Madison appreciated the heat because it had baked the horse-droppings dry and odorless. On second thought, it made him wonder about the fine dust being kicked up. He pulled a handkerchief to wipe the grime from his watery eyes and then held it in front of his mouth as he squinted against the onslaught of sun and grit.

Before they had closed half the gap, a man intercepted them and shook a bag of coins in their face. "Wager?"

"How many contestants?" Hamilton asked.

"Four, but separate races."

"Odds?"

"Two to one against the ol' man in the first race. Straight up for the second two."

"Do you know who that old man is?"

"Of course. Jared Ingersoll can't gather a crowd this size."

"Yet you set the odds against Gen. Washington."

"The general knows how to flog men, but that doesn't mean he can flog a horse. These boys are here most afternoons, and your general has matched against the best. Besides, by the third race, his bonny mare will be tuckered."

"How're the bets going?"

The man shrugged. "You'll bet the general—like the other delegates and sightseers."

"And the experienced betters?"

"How much do you wish to wager?"

Hamilton turned to give his companions a knowing smile. "Ten sovereigns."

The bookmaker scratched his chin. "A rich bet. On most days beyond my means, but—" He waved his hand over the crowd. "Let's see the coin."

After everyone but Madison set a bet, the men moved further down the street toward the champing horses.

"You didn't place a wager," Hamilton said.

"I don't gamble."

Hamilton laughed. "This is no gamble."

"Nothing's sure."

Gouverneur Morris looked over his shoulder. "This is, my boy. As sure a thing as you'll encounter. The general has the best riding seat in Virginia, and Robert Morris paid a princely sum for this mare. These boys will get a rude lesson from that ol' man."

"We have another edge," Hamilton added.

"What's that?"

"The general doesn't like to lose."

As they approached the starting point, Madison's attention was riveted on Washington's mount. He had never before seen such perfection. All the horses in the Robert Morris stable were first-rate, but this one looked like Michelangelo had sculpted it as the rightful companion for David. The shimmering red coat highlighted smoothly delineated muscles that looked taut and ready for the slightest nudge of the heel. As the well-groomed mare pawed at the ground, she occasionally threw her head in disdain for all those about her.

It took a while for Madison to notice Washington. He sat in calm dignity, seemingly oblivious to the pandemonium or the side-strutting horse beneath him. He wore a blue and buff trouser suit that carried a military hint but fell short of a uniform. Both man and horse clearly were in command of their purview.

Madison regretted not placing a wager.

"The man's in love."

"What? Who?"

Gouverneur Morris rollicked in laughter. "The general. I've never seen him so smitten."

"With whom?"

"The mare, of course."

"Oh."

"Robert had an agent buy her in Maryland. She arrived this week, and it was love at first ride. The general would mortgage Mount Vernon to get her, but Robert won't sell."

"She looks strong. Can she win three races?"

"The second two will be easy, if she can win the first one," Morris said, as he pointed at the challenger.

For the first time, Madison noticed the rider next to Washington. The small-framed boy could not have been more than seventeen, and he appeared over-matched. Looking nervous amongst all the commotion, he had a hard time controlling his wiry horse that stood two hands shorter than his rival's mount. His brown trousers, open-necked white shirt, and scuffed saddle contrasted with the general's proper attire and shiny black tack.

"You've seen him race?"

"That boy keeps me in tavern money," Morris said. "He and his horse may look common, but they run with uncommon speed."

"Did you bet on him?"

"Heavens, no. I wouldn't want to be seen collecting a wager against the general."

"But you think it'll be close?"

"The edge goes to the one with the greatest will to win. And they're equally matched in that category."

"Are you talking about horse or man?"

"Both, my dear boy. Both."

Suddenly, a man stepped in front of the two riders waving a handkerchief. The skittish horses snorted and stepped back, away from the flag-waving starter. Two other men ran down the road, shooing people out of harm's way. The race was about to begin. Everyone was shouting and cheering as a path cleared, and the mob surged back and forth as people strove for a place to see. Madison was shoved to the side and found himself separated from his friends.

As things grew almost hushed, the starter yelled, "Riders, get ready!"

Washington, if possible, grew even more still, his body posed slightly forward with his weight carried in the stirrups.

The starter raised both arms and held steady for a moment. The boy's horse seemed to settle on his rear legs and snorted with checked energy.

The starter's arms dropped.

The horses bolted. Hoofs flew, dirt sprayed, people yelled, and Madison found himself pushed and shoved as spectators fought to get a view of the riders dashing down the lane. He couldn't tell who led, but the cheering grew strident as the riders approached the finish. In what seemed like an instant, the race was over.

Madison looked around but saw nobody he recognized. Then he spotted the looping gait of Gouverneur Morris, fifty feet down the street. How could a man with one leg move so fast? Running, Madison caught up with Morris and realized that everyone was sprinting toward the finish.

"Who won?" Madison panted.

"Well, Jemmy, my boy, I think the general, but I'm guessing."

"From the cheering?"

"The people do love their hero."

Soon, the sea of people parted, and Gen. Washington emerged, trotting his horse back to the start line. The closed-mouth grin confirmed that he had won the race. Dozens of men raced alongside him, patting the horse, leaping to pat the general, or, if blocked by other well-wishers, they just patted each other on the back.

Madison decided he liked horseracing.

MADISON AND THE OTHER delegates decided to walk back to the Indian Queen. The commotion was too maddening to attempt to hire a coach. Gouverneur Morris had been right: Washington won the second two races easily after nosing out the first contest.

Hamilton tossed a bag of coins from hand to hand. "Easy money." Then with a laugh, he said, "I think Jemmy should buy dinner."

"I didn't bet."

"Penalty heaped on punishment. A Puritan tradition."

"We're not in New England, nor am I a Puritan. I trust you'll be a gentleman and part with one or two of your sovereigns."

"Very well, the night's entertainment is on me. I haven't played host in a while."

"If that is the measure," Morris said, "it would be your turn for the next two weeks."

"Gentlemen, my duty is not to pay but to entertain you poor souls and bring cheer into our little conclaves."

"Indeed. Every evening, I look forward to your relentless pessimism."

"Bah! You're a good-natured beast, Mr. Morris, but you need reminding that the common man carries a bag of faults he tosses to the wind with no discernible pattern."

"Man sins, but he can also be noble," Madison said, halfheartedly.

"As we prove with this convention," Hamilton said. "A noble enterprise, nobly achieved."

Morris looked irritated. "It *is* a noble enterprise. Perhaps not nobly achieved, but we'll achieve it nonetheless."

"We're not finished yet," Madison said.

"Don't worry, Jemmy. You shall have your republic."

Madison glanced at Morris. "What makes you so confident?"

"The general doesn't like to lose."

29

Wednesday, July 18, 1787

"How is Mrs. Sherman?"

"Lonely."

Sherman had returned late to his boardinghouse. As on his first night in her home, Sherman had found Mrs. Marshall knitting in the parlor. She beckoned him with a two-handed wave of indigo yarn and said, "Come in, Mr. Sherman. Sit a spell."

"Thank you." Sherman took a seat in an opposing chair positioned in front of the dead fireplace. "What're you knitting?"

"A cap. I have someone who sells them for me on Market Street."

"Isn't it a bit hot for a knit cap?"

Mrs. Marshall dropped the skewered heap of yarn into her lap. "Mr. Sherman," she said in an exasperated tone, "I thought you were a smart man. In the winter, I tat lace for summer sale."

"The house doesn't support you?"

"Boarding has been good this year, but a little extra never hurts. Besides, I enjoy ending the day with handiwork. It soothes me, and this room seems cool after a day by the hearth."

"You're an excellent cook."

"And I knit a tight cap—along with other talents." She set her knitting aside and bounced out of her chair. "Brandy? My treat."

"Thank you. That would be a tidy end to an unkempt day."

"Difficulties?" Mrs. Marshall asked as she handed him an expensive snifter that looked like Stiegel glass.

After she had settled into her chair, Sherman said, "Not exactly. Just the drudgery of a herdsman entrusted with a flock that tends to wander."

"How long before you return home?"

"Perhaps a few weeks."

"Then we'll soon know what you men have dealt us."

Sherman took a sip and discovered that the expensive goblet held a middling brandy. "What've you heard?"

"That you bicker and haggle like old women."

"The purpose of politics is debate."

Mrs. Marshall raised an eyebrow. "Debate?"

Sherman shrugged.

"Well, I hope you fix the money problem."

"I'm optimistic on that score."

"Good. That'll make it easier to run my house."

Sherman put his glass on the side table. "Mrs. Marshall, I apologize, but can you wait a few more days for our board?"

Mrs. Marshall leaped out of her chair, exclaiming, "Oh my!" She scurried out of the room. "I think the letter you're expecting arrived." She returned a moment later, carrying a smile and a post.

After Sherman sliced open the envelope, he grew his own smile. "I'll pay our delegation's arrears tomorrow."

"You received a draft?"

"Yes, Connecticut has appropriated an extension of our allowance."

"I'm happy for you. I know you worried so."

"Thank you for your patience." Sherman put the draft in his coat pocket. "I hope you didn't assume any debt on our account."

"Never. Too many people I know have taken up residence at the Walnut Street prison."

"I never would've let that happen to you."

"Mr. Sherman, *I* never would have let that happen to me."

Sherman, taken aback by the strident tone, didn't reply. In a slightly more relaxed voice, she said, "Debt is a vice I do not abide."

"Your husband?"

"When he died, it took me two years to pay off his debts. I sold most of my fine furniture and accessories." She made a dismissive wave at the fireplace. "Instead of chalkware figurines, that mantle used to display an ormolu clock and a pair of Sèvres vases." Mrs. Marshall tossed her hair. "Long gone."

That explained why a few expensive pieces sat among the mostly tattered furnishings. Sherman glanced at the mantel that still held Mrs. Marshall in a wistful trance. She sat quiet a minute and then met his eyes to explain. "My husband thought money should always be in motion, his and any sitting idle in another man's purse. I was ignorant of his dealings until the strain put him in an early grave. After I put his books in order, I swore to keep a clean ledger."

"You manage the house well."

"Thank you. I make the most of it. It's all I received from my husband's estate ... besides a drawer full of worthless bonds."

"You own Pennsylvania bonds?"

"So does Howard."

"Howard?"

"What surprises you? That a Negro had money or that he supported the Revolution?"

"Both I suppose. Stupid of me."

"We pay Howard a fair wage, and he believes in that document you signed."

Sherman took another sip of brandy. "All men created equal ... not self-evident to everyone."

"Nonetheless true."

Sherman felt humbled. He made a decision. "Don't sell your bonds."

She leaned forward, as if joining a conspiracy. "The new government is going to honor war debt, isn't it?" Sherman conveyed nothing in word or expression. "May I tell Howard?"

"Yes, but no one else until the convention concludes."

"Speculators have stepped up their purchase of old bonds."

"Guesswork at the moment. At least, I hope." Sherman had second thoughts. "Make sure Howard understands you must keep this to yourselves."

"Don't worry. More happens in this house than you think. Nothing has escaped."

Sherman relaxed a little. "Tell me your best boarder story."

Mrs. Marshall laughed with genuine gaiety. "Tawdry tales should be shared only with intimates. But we'll see. I do appreciate the advice. You gentlemen may have done a proper job. Now, if you could only make my western lands valuable."

"You own western lands?"

"Mr. Marshall threw money in every direction."

"Sell it."

"What? Sell my land and hold my paper." Mrs. Marshall took on a mocking tone. "Mr. Sherman, are you rich? Should I heed your advice?"

Sherman laughed now. "No, I foolishly put my money into Connecticut bonds."

"Then why should I listen to you?"

"Listen to Adam Smith. He said the price of anything is the toil and trouble it takes to acquire it. Squatters take all the land they want with no toil, no trouble."

Mrs. Marshall looked dubious. "Are you saying that the value of western lands will never swell?"

"Not in your lifetime." Sherman saw annoyance flash across her face. Figuring it was the indirect reference to her age, he added quickly, "It'll take a hundred years to populate a boundless frontier. Emigration is restricted by the number of ships at sea."

"Everyone buys western lands."

"Passion makes people do foolish things."

"Indeed."

Sherman became wary of her coy smile. "Did you ever hear about the tulip rage in Holland?"

"It went bust."

"And so will this craze. When this bubble bursts, many prominent people will become neighbors of your friends on Walnut Street."

Mrs. Marshall sat a moment and then said, "I'll consider your advice."

Sherman stood up and didn't bother to stifle a heavy yawn. "Excuse me, but I must get to bed." He gave her what he hoped was an engaging smile and said, "Since I was unable to pay my board until this evening, you may give the advice the weight it deserves."

Mrs. Marshall also rose. "I'll give it the weight due a wise and good man." She picked up the two brandy glasses, hesitated, gave Sherman a direct look, and then asked, "Mr. Sherman, are you lonely?"

"Don't tell Mrs. Sherman, but I'm far too busy. Good night … and thank you for the brandy."

ON THURSDAY MORNING, SHERMAN and Ellsworth wandered into the already stuffy State House chamber. Ellsworth arranged his papers for a moment and then asked, "What's our plan for today?"

Sherman became distracted when he saw several delegates migrate to a corner. Keeping an eye on them, he said, "I'd prefer a shorter executive term."

Ellsworth looked uncertain, but Sherman barely noticed. He continued to watch as delegates meandered around to bid good morning and chat with friends. He judged the mood businesslike, with no sign of frenzied exchanges driven by high emotion. Good. Perhaps he could get home shortly.

Gouverneur Morris started. "We must make the executive strong enough to pervade every corner of this vast land. If the executive is impeachable, some demagogue will hold him hostage."

Sherman didn't understand why Morris was against impeachment. As a judge, putting the executive beyond the reach of the law grated against his hardest-held convictions.

Gouverneur Morris thumped around and then delivered an oratory flourish he hoped would close the issue.

"If the executive is to be the guardian of the people, let the people elect.

"If the executive is to check the legislature, let him be unimpeachable.

"If the executive is to be reeligible, let his term be short."

Wilson observed that election by the people seemed to be gaining ground, but Paterson jumped up to bellow that the rabble was unqualified to select an executive. Sherman leaned over and whispered to Ellsworth, "If Wilson said the sun sets in the west, Paterson would insist that it sets in the east."

"But only after he first yelled treason and stomped around like a raging schoolmarm." Both men chuckled as Madison stood to speak. In order to hear his quiet voice, Sherman and Ellsworth stopped their banter.

"How do we design a strong executive unbeholden to another branch and avoid a monarch? I believe the people should appoint, but how do we give proper weight for Negroes in the South? The use of electors will give the South their proper influence."

Until now, Sherman had found it ironic that he had promised to help the South protect slaveholdings, while Madison, who owned slaves, condemned the institution. Madison now seemed to defend his fellow Southerners.

Ellsworth quickly clarified their coalition's preferred design. "I move to strike out appointment by the national legislature and to insert 'to be chosen by electors appointed by the legislatures of the states.'" Without debate, the motion passed. Sherman leaned back with satisfaction. Yes, he might be home soon.

Ellsworth next proposed a term shorter than seven years. "I move for a six-year term."

Sherman smiled. Six years was certainly less than seven, but by as small a decrement as possible. The proposal, however, passed.

Pinckney and Gouverneur Morris then passionately argued to delete the impeachment clause. Morris searched for a convincing argument. "Gentlemen, will impeachment suspend his duties? If not, the mischief goes on. If it does, the mere launch of an impeachment will render the executive inert."

Mason responded with a rare spate of anger. "Shall any man be above the law? Above all, should this man be above the law—the one who can commit the most outrageous wrongs?"

Franklin, always ready to soothe ill temper, spoke in a cordial manner. "Gentlemen, what is the practice when a chief magistrate becomes obnoxious?" Franklin gazed about the chamber as if he actually expected an answer. When none surfaced, he exclaimed, "Why, assassination!"

After a few gasps and some sprinkled tittering, Franklin continued in his unique, whimsical way. "The man's not only deprived of life, but of an opportunity to clear his name. To avoid unjust injury to a man's reputation, I suggest we provide some other form of punishment."

The chamber laughed, but Sherman saw that Franklin had pierced to the core of the issue. Franklin and Madison shared a trait; they each invariably centered on the pertinent issue. Franklin used droll humor, while Madison wielded logic like a scythe.

Madison's next comment did not disappoint. "A majority of an assembly cannot be bribed, so it would be difficult to get the legislature to act together in some devious plot. On the other hand, the executive, as a single man, can be corrupted. We must provide a defense against the duplicity of a chief magistrate. Term limits are not enough."

Gouverneur Morris thumped heavily to the front of the chamber and contemplated something on the ceiling. Evidently coming to a conclusion, he said, "I've changed my opinion. More correctly, the arguments have changed my opinion." Morris met Washington's eyes. "I now see the necessity for impeachment. We are designing a system for the ages, not the next few years."

With Morris now for impeachment, the vote came fast and decisive. The assembly voted eight to two to include a clause that allowed for the impeachment of the executive. Although Sherman hadn't become highly engaged on this issue, he felt as if he had achieved one more victory. More important, another controversial subject had been resolved, which meant they were closer to finishing their work.

"Unanimity Hall, what claptrap."

"What?"

"*The Pennsylvania Packet.* They wrote a mindless article on the convention." Ellsworth thrust the newspaper in Sherman's face.

"Oliver, I'm writing a letter." Ellsworth had barged into his room, eager to share the news. Sherman ignored the press because he found that newspapers seldom contained anything useful to his purposes. Since Ellsworth looked crestfallen, Sherman set his quill aside. "Read it to me."

Ellsworth read the text as if it held great portent. "'So great is the unanimity that prevails in the convention that it has been proposed to call the room in which they assemble Unanimity Hall.'"

"I prefer Harmony Hall," Sherman teased.

Oliver slapped the newspaper against his thigh. "Roger, nothing goes unchallenged. We debate minutiae, argue long-dead republics, and dispute the very quality of human nature."

"Oliver, relax. Things have been going smoothly of late."

"Smoothly? We seesaw like children. Two sides, tottering back and forth ad nauseam."

"Monday, we were on the verge of collapse. Think of the progress we made this week."

"It's still like pulling an ornery mule across a rickety bridge. We squabble over every gooseberry." Ellsworth looked back at the newspaper. "Who would feed the press such drivel?"

"Who has influence with Philadelphia newspapers?"

"Dr. Franklin?"

"Franklin pushes unanimity. He's always saying that we must hang together or surely hang separately."

"Does that mean our most senior delegate violated the secrecy rule?"

"I thought you said the article was claptrap."

Ellsworth shook his head. "What would be his purpose?"

"Mrs. Marshall told me that street gossip says we bicker and haggle like old women. The article counters those rumors."

"Does it matter what the street says?"

"We must nurse public opinion. Now we need patience, and later we'll need support for the final design. Remember the Revolutionary pamphleteering. They nudged people to wage war."

"The pamphleteers only hardened existing opinions." Ellsworth plopped down in the easy chair and nodded toward the letter in front of Sherman. "Rebecca?"

"Yes. I have pressing affairs in New Haven."

"Events will accelerate now that we've settled the executive."

Sherman picked up his quill and said distractedly, "Assuming it's settled."

"You're not sure?"

"Nothing's certain."

ON SATURDAY MORNING, SHERMAN entered the chamber and walked immediately over to his customary table. He didn't want to hear a Paterson whine, a Martin bombast, or a Gerry diatribe. The river had been forged, and he had lost patience with his allies who refused to dump excess baggage.

The delegates approved the Virginia Plan proposal that the Senate would select judges. The next subject was revisionary power. The Virginia Plan stated that the executive could revise laws passed by the legislature.

Wilson started. "Gentlemen, laws can be unwise, unjust, or dangerous." He tilted his head down to look over his glasses. "But we should give revisionary power to the judiciary, not the executive."

Sherman scribbled a note and passed it across the table to Ellsworth, who stood to endorse the idea. "Judges possess knowledge of law, which an executive may not. Connecticut approves of Mr. Wilson's proposal."

Sherman was pleased to see Madison also argue in favor of the concept.

Gerry huffed and stuttered until he managed a staccato rhythm. "I strongly object. This idea grants judges the power to legislate and ought never to be done."

Instead of projecting his normal self-assurance, Gouverneur Morris seemed thoughtful. "Some check on the legislature is necessary. The only question is, in whose hands should it be lodged? Bad measures are often popular. Some think the people can spot mischief, but experience has taught us otherwise. The press provides one means to diminish the evil, but it cannot prevent it altogether."

Morris sat without taking a position. Martin had no such qualms. "Gentlemen, this is wrong! If the judiciary opposes popular measures, they'll lose the confidence of the people. The constitutionality of laws will, in time, come before the judges in their official capacity. Judges shouldn't intervene before that time. I cannot conceive of a greater danger."

Madison took the floor and, uncharacteristically, seemed uncertain. "Our purpose is not to blend departments, but to erect barriers to keep them apart." Madison stopped his customary pacing and gave the assembly a long look. "Perhaps the revisionary idea ought to be discarded."

Sherman sat stunned but impressed. Madison ended up on the opposite side of the fence from where he had started. His switch in position and simple argument killed the entire concept of revisionary power. The assembly voted to give the executive the authority to veto bills in toto, but without the ability to revise laws.

"WHAT DO YOU THINK about the proceedings, Roger?"

He looked up to see Madison. Sherman sat in a cane lawn chair at the State House Inn. "I'm satisfied. And yourself?"

"My comfort increases daily. The design must change because of your Senate."

"Our Senate."

"It will be our Senate only after we leave the chamber. Now it's your creature."

"The Senate provides balance and a unique check," Sherman said.

Madison shrugged. "I want your support for the popular election of the executive."

"Not practical."

"Why not?"

"Our nation's too large. Results from some states would be known before the count was completed in other states."

"All counts could be disclosed on a single day."

"Too much opportunity for chicanery."

"Are you firm on this?"

The question gave Sherman pause. "I'm open to reasonable alternatives."

"Would you consider dinner with me and Rev. Witherspoon?"

"I'd look forward to it."

Madison gave him a friendly nod, then scurried across the lawn like an energized child who had spotted a new toy.

"What did the little titan want?"

Sherman turned to see Dickinson. "Now I remember why I avoid the State House Inn. Everyone bothers a simple man trying to write a letter to a friend."

"Every part of that sentence is a lie. You're not a simple man, delegates hurry in other directions when they spot you, and no one besides myself can abide you."

"I *am* writing a letter."

"Rebecca?"

"No, John Adams." Sherman set the letter aside. "Pull up a chair. I'll buy you lemonade or an ale."

Dickinson picked up another cane chair and positioned it beside Sherman. "What does John say?"

"He's frustrated. The English refuse to give him the recognition due an emissary from a sovereign nation."

"He expects too much." Dickinson raised a hand to signal a tavern maid. "The English will treat us like an errant child until we prove otherwise."

"That requires a sound government backed by a secure source of funds. We have neither."

"Nor in the future, I suspect."

This startled Sherman. "You think not?"

"We design a hodgepodge. We should follow the British model. They built a vast empire, and a British subject has greater liberty than a citizen of any other nation."

"Then why did we break away?"

"Need I remind you that I voted against the Declaration?"

Sherman had momentarily forgotten this pivotal episode in his friend's life. It seemed long ago, but it had actually been only eleven years. A comely tavern maid gave Sherman an excuse to avoid a response. "May I bring you gentlemen some refreshment?"

"I promised to buy this patriot a lemonade."

"You promised an ale."

"I suppose I did. Two ales, please."

As the maid retreated to the tavern house, Dickinson asked, "What's your intent with the executive?"

"I want the states to control his election."

"Why?"

"If the states elect the executive, and his term is short, and he's eligible for additional terms, he can't ignore any region of the country. He'll be forced to be a national leader. An executive from the South will need political friends in the North and vice versa. Nor will an executive feel free to turn a blind eye to new states."

"Madison wants the people to elect."

"The people elect the state legislatures."

"You think it's the same?"

"Better." The maid returned, and Sherman took his ale from the young girl. After a bracing swallow, he attempted to explain. "State politics are fought in tight quarters, and the closeness means that elected officials are held to account. If they choose a bad national leader, they'll have to explain it to their neighbors."

"This convention carries a severe prejudice against state legislatures."

"A few irresponsible houses have sullied the reputation of the rest." Sherman ran his finger around his damp shirt collar and took another sip of ale. "Their sin is a craven servility to popular demand, not exactly the kind of tyranny that suppresses the will of the people. Besides, will this sin be banned at the national level?"

The two men languished into silence a minute, and then Dickinson said, "I still fear we're designing a hodgepodge. It's not the balanced system Madison brought to Philadelphia, nor a copy of a working model. It's cobbled together each day from scraps and remnants. How can it possibly succeed?"

Sherman knew his friend needed an answer. "John, if the mix of interests crammed into the chamber can agree on a plan, then it has a good chance of working. It'll mean that all those political rivals feel secure. That'll happen only if we balance power, build checks, and erect defensive measures. If the diverse interests in the chamber are protected, interests not present will also be protected."

"If everyone feels safe in their defensive armor, who has enough power to lead?"

"The darling of Mr. Madison—the people."

30

Sunday, July 22, 1787

"Come, take a look," Witherspoon said.

Madison, Sherman, and Rev. Witherspoon had met at the Coach and Horses for Sunday supper. The tavern had been Witherspoon's choice. The Coach and Horses appealed to the merchant class and tradesmen, not the leisured affluent, but the food was good and the service cordial. Witherspoon selected this tavern because he wanted to show Madison and Sherman a novelty he found fascinating.

The two men followed Witherspoon into the kitchen. The first thing to strike Madison was the aroma of roasting meats. His mouth watered, and he realized that the long Sunday service had put many hours between his breakfast and supper.

The kitchen was a beehive. Two men stood at a central table, one butchering and the other skewering meat. A boy in the corner made a hasty swipe at the plates and glasses that had been dumped on a small table by a scurrying woman. Two other women, skirts hiked to protect against embers, moved in and out of the huge fireplace, adding kettles, stirring pots, and slicing meat off various spits. The bustle looked normal for a popular inn, but then Madison noticed three small dogs running inside wood cylinders to turn the spits.

Before Madison could say anything, Sherman asked, "Are they bitches?"

"How did you guess?"

Madison turned to see a rotund tavern owner looking as proud as a new father.

"In my experience, males don't tread the same path indefinitely," Sherman said.

The plump inn owner rolled in laughter. "Right you are. The male pups flip directions like a gull searching for another crumb."

"Are they hard to train?" Madison asked.

"My, yes. No one has been able to replicate my success." The innkeeper touched his nose with his forefinger. "I have my secrets."

Madison watched the small dogs relentlessly trudging toward an unreachable goal. "These animals and I are kindred spirits. I too run in circles, yap to no notice, and spend my energies to fill someone else's belly." Madison was pleased to see everyone laugh at his quip. Sherman even gave him a pat on the back, a rare display of intimacy from the stiffest man he had ever encountered. Perhaps this meeting would prove productive.

"They must draw customers," Sherman said.

"My whelps bring them in and my food brings them back. My place settings may not be fine china, but no one in Philadelphia serves better food."

"The food is good," Witherspoon said. "Otherwise, you'd be buying me dinner at an expensive tavern."

The innkeeper put a guiding hand on Madison's back. "Take a seat, and I'll have one of my daughters at your table faster than a dog can wag its tail."

"With pleasure," Witherspoon said. "Our appetites have been charged by the Lord Almighty."

The innkeeper was as good as his word. Within seconds, a stout young woman approached their table, wiping her hands on her apron. "Good afternoon, gentlemen. I hope you brought an … Rev. Witherspoon, good to see you again."

"And you, my dear. I brought some friends today."

"I see. What can I get you men?"

"What's your soup today?" Madison asked.

"Lentil. Made fresh and hearty."

"We'll start with a bowl of soup, a basket of bread, and Madeira, followed by a salver of meats and a platter of fresh vegetables." Madison turned to his guests, "Does that meet with your approval?"

"Indeed," Witherspoon said. "And load the salver with a generous portion of pork." Witherspoon cocked his head toward the kitchen. "They roast it slow with a constant turn by our wee canine friends. Delicious."

The maid bounced her ample hip against Witherspoon's shoulder and said, "I'd never forget your fondness for our pork, my dear man. I'll personally carve a crispy end piece for you." With that, she whirled away toward the kitchen.

"New admirer?" Sherman teased.

The reverend blushed. "I eat here often. It fits my budget."

Madison had a friendly, but somewhat formal, relationship with Witherspoon. Still, he decided to join in the ribbing. "That lovely maid seems very familiar with your habits."

"She's not that … James, you must guess at the extent of her knowledge. I'll not enlighten you."

Madison looked at Sherman, and they both started laughing. Any other response by Witherspoon would have tempted the two to throw additional ribald allegations at their ever-proper dinner mate.

Witherspoon looked askance at their jocularity and asked, "Did you enjoy the morning services?"

"I always enjoy services," Sherman said. "Even if the sermon proves less than enlightening, I always leave refreshed."

"As you should. God cleanses the soul so that when we converse with ourselves, we enjoy a guiltless companion."

"Then I should be grateful, because I spend a lot of time alone," Madison said.

"Too much James—you needn't be so intense."

"Much is at stake, Reverend. Opportunity cannot be discarded for frivolous pleasures."

"When do you intend to marry?" Witherspoon asked.

Madison felt his face flush. "You must guess, because I'll not enlighten you."

"Your father worries."

"You've been in communication with my father?"

"Only because you have not. Why don't you write?"

"About my amorous affairs?"

"You have some?" Sherman asked in a tone that said he was jesting.

"Excuse me, but we must change the subject," Madison seethed. His notes and research took all his private time. Besides, he had no news he could share with his father, certainly none about a future wife. Others might find time for dalliance, but he had a mission.

"All right," Witherspoon said. "Then tell me, what place has religion in your design for a new government?"

"None."

Madison looked at Sherman. They had both answered together and with equal forcefulness.

"None? What will guide the men that guide us?"

"We can't rely on the goodness of men," Madison said dismissively. "Bad characters, as well as good men, seek power."

"God chastens bad characters."

"We cannot rely on his thoroughness." Madison grew irritated.

Rev. Witherspoon gave Madison a long look, then shook his head and turned to Sherman. "Why does a pious man answer the same as our naïve young friend?"

Sherman sat very still for such a long time that Madison thought he resembled a marble statue. When he spoke his voice was even. "My faith is personal, and I grant the same privilege to others."

"We agree at last," Madison said.

Sherman smiled. "We agree more than you suppose."

The maid suddenly appeared with three bowls of soup and a loaf of uncut bread. A small sip of the soup convinced Madison that the quality of the food hadn't been exaggerated. He dug in with relish.

"You're making a mistake," Witherspoon said. "The soul, as well as the body, needs nourishment."

"Men seldom get nourishment in a government chamber," Madison said distractedly.

Witherspoon showed a hint of prickliness. "Make light, if you must, but the crass impulses of men can be tempered only by a reminder that a greater power will one day sit in judgment. God helps weak men do good."

"The design must assume otherwise," Madison said.

"Gentlemen," Sherman said, "let's enjoy our meal. Granted, our design doesn't impose piety, but neither does it preclude piety. Each man must make peace with the Maker. It shall be ever so, despite laws and admonishments."

"Admonitions are my profession," Witherspoon said.

Madison saw Sherman grow even stiffer. "Sir, do you admonish me?"

"Certainly not." Madison enjoyed watching Witherspoon's discomfort. The reverend cut the bread as he surrendered. "Roger's right; let's enjoy our meal."

AS THE THREE SATIATED men stepped out of the tavern, Madison turned toward Witherspoon. "If I could beg your pardon, may I have a moment with Mr. Sherman?"

"Do you mean to speak about me?"

His question caught Madison off guard. Witherspoon must still be smarting from their previous discussion. "No, I must check on an item concerning the convention."

"An item so sensitive that you must take him aside?"

"Our proceedings are secret."

"We spoke about your convention earlier."

"Our convention has never addressed religion, so our discussion was philosophical."

"More's the pity." Witherspoon gave a nod of his head toward the street. "I'll wait over there."

Madison hesitated until Witherspoon had walked a few paces. "I'm afraid we may have offended the reverend."

"Don't let your defenses down; he's over there regrouping for another charge."

"I believe you're right. I'll bet he brings the subject up again."

"As he said, it's his job. Stick to your principles. I never told you, but I agree with your Statute for Religious Freedom."

"That was not my statute. Jefferson wrote it."

"You got it passed by the Virginia legislature. The honor goes to the one that puts theory into practice."

"Perhaps there are other areas in which we agree."

"What's on your mind?"

"Ratification. Can you support ratification by the people?"

"The state legislatures should ratify."

"I intend to push for direct ratification."

"Do as you think best."

"Will you join me on this issue?"

Sherman looked at Madison. Finally, he said, "I'll propose ratification by the state legislature, but I won't insist."

Madison felt relieved. When Sherman insisted, events seldom took another course. He decided to move to the next issue. "Do you remember the suggestion that each senator would vote independently?"

"I accepted that procedure."

"With a single vote per state, only an odd number of senators can avoid split votes like we have here. Three senators per state would be too many and one too few. Two seems perfect, but only if they vote independently."

Sherman smiled. "James, I already agreed."

"I'm sorry. I practiced that argument assuming resistance."

"And a fine argument it was."

Sherman's agreeability unsettled him. He had left the most difficult item for last and would soon see how far Sherman's newfound cooperation extended. "On the election of the executive, I—"

"I believe we should end on a good note," Sherman interrupted, and with that, he made a formal bow capped with an informal smile. "Good day, Mr. Madison, and thank you for a wonderful meal and your engaging company."

Sherman gave a wave of his hat to Witherspoon and walked off.

MADISON CRINGED. HE HAD turned in the direction of a ruckus behind him and saw that New Hampshire had finally waltzed in—two months late. They had entered the chamber to the type of fraternal greetings used by politicians and horse traders to convey supposed intimacy. Their earlier presence would have given Sherman a greater edge in negotiating privileges for the states. At this late date, another small state made little difference.

The new delegation caused a delay because the keeper had to find an additional table. When the session opened, they debated a resolution that required national officers to take an oath to support the Constitution. Wilson objected. "I'm not fond of oaths. A good government doesn't need them, and a bad one doesn't deserve them."

Despite Wilson's reservations, the clause was approved. Because of his jittery anticipation of the next issue, Madison recorded the vote with quick strokes of his pen. They would now consider the clause requiring that the Constitution be submitted to the people for ratification. Ellsworth immediately moved to refer the new Constitution to the state legislatures.

Mason presented the counterargument. "Succeeding legislatures, possessing equal authority, can undo the acts of their predecessors. The national government cannot stand on such a tottering foundation. Where must we resort? To the people, the ones who retain all power."

The evidence for Mason's argument sat in the room. They were superseding the existing government, and they should make it difficult to do the same thing in the future. The most effective blockade would be approval by the people, not government agencies that could withdraw support at will.

Randolph sounded testy. "Gentlemen, I remind you, the popular mind remains fixed at May 25."

This offhand comment startled Madison. The journey that the men in this room had traveled included no outside passengers. He would have to put some thought into how to bring the populace beyond May 25.

Gouverneur Morris clomped to the front of the room and stared at the Connecticut table. "Mr. Ellsworth assumes that we proceed on the basis of the Articles. I thought we were beyond that. A majority of the people can alter the federal government, just as any state constitution can be altered by a majority of the people in that state." Morris sat with a finality that said he had squashed the argument once and for all.

As Madison scribbled his notes, he recognized that, true to their earlier conversation, Sherman would propose, but not insist upon, ratification by the state legislatures. He almost let out a whoop when the convention voted nine to one to refer the Constitution to special assemblies to be chosen by the people.

With this crucial issue settled, Gouverneur Morris moved that the Senate should consist of two members per state and that each vote independently. Ellsworth agreed, fulfilling the other Sherman promise. The delegates, without further debate, approved the scheme. Madison rejoiced. This somewhat weakened the small states' great victory. The states would be equally represented in the Senate, but good men might break their state allegiance when conscience dictated.

Gerry next moved to appoint a committee to prepare a draft constitution.

Assuming there would be no objection, Madison received a surprise from Pinckney. "Gentlemen, if the committee fails to insert security for the South against an emancipation of slaves, I'll vote against their report."

Before Madison could figure out the meaning behind this statement, the convention agreed that tomorrow, a committee of five members would be appointed to draft a constitution.

"MR. PINCKNEY, HOLD UP a minute."

"I'm in a hurry."

Madison had scrambled down the sidewalk to catch up with Pinckney. Irritatingly, Pinckney, a few steps ahead, did not slow his pace. Madison juggled his valise under his arm and hurried to pull alongside. "What was the meaning of your last remark?"

"I thought my meaning clear." Pinckney continued his brisk pace and kept his eyes forward. "You must pay better attention. Were you distracted by your note taking?"

"I heard what sounded like a threat."

"Then you were listening."

"Charles, we're almost finished. Why are you throwing sand into the inkwell?"

"Because that inkwell will scribe a new constitution."

"The Senate protects your interests."

"The Senate represents but half of one branch."

"What more do you want?"

"A greater weight in the selection of the executive."

Madison saw something. "Did you cut a deal with Sherman?"

Pinckney stopped and turned toward Madison. "If you want something in a political sphere, you go to the one that has the power to deliver it."

"I could have helped."

"Face reality, James. A new coalition controls this convention."

"New England and the South make strange bedfellows."

"Desperate men go to bed with anyone willing to prostitute himself." With that less than flattering comment about his new ally, Pinckney charged down the street. Madison declined to follow.

TUESDAY STARTED ANOTHER ARGUMENT over how to elect the executive. The rancorous debate extended into Thursday. Madison realized that the executive provided yet another issue that stymied progress, but this time it was an honest bafflement over design, not an emotional fight over power.

Madison placed his quill down and asked for the floor. After summarizing the various positions, he informed the delegates that he had changed his opinion. "I've decided to support electors—chosen by the people."

A battle line had been drawn. Electors had gained the upper hand, but who would elect the electors?

Their energy finally spent, they elected a Committee of Detail. The committee—James Wilson, Oliver Ellsworth, Edmund Randolph, John Rutledge, and Nathaniel Gorham—would organize their sundry resolutions into a draft constitution.

To give the committee time to prepare a draft constitution, the convention adjourned until Monday after next.

"Mr. Madison, may I have a word?"

Madison immediately slowed his pace. "Of course, General."

Washington descended the few steps leading from the State House and walked close to the building until he was out of earshot. Madison followed.

"I believe the executive should serve a short term, be reeligible, and be subject to impeachment."

Madison nodded. "And who is to elect?"

"I lean toward electors. Prudent men who understand the required skills."

"I concur." Madison hesitated. "But who elects the electors?"

Washington gave one of his closed-mouth smiles. "That seems to be the remaining question."

"I support the people."

"We all support the people."

Madison was not sure what that answer meant, but he knew that he shouldn't take it as an endorsement of his preference.

Washington started toward his carriage. "Jemmy, what do you plan for recess?"

"I'm not sure," Madison said. "What will you do?"

Washington beamed. "I'm going fishing."

"Fishing?"

"Yes, trout fishing at Valley Forge."

"I'd think you'd want to avoid that dreadful place."

"A man should face his devils. Besides, it is only dreadful in winter."

"Then I wish you fair weather."

"Thank you, James. My advice is that you should do something fun. Don't obsess about the convention."

"General, obsessed men have fun only when allowed to work on their obsession."

31

Friday, July 27, 1787

The coachman closed the door with a satisfying click. Sherman felt the carriage rock as the big man climbed into the driver's seat. The mild dawn predicted a good day for travel, and a hearty breakfast had made him drowsy. He closed his eyes and saw home. Tomorrow night, he would be in New Haven.

"Don't go to sleep, Roger," Baldwin said. "You need to restrain me from throwing this rascal out."

"Yes, Roger, stay awake," Hamilton insisted. "Otherwise, I'll throw myself out if I must converse with this backcountry lout."

Sherman opened his eyes. Alexander Hamilton and Abraham Baldwin sat smiling on the opposite side of the coach.

"Children, behave. It's going to be a long trip."

"At least His Highness will depart our company in New York," Baldwin said.

"With great relief, Mr. Baldwin," Hamilton responded. "After a boring day of banter about pigs, chickens, and savage Indians, I'll be desperate for urban company."

"Now, now," Sherman said. "I'm looking forward to this journey. I get to go home, and I have the pleasure of making the trip with my best friend and my favorite politician. We'll avoid discussing chickens and pork until we eat."

"I'm not your friend?" Hamilton asked.

"I thought you would be more impressed with being my favorite politician."

"Actually, I am." Hamilton gave Baldwin a grin. "Friends are overvalued."

"As seen by your lack of surrounding admirers."

"Of the male variety only. I boast many women admirers."

"A gentleman does not boast—whoa!" The coach had bounced hard, introducing the three men to the ceiling of the closed carriage. Their speed had picked up to signal that they had left the city for open road. Sherman grabbed his tricorn and snugged it back onto his head to pad the next bounce.

Since a ten-day recess was too short for a return to Georgia, Baldwin had decided to visit friends and family in New Haven. Sherman was glad for his company. Hamilton and Baldwin, if not friends, were friendly. Both men enjoyed ribald bantering, which promised to make the trip entertaining.

"Any word from New York?" Sherman asked Hamilton.

"Not yet, but I hope to hear something when I arrive."

"If that falls through, I might as well return to Georgia to herd pigs."

"The deal's been struck," Hamilton said.

Baldwin looked skeptical. "You trust the word of bandits?"

"Clinton might make additional last-minute demands," Sherman mused.

"A true scoundrel." Hamilton laughed. "But you must admire his mastery of the game."

"I know the blackguard only by reputation," Baldwin said. "I see nothing to admire."

"His political network runs like a well-tended gristmill. Every part reliably does its assigned task. If government's job is to make things happen for its constituents, then New York compares favorably to the mayhem in your respective states."

"In Georgia, we prefer our politicians' hands in their own pocket."

Hamilton shrugged. "Graft is a disguised tax that lubricates the wheels of government." Hamilton gave Sherman a theatrical wink that said he was enjoying himself. "Tell me, Mr. Baldwin, have you eradicated the vice in Georgia?"

"We endeavor to control the scale."

Hamilton laughed. "Bravo. But we take pride in doing things big in New York."

Turning to Sherman, Baldwin said, "You've been unusually quiet."

"Guilty."

"We're all guilty," Hamilton said.

"I merely played a bit part," Baldwin said.

"An all too crucial part. We're in your debt."

"And I shall collect—"

Another rude bump sent the men bouncing. Hamilton rapped on the ceiling. "Watch the road, man!"

Sherman smiled. "I'd rather not dally."

"Oh, it does no good. Drivers relish tossing their fancy guests around." An impish grin appeared on Hamilton face. "I yell to bolster their amusement."

"Why, Mr. Hamilton," Baldwin said, "your regard for the common man surprises me."

"I admire the common man; I just don't trust his judgment in government matters."

"All of us come from common roots," Sherman said.

"Yes, and I the bastard of a common whore. But wits, not lineage, define the egalitarian aristocrat. By that measure, I'm a prince."

Hamilton had veered from chitchat to a personal disclosure. Adversaries often called Hamilton a bastard behind his back, but this was the first time Sherman had heard Hamilton use the word himself.

"That explains things," Baldwin chided. "You've adopted *The Prince* as your handbook."

"Machiavelli understood the nature of man."

This comment caught Sherman's attention. Leaning forward, he asked, "Do you believe man's base nature can be harnessed by a well-constructed constitution?"

"I have a less elevated goal than our little friend," Hamilton responded.

"What's your goal?" Baldwin asked.

"A sound government that can protect the nation and manage commerce."

"You don't fear a union too strong?" Sherman asked.

"I fear weakness. Defective constitutions sow the seeds of tyranny. When men are forced to go outside the limits set by their constitution, despotism reigns. The nation must meet emergencies without abandoning the constitution."

"Are you suggesting that we draft a flawless constitution?" Baldwin asked.

"I'd never propose such a goal. Flawlessness is the aspiration of fools."

Some additional jolts jostled the three men, so Sherman waited for the carriage springs to settle down to predictable rolls. "If not flawless, what's our aim?"

"Adequacy. The dominion of misbegotten man."

An odd turn of phrase, Sherman thought, considering Hamilton's earlier reference to his illicit parentage. "How do you define adequacy?"

"Sufficient to satisfy the present need. None of us are seers." Hamilton smiled. "How, may I ask, would Mr. Sherman define success for our grand undertaking?"

The question did not catch Sherman by surprise. "Alex, I believe we can trust our liberty to any constitution that disperses power and provides enough checks to reassure Paterson, Pinckney, and our other malcontents. If the disparate interests in the chamber feel safe, then any faction, alive or on the horizon, can tuck their fears in a closet."

"You ol' reprobate," Baldwin exclaimed. "You've rationalized your compromising."

"A politician slithers through any opening."

"A colorful choice of words," Baldwin said.

Sherman felt an unintended smile. "I'm a colorful man." This brought so much laughter from his traveling companions that Sherman changed the subject. "Paterson won't return from recess."

"More good news," Hamilton said. "I shan't miss that beady-eyed little prosecutor."

Baldwin stretched his legs. "I'm glad no one else chose this coach."

"I bought the remaining seats," Hamilton said.

"What?" Baldwin looked askance at Hamilton. "Why?"

"So we can have a private ride. New York can afford it."

"A true New Yorker. You rape the public treasury for your own comfort," Baldwin said.

"I felt the expense worthwhile so we could discuss the convention." Sherman saw a foreshadowing smile grow on Hamilton face. "But don't get your hopes up; I purchased the seats only to New York."

"You miser," Baldwin blustered. "You said you were in my debt. You could have considered our comfort after you departed our company."

"I'm a royalist. You, on the other hand, are men of the people. I thought you should meet some."

"With pleasure," Baldwin said. "I prefer the common sense of the common man."

"I strive to avoid the common," Hamilton said with surprising earnestness.

"Roger, tell this Tory he should be mixing with the masses before he ordains himself architect of our new republic."

Sherman was enjoying the trip, and he felt even better when the predictable sway of the coach signaled they were making good time on decent road.

AFTER A FEW HOURS, the coach rolled to an abrupt stop, and Sherman felt the driver dismount. Soon the door snapped opened to reveal a grizzled face that didn't bother with pleasantries. "You have a half hour to eat. I leave on time. If you dally in the privy, you'll spend the night here."

As they dismounted, Hamilton said, "One of the commoners you're so fond of."

Baldwin ignored the gibe and headed for the yard behind the tavern. "I'll meet you men inside."

"Be swift. I've traveled this route many times, and I don't recommend that privy."

"God, I hate traveling," Baldwin said to himself as he walked away.

Sherman inhaled the fresh country air. He could see nothing in either direction but a rough-hewn road that tore a gash between unending fields of trees. As soon as they had planted their feet on solid ground, a tavern liveryman drove the coach over to rickety shelter to change horses. The tavern itself was a clapboard affair that looked in dire need of repair.

"Did you bring food?" Hamilton asked.

"No."

"A mistake. The fare at this desolate tavern is invariably a rancid stew made with suspect meat and vegetables boiled to an indiscernible mush."

"I'm not hungry."

"Then I'll reward you with a pear. I recommend we eat outside."

"Dank inside?"

"The tavern reeks of their perpetual stew pot, the sweat of men oblivious to even elementary hygiene, and decades of harsh tobacco."

"You've convinced me. Let's sit on that fallen tree across the road."

When Baldwin emerged from behind the building, he failed to notice the men on the other side of the road and walked into the tavern. He spent only a few minutes inside and emerged with a wooden bowl and an oversized spoon. Looking around, he finally spotted Sherman and Hamilton on the log across the way.

As he took a seat next to Sherman, Baldwin asked, "What's this?"

Hamilton leaned forward to look around Sherman. "Squirrel, I think."

"God, I hate traveling."

"Throw it away, and I'll give you a pear."

Baldwin dipped his spoon deep into the concoction and let the goo plop back into the bowl. "This looks like pig swill." He ceremoniously turned the bowl over, and they all watched the pottage spill onto the ground in bumpy chunks.

"My money says that blob will still be there on my return trip," Hamilton said.

Baldwin turned the pear a couple times and then took a huge bite. After a noisy chomp, he spoke with a mouth half full. "I'll not take that bet; forest animals have more dignity."

"How'd you like the privy?"

"My God, can't they dig another one?"

"Takes work." Hamilton absently wiped pear juice from his chin. "There's no place more convenient to stop."

"If you'll excuse me, gentlemen," Sherman said, "I think I'll stroll into the woods for my respite."

When Sherman returned, he noticed that the coach had reappeared in front of the tavern, and Hamilton and Baldwin were talking to two men on horseback. As Sherman approached, he saw enough resemblance to realize it was father and son.

"I kick myself for being so foolish," the older man said.

Baldwin saw Sherman approach. "Roger, meet Mr. Russell and his son, Charles." Sherman shook both men's calloused hands. "They own a farm six miles north. Seems they intend to foreclose."

"Bastards." The man gave his son a forlorn look. "Headin' down to Trenton to see if I can talk 'em into more time."

"How much do you owe?" Sherman asked.

"One hundred and sixty shillings. More'n I got. And the bastards won't accept my New Jersey bonds. Three years I fought, and all I got was bloody worthless paper. Makes a man want to fight a revolution all over again."

Sherman thought a minute. "How much money do you have?"

"Sixteen shillings, five pence. Sold my hogs."

"That won't stop them," Hamilton said.

Sherman opened his purse and found his last sovereign. He didn't know the measure of a British sovereign against a New Jersey shilling, but he knew hard money carried a heavy premium. Sherman held the heavy coin up and raised an eyebrow at Hamilton and Baldwin.

Baldwin paused and then pulled out some coins that amounted to almost two sovereigns. "How do you expect to buy ale this evening?"

"Keep one sovereign." Sherman held his hand out to Hamilton. "Alex?"

"You're mad. We don't know these men. And besides—"

"We're good, honest farmers," the boy exclaimed, "and my father carries a ball in his shoulder to prove he's a patriot. We don't want your money."

"The boy's right. It's not enough. We didn't come begging."

"How much can you spare, Alex?" Sherman asked.

"You ol' skinflint," Baldwin said. "As a founder of the Bank of New York, you can afford it better than we can."

Hamilton looked as angry as Sherman had ever seen him. Finally, his features softened, and he said, "I'll contribute another sovereign, but if they want his land, they'll foreclose anyway."

"They want my land, all right. It's fertile, with a ready supply of water."

The coachman walked over and insisted that they climb into the carriage. Sherman gave him a no-nonsense look and said, "We'll be five minutes, and you *will* wait."

The driver looked ready to argue but instead said, "Five minutes, and you'll hear the crack of my whip."

Sherman followed the coachman back to the carriage and took out his satchel. He extracted a piece of fine paper and his travel writing materials. It took him only a minute to write the brief letter. Walking back to the group, he waved the paper to dry the ink. "Here, each of you sign." Hamilton and Baldwin quickly scribbled their signatures. Sherman blew the ink dry and handed the letter to the farmer still mounted on his mare.

Embarrassed, the farmer handed the letter to his son. "I can't read."

After reading the note to himself, the boy sounded incredulous. "These men are congressmen. One is Alexander Hamilton."

"Aid to Gen. Washington?"

The boy handed the letter back to his father. "The letter pleads to accept a partial payment and to extend the final payment until next September."

"That might work. It'll look like I have powerful friends. To think, a mile back I damned Congress."

"As well you should," Baldwin said. "A useless enterprise. We're members of the Federal Convention that will put an end to the tomfoolery."

"How can I ever repay you?"

"With three sovereigns mailed to me in New Haven, care of Yale University," Sherman said.

The man looked down at the letter. "It may be a while."

"I'm a patient man. Now we must get along." Sherman handed him the coins. "Good luck."

"Bless you. I'll remember you in my prayers."

"Remember us with a post," Hamilton said. "In the meantime, when you hear of our work, support the new Constitution."

"I'll support anything proposed by you gentlemen. You've saved my family."

Sherman grabbed his companions by the shoulders. "We must go." As the three men raced for the coach, Sherman saw the driver make a show of whirling his whip. After scrambling into their seats, Baldwin sighed and said, "I haven't felt so good since I left Georgia."

As the coach lurched forward, Hamilton suddenly seemed to find something amusing. With a head bow, Hamilton touched two fingers to his tricorn and said, "Roger, I apologize for laughing when you said you were colorful. I had no idea."

THE COACH STOPPED AT an inn less than ten miles from New York. From here, Hamilton would catch a hansom buggy to his home. Unlike their midday stop, this area had the appearance of a small village. Several homes were scattered around the inn, a blacksmith shop, a livery stable, a general store, and two churches.

Sherman dismounted and stretched to his full height. "Only seventy-six miles from home."

"Well, I don't want to make you feel bad, but I'm only a few miles from decent food, fine wine, and my own bed."

"Oh, you'll be sleeping in your own bed this evening?" Baldwin asked.

"Yes, I need rest before my admirers discover I'm back in town."

Sherman walked over and shook Hamilton's hand. "Thanks, Alex. The country owes you a debt."

Hamilton laughed. "So does some woebegone farmer in New Jersey."

"Could you send a messenger if there is any news about the Cutler deal?"

"Why not join me at my home?"

"The coach leaves before dawn. I don't want to miss it."

"I'll send a messenger if there's any news, but our sluggish Congress has probably not moved their collective derrière."

"Thank you. We'll see you in nine days. Hopefully, we can wrap up quickly."

Hamilton looked concerned. "Roger, when we report out a constitution, the real work begins. Powerful forces will fight us."

He grabbed his bag and sprinted toward a waiting buggy. After he had climbed aboard, Sherman and Baldwin reluctantly walked into the dowdy-looking inn to be greeted by a portly man and a small boy. "Welcome to the Black Mare."

"Thank you." Sherman handed his bag to the boy. "Separate rooms, if possible."

"Heavens, I'm afraid that's quite impossible. Yours is one of many coaches that stop here—one room per coach. You're lucky you're the only two passengers on the Philadelphia route."

"Luck had nothing to do with it," Baldwin muttered. Turning toward Sherman, he added, "Remind me to thank Hamilton for his generosity."

The innkeeper looked perplexed but didn't pursue the matter. "Billy will take your bags to the room. The coach will leave one half hour before daybreak. The boy will give just one knock on your door, so move sharply. Now, would you care for some ale and food?"

"Indeed, we're famished." Baldwin handed his bag to the boy, and both men took a seat at the end of a long table.

"What do you think of Hamilton?" Sherman asked.

"The smartest man I've ever met but driven by inner demons."

"He'll be powerful in the new government."

"I'll sleep at night. I'd rather see him in a financial role than Robert Morris. Hamilton's a bit of a royalist, but Washington has his mark."

"His womanizing offends me, and the man has no religious underpinnings."

"He worships Washington," Baldwin said.

"A surrogate father?"

"Us backcountry folk don't complicate things. If they choose each other, then it speaks well for both their judgments." Baldwin gave Sherman a friendly grin. "Roger, mostly you keep your religion to yourself, but underneath you're a strident prude."

"I try not to be judgmental."

"You mean you try to keep your mouth shut."

Sherman laughed. "You know me too well."

"Who else offends you?"

Sherman used two fingers to pinch his mouth shut.

"Come on. It's just us now, talking over tankards of ale."

Sherman glanced around to see if anyone was paying attention to their conversation. "Gouverneur Morris."

"What? My favorite delegate. There's not a pretentious bone in his body. The man knows how to enjoy life, and he's a good republican."

"He ridicules religion, treats women as entertainment, and uses the Lord's name in vain. He sets a bad example."

Baldwin found this amusing. "You ol' humbug. The closer you get to home, the more puritanical you get. Well, you shan't change my mind. I like Morris, and I think he's one of the most balanced thinkers in the chamber."

"I trust his political judgment, and I can't help liking him. At least he's not a hypocrite. He never pretends to be pious."

"Roger, most of the men in that chamber lack piety. Why won't you excuse Gouverneur Morris?"

"Because he makes a cause of being irreverent."

"I know this'll come as a surprise to you, but some politicians project an image like a woman shows cleavage. It doesn't mean they'll jump in bed with the first rogue they encounter—they just like the attention."

"That's foreign to me."

"Obviously."

"You think I should be more tolerant?"

"More?"

Both men laughed. "I'll endeavor to be forbearing—and if I fail, I resolve to keep my mouth shut."

AFTER AN ADEQUATE SUPPER, Billy led them to their room with a lantern. To light a candle sconce, the boy had to shimmy sideways in the scant space between the bed and the wall. The room was devoid of any other furnishings, and the bed's lumpiness was evident even in the poor light.

"God, I hate traveling," Baldwin muttered.

Sherman tried to step to the other side but stumbled over their bags, which had been dropped at the foot of the bed.

Regaining his balance, he asked, "They board an entire carriage in this room?"

"Since there's only two of you, Mr. Wilson put you in the women's chamber."

Baldwin found this hilarious. "We must quit spoiling our womenfolk." Looking back at the door, Baldwin asked, "How did they ever get that bed in this closet?"

"Don't know, sir. It's been here as long as I have."

Sherman handed the boy a two-penny coin. "Thank you, son."

Baldwin had to sit on the bed in order to give the boy enough room to close the door. "I hope that's only mildew I smell."

A few minutes later, they heard a rude knock on the door. When Sherman opened it, the innkeeper held out an envelope. "This was delivered moments ago."

Sherman took the envelope and examined the wax seal. "It's Hamilton's mark." Sherman used his finger to break the seal and then extracted the letter. Looking up, he said, "Congress approved the Cutler deal this afternoon."

"Any other news?"

"The Scioto Company allocation also passed." Sherman handed the letter to Baldwin. "When their interests are on the line, Congress moves swiftly enough."

After a moment, Baldwin looked up from Hamilton's note. "A lot of men are now wealthy."

Sherman plucked the letter out of Baldwin's hand and edged the corner of the paper into a candle flame. As the letter burned, he kicked the chamber pot from under the bed and dropped the smothering remnants into the bowl. "Not wealthy. They have an interest in a lot of wilderness that'll prove worthless in their lifetime."

"You believe that?"

"There's such a vast quantity of frontier that we bribed them with a fool's paradise."

"You're not rationalizing?"

Sherman shrugged. "Let's go to bed."

SHERMAN STRETCHED AS MUCH as he could in the close quarters. He reminded himself that he should also thank Hamilton for buying the extra seats to New York. On this leg, there were seven men crammed into a space that would crowd four. The width of the carriage wouldn't accommodate three sets of shoulders, so one man had to lean forward. An unspoken protocol dictated that when the pain became unbearable, a little shuffling would ensue so the man could rest his back.

The seventh man sat on the floor with his back against the door, so no one could stretch his legs. Sherman told himself to be grateful he wasn't on the floor. Once he had volunteered for the position because he thought it would be more comfortable for his long legs. He learned a lesson quickly. Every bounce of the carriage reminded him of his father's paddle. After that experience, Sherman never hesitated to use his age to get a seat.

He was surprised that all the other passengers were strangers. New Haven had a population of about twenty thousand, but Sherman was the mayor, a congressman, a superior judge, and had been the treasurer for Yale and a major town merchant. He normally could recognize most of the residents and frequent visitors. Three of the men were really boys anxious to arrive early for their term at Yale, while the other two men were making the trip to buy oysters and clams, the economic mainstay of the New Haven harbor.

Sherman and Baldwin didn't mention their convention membership. If they had let it be known, they would have had difficulty fending off questions without appearing rude. Politics dominated the conversation, and the discussion reminded Sherman of Randolph's comment that the popular mind remained fixed at May 25. Sherman reviewed his own shifting opinions since the beginning of the convention. Hamilton was right—once they reported out a constitution, their work would have just begun.

Sherman gave Baldwin a gentle nudge with his elbow when he spotted the outer neighborhoods of his hometown. Like Philadelphia, New Haven was laid out in a grid, with thirty-two blocks covering an area of about six square miles. The population was comfortably scattered in neat two-story wooden homes generously spaced along wide parallel streets. A French visitor had once told Sherman that a European city would pack six times as many people in the same space. Despite having nearly half the population of Philadelphia, New Haven retained the appearance and attitude of a small town.

Sherman felt the coach roll to a gradual stop at a central square simply called the Green. He leaped out, not waiting for the driver to come around to open the door. He immediately marched around the back of the coach and stood facing the Green. Taking a deep breath, he felt a surge of tranquility. The well-groomed Green was one of the most beautiful spots in New England. Tall elms bordered the grass plot, but Sherman could see through them to the stately Yale brick buildings set back on the far side. In the morning, he would attend services at his own church, the one that stood guard at the top of the Green. The northwest side sloped up to a calm burying ground Sherman knew would be his permanent refuge.

"Rebecca not meeting you?"

"I arrived faster than the post."

"Then I shan't interrupt your reunion. I'll be off to my brother's."

"That's neighborly of you." Sherman caught his bag as the driver tossed it. "See you in church."

Lugging his bag of dirty clothes, Sherman cut the corner of the Green and headed for College Street. Unlike Philadelphia, where brick or stone facades crowded the sidewalk, New Haven's wood homes stood comfortably back from the street. Trees and shrubs decorated the median that put a civilized distance between a man's home and clattering carriages.

When Sherman passed a house once owned by Benedict Arnold, a splinter of disquiet intruded on his reverie. Sherman's relationship with Arnold had been long and bumpy. Twenty years ago, the youthful Arnold had been arrested for breaking into a house, and Sherman had sentenced him to a public whipping. Later, when Sherman was treasurer for Yale, Arnold had contributed generously to the college and had grown to become a respected member of the community. His bravery and Revolutionary victories had made him a hero in New Haven and throughout the nation. Now Sherman wished he could get Arnold back into his courtroom. He would never understand how anyone could betray their neighbors and country for money or petty grievances. The mercurial traitor had escaped to England, but Sherman hoped his conscience denied him a peaceful sleep.

Sherman found himself standing in front of his own home. Dusk had started to mute the summer colors, and the faint glow of a lantern lit the parlor window. He jostled his bag and stepped with purpose down the stone walkway. As he opened the door, he smelled baked apples and heard the rhythmic twirl of a spinning wheel.

Lost in concentration, his wife hadn't noticed him enter. He set his bag softly on the floor. "Rebecca?"

"Roger!"

Sherman was sure his grin looked silly on his normally stoic face. She waited until the wheel spun down and then leaped at him. "Oh, Roger, I'm glad you're home." She threw her arms around his neck and gave him a kiss that validated her words. Sherman felt wetness on his cheek, and he knew he wasn't crying.

"Mrs. Sherman, I must leave home more often just so I can enjoy this welcome."

Rebecca feigned a firm face and slapped his forearm. "You do and I might just get a proper husband."

"Not a sea captain, I hope. You're the type of woman who needs a farmer, one with a small farm so he'd never be out of sight."

"Go ahead. Make fun. I married a merchant with two successful general stores. I could keep my eye on you in those days."

"Before you get too excited, I have bad news. I'm home for only six days."

"Damn it, Roger."

"Rebecca."

"I'm sorry for swearing, but damn—" She took a quick swipe to dry her eyes. "How much longer?"

"Not long. We're on a ten-day recess for the Committee of Detail to scribe a document."

"First the war, then Congress, and now this interminable convention. At least when you're in New York, you get home."

"Rebecca, all that remains is the ceremony."

"Then why do you have to return?"

"I mean to sign our new Constitution."

Now she actually looked apologetic. "Of course you do." She threw her arms around him again and hugged a bit too tight.

When she broke, Sherman could tell the momentary anger had passed. "I need to put more meat in the pot."

"No hurry."

"You're not hungry?"

"Starving, but it can wait. I'd like to bathe first."

She smiled coyly. "Good idea. I'll put some water on the fire."

THE NEXT MORNING, SHERMAN returned from his walk to find breakfast ready. Rebecca was a great cook, and the house smelled so good that he could eat the banister. "Good morning."

Rebecca was crouched in the hearth. Without rising, she spun and gave him a welcome smile. "Ready when you are. I've already fed the boys, and they're off to work."

"Now would be just fine."

"Then bring over a couple of bowls."

Last evening, Sherman's two youngest boys had returned home while he was still in the tub, and he caught up with their lives while he soaked. Both were apprenticed to accomplished craftsmen and, before his morning walk, they had gobbled their breakfast and charged out of the house.

As they sat down to porridge, bacon, and the best biscuits in the world, Rebecca brought up her big worry. "Roger, can you do anything about money while you're here?"

Sherman floated a generous amount of maple syrup on his porridge. "I've already set up a couple of trials to judge, and I've corresponded with people who owe me old debts. I'll also see about getting my allowance for the convention extension."

"There was a huge row over the last extension. It was the talk of the town. A lot of people didn't want to fund a secret meeting."

"Some people don't like what we're doing, public or private." Sherman wiped his mouth with a napkin. "But they'll continue to finance our delegation because they desire a voice more than they desire money."

"And our bonds?"

"If all goes well, I think we can trust Alex to make them good."

"Alex?"

"Rebecca, I can't talk about our proceedings, but it's no secret that Washington will be the first executive. Alex will surely head Treasury."

"And you?"

"The young can take their turn."

"It may be years before we can cash those bonds."

"So, the truth comes out. You like it when I'm away."

"Will New York be the capital?"

Sherman scratched his nose. "I think some have other designs, but it's likely—at least for a while."

Rebecca came around the table and picked up his dirty bowl. "Roger, you're a great politician and a good man. New York is only a day away. You should explore the possibilities."

"How do you know we're not designing a monarchy?"

She gave him a bump on the head with the bowl. "Because you want to return to New Haven."

Sherman gave her a hug around the waist. "I'll talk to some people."

"You do that. Besides, you didn't act sixty-six last night."

"Talking isn't my only talent."

"Talking? You're a terrible speaker. All the wives ask me what you're really like. They can't understand how such a cold, stiff man gets his way in politics."

"And what do you tell them about your stiff man?"

Rebecca blushed. "Nothing."

Part 5

Slavery

32

Monday, August 6, 1787

"Mr. Madison, may I—"

"Not now, perhaps later." Madison did not slow his pace or even give an acknowledging nod. He walked past the clusters of delegates in idle conversation and marched directly into the chamber. When he reached his table, he immediately distributed his notes and writing materials, snapping his inkwell on the baize-covered table with enough force to draw inquisitive glances. Sitting down, he rifled his papers until he realized that everything was already in order.

Several times, he had approached Randolph, who had steadfastly insisted that the Committee of Detail could handle their assignment without Madison's assistance. The five committeemen had locked themselves in the upstairs Council Room during the workday and studiously avoided other delegates at night. Why had they been so secretive?

Most of the delegates had left the blistering city, either to visit home or to venture into the cooler countryside. Madison had neither enough time to go home, nor the inclination to face his father, so he had remained at the Indian Queen to work on his notes.

He worried that Randolph lacked resolve and would easily bend to the other committee members. His notes could have been invaluable to the committee, but they never asked to see them. Now, as the assembly reconvened after a ten-day recess, Madison feared that the document they were about to distribute would veer from the convention's directives.

Everyone filed to their seats, and Washington immediately awarded the floor to Rutledge so he could present the committee report. While he made his preliminary remarks, Gorham and Ellsworth walked around the chamber distributing copies of a document. When Madison received his copy, he flipped the pages like a raccoon sorting through trash. What he saw confirmed his fears. They had remained faithful to the votes on decided issues, but there were many other areas, some quite extensive, where they had borrowed from other sources. Madison was immediately struck by how little they had accomplished in two months.

He picked up Rutledge's words: "We the people of the States of New Hampshire, Massachusetts, Rhode Island, Connecticut..."

The committee had gone to the expense of having their report typeset and printed as a folio pamphlet. The first page bore the imprint of Dunlap and Claypoole, one of the most prestigious printing houses in Philadelphia. They had shown the courtesy to restrict the printing to the right side of the page, so delegates could make notes in a broad left margin. At least they knew this wouldn't be the final document.

Rutledge stopped reading to make a parenthetical comment that caught Madison's attention. "We choose *Congress* as a name for the national legislature to appeal to our present congressmen. If the members believe the body is the same, they'll assume they can be easily elected to the new body."

Madison had no qualms about their choice of names for the various government departments, but he suspected that they had spent too much time on such a small matter. The convention had already informally adopted *Senate* for the upper house and the committee now specified *House of Representatives* for the lower house and *Congress* for the combined bodies. The *Supreme Court* showed little imagination, but the name fit the task. They avoided words that had become sensitive during British rule and selected the neutral *president* for the executive. The controversial parts didn't appear on the first page, so Madison went back to reading. The biggest problems appeared to be with the executive, this new president.

Rutledge took several hours to read the report, seldom adding any explanation. Madison calmed down after studying the document. The deviations arose from issues in which the convention had never bought finality with a vote. Without guidance, the committee had no choice but to invent solutions. Madison believed that they should be able to quickly move through the document and button up the remaining issues. He tossed the folio onto the table and sighed. The committee had done a service by exposing their omissions.

"DID YOU HAVE A pleasant visit home?" Madison asked.

He had found Sherman in the yard, and both men had started walking together. Strolling the tree-lined path, Madison wondered how they could accomplish any proper work in a room that felt like a blacksmith shed.

"Excellent. Did you enjoy the recess?"

"Mine was quiet. I stayed in Philadelphia to recuperate."

"How's your health?"

"Much improved. I caught up on my sleep."

Sherman looked over his shoulder. "The general looks sunburned."

"I understand he traipsed around Valley Forge and went trout fishing at Trenton. What'd you do in New Haven?"

"My wife and I hosted several large family gatherings, I enjoyed my own church services, and I performed some judicial duties." Sherman gave a rare smile. "A pleasant and gratifying life to which I'm anxious to return."

"If I had gone home, my father would have made me follow him around the plantation while he lectured me."

"He appears to be a devoted father."

"Appearances deceive."

Madison felt uneasy because Sherman looked as if he might probe, but he merely asked, "And your mother?"

"Very supportive. I wish I could write her about the proceedings. She's taken to bed again, and it would lift her spirits. Instead, I write about Philadelphia." Madison looked up into Sherman's impassive face. "What's New Haven like?"

"Peaceful—and pretty. Green neighborhoods filled with friendly people. The college adds both a scholarly and a rambunctious note."

"I'll bet I'd like New Haven. I loved Princeton."

"Then you must visit."

"I shall. Did you have any interesting cases?"

"Just tedious debt issues. I broke the monotony by giving a rambling speech to dedicate a bridge."

"You've never given a rambling speech here."

For some reason, this made Sherman laugh. "I didn't know what to say, so I stomped my foot and said, 'This bridge looks sturdy built.'" He laughed again. "Some were critical of my brevity."

"That's all you said?"

"What more needed to be said?"

Madison contemplated the strange man who walked beside him with the gait of a plow horse. Despite his physical awkwardness and poor speaking style, he projected self-assurance and seemed comfortable with himself. Was the man smart? Without a doubt, and he was savvy. Madison realized that Sherman was not oblivious to his shortcomings. The evidence lay in the way he used other people. There was a lesson here that he would have to think about.

ON TUESDAY THEY DEBATED the committee report. Madison settled in for an easy day, because the initial clauses held little potential for conflict. The debate meandered, so Madison decided to ask why the committee had fixed a date for Congress to meet. He suggested that the Constitution should require only that Congress meet once a year.

Gouverneur Morris interjected that they shouldn't be required to meet annually because there might not be enough business for an annual session.

Ellsworth, a bit exasperated, explained. "Until they meet, Congress won't know whether a session is required or not. Nor will they know when to send their members."

"Gouverneur Morris is right," King argued. "Legislating too much is a vice. And the vast majority of legislation belongs to the states."

Sherman made a typically terse statement. "I'm for fixing a date. The great extent of our affairs will supply purpose enough."

They voted to leave the date in December but allowed Congress the authority to set a different date if it chose.

The report recommended that persons qualified to vote for state offices would be qualified to vote for the House of Representatives. Gouverneur Morris spoke with a level of emotion that surprised Madison. "The states should not establish qualifications. We should set the standard, and we should limit the vote to men of property."

Wilson spoke with a note of condescension. "Does Mr. Morris wish to tell a man he can vote for his state representative, but he cannot vote for his national representative? That makes no sense."

Gouverneur Morris thumped his wood leg. "Balderdash! I object to letting the states set the qualifications." Another thump. "It's not proper."

Ellsworth explained. "Eight or nine states have already extended the right beyond freeholders, and the people will never rally behind a constitution that disfranchises them." Ellsworth put his fingers in the waistband pocket where he kept his snuffbox. "Every man who pays taxes owns the right to vote for the man who spends his money."

Morris was unconvinced. "May I remind the delegates that children don't vote? Neither can the ignorant and dependent be trusted. The time is not distant when this country will abound with men who receive their bread from employers. Will such men guard liberty?" Morris sat back down but threw out one final taunt. "As for merchants, if they want to vote, they can acquire property."

Madison caught Washington's eye and signaled that he wanted the floor. "In the future, a great majority of the people will be without land and possibly without any form of property. They will combine their interests and threaten property rights. Despite these considerations, we must remain pragmatic. A few states still require a freehold, but more have granted suffrage to every man. Keep in mind, the people must ratify our work."

When Madison took his seat, he saw a faint nod from Gen. Washington. As he picked up his quill, he felt chagrined to discover how much he craved approval, so he immediately made himself busy to suppress the uncomfortable emotion.

Franklin gathered himself up and spoke to the assemblage like he was their kindly guardian. "Gentlemen, I'd like to remind you that American seamen, who were carried in great numbers to British prisons, refused to free themselves by serving on the ships of our enemy. Contrast their patriotism with the British seamen, who readily served on our ships. This difference stems from our just treatment of commoners. We don't have the right to narrow suffrage, and such a restriction will create ill will with many of the men in this chamber."

Everyone knew that "many of the men" included Benjamin Franklin. After this upbraiding by their most senior delegate, the assembly dropped the matter and quietly adjourned.

"JAMES, MY GOOD MAN, I'm glad I found you."

Before his jolly greeting, a thumping dowel had signaled Morris's approach. Madison held aloft a silver teapot. "Gouverneur, may I offer you tea?"

Morris plopped into the opposite chair. "That you may, my boy, that you may."

Madison set the teapot on a silver platter and signaled for another teacup. The Indian Queen, in patriotic fervor, had sold all their European tea services and replaced them with sets crafted by Paul Revere. He would never voice the opinion, but Madison preferred the more elegant European designs to the simple American tooling. When a maid delivered another teacup, Madison covered the bottom with cream and added two teaspoons of sugar before pouring hot tea to the brim. "You're not going to flail me about a property requirement, are you?"

"Heavens, no." Morris took a cautious sip to test the temperature. "We have bigger game to hunt."

Madison laughed. Morris never took defeat to heart; he just rotated the angle of attack or gracefully slid to a whole new issue. The man could not be deflated. "And what new conquest do you have in your sights?"

"The slave trade," Morris replied. "We intend to kill it."

Madison felt his good mood evaporate. "I think most of us consider that issue settled. You might unravel some painful negotiations."

"Better than unraveling our budding empire. The South got the better of that deal, and we mean to balance the scale."

"Who's we?"

"Massachusetts and Pennsylvania."

"Sanctioned by?"

"We don't need permission." Morris waved his hand dismissively. "Where do you stand?"

"I've placed that issue in the completed pile. What do you mean, balance the scale?"

"We must stop importing these poor souls onto our shores."

"Make slave trade illegal?"

"As in Virginia."

The Deep South had threatened to abandon the convention if there was any restriction on slave trade. Now Morris threatened to stop a lucrative commercial enterprise. On the other hand, he had promised Witherspoon to work toward prohibiting this heinous practice. Madison set his teacup down. "I'll not be in the forefront, but if you create a breach, I will lend my influence, for whatever it may be worth."

"A slaveholder and Virginian?" Morris threw his arms out.

"Gouverneur, I'll not jeopardize the entire Constitution on this issue."

With that, Morris swallowed the last of his tea and lurched onto his wooden leg. "Thank you, James. I shall count on you."

ON WEDNESDAY THEY WERE supposed to take up the qualifications required to be a member of Congress. King asked for the floor and walked to the front of the chamber. He stood silently for a long time, gathering attention. When he started, he spoke slowly. "The issue of slavery grates on me. I've previously not made a strenuous objection because I hoped this convention would restrict the vice."

The best orator in the chamber had launched the first salvo to reignite the slave trade question. Again, Madison wished he had a seat that allowed him to see the reaction of the delegates. Glancing up, he noticed a twinge of disapproval on Washington's face.

King walked in a measured pace across the front of the chamber, shaking his head like a man perplexed. "There is so much inequality in all this. I had hoped some accommodation might take place."

King stopped his pacing, as if coincidentally, in front of the South Carolina table. He suddenly waved the committee report over his head and spoke in a voice that shook the chamber. "This report is an abomination. Slaves are represented. The importation of slaves cannot be prohibited or even taxed. Exports cannot be taxed. I ask, is this reasonable?" King slapped the report onto the South Carolina table. "The South cannot have it all!"

Madison saw Rutledge bristle. "I don't know where you got this idea that slaves are represented. That's foolishness."

"I read it in the report!" King boomed. "Do not twenty-five slaves have the same representation as fifteen freemen?"

Instead of answering, Rutledge crossed his arms against his chest and glared until King marched back to his seat.

Sherman asked for the floor. "The point of representation has been settled. As for the slave trade, I consider it sinful but don't believe myself bound on the issue. That is my position on the matter."

Madison was stunned by Sherman's feeble response, but before he could think it through, Washington banged his gavel. "Delegates, confine your comments to the report—in sequence. We'll consider the entire report in due course." He ended this order with a single sharp rap of the gavel.

The next section set the ratio of one representative per forty thousand "inhabitants."

"I move to insert *free* before the word *inhabitants*." When Gouverneur Morris uttered this incendiary sentence, Madison sensed a silent gasp from the delegates. Morris had had the effrontery to ignore Washington's admonition and return the debate to slavery. Morris stood but did not bang his wooden leg. With a sad note in his voice, he said, "Rather than saddle posterity with a Constitution that tolerates slavery, I'd sooner pay a tax to free every Negro."

Madison scribbled in increasing agitation. He knew Morris would not relent on the slave issue, which meant that everything closed could be reopened. Madison wondered if the leaves would turn color as he sat in this chair. Then a horrible thought struck him. He cringed at the thought of seeing snow piled on the windowsill.

As Madison entered the Indian Queen, he asked the doorman to send tea and a barber to his room. When he entered his quarters, he laid his valise on the bed and collapsed into the easy chair. This was a dangerous moment. Things could easily go astray. After a few minutes, he decided to seek help. He had ridden events ever since Sherman engineered a successful challenge to the Virginia Plan, but he vowed to assert himself. He wouldn't allow his dream to be dashed because of passivity.

He hoped the knock at the door meant his tea had arrived but discovered the barber instead.

"Come in."

"Thank you, sir." The barber looked around and said, "May I move the chair nearer the light?"

"Of course."

He picked up a ladder-back chair and set it carefully by the window. As Madison took a seat, the barber asked, "How would you like it cut?"

"Short. Crop it short enough to feel a breeze on my head."

"And where will you find this breeze?"

"I shall find it in the bluster of my fellow delegates."

33

Sherman stared at a small ship supposedly powered by steam instead of wind. The polished brass machinery looked heavier than a printing press and seemed to take up the entire deck. He thought it a poor idea.

"Absolutely brilliant." Ellsworth looked like a child who had just peered through his first telescope. "I must meet the inventor."

Sherman, Ellsworth, and Dickinson stood at the midpoint of a narrow dock that extended into the Delaware River. It felt like a parade, with about thirty men shoulder to shoulder on the dock and hundreds more on shore. John Fitch had brought his steam-powered ship to Philadelphia to impress the delegates and garner investors. The steam engine supposedly used twelve powered oars, six to a side, to propel the boat without sails. Sherman thought the wind undependable but easier to gather than a cord of wood.

He shifted his stance a bit wider to balance against the rolling dock. "We've not yet formed our government, and the rapacious already want to pillage the public treasury."

"Fitch wants private investors," Ellsworth said.

"Then why did he bring his novelty to us?"

Sherman felt Dickinson's hand on his shoulder. "In case you haven't noticed, most of the rich are here."

"Just because something can be done, doesn't mean it should be done. Ships move cargo." Sherman looked at Ellsworth. "That metal barrel with its levers, treadles, and cranks takes all the space and tonnage. Water is plentiful in the Atlantic, but trees are scarce." Ellsworth and Dickinson laughed, trading a knowing glance. "Could you gentlemen explain the humor in my comments?"

Dickinson squeezed Sherman's shoulder. "Roger, you may be inscrutable in chamber, but you're predictable outside."

"You think this has merit?" Sherman said in disbelief.

Ellsworth swept his arm across the ship. "Fitch proposes his steamship for the Mississippi River. Environs with plenty of trees, if I recollect."

Dickinson used his foot to caress the gunwale. "Innovations like this will increase the value of western lands."

Sherman grunted. "Driving the Spanish from our frontier will—"

A loud voice yelled, "All those game, climb aboard! We'll push off in a moment."

Ellsworth immediately squeezed onto a deck crowded with an unbelievable menagerie of rods, tubes, and struts. Madison suddenly exploded from the crowd and slipped on the wet wood as he tried to board. Sherman gripped him by the scruff of his coat and gave a gentle tug that righted the little man squarely on the ship's deck. Madison beamed. "Thanks. Aren't you coming?"

"I'll forego the experience, but I'll expect a report."

Seamen pushed the boat away with long poles and let it drift until it slipped a dozen yards into the river. About a dozen delegates had jumped aboard for the promised ride against the river's current. Suddenly, the weird boat issued a deep-throated growl that made conversation impossible. Twelve oars thrashed the water, lifted, and then thrashed again, until the river was a carpet of white foam. Despite a deafening roar and a frenzied whipping of the river, Sherman guessed the boat moved at less than two knots.

Turning to Dickinson, he shouted, "Let's step away."

When they reached the shore, Dickinson was laughing uproariously. "I believe that thrashing may kill all the fish within a hectare."

Sherman took a moment to catch his breath and suppress his own laughter. "Now I know what prompted Fitch to bring his boat to us. He spotted a kindred spirit in our braying and pointless thrashing."

GOUVERNEUR MORRIS OPENED THURSDAY'S session with a motion to require senators to be citizens for fourteen years.

Surprisingly, Butler backed the motion. "I oppose foreigners in the Senate. I was called to public life within a short time after coming to America, but my foreign attachments should have made me ineligible."

Madison said, "The parts of America that encourage emigration advance faster in population, prosperity, and the arts. The issue is negligible, because foreigners are rarely elected to office."

Gerry jumped in. "Eligibility ought to be restricted to native-born Americans. Otherwise, foreigners will infiltrate our councils and meddle in our affairs. Everyone knows the vast sums Europe lays out for secret services."

Wilson reminded Sherman of a neglected stew pot ready to spew. "I'm not a native, and if these ideas are approved, I'll be ineligible to hold office under the Constitution I'm entrusted to write. I'd feel humiliated."

Gouverneur Morris thumped his leg and said, in a snit, "Reason, not feelings, man. We should never strive to be polite at the expense of good sense. Some Indian tribes carry their hospitality so far as to offer their wives and daughters to strangers. I'll admit foreigners into my home, invite them to my table, provide them with lodging, but I don't carry hospitality so far as to bed them with my wife."

Morris limped across the front of the chamber but kept his eyes on Wilson. "The privileges we allow foreigners exceed those in any other part of the world. As for those philosophical 'citizens of the world,' I don't want them in public councils. I don't trust a man who shakes off attachment to his country."

Gouverneur Morris plopped into his chair with a finality that conveyed his firmness, but his motion to extend the citizenship requirement to fourteen years failed. Someone immediately made a motion for thirteen years, which also failed. Then a motion for ten years failed. Finally, a motion for nine years passed.

Pinckney again raised the issue of property requirements. "The members of the legislature, the executive, and judges should possess enough property to make them independent. If I were to fix an amount, I should think not less than one hundred thousand dollars for the president and half that sum for judges and members of Congress."

Franklin spoke in a lilting voice as he gently scolded Pinckney. "If honesty always accompanied wealth, then I'd agree with my illustrious colleague from South Carolina, but some of the greatest rogues I know are rich."

Sherman wondered if Pinckney's idea would have found acceptance if he had prescribed a more reasonable property requirement. One hundred thousand dollars would have prevented many men in the chamber from seeking the presidency.

"MORRIS HIT WILSON HARD today."

Sherman tilted the book he was reading so he could see Ellsworth. "Don't step into a family feud."

"Family?" Ellsworth asked.

"Political family. Morris and Wilson tussle for leadership of Pennsylvania."

The two men sat on chairs they had hauled to Mrs. Marshall's backyard. Sherman had strategically placed his chair so he could rest his legs on the stump of an elm, which in its day must have been a magnificent tree. He briefly lamented its foregone shade but appreciated the utility of the carcass.

Ellsworth broke his reverie. "What about Franklin?"

"Franklin devotes his time and fortune to Philadelphia. He leaves the state to younger men."

After fiddling with his snuff, Ellsworth said, "So Morris took umbrage that Wilson didn't follow his lead on citizenship."

"And Wilson didn't like Morris trying to exclude him from national office."

"You didn't take offense when Pinckney tried to exclude you."

"Pinckney's motion was flummery."

"How rich do you think he is?"

"Somewhere in excess of one hundred thousand dollars," Sherman said distractedly.

Ellsworth laughed. "Indeed." After a moment, he mused, "We must be nearing the end."

Sherman dropped his book again. "Why do you say that?"

"Because Morris tried to exclude his competitor from national office, and Pinckney tried to exclude all but the crème de la crème. The ambitious already assume a new government."

"Why, Mr. Ellsworth, you embarrass me. I was so engrossed in this book, I missed that."

Ellsworth beamed at the roundabout praise. "What're you reading?"

"*Robinson Crusoe.*"

"You like it?"

"No."

"It's very popular."

"It is popular because it's a tale well told. I object to the underlying message. It means to teach religious tolerance, but it goes too far."

"Too far?"

"It preaches that all religions are equal."

"I can see why you'd have difficulty with that."

"As would anyone devout."

"Some are open to other possibilities."

"If you believe in one God, and you have faith that you have found him, you can admit no others."

"But you've always been highly tolerant."

"Tolerant of other Protestant faiths. They worship the same God."

"What about the Hebrews?"

"I pray for them daily."

FRIDAY AND SATURDAY'S SESSIONS had covered old ground and frustrated Sherman, who was anxious for progress. On Monday, Randolph opened with an emotional plea to give the House of Representatives control of finances. He wanted the House to have sole authority over revenue and expenditures. The Senate would be prohibited from any modification to amount, source, or use.

Mason leaped to agree and ended with an angry harangue by saying, "I may consent to a Senate veto of money bills, but they're not entitled to it."

After a spout of stuttering, Gerry threw his words as a farmer might hurl stones at a mule's backside. "The people will never allow anyone but their immediate representatives to meddle in their purses." He glared across the chamber and then blurted, "If the Senate is not restrained from originating money bills, this plan will fail."

Sherman felt a piece of paper slipped under his hand. When he looked up, Ellsworth looked troubled. The scratched note read, "*Why are Randolph, Mason, and Gerry so angry?*" Sherman thought a moment. He picked up his quill and wrote, "*Mason due to principle. Randolph, because he lacks principles. Gerry due to his nature.*" After Ellsworth read the note, he looked no less troubled but gave a nod just the same.

Madison received the floor and started a monologue. "The word *revenue* is ambiguous. In many acts, particularly in the regulations of trade…"

Sherman's concentration lapsed. He knew Madison would deliver a long, logical argument, but he could anticipate the points and couldn't sustain the effort to follow his soft voice. He worried that progress remained painstakingly slow after the recess. Except for a few details, he felt he could predict where they would end up, but how long would it take to get there? Sherman settled in his chair, crossed his gangly legs, and told himself to be patient. The convention needed unanimity, or close to it, and that would take time.

After recess was called, Sherman watched Randolph, Mason, and Gerry leave the chamber. They had argued the same positions today, but they left separately. He decided that they didn't comprise a threatening coalition.

"Where are you headed?"

Sherman recognized the voice of Dickinson. "Across the street for lemonade."

"I'm with you."

As the two men dodged horses, carriages, and wagons, Sherman yelled above the din, "Is this social, or do you have an agenda?"

Dickinson gave a thank you wave to a teamster who had pulled up to give him room to scurry across. "Do you have social calls?"

"Not since I left New Haven. What's on your mind?"

"Let's get the lemonade first."

"Since you're the one with business, this is your treat."

"I'd gladly bribe you for the price of a lemonade."

"I don't barter my opinions, only my time."

"Really?"

Sherman gave him a friendly smile in response.

The State House Inn had taken advantage of the sweltering heat to set up an outdoor shelter to sell iced lemonade. Rough-hewn logs supported a canvas cover with brightly colored pennants over a makeshift table. Having bolted the chamber, they had beat the convention crowd and had to wait behind only a few strollers. When they reached the table, Sherman was impressed with the inn-keeper's business acumen. The comely young maid had conveniently forgotten to tie the string on her loose cotton blouse, and when she leaned over to pour each glass, she invited a tantalizing peek.

As they walked over to the shade of a tree, Dickinson said, "I'll bet not many men pass that stall without stopping for a respite."

Sherman lifted the glass in salute. "Since you've already received good value for your money, I question whether I owe you my time."

"Then will you lend me your ear?"

"Ha, for that repartee, I'll make a donation. You look a charitable case."

"As a matter of fact, I wish to discuss money."

"How so?"

"I'll propose this afternoon that members of Congress be paid by the na-tional treasury."

"I thought we agreed the states pay."

"I'm concerned that some states will set salaries so low, only the rich can serve."

"Pinckney's motion failed."

"There's more than one way to rig a scale. I want the wages secured by the national government so men such as yourself can serve, as well as men like Pinckney."

"That's considerate of you, especially since you can satisfy Pinckney's admis-sion price."

Dickinson made a dismissive shrug. "A silly, transparent proposition. I want equal compensation to avoid hard feelings and elitism."

Sherman thought Dickinson's argument sound. Previously, he had argued for state compensation so Connecticut could control its delegation. Now he saw it as a hindrance to a truly national government. He wondered at how far his thinking had evolved since arriving in Philadelphia. "I agree. Anything else?"

"I want to restrict members of Congress from holding other national posi-tions."

"Agreed."

Dickinson's head snapped and then he laughed. "This from Madison's great-est dread."

"I don't follow."

"Separation of power. Madison's sacred incantation. You're the mayor of New Haven and a judge of the Connecticut superior court and, for many years, you were simultaneously a member of Congress." Dickinson laughed again. "You must give the man fits. Executive, judicial, and legislative powers, all tightly gripped in the hands of one man."

"Those are separate jurisdictions. National, state, and city. I couldn't support my family on the wage from a single position."

"You prove my point. Congress must be paid from the national treasury. You deftly juggled multiple posts, but the task is beyond mortals."

"Mr. Dickinson, you're enjoying yourself far too much. If we had more time, I would make you buy me another glass of lemonade."

"Unfortunately, we must get back so you can earn that handsome allowance Connecticut pays you."

Sherman felt Dickinson's hand on his shoulder as they walked over to the table to return the empty glasses. He had tried to make light of Dickinson's taunts, but in his heart, he knew he would trust few others with such a broad expanse of power as he had wielded in Connecticut.

DICKINSON HAD FORESEEN CORRECTLY. Pinckney opened the afternoon session with a motion that members of Congress should receive no salary or expenses. He also proposed that members could be appointed to positions in the executive branch.

Luther Martin stood unsteadily and made a point of pulling down his soiled waistcoat. Sherman heard someone at another table say a bit too loudly, "The man's drunk." Sherman wished that Martin had taken his refreshment from the maid with the décolleté blouse. Martin coughed into a filthy handkerchief and then waved the offensive fabric at buzzing flies. "Gentlemen, without patronage, the Senate won't let the president in for his share of the plunder." He weaved a bit and then blew his nose before resuming his semaphore. "I ask, is that fair?" Martin seemed to instantly regain sobriety, and his voice lost its flippant quality. "If our senators carry such mercenary views, we should choose a despot, because it's easier to feed the rapacity of one man than the rapacity of many."

Sherman gained the floor. "I move that members of Congress be paid out of the United States Treasury."

When his motion passed, Sherman gratefully voted to adjourn for the day.

"MR. SHERMAN!"

Sherman stopped midstride to see Pierce Butler charging at him like an enraged bull. "Yes?"

"We have an agreement."

"It doesn't extend to compensation."

"It extends to a Senate committed to protect the sensitive issues of my state."

"The Senate has enough control to protect your interests."

"Not if we can't control our senators."

"I was unaware the type of man selected by South Carolina could be controlled by an allowance."

Butler's lips quivered, and several seconds passed before he could speak. "We don't control Georgia."

"They'll be pleased to hear that."

"Mr. Sherman, do not trifle with me. You know what I mean."

"We never discussed this issue. It's not part of our agreement."

"You cannot parse clauses like a pettifogger. Our word, as gentlemen, is supposed to be our bond."

For the first time in recent memory, Sherman felt his face flush with rage. "Mr. Butler, no one has ever challenged my word. Ever. I'll abide by our accord, but I won't allow you to dictate Connecticut's position on all matters."

Sherman could see by Butler's face that he knew he had gone too far. When he spoke, it was with an even tone. "So be it, Roger, but don't split hairs. We didn't sit down and negotiate a contract. We promised each other to support our respective states' interests." Sherman said nothing. "The next time you consider a change in position, would you be kind enough to check with me to see if it is a crucial cog in our scheme?"

Sherman hesitated to regain his composure and then said, "If I deem it relevant to our accord, I'll seek you out."

Butler almost said something, then shook his head and walked away. As Sherman watched him retreat, he reminded himself that political alliances were as fragile as chalkware. He had to be careful.

34

Tuesday, August 16, 1787

Madison felt a rush of excitement as he entered the shop, his third visit since he had arrived in Philadelphia. He was ready to order. The price would be high, but he wanted this extravagance more than anything else offered by the indulgent city. Tom Jefferson surrounded himself with clever novelties, but he didn't have one of these, and Madison looked forward to making him jealous.

The shop looked like a disheveled laboratory. David Rittenhouse, a renowned astronomer and mathematician, built clocks, surveyor tools, and scientific instruments. Cluttered benches edged the periphery of his workroom, and each bench displayed mechanical pieces strewn haphazardly around half-built contraptions. The laboratory made Madison's heart pump with the promise of magic. In addition to his other endeavors, Rittenhouse had built the first telescopes in America, and Madison had come to buy one of these miraculous instruments.

"Welcome, Mr. Madison. Did you get your father's permission?"

Madison winced. It had taken several beseeching letters to get his father's approval, but he didn't like to be reminded who controlled his purse. "An expenditure this large required consultation."

"Of course," Rittenhouse said.

Madison picked up a piece of beveled glass and moved it back and forth in front of his eye. "How long?" Madison asked.

"About eight weeks." Rittenhouse waved his arm to encompass the shop. "I have a large backlog." He looked as disheveled as his shop. In his mid-fifties, he had become a fixture in the city since his arrival seven years before. A close friend of Franklin, he had quickly established himself as one of the intellectual leaders of Philadelphia and a prominent member of Franklin's American Philosophical Society.

"Damn. I wanted to take it with me when I return to Montpelier."

"The convention goes well?"

"I'm not allowed to say, but it won't take eight weeks."

Madison walked over to a bench that held a partially finished telescope. With the back of his fingers, he caressed a shiny brass tube. "Who's this telescope for?"

"The Philosophical Society. I'm sorry, I've made commitments."

"Perhaps they can wait?" Madison picked up a machined brass ring that was pretty enough to adorn a lady's wrist. "I can be generous."

"I can't break my promise."

Madison carelessly flung the ring back onto the bench, where it pinged against the tube and then briefly spun like a child's top. "How noble of you."

When Madison turned, Rittenhouse looked angry. "If you had ordered on your first visit, you'd have your telescope by now."

Madison deserved that. He had allowed his disappointment to make him rude. "I apologize; I didn't mean to insult you."

Rittenhouse relaxed. "Never mind. I feel complimented that you want my instrument so badly. I'll rush it."

"Thank you. If it takes eight weeks, you know where to post it."

"Montpelier, Orange County."

"May I visit occasionally?"

"I don't encourage customers in the shop—but for you, anytime. I may not get started for weeks though."

"You'll be completing this one. I'd like to watch."

Rittenhouse looked wary and then affected a polite smile. "You don't intend to supply the Virginia market, do you?"

This triggered a genuine laugh. "I'm all thumbs. I merely hope to fix simple things that might break."

"In that case, come ahead. I'll explain some of my other devices. Give me opportunity, and I'll own your next tobacco crop."

"Perhaps Virginia's entire crop. I intend to drive my neighbors green with envy. Expect a rash of orders from the Old Dominion."

"In that case, I shall include my calculations for the transit of Venus. That should impress them."

"That would be very gracious of you."

Madison could tell that he had repaired the damage of his intemperate remark, so he picked up his hat, preparing to leave. "Have a pleasant afternoon, Mr. Rittenhouse."

When he turned to lift the door latch, Rittenhouse's voice gave him pause. "I'll build you a good telescope, Mr. Madison. You build us a good government."

"Yes, sir. I shall do my best."

"How?"

"Indirectly, my dear boy, indirectly. When you want to catch a big fish, you must first capture the bait." Gouverneur Morris took on a self-satisfied look. "We'll not attack the slave trade directly but attack another piece of the equation."

"The prohibition to tax exports?" Madison asked.

"I knew you were a clever lad."

Madison grew irritated with Morris's phony gregariousness. He had been the architect of this convention and was tired of being treated like a junior partner. Morris had invited him and Wilson over to his home to plot and scheme, a pastime Morris relished. Despite his rakish image, Morris's home was formal and dignified. Unlike Robert, this Morris did not use a rococo painting to lend a ribald touch to the decor. Gouverneur Morris needed no other props than his personality.

"What part do I play?" Madison asked.

"We want one of your logical arguments."

Madison grew wary. "When?"

"Tomorrow."

"That puts me far too much in front."

"I understood you had promised," Wilson said, with a shade of haughtiness.

Madison turned toward the owlish man. "I said I'd help after you created a breach."

"Don't worry, my boy, we shall precede you and blast a big hole in their lines."

"You ask a lot." Madison sat thoughtful. "There's a price."

Wilson looked annoyed, but Morris rocked with laughter. "Of course, of course. There's always a price. What do you want?"

"A stronger check on the legislature."

Wilson gave Madison a condescending look. "That's a piddling price."

Madison felt embarrassed at the dismissal, but he wanted this more than anything else at the moment. "Then you'll agree to a three-quarters vote to override a veto?"

"If that's what you want, then you must demand an absolute executive veto."

"That's already been defeated." As soon as the words escaped, Madison regretted them. He wanted the respect of these men, and he would never get it if he always let logic dictate his thinking. "Let me be clearer. Since an absolute veto has already been rejected, we need a red herring. I'll propose that laws must be approved by both the executive and the Supreme Court."

"Splendid. We'll make a backroom brawler of you yet."

Madison bristled. Where was Morris when he had pulled every ploy possible to get this convention assembled? Who had convinced Washington to leave his precious Mount Vernon? Morris had never even espoused a consistent theory of government, yet he believed himself the master and Madison the student. Suddenly, a realization struck Madison. It didn't matter. Every politico used others to get what they wanted, even if it meant turning a blind eye to their fellow conspirators' frailties.

Madison sat a bit straighter, in complete control of his emotions. "Thank you, Gouverneur. You're a master at dissimulation. I've learned more from you than from any other delegate." Madison gave a tip to an imaginary hat. "I hope I can count on additional lessons."

Morris puffed up like a satiated rooster. "That you may, my boy, that you may."

Madison shifted his gaze. "With Mr. Wilson's fine legal mind and your shrewd navigation, I'm confident we'll capture the opposition flag."

"Intelligence has not been dealt equally," Wilson preened.

Madison sat amazed. This was far too easy. Men, especially men of this stature, should not be susceptible to such thin flattery. But they were. The evidence sat before him. He decided that Morris had indeed taught him an invaluable lesson.

ON WEDNESDAY MORNING, MADISON moved that both the president and the Supreme Court have veto power over legislation. He felt bitter when his motion went down to overwhelming defeat without rousing the slightest argument.

As he brooded, Gouverneur Morris—never one to accept defeat easily—raised the ante. "I move for an absolute executive veto."

Madison watched Sherman stand in his typically rigid posture. "Gentlemen, I understand the concern, but one man cannot be wiser than two-thirds of both houses."

After additional speeches, the coordinated effort of Madison, Morris, and Wilson finally exhausted the delegates, causing them to vote for a three-quarters veto override. Madison knew the harsher restraint on the legislature had not passed due to reasoned persuasion, but because the assembly wanted to move to a different subject. Still, he felt satisfied. A victory, however achieved, was a victory nonetheless.

The next clause was the power to tax. Rutledge gave an angry speech, concluding with, "I'll vote for the tax clause on the condition that parts protecting slavery remain intact."

Gouverneur Morris leaped up without being recognized. "It's not equitable to tax imports without taxing exports!"

Washington gaveled Morris down, and an uncomfortable silence ensued. Madison waited for Wilson or Morris to push the issue, but when neither made a move, he signaled that he wanted to speak.

He picked up a piece of paper from his table. "Gentlemen, I oppose a prohibition against export taxes." Consulting his notes, he presented the logical arguments to support his case. Wilson followed with a long speech that reinforced his points. Madison hoped that their strategy of wearing down resistance would work again.

Gouverneur Morris took his turn. "Every country taxes the exportation of unique articles. France taxes her wines and brandies." As was his habit, Morris thumped across the front of the chamber. "Export taxes can also be used as a weapon. If we impose a tax on lumber, for example, we can punish the West Indies for restricting our other trade."

Sherman displayed an atypical tone of exasperation. "Gentlemen, I thought this matter settled. Imports are taxed and exports are not. Complexity renders an equal tax on exports by region impractical." Sherman moved to postpone and the assembly quickly agreed.

"THAT'S WHAT YOU CALL a big hole in their lines?"

"That was a trial salvo, my dear boy. Something to rattle the troops. I didn't expect you to charge in."

"I thought Washington's gavel forced your retreat."

The genial Morris countenance flashed anger. Madison took pleasure in setting him on his heels. Perhaps he could grow to like backroom politics.

He felt even more pleased when Wilson added, "You left us in the lurch."

The rare Morris anger flashed between the two men. "Strategy is important, but timing is everything. You jumped the bugle."

"I distinctly remember that you said today." Madison could not help throwing salt on the cut.

"And I distinctly remember that your price was a three-quarters override. I got you a stronger veto, but your feeble foray put the delegates into a slumber."

Madison felt the sting and remembered why he didn't like combative politics. He decided to revert to the tactic that had worked so well the night before. "You're right, Gouverneur. I may have been overanxious."

Morris laid a hand on Madison's shoulder. "Not to worry, my boy, no harm. These naughty little trysts always start with some awkward fumbling before they reach a fluid crescendo."

Madison returned a smile and ignored the disdain on Wilson's face. When Madison stood to leave, Morris grabbed his attention. "The general wants us at Ben's courtyard."

"When?" Wilson sniffed.

"Now."

Damn it. It was bad enough that Gouverneur played the *Kapellmeister* of their little troupe, but it jarred Madison to be summoned by this braggart. After all, Washington was a Virginian. When would it be his turn to fetch Gouverneur to the great man's presence?

Wilson looked anxious. "Is the general upset with our position on export taxes?"

"I don't think so," Morris said. "All the senior delegates will be there."

"Is there a crisis I'm unaware of?" Wilson asked in an annoyed voice.

"That's best left for the gathering," Morris answered.

The response pleased Madison because it meant that Morris didn't know why they had been called together. "Who else will be present?"

"Robert and Alex," Morris said.

"Virginia, Pennsylvania, and New York," Wilson mused. "The three big states. Something's in the wind."

"The important part is that we're not meeting at Robert Morris's home," Madison said. He answered their bewildered expressions by explaining, "The general wants Ben's advice."

"Why do you say that?" Wilson asked.

"Franklin's health limits his mobility. When Washington wants his counsel, he goes to the doctor."

Madison enjoyed the look on their faces. His logical mind, plus knowledge of the habits of the two patricians, had momentarily placed him on an equal plane with these two men who saw themselves as master politicians.

Morris waved his arm in an elaborate gesture that meant they should depart. "We'll know soon enough."

WASHINGTON STOOD TO GREET the new arrivals. After Madison, Morris, and Wilson took seats, he said, "Thank you for coming. I won't keep you in suspense. I asked you here to discuss Clinton."

"What mischief has he been up to?" Morris asked.

"Our fear is that we only know the half of it," Franklin answered. "Since Clinton pulled Yates and Lansing from the convention, he's been spreading ugly rumors."

"And we can't violate our secrecy oath to dispute them," Washington inserted.

"They violated it," Hamilton nearly yelled.

"Did they?" Washington gave Hamilton a stare that Madison wouldn't want aimed at him. "The rumors describe a convention I've not attended."

In a level tone, Hamilton said, "They violated the intent of the secrecy accord."

"And how should we punish them?" Washington asked. When he received no answer, he said, "Dr. Franklin has been informed that articles will appear in all the major newspapers alleging that we intend to anoint the second son of George III as king."

"Clinton also called out the state militia," Franklin added.

"To what purpose?" Wilson seemed startled.

Franklin shrugged. "Ostensibly for training." He removed his spectacles to rub his eyes. "The worrisome part is that New York's militia is rife with Cincinnati."

"Training be damned. He means to intimidate us—or perhaps worse," Hamilton said with disgust.

Wilson looked at Franklin. "We must prepare for attack."

Now Franklin looked annoyed. "Who should prepare? The guards surrounding the State House?"

"The Pennsylvania militia." Wilson looked determined.

About ten years before, a mob had stormed Wilson's home because he had defended Robert Morris in a corruption case. Wilson had gathered thirty friends and fought off what could only be called a riot. Ever since, Wilson preached meeting force with force.

Madison felt compelled to defuse the growing alarm. "If I may, I think the message is aimed internally. Clinton wants to show New York that they have the military strength to remain independent. He's started the ratification engagement before we have even laid ink to parchment."

"That makes more sense," Franklin said. "Clinton's a rogue, not reckless. He'd never threaten war against the combined forces of the other states."

Wilson scowled. "Don't underestimate Clinton's treachery."

Hamilton stood and paced in front of the men. "If Jemmy's right, Clinton's militia is still a threat, perhaps not immediately, but in the years ahead." He stopped in front of Washington. "Let me return to New York and start a campaign to impeach the son of a bitch. Powerful men have grown tired of paying tribute to that martinet."

Franklin took on a thoughtful pose. "There's risk. Clinton could make public our negotiations with Congress."

"The doctor's right—we must engage on the periphery." Washington looked up at Hamilton. "Alex, I'd like you to return to New York. Investigate this newspaper story and see if you can determine its source. Also, ascertain the risk from your fellow members in the Cincinnati."

Hamilton retook his chair. "Of course, sir. Anything else?"

"Wrap your extraordinary mind around the New York ratification. Clinton knows we must have them in the union. Figure out a way to mitigate the price." Washington patted Hamilton on the knee. "You're a good warrior, Alex, but this battle will be fought with your other admirable quality—your wits."

THE NEXT DAY THEY came to the clause "to make war." Pinckney opened. "I oppose vesting this power in the combined Congress. I propose the Senate alone."

Butler argued that the power should be vested in the president, and Gerry huffed, "I never expected to hear a motion to empower the president to make war."

Madison moved to strike out "make" and insert "declare," which he believed would leave the executive free to repel sudden attacks.

He was irritated to see that Sherman again disagreed. "The current provision stands well. The president should be able to repel an invasion but not commence war. *Declare* narrows congressional power too much."

Madison could not restrain a small smile when the convention overruled Sherman's objection and then voted to replace the word *make* with *declare*.

Rutledge gained the floor in a snit. "This convention is interminable. I'm sure the public grows impatient—I know I do. I move that the convention henceforth meet precisely at ten o'clock and never adjourn prior to four o'clock."

Madison smiled. Rutledge intended to punish their dalliance. Nothing would light a fire under an assembly more than hampering their freedom to entertain each other with public money. But when the vote came, Madison saw that he had underestimated the delegates' impatience. Only Pennsylvania voted against the motion, because its members could conduct business outside of session hours. Good. It would be difficult to keep his notes current, but Madison would rather things moved fast.

Mason brought up a new war powers issue. "Except for a few garrisons, there should be no standing army in time of peace. Therefore, we must rely upon the militia to defend the nation. I move to add the power to regulate the militia to the general government."

Gerry flicked his head as unconsciously as a horse swiped its tail at pesky flies. "Gentlemen, a standing army is like a standing member: an excellent assurance of domestic tranquility, but a dangerous temptation to foreign adventure."

Instead of laughter, Gerry received stony silence. He sputtered unintelligibly and then continued pugnaciously. "As we speak, preparations are being made to use force against us. The governor of New York has rallied his militia and drills them for war against those who support this plan. Power over the militia must be taken from ruthless demagogues." After more comments supporting a militia controlled by the general government, Gerry offered an inane stipulation. "We should never need a standing army of more than a thousand troops."

Washington, in a stage whisper, muttered, "Then the Constitution should include a rule that invading forces must be limited to the same number."

Madison's head bounced in surprise. That might have been the first full sentence Washington had uttered in these long months, but by the time he raised his sight, Washington had shrouded himself in a placid expression that conveyed not the slightest emotion.

Sherman stood and clasped his left wrist with his right hand. "The states want their militia to defend against invasions and to enforce their laws. They'll not give on this point."

As Madison gathered up his things for the day, he shook his head in disbelief. Sherman's comment showed that his biases had not been totally shed.

"What are your thoughts on the assumption of state debts?" Sherman stood at Madison's elbow.

"My thoughts, or the Virginia delegation's position?"

"Both, if you can convey them."

Madison ceased gathering up his belongings. Sherman had been assigned to a new committee to work out the remaining open issues. "Have a seat. The chamber is about empty."

"Thank you." Sherman pulled a chair around catercorner to Madison.

"We've repaid much of our war debt," Madison said. "Other states have not. Virginia feels it's unfair to punish responsible states."

"How does James Madison feel?"

Madison needed a moment to think. "I think it's a good idea."

"Why?"

"I wish I could give you a new argument to take into committee, but the only reason I can think of is to improve ratification."

"Would you put your head to it?" Sherman looked thoughtful. "Despite the unfairness, we still need Virginia to ratify."

"I'll scratch out some thoughts. What's your opinion?"

"I believe it is an issue for the First Congress. I'd rather we stay mute on the subject."

"Because?"

"Because it'll require hard bargaining. Too hard to allow us to conclude our proceedings in a timely fashion."

"Do you own Connecticut bonds?"

"I do."

"Then federal assumption would benefit you personally."

"I am here to serve my country."

"Which country is that: the United States or Connecticut?"

"Connecticut today, the United States the day I sign the Constitution."

Madison was startled by the forthrightness of Sherman's response. "I appreciate your honesty."

"Which country demands your loyalty?"

"The United States of America—since the Annapolis Convention." Madison hesitated. "No. Long before."

"That may account for the friction between us."

"Perhaps, but I'm pleased to know we'll be allies after the signing ceremony."

Sherman gave a rare, wide smile. "That, my good sir, is yet to be seen." Sherman stood and nestled his tricorn under his arm. "Good afternoon, Mr. Madison. And thank you."

35

Saturday, August 18, 1787

Sherman gave two raps with the door knocker and was pleasantly surprised to see Gen. Washington answer the door. "Mr. Sherman, thank you for accepting my invitation."

"I'm always at your disposal, General."

"Then perhaps you'll not object to a walk?"

Sherman involuntarily glanced into the Robert Morris house. "Sir? For privacy or pleasure?"

"Pleasure and business. I have ordered a carriage built, and I check the progress daily. We can talk along the way."

"A walk will do my constitution good." Sherman stepped aside to give Washington room to pass him down the steps. "I'm stiff as a ramrod after sitting in that steamy chamber."

Instead of marching past Sherman, Washington held out an uplifted palm, signaling that Sherman should descend the stoop first. "Perhaps rheumatism is God's curse on politicians. Military service has its hazards, but at least a military man lives outdoors."

Sherman laughed as he walked down the three steps to the broad sidewalk. "Yes sir, politicians are indoor creatures."

Washington descended the steps, apparently oblivious to the deferential glances from the people in the street. "Not a smidgen of fresh air lightens our stale breath. I fear we shall expire in our own gases."

"Some would say we deserve such a fate."

"Some would say." Washington marched off at a brisk pace.

They didn't speak for half a block. Washington had a motive for this invitation, so Sherman remained silent to allow the general to lead the discussion.

When people became rare on the sidewalk, Washington asked an odd question. "Whom do you know in Fairfield?"

Sherman thought a moment. "Politicians and merchants. It's along the route to New Haven."

"Is it a hotbed of Connecticut loyalists?"

"No." Washington gave him an odd look, so Sherman added, "It is a hotbed of plowmen."

Washington nodded. "You've heard the rumors about Frederick Augustus, the Bishop of Osnaburg?"

"Yes."

"I dispatched Hamilton to investigate. He discovered that the rumor surfaced first in a broadside printed in Fairfield."

This was news to Sherman. He had heard the rumor that the convention was going to anoint the second son of George III as king of the United States, but he hadn't known that the story had originated in Connecticut. "That doesn't sound in character with the town," Sherman mused.

"Someone in Fairfield wants to harm this convention."

"This rumor spread too fast and furious to be propelled from a coastal village."

Washington smiled. "I believe you're right. Someone probably used a Fairfield sympathizer to hide his identity. Once the printed word had lent respectability to the falsehood, they got the rumor spread through larger newspapers." Washington gave Sherman a sideways glance. "Who would you suspect?"

Sherman didn't hesitate. "Governor Clinton. He's devious enough, and Fairfield is close by New York."

"Then Alex isn't overly suspicious?"

"I can't render judgment on that score, sir, but if Alex believes the most likely culprit is the esteemed governor of the sovereign state of New York, I agree with him."

Washington walked a few more paces and then said, "New York may ruin this convention yet. We need to squelch this rumor."

"You think people give it credence?"

"An outrageous lie, if repeated often enough, and with fervent indignation, will eventually be accepted as truth."

Sherman took half a step to avoid the leavings of a dog. "They can accuse us of anything."

Washington drew a folded piece of paper from his coat. "I'd like you to read this."

Sherman stopped walking and rested his buttocks against a low fence as he withdrew his glasses. He recognized Hamilton's handwriting.

"Many letters have been written to the members of the Federal Convention from different quarters, respecting the reports that we intend to establish a monarchical government and to send for the Bishop of Osnaburg. Although we cannot tell you what we are doing, we can tell you what we are not doing—we never once thought of a king."

Sherman extended the single page back to the general. "What do you want me to do?"

Washington made no attempt to accept the piece of paper. "Agree with the text and have it printed in Connecticut newspapers."

Sherman refolded the paper and slipped it into his own pocket. "Anything else?"

"After the notice has been printed, send letters to influential people and tell them that powerful forces outside the convention have spread this rumor because they want to put public pressure on us to create a monarchy. Plead with them to support our work, because otherwise a king might be thrust upon us."

Most politicians would be pleased to squash a harmful rumor, but Washington went a step beyond. After deflecting the blow, he used the force of the thrust against the perpetrators. People underrated the general's political skills, owing to his deft sleight of hand.

"Other states?" Sherman asked.

"The statement will be printed in the *Pennsylvania Herald* and then throughout the country. Ben has broad influence."

Sherman thought that an understatement. Washington suddenly started off again and quickly stepped into an alleyway that ran alongside a leather shop. After they entered a courtyard in the center of the block, Sherman spotted the carriage maker. A furniture shop shared the small courtyard, and about half a dozen smocked men worked on sundry pieces scattered around the open area. Sherman briefly admired the quiet professionalism of the craftsmen before noticing the handsome carriage sitting just inside the wainwright's wide double doors.

"Watch out, man!"

The shout threw Sherman against the wall. Two gruff men rolled large wheels with remarkable speed by slapping their hands against them in an upward motion. The dirt pathway had muffled the noise, catching Sherman by surprise.

"Are those wheels for your carriage?" Sherman asked as he brushed off his shoulders.

"Mine are mounted. I watched them being made across the street. Good solid craftsmanship."

Wheels were a specialty trade, and most people would have been satisfied with a brief inspection of the wheel maker's shop. The way Washington simultaneously handled so many interests fascinated Sherman. He orchestrated political events taking place in front of the curtain, directed the intricacies behind the curtain, and at the same time, paid close attention to the small details of his personal business.

"Your carriage?" Sherman asked, pointing to the nearly finished carriage in the doorway.

"Yes. What do you think?"

The black and gilded carriage was too pretentious for Sherman's taste, but he said, "The workmanship looks exceptional."

"Even fine workmen need to feel the watchful eye of an overseer." With that curt statement, Washington marched into the shop. The barnlike structure had an expansive feel, housing three carriages in varying states of construction. The two wheelmen were situating their handiwork against a wall, and five other workmen bustled around the carriages.

A beefy man approached the general. "We didn't expect to see you today, General."

"You should always expect me, Mr. Greer."

The man grimaced and looked back at the carriage. "It'll be ready in ten to twelve days, as I explained yesterday."

"The upholstery?"

"The leather has not yet arrived, but that won't delay us."

"You said that yesterday."

The large man's eyes grew hard and he leaned ever slightly toward Washington. "General, with all due respect, our work is impeccable and on time." The man gave another glance at the coach behind him and continued in a voice loud enough for his workmen to hear. "Constant interruptions are the only thing that might delay us."

"I'm sorry if my visits disturb you, but I'll never relinquish the right to oversee my interests." Washington leaned toward the man's ear, but he spoke with his stage whisper. "Let me be clear: I will not discontinue my inspections nor limit my remarks to avoid hurting your feelings."

Greer retreated half a step and then bowed his head respectfully. "Of course, sir. I apologize if my meaning was misunderstood. I only meant that the work is at a delicate stage that requires concentration. The gilding must be done to exacting standards."

"So must the coachwork. I insist on inspecting the calfskin and horsehide."

"The horsehide for the coachman's seat is in the back. I assumed you were only concerned with the passenger compartment."

"You assumed incorrectly. May I see the material?"

"Of course. If you'll wait, I'll bring it into the sunlight."

The burly man moved with unusual speed to the back of the shop. Washington turned to Sherman. "Your committee will make a recommendation on the militia. I would take it as a personal favor if you didn't preclude a standing army."

The abrupt change startled Sherman. "We have a tradition of relying upon a citizen militia."

"We must face our defects and provide cures. I fought a war with well-meaning, but undisciplined, volunteers. We should not do so again."

"You were successful."

"Barely."

"You're asking only that there be no stipulation against a standing army?"

"Correct."

"I will work to that end."

"Thank you." Washington turned to the returning coach maker, who held the horsehide in his outstretched arms.

Washington reached out and turned over one corner of the hide to examine the back. "What do you think, Roger?"

Sherman didn't need to touch the hide. "These are remnants. Serviceable, but not top grade."

"Mr. Greer?"

"Sir, I beg to differ. This hide is tanned to the highest standards. In this business, we use all our materials."

Washington raised an eyebrow in Sherman's direction. He felt uncomfortable that Washington had put him in the middle, but Sherman stepped closer and took a careful look at the remnants. "Mr. Greer, if you use these hides, how will you handle the seam?"

The man looked uncomfortable. "Yes, I see. The seam would go down the middle of the seat."

Washington nodded toward the other carriages. "Use these remnants on one of those."

"Yes, sir, of course. I'll get you a hide that'll require no seam."

"Thank you, Mr. Greer. I'll leave you to your work."

Washington turned on his heels and walked toward the alleyway. Sherman scrambled to catch up and expected the general to remark on the scene that had just transpired. Instead he asked, "What will your committee recommend about state debts?"

Without hesitation, Sherman said, "Assign the power, but not the obligation."

"Why?"

"We don't have the information in front of us. It will take weeks, perhaps months, to negotiate and separate war debts from other borrowings. I also don't believe we have authority on this issue."

"We don't have the authority to write a new constitution."

"Excuse me, sir, but do you want us to address state debts?"

"No. I believe your reasoning valid." Washington gave a small wave to a passerby. "We'll let the First Congress sort that mess out. Assigning the power serves the purpose."

Sherman smiled. He walked the rest of the way, confident that the first executive under the new government could handle the troubles plaguing this youthful nation.

"AND TO MAKE ALL laws necessary and proper for carrying into execution the foregoing powers, and all other powers vested, by this Constitution, in the Government of the United States or any department or officer thereof."

Sherman felt a twinge of unease. He had read the clause several times, and it had never given him pause, but hearing it read aloud raised an instinctive alarm. Could "necessary and proper" create a breach? Before Sherman could put his qualms into words, the measure passed without objection.

Sherman listened to the next clause. "Direct taxation shall be regulated by the whole number of white and other free citizens and inhabitants of every age, sex and condition, including those bound to servitude for a term of years, and three-fifths of all other persons not comprehended in the foregoing description (except Indians not paying taxes), which number shall, within six years after the first meeting of the legislature, and within the term of every ten years afterwards, be taken in such manner as the said legislature shall direct."

A motion was passed to delete the redundant "white and other." Then a motion passed to take the first census in three years instead of six.

As planned, Ellsworth made a speech supporting prohibition of export taxes. Sherman wanted to send South Carolina a signal that Connecticut would help fight off the coordinated attack by Madison, Wilson, and Morris on slave trade.

Sherman listened expectantly as Madison renewed his assault, but with a new twist. "Gentlemen, most of the revenue will be drawn from trade, and it makes no difference whether it comes from imports or exports. We should examine both, including *any* prohibitions on import taxes."

Clever, Sherman thought. Madison was telling South Carolina to accept export taxes or to allow an import tax on slaves. As Madison took his seat, Sherman saw him give the slightest of nods to Wilson and Morris. They both gave long-winded speeches supporting an export tax.

After a midday break, Luther Martin stumbled to the front, weaving between the tables until he passed close to the Virginia table. Martin looked pointedly at Madison and said, "Fool," in a voice loud enough for Sherman to hear in the back row.

Martin, looking as rumpled as ever, swayed as if on a roiling sea. Sherman thought the man could dismay him no further—then he began to speak. "Gentlemen—" Martin bowed slightly toward the South Carolina table and continued, "and pharisaical delegates from the South... the slave trade, not an export tax, is the issue. We ought to prohibit this disgusting practice. Or place a heavy tax on it."

An audible gasp went up in the chamber. Martin, inebriated and bored, decided to mount a frontal assault, one aimed at the true sticking point. Raising the slave trade directly would inflame tempers and erase any pretense of civil debate. And he wasn't done.

"The slave trade is dishonorable to our character. It has no place in our Constitution. Since five slaves count as three freemen, the Constitution encourages traffic in human chattel. We must offset this incentive by attacking the purse of those who engage in this ugly business."

Martin's gait grew steady, and then he said, "You should all be ashamed."

Madison had whirled around to watch Martin retreat to his seat. His face looked incredulous as he held his quill motionless above his inkwell. Normally, Sherman took pleasure in a discombobulated Madison, but Martin's outburst meant greater problems for him than for his bright little colleague. The chamber grew so still that Madison's resumed quill scratching sounded like a chair grating across the floor.

When Pinckney spoke, Sherman winced at the sharpness of his words. "If South Carolina is left alone, it may prohibit the trade, but if we're bullied, we'll walk from these proceedings."

Mason owned nearly a hundred slaves, but he seemed oblivious to the apparent hypocrisy of his remarks when he followed Pinckney. "Slavery is an abomination. It discourages the arts and manufacturing. The poor despise honest labor because slaves perform it. Every master is a petty tyrant. Gentlemen, make no mistake, slavery will bring the wrath of God on our country! The government must be given the power to stop importing Negroes!"

The delegates at the South Carolina table bent together in a whispered exchange, and then Pinckney asked for the floor. "It might be reasonable that slaves be taxed like other imports, but South Carolina will reject the union if the slave trade is abolished."

Sherman's head lifted with that comment. Did Pinckney just offer a compromise? His next sentence answered his question.

"I move to commit a clause that slaves be liable to an equal tax with other imports." Disdainfully, he added, "That should remove the difficulty."

"THANK YOU FOR OFFERING a compromise."

Pinckney busied himself gathering up his belongings. "If you'll excuse me, I have other affairs."

"I take it you're unhappy to have been placed in a position to compromise."

Pinckney gave Sherman a cross look. "That sanctimonious little prick. He should free his own slaves before instructing us. And you shouldn't look so pleased. We had a deal."

"I'm upholding my end."

"Not well enough."

Sherman kept his voice even. "South Carolina and Connecticut agreed on a set of accommodations, but there are eleven states. The ones that fight against the trade were originally on your side."

Pinckney slapped his portfolio closed. When he looked up, the usual arrogant expression was absent from his handsome face. "Roger, this is not done. You would be wise not to waiver." With this, Pinckney tucked his portfolio under his arm and marched out of the chamber.

Ellsworth walked over and asked, "What has Charles so bothered?"

"He's angry that Madison figured out that South Carolina would rather see a tax on the import of Negroes than a tax on exports."

"South Carolina would rather cut a deal to make Madison president than see slavery hampered."

Sherman gave a hearty laugh. "Now you go too far. Pinckney's angry, not mad. Come on, let's take a brisk walk before we return to Mrs. Marshall."

Part 6

Unanimity

36

Thursday, August 23, 1787

Madison bounded down the stairs. After he made the turn at the landing, he saw Pinckney in front of him. "Charles, may I join you for breakfast?"

Pinckney stopped his descent and turned toward Madison. "You may not."

Madison stopped a few steps above Pinckney. "You're angry?"

"What did you expect?"

"Sarcasm, not sulking."

"I don't sulk." Pinckney turned to continue down the stairs and mumbled, "I reserve my sarcasm for friends."

Madison laughed out loud. Pinckney whirled and gave him a piercing look. "Mr. Madison, do not provoke me."

"Of course not. I apologize." Madison bounced down the remaining stairs. "Charles, please. We must talk."

"Why?"

"Because we—"

"Never mind. Let's eat. I'm famished."

Madison and Pinckney walked into the Indian Queen's elegant dining room and were immediately seated. After ordering, Pinckney said, "You're a dastardly turncoat."

"I fight for principles. A turncoat has none."

"Principle is a fancy word. I see self-interest—and hypocrisy."

A server arrived, balancing a crowded salver on his fingertips. The man fastidiously arranged their breakfast and then asked if everything was to their satisfaction. Pinckney gave the dismissive wave he used with servants. After the servant bowed and backed away, Pinckney leaned toward Madison. "You betrayed the South."

"You can accuse me of betraying slavery, but not the South. The South is more than slavery."

"The South is less without slavery, you fool. How would your plantation fare without slaves?"

353

"I merely want the slave trade curtailed. No one has raised emancipation. The South has quite enough Negroes."

"Virginia does not comprise the entire South. The rest of us need more slaves, and we don't want to buy them from Virginia."

"This idea that Virginia has too many slaves is ludicrous. Where did it come from?"

"So, our little master wants to enlarge the slave population of Montpelier."

Madison looked at his oatmeal and pushed it away. He had inadvertently filled the bowl to the brim with maple syrup. Madison looked at Pinckney. "You must admit the deal was weighted heavily in your favor."

"I admit no such thing."

"No tax on exports, no import tax on slaves, and slaves counted as three-fifths of a person. All in exchange for a bastardized Senate."

Pinckney made a show of sniffing his melon. "A small price for empire."

"We're building a republic."

Pinckney dug out a spoonful of melon and poised it in midair. "A small price, nonetheless."

"You must relent on this infernal importation of Negroes."

"A small tax is acceptable, but in exchange, we have other demands."

"What other demands?"

"The obligation of every state to return fugitive slaves. As it so happens, also part of the Northwest Ordinance."

Madison fumed. "Slavery cannot dictate every aspect of our government."

"Why not?"

"Because I won't allow it." Madison crisply tapped one egg with his knife, and a perfect serrated circle appeared one-third of the way down from the top of the shell. He lifted the top off in a single twisting motion, swirled a knife under the remaining shell bottom, and slipped the egg into a small bowl. After he replicated the ceremony with a second egg, he lifted his eyes to see Charles Pinckney wearing a bemused smirk.

MADISON LISTENED AS KING read the report from Sherman's committee. King's smooth voice wafted through the chamber. "To make laws for organizing, arming and disciplining the militia, and for governing such part of them as may be employed in the service of the United States, reserving to the states respectively the appointment of the officers, and authority of training the militia according to the discipline prescribed."

"This turns the states into drill sergeants!" exploded Gerry. "I'd rather disarm the citizens of Massachusetts than submit to this despotism."

Martin blustered with indignation, "Are you men fools? The states will never give up control of the militia. How will they protect their liberty?"

Madison sighed. Gerry's and Martin's negativism exhausted him. He snapped his quill into his inkwell too hard and jammed the tip. As he used his penknife to cut a new point on his quill, King read the next clause. "The national legislature shall fulfill the engagements and discharge the debts of the United States and shall have the power to lay and collect taxes, duties, imposts, and excises."

Gerry remained in a snit. Shaking his head, he said, "To not require assumption of state debts is tomfoolery."

Sherman immediately said, "The First Congress can decide the extent of the 'debts of the United States.'" Before Madison could turn his head, Sherman had already taken his seat. Even for Sherman, the comment was unusually terse. Gerry's reflexive assaults on anything and everything must be frustrating his adversary. Good.

Butler surprised Madison with an emotional outburst. "If this compels payment to the bloodsuckers who took advantage of our soldiers, then I strongly object. I insist we exclude speculators."

After some additional complaints about speculators reaping a windfall, King proceeded to the next clause. "The Senate of the United States shall have the power to make treaties, and to appoint ambassadors, and judges of the Supreme Court."

Gouverneur Morris moved that the Senate should ratify the treaties made by the executive, but the Morris modification failed, and they called it a day.

WANDERING INTO THE BARROOM at the back of the Indian Queen, Madison spotted Gouverneur Morris. Sliding onto the bench across from him, Madison said, "I agreed with your motion."

Morris looked up from a legal document. "That's because you're a smart boy, James."

"I think I mentioned this 'boy' thing before."

"Just a figure of speech. You must learn to be less sensitive."

"I'll talk to Gerry. He can instruct me on how to shrug off little irritations."

"Ha, good, my boy." Morris waved the barmaid over to their table. Without asking, he ordered Madison a glass of Madeira. After the barmaid scurried away, Morris said, "We must bar the committee doors against malcontents."

"What committee?" Madison asked.

"Oh, there'll be another committee. *The* committee. I'm working to get us both assigned."

Many believed that political bodies debated issues, voted, and that was the end of it. In truth, assemblies cobbled together something closer to a rough draft. Committees smoothed phrasing, added nuance, adjusted points, and even deleted great volumes of verbiage. Their final committee would have inordinate influence over the Constitution.

Madison felt chagrined. "I should've thought about the next committee. Thank you." Madison sipped his Madeira. "Do you think it's close? I feel like I've been in a death struggle for months."

"Skirmishes, mere skirmishes. You must learn to husband your energy for the coming Armageddon."

"That seems overstated."

"My bread and butter, my boy. Without hyperbole, your hobbling friend would find himself without an audience."

"You mean to entertain?"

"I mean to ladle my bluster with a touch of maple syrup." Morris looked momentarily pleased, but his face quickly grew serious. "The general wants unanimity."

"Wishful thinking," Madison snapped, irritated by Washington's compulsiveness.

"The doctor wants to discuss it nonetheless."

"When?"

"Shall we finish our Madeira and see if the good doctor is lounging under his mulberry tree?"

As MADISON CIRCLED BEHIND the house, he was not surprised to see a tired-looking Franklin sitting in a cushioned rocking chair under his famed tree. The absence of guests did surprise him. Usually in the late afternoons, admiring females or conniving men surrounded Franklin. Today, when they rounded the corner of his house, they had heard neither self-conscious giggles nor conspiratorial whispers. The old man sat alone, quietly reading a book.

"Gentlemen, please sit. May I offer you lemonade or porter?"

"We don't mean to disturb your peaceful afternoon," Madison offered.

"I chased away some people earlier, but only in the hope that you two would visit."

Morris swung a straight-backed chair closer to Franklin. "You'll never see me pass up your superb porter."

John miraculously appeared, and Franklin gave him a nod. Madison pulled his own chair closer to Franklin. "I understand you wanted to see us together."

"We must plot the last scene in our little drama."

"The final committee?" Madison asked.

"We'll trust the two of you with that episode, I was referring to the final vote."

"The general seeks unanimity?"

Franklin leaned forward. "Can we get it?"

"No."

Franklin leaned back and slowly rocked his chair. "Even if not everyone in the chamber agrees, we think we can finesse a unanimous vote of the states."

Madison thought a moment. "What about New York?"

"Hamilton will sign, but New York is not officially represented." Franklin stopped rocking and leaned forward again. "Jemmy, who will refuse to sign?"

Madison knew that Washington and Franklin had already discussed this question, so he took time to think through the possibilities. "Gerry and Martin will refuse to sign. I think Patrick Henry has warned Randolph not to sign. Mason worries me, as does Gorham."

"Gorham! Why Gorham?" Morris exclaimed.

"Because he's astute," Madison said, pleased with his companions' startled expressions. "He knows Rufus is solidly with us and Gerry adamantly opposed. It gives him the swing vote. He'd be foolish to give that away without exacting a price."

"My God, you're right," Franklin said. "What will he demand?"

"Something valuable to Massachusetts, I should think," Madison answered.

Franklin seemed to contemplate for a moment. "Gouverneur, can we trust Rufus to intercede with Gorham?"

"Normally, I would say yes, but this may present too much of a temptation. They could collaborate to extract the maximum price."

"Alex can get Gorham's measure," Franklin said. "He's supported him many times in Congress."

When Morris gave a nod, the issue seemed settled. John conveniently chose this time to bring out their drinks, and Morris made a show of taking a long draw on the porter. "Excellent," he said.

Franklin smiled and then turned to Madison. "Do any other states worry you?"

"No. Martin can't sway Maryland, and if both Randolph and Mason bolt, the remaining Virginians will override them."

"That's our assessment as well. What do you think it would take to get Mason, Randolph, Gerry, and Martin to sign?"

"Nothing political will move Gerry or Martin, but the general might ask for a personal favor."

"Already broached with the general," Franklin said. "He might approach Martin, but he refuses to barter with Gerry. What about Randolph and Mason?"

"Mason's a puzzle." Madison took a sip of his beer. "Randolph is easier to understand. A signature requires commitment."

"Something he's loath to do," Franklin said.

"Exactly." Madison set his drink down. "He won't sign."

"We should concentrate on Mason, Martin, and Gorham," Franklin said. "If we succeed with two or more, then we'll figure out if there's anything to be done with Gerry and Randolph." Franklin looked in dire need of a nap, but he wasn't done. "One more item. Sherman must get Paterson back for the signing."

Madison shifted in his chair. "I'll talk to him."

"Good." Franklin looked peeved. "As soon as that whelp Paterson got the Senate he wanted, he ran home. Tell Sherman the general and I insist on Paterson's signature." Franklin raised his hand toward the house, and John appeared directly. "Anything else, gentlemen?" the doctor asked.

"Only that I'm beginning to worry about Virginia ratification," Madison said. "Patrick Henry is lining up against it."

"Too far in the future for this old codger," Franklin said, as he rose. "We must first get an approved plan with the appearance of unanimity before we worry about ratification."

"Gouverneur counseled me to think further ahead."

Franklin winked at Morris and said, "This from a man incapable of thinking beyond his next meal and wench?"

Morris rose and gave Franklin a gracious bow. "My good doctor, I must object. My female companions are of a higher class than wenches."

Franklin's eyes took on a glint that swept away the fatigue. "Mr. Morris, in my considerable experience, the difference between a lady and a wench has less to do with their position in society than their willingness to be put in a compromising position."

As the three men laughed and bid their farewells, John assisted his aging, gout-ridden master into the house. Madison walked with Morris around the house and through the archway leading to Market Street, once again marveling at how well the surrounding buildings shielded the courtyard from the street's bustle.

"The doctor looked tired," Madison said.

Morris didn't answer immediately. When he did, his voice sounded more solemn than normal. "Our nation may never know how fortunate it was to have him with us at this hour."

ON SATURDAY, KING STARTED by reading a committee recommendation. "The importation of such persons as the several states now existing shall think proper to admit, shall not be prohibited by the legislature prior to the year 1800, but a tax may be imposed at a rate not exceeding the average of the duties laid on imports."

Madison liked the proposal but suspected that it went beyond what the South would accept. He was surprised when Pinckney, instead of objecting, made a motion to change the deadline for ending the slave trade from 1800 to 1808. Madison winced when Gouverneur Morris angrily said that the clause ought to be honest and use the word *slave*.

Sherman said, "I prefer the current wording. The old Congress avoided the use of the word *slave* because it offends people."

He added in an unusually testy voice that the small duty showed that revenue was the purpose, not discouragement of the trade. When Sherman would not relent, the wording was changed to "a tax or duty may be imposed on such importation not exceeding ten dollars for each person."

Madison gave a low whistle. He wanted to stop the trade, but ten dollars per head would do the job almost as well. It looked like an adequate compromise, especially if in later deliberations they rolled the twenty years back to a reasonable deadline.

"How does it feel to be a thousand dollars richer?"

"Excuse me?"

Pinckney plopped his portfolio onto Madison's table and sat down. Madison was always the last to leave because he normally had additional notes to scribe.

"Mr. Madison, squire of Montpelier, you can't deny that your hundred slaves have appreciated with this new tax."

"The market determines the price of slaves, not taxes."

"How naïve."

"Mr. Pinckney, I don't have time for your insolence."

"How would you run your plantation without slaves?"

"With wage labor—indentured servants, if necessary."

"You believe a seven-year slave moral?"

"He's earning passage. A wage paid in advance."

"Commercial passage costs more than a slave, and slaves last a lifetime—and they replicate. With very little urging on our part, I might add."

"If they're such a bargain, ten dollars ought not to harm such a lucrative enterprise."

"The enterprise that benefits from this nasty tax is the sale of Virginia's excess slaves to neighbors."

"My slaves won't leave Montpelier unless I free them."

Pinckney picked up his portfolio. "Then they'll surely be shackled for life." Pinckney made an elaborate show of tipping an imaginary hat. "Good day, Mr.

Madison. I'm so proud of you for using the personal pronoun. Often, one must measure progress in tiny steps."

Madison sat dead still until Pinckney had left the chamber. After a few additional moments, he suddenly slammed the flat of his hand against the table.

ON WEDNESDAY, BUTLER PROPOSED harsh wording for the fugitive slave clause. "If any person bound to service or labor in any of the United States shall escape into another state, he or she shall be delivered up to the person justly claiming their service or labor."

The convention agreed to this wording to mollify states wounded by the ten dollar tax on slaves.

The next issue was ratification. The committee hadn't specified the number of states required to put the new constitution into force. Wilson proposed seven, a majority of states. Sherman wanted ten. Mason suggested nine, and the assembly quickly passed the motion. Madison grew excited. When they finished the final touches, only nine states would be required to make this new Constitution the supreme law of the nation.

Gouverneur Morris suggested that state legislatures be instructed to call the conventions speedily. Morris said, "When it first appears, people will approve of our work, but by degrees, state officers will turn the popular current against the Constitution."

Martin weaved to the front of the chamber and leaned against a table with the tips of his fingers. After steadying himself, he said derisively, "Mr. Morris is correct. After a time, the people will oppose it, but for different reasons. They'll reject this travesty not because of unscrupulous state officers, but because they'll come to know it. The people will ratify this Constitution only if caught by surprise."

Mason asked to postpone debate on ratification. "I'd sooner chop off my right hand than put my signature to this Constitution. I recommend that the whole subject be brought before another general convention."

"I heartily agree!" Gouverneur Morris yelled. "Yes, by all means, let's convene once again in this dreadful room and wile away our lives in fruitless adventure."

Madison tried to figure out what point had turned Randolph, Gerry, and Mason against the plan. They weren't natural allies. He decided each man acted from different motivations.

Mason still smarted from the decision on a single executive. He had arrived in Philadelphia confident of an executive position in the new government, but he had no illusions that he could win against Washington—or outlive him.

Randolph was scared. He had lost touch with the mood in Virginia and didn't have an inkling of what his constituents were thinking. The long convention had prevented him from putting his finger to the wind, and the man loathed taking a blind stand. Madison guessed he had already worked on public statements that would give him room to either support or fight ratification, depending on the reception back home.

Gerry was cantankerous, but it had to be more. He would have preferred a government in which the elite ruled. The man feared what he called "the leveling spirit." Above all, this odd scarecrow of a man always aligned himself with whichever side seemed to be winning.

This realization brought Madison up short. Gerry had decided that the new Constitution would fail. Why? Mason and Randolph were one good reason. These two powerful Virginians could tip the state against the plan, and they had Patrick Henry in the wings, ready to mount the stage to slay the monstrous dragon from the North. Virginia split the country in the middle and would make it nearly impossible to form one nation if it stayed outside. The second most critical state was New York, obviously problematic under Clinton's devious leadership.

Gerry's cynical calculations caused Madison's heart to beat so hard he had to concentrate on long, slow breaths to regain his composure. After he calmed down, Madison vowed to work relentlessly for ratification in New York and Virginia. They had come too far to lose it all in the closing stages.

When his mind returned to the proceedings, Sherman moved to refer the remaining issues to another committee. Madison gave a knowing glance at Morris when it was announced that they would both be members. This time, the composition showed balance. Although Sherman had Baldwin and Dickinson, Madison could count on Morris and King. Unfortunately, this put the mercurial Pierce Butler in a pivotal position. It might not be Morris's hyperbolic Armageddon, but the committee had all the hallmarks of a pitched battle between evenly matched forces.

37

Friday, August 31, 1787

The Committee on Postponed Matters met in the Council Chamber, the small room on the second floor of the State House. Sherman had worked on the committees that wrote the Declaration of Independence and the Articles of Confederation, but this was the most important of his long career. A Committee of Style would eventually craft the language of the Constitution, but this one would finalize four months of work and make recommendations on the few remaining issues.

When the convention had adjourned earlier that afternoon, Sherman, Madison, Morris, King, Baldwin, and Butler had climbed to the second floor for their first meeting. Everyone was present except Dickinson, who felt ill. Their first order of business had been to catalog the issues they needed to address in the next few days.

After resolving one issue, Butler moved to adjourn. Sherman scanned his two pages of terse notes to make sure there were no crucial issues that needed immediate attention. He looked up from his meager scratches to say, "I agree. Let's adjourn. Nine o'clock tomorrow morning?"

As Sherman packed his valise, he noticed that Gouverneur Morris looked unhappy. He was contemplating whether to probe into the cause of his dissatisfaction, when the door suddenly burst open.

"Gentlemen, I apologize," Dickinson said.

"John, you look terrible," Sherman said. "We've just recessed. Get some rest."

"You're done?"

"For the day," Butler answered.

"Have you made any decisions?"

Butler didn't stop packing his writing materials. "Only on the executive," he said offhandedly.

"How did you decide?"

"Selection by Congress," Morris snapped.

"Damn it, no."

Dickinson's outburst startled Sherman. "John, we merely endorsed the convention's vote."

Dickinson began pacing the room. "I know how the convention voted."

"Then you know it is not within our purview to decide differently," Butler said with an edge of irritation. "We're supposed to resolve postponed matters."

Dickinson pleaded. "We cannot give the president enough power unless he's independent of the legislature."

"Hear! Hear!" Morris said. "Finally, someone talks sense."

Butler shook his head as he prepared to leave. "I refuse to open the issue again."

"Do you have a suggestion?" Madison asked Dickinson.

"No!" Butler shouted. "Leave it be."

"Just a minute," Morris said. "It's a simple question."

Dickinson quit pacing and looked at Madison. "Electors chosen by the state legislatures."

"Not that tired ol' horse." Butler started for the door. "I'm leaving."

Morris, who had stayed seated, leaped up. "Pierce, please, give it a moment."

"A moment? Good God, man, we've been over this matter innumerable times." He turned to Dickinson. "Do you have anything new?"

Dickinson started to say something, stopped, and then fixed Butler with a firm look. After a moment, he said, "Yes."

Sherman knew his friend was lying.

"I want to hear," Madison said eagerly.

Morris took his seat. "Yes, everybody sit back down."

Butler whirled on Morris. "We've already adjourned."

"We can reconvene," Morris insisted. "Shall we vote?"

"Hell, the president might be the only thing my people back home care about," Baldwin said. "Let's hear John out."

Butler didn't say another word, but he plopped his portfolio on the table with a loud slap to show his irritation.

King looked skeptical, but he sat back down. "What's new about electors?"

"People must trust the president," Dickinson said.

Sherman wanted to help, but he disagreed. "People trust the legislature."

"They trust their representative, not the body," Dickinson said. "Only the president can represent the nation as a whole."

"So let the people elect," Madison said.

"If I may," Dickinson said. "We have three choices that have been bandied about. Election by—"

"Bandied? Where have you been, man?" Butler remained angry. "They've been argued to the point of nausea."

"Let him finish, please," Sherman interjected mildly.

"Yes, I want to hear," Morris insisted.

Dickinson took a deep breath. "The three include election by the people, election by Congress, and election by the state legislatures. The delegates split numerous times on these three choices. We need another option."

"We don't have the authority!" Butler screamed.

"Hell, why should that stop us," Baldwin said. "Everything we've done has been outside of our sanction."

"If I may," Madison said in his soft voice. "We're charged with resolving postponed matters, but it's within our purview to recommend further changes for symmetry."

"You just want a popular election," Butler said.

"Let's hear John out." Baldwin and Morris had spoken in a single voice.

Butler made a show of throwing his arms open in surrender. Everyone turned to Dickinson, who took another deep breath before saying, "We let the state legislatures decide how electors are chosen."

Madison looked intrigued. "You mean they can authorize popular election."

"Or not," Dickinson answered.

Everyone sat quietly for a moment.

"It might work," Morris said.

Dickinson started speaking rapidly. "This'll give the executive independence, so we can grant him additional powers. We can simplify impeachment, the presidential term, and reeligibility. We can eliminate cabals by requiring the electors to vote in their own state on the same date. The extent of the country will make collusion impossible."

Madison cleared his throat. "I can support this. Even if only a few states allow popular choice, the people will apply pressure to the other states."

Sherman turned to Morris. "Gouverneur?"

"Not perfect, but better than Congress."

"Pierce?"

Butler hesitated, so Baldwin interrupted, "My constituents will reject a powerful executive chosen by the ruling class. We must emaciate him or give the people voice."

"This doesn't exactly give them a voice," Butler said.

"Give Georgia the choice, and my people will make sure that they're heard."

Sherman gave Butler a hard look. Butler looked down at his closed portfolio and gave it a dismissive spin. "I can live with this—if the convention can."

Although he remained planted in his chair, Madison looked as if he were bouncing. "May I take the liberty to sketch out some ideas around this proposal?"

"I think that an exceptional idea," Morris said.

Sherman was not enthralled, but he said nothing because he didn't want to jeopardize the progress just achieved. Besides, despite a purist bent, Madison did have a talent for symmetry and balance.

"Then may we call it an afternoon?" Butler asked testily.

"Indeed," Morris answered. "Thank you for your patience, Pierce." Butler's whole body tensed, but Morris quickly added, "I meant that sincerely. Good God, man, we're all frustrated."

Butler picked up his portfolio and scooted his chair away from the table. "Perhaps I was a bit brusque." He stood and tugged his coat taut against his shoulders. "I'll see you all in the morning."

"If you have no other plans," Morris said, "I'd be honored to host the committee at the City Tavern."

Baldwin leaped to his feet. "Now that's the best idea I've heard today." He gave Dickinson a friendly smile. "Beggin' your pardon, John."

Butler looked dubious. "Will we discuss committee business?"

Morris rolled in laughter. "Absolutely not."

"Then I'd be pleased to join you."

"Great. Roger?"

"Of course, but in a bit. I'm going to see that John gets immediately back to bed."

"We shan't wait," Morris warned.

"Nor did I expect you to."

"Gentlemen, let's see how much damage we can do to my purse." Morris draped his arm lightly around Butler's shoulder and led the small procession out of the room.

"How do you feel?"

"As bad as I look." Dickinson walked slowly alongside Sherman. "I want to go home."

"So do we all," Sherman said.

"No. I mean I'm leaving."

"We're almost done."

"So am I."

"But you'll miss the signing."

"I authorized George Read to sign for me."

"John, all you need is rest."

"I've done nothing but sleep, yet I can't wait to get back to bed." Dickinson made a weak wave of his arm to take in crowded and noisy Philadelphia. "This dirty city has made me sick, and I don't intend to die away from home."

Sherman, taken aback, put his hand on his friend's shoulder. "Then go. Get some clean air and regain your health. You've done a yeoman's duty already."

"I will, now that I feel more comfortable with the plan's direction."

They walked in silence for a few minutes, and then Sherman asked, "When did you come up with your brilliant compromise?"

"It wasn't brilliant."

"Of course it was."

"Election by the state legislatures had already been proposed. By someone currently at my side, if I remember correctly."

"Giving the state legislatures the option to provide for popular elections took something old and made it fresh." Sherman gave his friend a grin. "In politics, that's brilliant."

Dickinson gave a slight bow. "Due to your reputed expertise in these matters, I concede the point."

"As well you should, but you haven't answered my question. When did you come up with the idea?"

"In the room. I thought you'd come to my assistance, but you just sat there enjoying my predicament."

"I was testing your health." Sherman patted his friend's shoulder. "You'll live."

"Thank you, Doctor, but I'm going home anyway. One more thing. I'm giving George money for a celebratory dinner. Manage events so George will have a good reason to spend my money."

"Leave it in my capable hands."

"The obligation, of course. The money I'll trust to George."

THE NEXT MORNING, SHERMAN looked out the Palladium window to the State House yard as he trudged up the stairs to the second floor. He was about ten minutes early. When he entered the Council Chamber, he saw that Madison was the only one to precede him.

"Roger, I'm glad you arrived early. There's something I wish to discuss with you."

Sherman plopped his valise on a chair and walked around the table. "Good morning, James. What's the subject?"

"William Paterson."

"Paterson? I thought you'd want to discuss presidential powers."

"I had no difficulty outlining the powers."

"What are they?"

"That can wait for the committee. Will Paterson return for the signing?"

"Is that important?"

"Paterson browbeat the convention until he caused a schism. Now he owes us his signature."

"The New Jersey delegation will sign."

"We need everyone's support—especially the malcontents."

"Randolph and Mason?" As Sherman watched Madison cringe, his mind raced to figure out why this subject had arisen. Madison must be thinking ahead to ratification, or more likely, Washington desired the appearance of a solid consensus.

"Randolph and Mason present difficulties, but their objections pale next to Martin's and Gerry's bombast."

"Both sides harbor dissidents."

"I thought we were beyond *sides* by this point."

"My apologies." Sherman looked toward the door. Others would be intruding in a few moments. "James, we'll never convince everyone."

"We can achieve unanimity among the states represented."

Sherman nodded. "What state presents the highest risk?"

"Massachusetts."

"Agreed."

"Will you work with me on this?"

"Of course."

"And Paterson?"

"I wrote him two weeks ago. He'll be here for the signing."

MADISON BEGAN THE MEETING by presenting his outline for presidential powers. "The opportunity for popular election allows a stronger executive, and we can use the Senate to advise and consent. Our prior approach used a weak executive to check Congress. Now both branches provide checks on each other."

Sherman didn't like the way Gouverneur Morris nodded as Madison read. At dinner last night, the two had engaged in numerous whispered exchanges, and they took a common carriage back to the Indian Queen. Madison's plan intuitively made sense, but Sherman resented that they failed to bring other committee members into the discussion.

"The convention session is about to begin," Morris said. "I suggest we meet again directly after adjournment." As they prepared to go downstairs, Morris said to Sherman, "I hope we reach agreement this afternoon. I have plans for tomorrow."

"We all have plans for the Sabbath," Sherman said. Morris coughed in a way that told Sherman he had a more earthly commitment.

SHERMAN LEFT THE STATE House with Baldwin. The afternoon session had been dull and focused on triviality. The committee had thrashed around numerous points but had come to no conclusions, so they scheduled the next meeting for Monday, which gave Sherman his Sabbath and Morris his diversions.

They walked quietly, until Baldwin interrupted his thoughts. "What are you cooking up in that scheming mind of yours?"

"Nothing."

"Liar."

"Who becomes president if he dies in office?"

"The same man who succeeds him when he's impeached."

"Very helpful."

"The president of the Senate?" Baldwin asked.

"I don't like that. Under the Articles, the president of Congress is the executive. If we—"

"If the president of the Senate succeeds the president, he might grab too much power."

Sherman nodded. "As our little friend likes to remind us, we need to keep powers separated."

"So who? Someone from the executive side, but the president can't appoint his successor."

"At first, I thought that might work, but I decided an unscrupulous executive could barter the vice presidency."

Baldwin smiled. "Vice president?"

"You have a better title?"

"No."

"Madison's plan looks good, but I think this is a hole."

"What'll the vice president do besides pray for his superior's demise?" Baldwin asked.

"We must give him work."

Baldwin took a moment. "Secretary of state?"

"Something less competitive."

"President of the Senate? It denies the ambitious a job they might turn into something more."

"I need to think about it," Sherman said. "Our current president of Congress sets a bad example."

They arrived in front of Mrs. Marshall's boardinghouse. Baldwin was staying a block further east. "Mrs. Marshall will be serving supper soon. Do you want to sample her cooking?"

"Will there be room?"

"Saturday evening? I presume so."

"As your guest?"

"If you behave yourself."

"Then lead on, Mr. Sherman. A meal at your expense will be a rare treat."

When they entered, Howard was setting the table. "Good evening, Mr. Sherman. I hope you're staying for dinner."

"I am. Do you have room for another guest?"

"You've made Mrs. Marshall a happy woman. The other boarders have engagements. You have just enough time to wash up."

The two men climbed the stairs to Sherman's room to find a clean towel and fresh water beside the washbowl. After washing, Baldwin said, "Mrs. Marshall runs a good house. Are there any open rooms?"

"Full," Sherman said distractedly.

"Damn city."

"What?"

"Roger, where's your head?"

"A vice president solves another problem."

"Which is?"

"The electors can vote for two men. The one with the most votes becomes president, and the one with the next highest number becomes vice president. If both must be from different states, then the president will always be someone of national stature."

"Thank God tomorrow is the Sabbath."

"I usually need to pray for forgiveness because I think about politics on the Sabbath."

"You think that surprises me? By the way, good solution."

"Let's eat."

When the men walked downstairs, the aroma of freshly cooked meats and vegetables greeted them. As they took their seats, Mrs. Marshall distributed a series of bowls and platters as she clucked over the men like they were esteemed dignitaries. She quickly laid out generous portions of chicken, roast beef, dumplings, boiled potatoes, and fresh green beans that Sherman knew she had harvested from her garden within hours of preparation.

After Baldwin had served himself a heaping plate of food, he asked Mrs. Marshall, "When do you expect an open room?"

She stopped in mid-motion. "Don't you gentlemen understand how anxious we are for you to finish your work?"

"We're close," Sherman said.

"Then why does Mr. Baldwin consider changing boardinghouses?"

"Mr. Sherman is correct," Baldwin said. "We have only a few things to tidy up. I was just overcome with your cooking."

Mrs. Marshall, arms akimbo, said in her matron's voice, "Gentlemen, time is running out. I suggest you get on with your business."

"As we shall, Mrs. Marshall. After the meal, Mr. Baldwin and I will tidy up those loose ends." Sherman glanced over at Baldwin to see disappointment written on his face. "Eat up, Abe. You didn't expect a free meal did you?"

ON TUESDAY, SEPTEMBER 4, the Committee on Postponed Matters presented their report. They had spent Monday arguing, cajoling, and at times bickering, but in the end, they voted out a plan that put the various pieces together in a coherent whole.

King explained that the president, with the advice and consent of the Senate, could make treaties and appoint ambassadors, the Supreme Court, and all the other officers of the United States. The president could be removed from office for treason or bribery when impeached by the House of Representatives and convicted by the Senate. Money bills had to originate in the House but could be amended by the Senate. Military appropriations were restricted to two years. Members of Congress were barred from holding any other government positions. The government could grant authors and inventors the exclusive right to their respective writings and discoveries.

Sherman noticed some uneasy shuffling as King spoke, but the room became still as he read the next clause. "The president shall hold his office during the term of four years, and together with the vice president, chosen for the same term, be elected in the following manner. Each state shall appoint in such manner as its legislature may direct, a number of electors equal to the number of senators and members of the House of Representatives to which the state is entitled."

King explained that electors would vote for two persons, one of which could not be from their state. The president would be the individual with the most votes, and the vice president would be the one with the second highest count. In case of a tie, the Senate would select the president. The vice president would be president of the Senate, except during presidential impeachments, and the vice president did not have a vote unless there was a tie. Upon death or incapacitation of the president, the vice president would assume the office.

Randolph immediately asked for the floor. "If I may beg the speaker's pardon, how did the change in the electing of the executive come about?"

Morris answered. "First, to avoid intrigue if appointed by Congress. Second, to allow reeligibility. Third, to establish an impeachment court separate from the election body. Fourth, many wanted the people to choose. Fifth, to make the executive independent of the legislature."

"I'm heartened to learn that the esteemed delegate from Pennsylvania can count," Pinckney said. "In like mind, I will enumerate my objections. First, this process throws the appointment into the Senate. Second, the electors will be strangers to the candidates. Third, it makes the executive reeligible."

Baldwin recommended a postponement to give the delegates an opportunity to digest the recommendations. Before adjournment, the committee received another assignment: "to prepare a plan for defraying the expenses of the convention."

"WASHINGTON WANTS ANOTHER RECOMMENDATION," Madison said at the beginning of yet another committee meeting.

"Will this interminable convention never end?" Butler said, in exasperation.

"What is it?" Sherman tried to sound noncommittal.

"He wants the national capital independent of any state."

"What?" Butler bellowed.

"The national capital will be a huge plum. See how Clinton turned it to his advantage. Also, the general fears hot political battles between New York and Philadelphia."

"Not if the general sides with Philadelphia." Morris waved his arm to encompass the room. "This city has a birth right. The nation was invented in this building."

"You prove the general's point, Gouverneur," Madison said.

"This is Hamilton's work," Morris muttered. The slight shrug meant he would not fight the motion.

"Perhaps, but a good idea nonetheless," Sherman said. "We must get the capital away from Clinton."

"To where?" Butler demanded.

"Washington believes that should be left to the First Congress," Madison answered. "For now, we just make the provision."

Baldwin shook his head. "The Virginians want the capital close by their plantations."

"This is not a Virginia plot," Madison blurted.

"Perhaps not," Baldwin said, "but the capital will not be located in Georgia."

"That would make no sense," Madison said in a rare snit. "Georgia is at the extremity of the nation."

"By Jove, I think you're right," Baldwin said. "Let's get a map and see what state is at the center."

"That's enough." Sherman believed Baldwin had a point, but he still liked the idea. He turned to Madison. "Do you have wording?"

Madison handed Sherman a piece of paper. He read it aloud. "To exercise exclusive legislation over such district (not exceeding ten miles square) as may by cession of particular states become the seat of the government of the United States."

Sherman passed the page back to Madison. "I concur with this. Unless someone objects, let's move on."

On Wednesday, the committee presented their complete report. Sherman was a little startled to hear no objections to the recommendation on the seat of government. Either everyone was eager to take the capital away from Clinton, or Washington had discreetly let it be known that this was his suggestion. Neither did anyone object to their recommendation that they each be paid equal to the compensation received by congressmen and that all of their expenses should be reimbursed.

George Mason won an amendment to add high crimes and misdemeanors to treason and bribery as causes for executive impeachment.

Gerry opposed the idea of the vice president acting as an ex officio head of the Senate. Sherman answered, "If the vice president is not president of the Senate, then he'll be without employment—other than mischief, of course." Sherman sat down to enough laughter that he knew the vice president would be approved when it came to a vote.

"Can we take a walk around the yard?"

Sherman looked up to see Hamilton. "Of course."

When they walked out the central corridor and into the yard, a warm sun and soft breeze greeted them. Sherman stopped after he descended the steps.

"Something wrong?" Hamilton asked.

"No." Sherman looked up at the line of elm trees. "I'm just listening to the leaves rustle."

"I fear autumn will be upon us before we finish our business."

"We're close to the end."

"We merely approach a milestone," Hamilton answered.

With a long stride, Sherman started in a counterclockwise direction. "What worries you?"

"Ratification. New York and Virginia will be difficult. If either opts out, it won't matter if nine states ratify. They're large powerful states that will split the new nation, both geographically and politically."

"You want something."

"Of course." Hamilton had no trouble keeping up with Sherman's pace. "Will the small states ratify?"

"Yes."

"No equivocation?"

"None. How will you handle New York and Virginia?"

"Madison will go immediately to New York to shepherd the Constitution through Congress, and then he'll travel posthaste to Richmond. He'll also be the focal point for a committee of correspondence to coordinate the states. Will you join?"

"Of course, but that's not why we're taking this walk."

"We want your commitment to accept whatever's necessary to secure Massachusetts' approval."

"What's the price?"

"Not yet determined."

"Then how can I commit?"

"With faith that whatever price is extracted, it is the lowest possible."

Sherman walked for a few paces and then stopped under a full elm tree. "Agreed."

"Washington wants more than Connecticut's commitment. He wants support from your coalition."

"I have no coalition."

"Of course you do."

Sherman smiled. "You may give the general my assurances."

Hamilton nodded and they started walking again. Sherman enjoyed the afternoon sun on his face. When they reached the far corner of the yard, he posed a question. "Alex, Clinton is sure to preside over the New York ratification committee. How do you plan to win?"

"Our first task is to win overwhelmingly in New York City to counter Clinton's rural delegates. John Jay is already working toward that end. Beyond that, we're still trying to figure out a strategy." Hamilton gave a small laugh. "Any suggestions?"

"Find a way to use Madison."

"We've already had discussions. Anything else?"

Sherman stopped walking again and faced Hamilton. "Don't equivocate. Defend every word."

"Do you believe every word is worth defending?"

"I do." Sherman looked toward the State House. "When I first arrived, I wrote my wife that I was about to engage in a battle with desperate and able men. I've moved a long way since that day. The country's dire situation instilled the desperation." Sherman looked back at Hamilton. "But I was also right about the assembly being able. These are fine men dedicated to doing justice to our grand republican experiment. We toiled, argued, and sweated over each clause until it was the absolute best we could bequeath to our nation."

Sherman resumed walking. "Alex, defend every word."

38

Sunday, September 9, 1787

"Where do we stand?" Washington asked briskly.

Washington, Madison, Hamilton, and Gouverneur Morris once again enjoyed Franklin's hospitality under his mulberry tree. On Saturday, the convention had made numerous minor modifications but had eventually approved the report from the Committee on Postponed Matters. Madison had been elated when they appointed a Committee of Style to organize their resolutions into a final document.

After an uncomfortable silence, Hamilton attempted to answer the general's question. "Sherman says the small states and the South will vote for the plan."

"I assumed *that*." Washington took a sip of Madeira.

Morris shifted in his seat. "Luther has agreed to fade away. He'll depart before the signing ceremony."

"That merely transfers his objections to the Maryland ratification," Washington said. "Please stop avoiding the issue."

Morris cleared his throat. "I'm sorry, sir, but we've made no progress with Randolph or Mason."

Washington leaped to his feet. "Goddamn it, Randolph presented the plan. Can we not make him see reason?"

Madison cringed but dove into the maelstrom anyway. "I believe Patrick Henry put the fear of God in him."

"Henry is not a god," Washington barked with a vehemence that made everyone flinch.

After a still moment, Morris asked, "Have you informed him of that fact?"

Washington whirled on Morris and gave him a withering stare. After a moment, he took his seat and asked mildly, "What will induce them to support the plan?"

"Are you sure we should make further entreatments?" Hamilton asked.

"Loud dissent from the convention threatens ratification." Washington slammed his fist against the arm of the chair. "Goddamn it, I want unanimity."

Morris fidgeted and then said, "They insist on state conventions that can offer amendments for consideration at a second national convention."

Madison almost bounded out of his seat. "No! Another convention will unravel our work instead of darning holes."

Hamilton said evenly, "We must abandon these two. We still have a solid Virginia."

"Virginia solid?" Washington said in a testy voice. "Without the governor?"

Madison knew why Washington was so angry. He understood Randolph's tendency to vacillate but had insisted on having him present the plan in an attempt to buy his commitment. Nothing made the general more furious than one of his schemes going awry.

Franklin interceded with a question meant to return the general to a more reasoned discussion. "General, are you unconcerned with Mason?"

"Concerned, but fatalistic. The Grand Lord of Gunston Hall deigns to withhold his consent to any government that fails to make room for him."

Madison thought Mason might have loftier objections, but then he remembered his disagreeable conversation with him nearly three months ago at the Robert Morris ball. He had been irascible ever since.

Washington stiffened into a posture reminiscent of a primeval oak that had weathered innumerable storms. He turned to Hamilton. "Alex, make a motion that gives the states authority to propose amendments."

"No!" Madison could not help himself.

Franklin put a hand on Madison's arm. "It won't pass."

"It's too dangerous," Madison said.

Washington's angry face dissolved into something worse, a condescending expression that deeply wounded Madison. The same look his father used, it never failed to make him feel inadequate.

"Let me explain, if I must." Washington leaned a tad closer. "We spoke of Henry and his exalted opinion of himself, but make no mistake: he'll be a powerful figure in Virginia's ratification. When facing a powerful foe, you first isolate him from his alliances." Washington gave Madison a stern look. "This may not work, but the risk is minimal. We can tell Randolph we tried to meet his demands, but the convention thwarted our effort. It should give him the political cover he seeks."

Washington settled back in his seat and took another sip of Madeira. "If he still refuses to acquiesce, then I shall bribe him with an important position in my administration. We must deny Henry the governor's support."

Madison felt chagrined. He knew Washington disliked explaining his connivances. He also understood that he had just witnessed politics played on a scale he would need to learn if he wanted to play a role beyond resident logician. He tried to keep his face blank as he said, "I understand, sir."

"Excellent. Now, Ben says that you made an astute observation about Massachusetts. I appreciate your bringing that to our attention."

"Thank you, sir." Having just received praise, Madison hated to bring up the next point. "Gerry wants an easier amendment process, but if we give it to him, I believe he'll still refuse to sign."

"Not worth the breath," Washington said. "What does Gorham want?"

"Nothing," Hamilton said. "Either he is a stalwart believer, or he does not grasp the power of his vote."

"I always thought he was an agreeable sort," Morris said.

Washington looked thoughtful. "Perhaps, but I'm not. If Nathaniel chooses to pass up this opportunity, we'll grasp it." Washington's comment intrigued Madison, and he became riveted when Washington looked directly at him. "Sherman got his equal representation in the Senate; now we must throw some large state weight to the House."

"How?" Hamilton looked puzzled.

"One representative for every thirty thousand people," Madison answered.

"Exactly," Washington said. Madison struggled to keep from beaming

Morris twitched with excitement. "If we lower the benchmark from forty thousand, the populous states will have more votes."

"I presume you want Gorham to make it a condition of his vote," Hamilton said.

"Your assignment, Alex," Washington said. "Massachusetts benefits, so it should be easy. But make sure he understands that this must appear to be an ultimatum of his own making."

"Consider it done."

Washington looked around. "Anything else?"

Franklin waved at Madison, Hamilton, and Gouverneur Morris. "We have three of the five members of the Committee of Style. Any instructions?"

"Yes." Washington spoke earnestly. "Gentlemen, do a superb job."

ON MONDAY, GERRY WANTED to reconsider the way the Constitution could be amended. As the clause now stood, two-thirds of the states could request a convention to consider amendments. After extensive debate, they decided a two-thirds vote by both houses of Congress could also call conventions. Wilson then moved to require a three-fourths majority of the states to ratify amendments.

Rutledge interrupted. "I refuse to agree to a power that might alter slavery."

Damn slavery, Madison thought. Must it dictate every issue? His mood didn't improve when the amendment process passed after they added a phrase that restricted slavery amendments until after 1808.

Hamilton asked for the floor. Madison knew what was coming and scooted his chair aside to get a view of at least a few delegates. As Hamilton walked to the front of the chamber, Madison marveled at how this small man, someone not much taller than himself, could fill a room with his presence.

"Gentlemen, we have nearly fulfilled our obligation to design a grand republic. It's time to turn our attention to how our work is sanctioned. The plan must be sent to Congress for their approval and then communicated to the state legislatures for their approval and amendment."

Randolph asked for the floor. "Last May, I presented a set of republican propositions, but we've departed from those sound propositions. State conventions should also be empowered to offer amendments at a second federal convention."

King said, "Congress loathes taking sides in a heady dispute. We shouldn't put our dear friends in such peril."

After a few more hours of heated debate, Mason requested that the motion lie on the table for a day or two to see what steps might be taken to satisfy Randolph. Agreeing to table the motion, the convention adjourned.

GOUVERNEUR MORRIS MADE A motion with his hand that Madison interrupted as a sign to gather around his table. By the time Madison had packed away his notes and writing material, Hamilton and King had already pulled chairs around the Pennsylvania table. As Madison took a seat, he noticed that other delegates lingered in small conversational groups, in no hurry to depart the chamber.

Morris looked around and said, "We need to set a meeting time and place. May I suggest my home in one hour? I've done a count. There are twenty-three articles we need to mesh into a coherent plan."

"We must aim for more than coherency," Madison said. "The plan must be eloquent."

"Make a purse out of a sow's ear?" Hamilton's derisive tone grated on Madison.

"The plan holds together better than I would have expected," Madison said. "Every article must be defended."

"That's the second time I've received such advice," Hamilton said in a distracted manner.

"Who else?" Madison asked.

"Never mind," Hamilton answered.

The resolutions before them were a far cry from the plan Madison had brought to Philadelphia, but they still overcame the deficiencies of the Articles of Confederation. Besides, there would never be another opportunity. They must all stand resolutely behind this plan or surrender to a rapid deterioration.

"I have an alternate proposal," Morris said. "With your consent, I'll organize the resolutions and work on some phrasing; then we can meet in the morning to edit my work."

"Excellent," King said. "When orderliness is the goal, one man's point of view exceeds a committee. Tomorrow morning is soon enough."

Madison felt disappointed that he hadn't been selected for the task. After all, he had put together the original Virginia Plan. He kept quiet for one reason: he recognized that Morris had a facility with words far beyond his tortuous turn of phrase.

"Gentlemen, I must get to work. I'll see you in the morning."

After they stepped outside, Hamilton put his hand on Madison's shoulder. "It was your friend Sherman that advised me to defend every word."

"Roger's not a friend."

"Colleague then?"

"Still a generous description."

"Our bickering resulted in a better plan. We owe a debt of gratitude to the otheriness of Mr. Sherman."

Madison turned so that Hamilton's arm fell away from his shoulder. "He's made his contributions."

"As have you, Jemmy. Your work has been invaluable. If this odd thing we created finds glory, future generations will revere you."

"And if it fails?"

Hamilton looked sad. "Then you and this fair nation will be forgotten."

"Your estimation?"

"I'm not content with every aspect of this plan, but it is a damn site better than the Articles." Hamilton's prideful face took on a determined look. "We must make it work."

"Make it work?"

"It provides the scaffolding to build an empire."

"I prefer republic."

Hamilton smiled. "A republican empire then."

HAMILTON GAVE OUT A low whistle. "Gouverneur, you've outdone yourself."

Madison had to agree. The twenty-three disjointed sections had been ordered and logically consolidated into seven articles. Awkward phrasing and stilted words had been replaced with sentences that were clear and easy to read. It was the preamble, however, that made the document appeal to patriotic urges.

They had gathered in Morris's elegant parlor. After coffee and tea had been served, Morris handed each man a copy of his edited manuscript. Madison was startled. The cost of copies would not noticeably deplete his purse, but where had he found the time? He could tell by the poor quality that the documents had been made by applying ink to glass so that an image could be transferred to successive sheets of paper, but still the process took hours.

Madison let the manuscript fall to his lap. "Our ramblings look consistent and rational. You've done a masterful job."

"Thank you for the compliments, but this is hardly a finished document."

"Then may I make a suggestion?" King asked.

The men shifted in their seats to face King.

"The country is accustomed to the legislature wielding sole power. An energetic executive is an innovation that will frighten many. I suggest we reorder the articles so that we lead with the legislature."

In the Morris draft, the first article defined executive powers. Madison immediately saw the advantage in changing the order. The balance of the powers would be more evident to people if they first saw that the legislature could hold the executive in check.

"Are you suggesting the executive article be third?" Morris asked.

Hamilton stiffened. "The executive is the most important. It cannot be relegated to the back."

"I was thinking second," King said.

Everyone waited, and then Morris said, "I think that improves the presentation."

"Since each branch is equal, I have no objections," Madison said.

Hamilton seemed tense. "It'll make no difference."

"I think it does," Morris said. "The plan remains the same, but the people will feel reassured if we give the legislature prominence."

"You delude yourself," Hamilton said.

"The price is insignificant," King interjected.

Hamilton shrugged. "Change the order. It won't change the substance, nor resistance."

"Shall we move on to phrasing?" Morris asked.

They started with the preamble. After an hour, they had made some minor refinements, and they all nodded when Morris read the final draft.

"We the people of the United States, in order to form a more perfect union, establish justice, insure domestic tranquility, provide for the common defense, promote the general welfare, and secure the blessings of liberty to ourselves and our posterity, do ordain and establish this Constitution for the United States of America."

The end result pleased Madison enormously. Morris had dropped the listing of the states to give the power directly to *the people of the United States*. They had picked their verbs with utmost care, using *establish, insure, provide, promote*, and *secure* to convey emphasis and priority. He didn't believe even Tom Jefferson could have so succinctly articulated the source of authority and functions of government.

It took them the rest of the afternoon and the following day to go through the seven articles. When they finished on Wednesday afternoon, Morris introduced another political element. "We need to decide on how to address Congress. I suggest we draft a separate letter."

"Congress has already been bought and paid for," Hamilton said.

"Nothing can come unbound faster than a group of self-serving politicians," Morris said.

"What are you suggesting?" King asked.

"Instructions to Congress on the measures to put this Constitution in place. No leeway. A letter would carry the authority of the entire convention."

"And what authority would that be?" Hamilton asked.

Madison ignored Hamilton. "Why not include it in Article VII?"

"I believe it better done outside the formal document. Separate, it carries more weight than something embedded deep in a long document."

"It will carry more arrogance," Hamilton said.

"What can possibly be more arrogant than disbanding a duly established government and replacing it with one of our own design?" Morris gave Hamilton an uncharacteristically hard look. "We might as well go the next step and instruct Congress on how to implement it."

Madison shook his head. "I'd still feel more comfortable adding the instructions to Article VII."

"We don't need to burden future generations with the gritty details." This indirect endorsement came from Hamilton.

"I thought you believed it arrogant," Madison said.

"I do." Hamilton smiled. "But humility is not one of my virtues."

Madison looked around. The other men returned his look. Now it was Madison's turn to shrug. "Let's draft it."

When they had finished, Madison knew that the other men had been right. The sequence of events to establish the government would occur only once, and they deserved the special attention bestowed by a separate document. The letter blandly stated that the Constitution was presented to Congress for them to forward to the states for ratification by conventions of the people. After the conventions, the states were to notify Congress of their assent or rejection. After senators and representatives were elected, the electors would meet on the same date in their respective states and forward their certified, signed, and sealed votes to the secretary of the new Congress. The Senate would open and count the votes.

The only sentence that bothered Madison was the last: "By the unanimous Order of the Convention." Unanimity was not yet a given, and Congress might take umbrage at an order coming from a mutinous convention.

With the Constitution ready to present, Madison collapsed in exhaustion against the back of his chair. Despite his weariness, he felt exalted. Five months ago, he had embarked on the perilous course to overthrow a standing government without bloodshed. A truly historic moment was within grasp. They held before them a Constitution built clause by clause through debate and deliberation that were sometimes raucous, but many times thoughtful and principled. All that remained to seal its Lockean legitimacy was for the general populace to ratify their work.

As they were preparing to depart, Morris volunteered his coach to take them back to the Indian Queen. After Morris returned from giving instructions to a servant, Madison asked, "How did you get copies made so quickly?"

Morris looked pleased with the question. "When I left you gentlemen at the State House, I went to my printer and paid them to stay ready throughout the night."

"That must have been expensive."

"Speed is of the essence now, my boy. We mustn't give our enemies the time to marshal resources."

It had taken five years to ratify the Articles, and if the Constitution took that long, it could prove disastrous. Madison felt drained, but he had to find strength to bring his dream to fruition.

"How can I help?"

"Talk to Sherman. We need the small states to ratify immediately."

"Why does everyone think I have a relationship with Sherman?"

"The two of you got us to this point. Work with him to finish the job."

Madison nodded. "I'll do my best."

Morris put a hand on his shoulder. "Jemmy, when you're at your best, you inspire all those about you."

Madison flushed. "Thank you. I'm always concerned I may be deficient in the hard political skills."

"Many possess hard political skills; inspiration is rare." Morris patted Madison's shoulder. "You possess a unique talent."

They moved outside and clambered aboard the coach positioned at the front door. As they settled in, King said, "Our gambit with Randolph didn't work."

"What do you suggest now?" Hamilton asked.

"Let him go." Madison placed his valise between his feet. "He said an attempt alone is insufficient because no one will know he wanted additional scrutiny of the plan."

Hamilton harrumphed. "An entire army couldn't provide enough cover for that insipid poltroon."

The carriage gently rocked as the driver climbed into his seat. Madison rested his elbow out the carriage window and reclined against the upholstered seat back. "Alex, we must push for a quick ratification."

"I have plans."

"What?"

"A series of papers. *The Independent Journal* has agreed to publish them."

"Who will write them?"

"Not settled yet, but New Yorkers. Jay agreed, but Morris declined."

"Morris lives in Pennsylvania."

"He left New York when the Clinton clique drove him out of Congress, but he still has his Morrisiania estate in Westchester."

"Too bad. We've seen the proof of his pen."

"He still carries scars from New York politics."

"Let me know if you can use my assistance." Madison felt the carriage jerk forward and realized he was looking forward to a quick meal and bed. Turning to Hamilton, he asked, "Alex, do you have a plan for these papers?"

"Yes. I shall defend every sentence."

39

Wednesday, September 12, 1787

"Thank you for joining me for breakfast."

"My pleasure." Sherman took a seat opposite Madison in the Indian Queen dining room. "I look forward to seeing your committee's work."

"I think you'll be pleased. Gouverneur did a masterful job."

"I'm sure you contributed as well." Sherman spread a linen napkin across his lap and realized that the walk from his boardinghouse had made him hungry. "I hear the ham comes from Virginia."

"A small contribution from my humble state."

"An interesting adjective for Virginia."

"People misjudge us."

"As they do my stiff Yankee accent. But I assume this meeting is about our states working together on some agenda."

"Ratification."

A nattily dressed servant interrupted Sherman's response. After they had placed their order, Sherman started to speak, but the rich aroma of roasted coffee caught his attention. A second servant appeared at his elbow to expertly pour steaming coffee from a burnished silver urn. After an exploratory sip, Sherman had to admit that there were things the Indian Queen did better than Mrs. Marshall.

"You were talking about ratification," Sherman said.

"It must be fast. A few states must ratify immediately."

"Small states?"

"You have the Senate."

"And you have protection for slavery."

Madison winced. "The South won't ratify easily. In their eyes, they have more to lose."

"Georgia'll be quick."

"Exactly. They're small. If you use your influence with the other small states, a momentum can be established."

Their meal arrived, which gave Sherman time to think. He cut a piece of ham and savored the distinctive Virginia cure. "The ham's excellent. My compliments to your 'humble' state."

"Can you engineer a quick Connecticut ratification?"

"How quick will Virginia be?"

Madison looked frustrated with Sherman's deflection. "I'll do what I can."

"Henry a thorn?"

Madison gave one of his little laughs. "A sword of Damocles, I'm afraid."

"What's in it for us?"

"A competent government."

"A goal worth striving for." Sherman finished another mouthful of ham. "I'll do my best."

"That should be sufficient. When you are at your best, you always seem to get what you want." Madison picked up his fork and ate with relish.

"Welcome back, William."

"This is historic," Paterson said. "I intend to be part of it."

"You're aware of the latest developments?" Sherman asked.

"I met with my delegation last evening. The presidential powers are a bit worrisome, but I won't quibble." Paterson looked at the delegates gathered in the hall outside the Council Chamber. "People look serious."

Sherman thought even Paterson appeared somber. "This business carries enormous risk for the country—and our families." Sherman led Paterson to a corner of the hall. "What do you hear from New York?"

"The battlements are going up."

"Little Mars has been planning a campaign. He's been returning to New York to cajole or buy allies."

"New Jersey will ratify easily."

"Good. It helps New York and Virginia if several states ratify quickly."

"Small states." Paterson seemed reflective. "In May, the big states championed an energetic central government, but after your Senate victory, support for this new government shifted to the small states."

"This has always been about power."

"Power for Virginians. New Jersey just wanted to protect herself from their ambitions."

"Put it away, William. It's a good plan."

Paterson looked reluctant to forego the anger that had given him energy, but he finally smiled. "Yes, it is."

At the opening of the session, Gouverneur Morris distributed printed copies of the Constitution from the Committee of Style. Although they couldn't leave the chamber, a recess was called so delegates could read the polished document. Madison had been right: the committee had done a masterful job. Sherman admired the eloquence and logical presentation of their resolutions.

After an hour, the convention reconvened to consider final modifications. Sherman hoped there would be few. A motion to revert back to the two-thirds override of presidential vetoes passed with little comment.

Gerry sputtered and spewed words like a teapot ready to blow. "I move for a right for trial by juries."

"The plan should be prefaced with a complete bill of rights," Mason said with equal anger. "One can be prepared in hours."

Sherman didn't believe the task could be completed in hours and felt it was time to bring the proceedings to a close. "I support securing the rights of the people, but the Declarations of Rights in the states are still in force, and their authority sufficient."

Sherman was surprised when Mason responded with more emotion than he thought the issue deserved. "The laws of the United States are paramount to the states, including their Declarations of Rights."

Sherman didn't believe words guaranteed people's rights. Untold hours in backrooms had taught him that unscrupulous political operators searched until they found ways around stipulations that supposedly obstructed them from achieving their ambitions. Frequent elections and checks on the abuse of power provided better protection. The system itself must guarantee rights.

Without further discussion, a motion for a committee to prepare a bill of rights failed unanimously. The end was too tantalizingly near to closet another group of men to complete an arduous task that could stretch into weeks.

"You're wrong."

Sherman turned toward the State House door and raised his hand to shield his eyes from the bright sun. "About?"

"The bill of rights." Madison remained on the State House stoop, which required Sherman to look up.

"Laws govern nations, not platitudes."

"A bill of rights has the force of law."

Sherman tried to keep exasperation from his voice. "I've been through the process numerous times. Nothing excites debate more than an attempt to build a far-reaching list of rights. The end result is too general for practical use."

"A bill of rights can be precise."

Sherman grew annoyed. He paused to figure out why he felt so irritated by Madison's comments. Sherman sloughed off affronts from fools, knaves, and the ignorant, but he took to heart the critiques of people he respected "James, the process to achieve precision in a bill of rights must go through a messy course before the list can be whittled down to the salient themes. We don't have the time. The country disintegrates before our eyes."

"We can start with the state bills."

"We don't have time."

Madison looked worried. "Roger, you're making a rare mistake."

"Perhaps, but it's one I cannot be dissuaded from." With that, he lowered his hand, turned away from the elevated Madison, and walked in the direction of Mrs. Marshall's house.

ON THURSDAY, THEY CONTINUED their review of the final draft from the Committee of Style. Sherman was pleased that only a few inconsequential changes were made, and they progressed rapidly through the document. The Constitution was long, and as the afternoon droned on, it became increasingly difficult for people to remain in their seats. Everybody just wanted to be done. Some leaned against the back wall with their arms folded across their chests, while others whispered in small groups toward the sides of the chamber. Many left for a spell. At times, Sherman could count only a dozen delegates in their seats.

Washington, who had previously enforced strict decorum, ignored the disorder and plowed ahead without recess. Sherman shared the others' impatience, but he felt the best way to leave this chamber for good was to stay in his seat. Just when he thought things couldn't get any more discourteous, he heard a loud thumping behind him. He did not need to turn around to know that it was Gouverneur Morris showing his displeasure by pacing with excessive weight thrown to his wooden leg.

This proved too much for the general's newfound tolerance. Bang! Bang! Bang! Sherman had never heard a gavel rapped with such authority. "Order in the chamber. Delegates, take your seats or remove yourselves. Immediately." Morris made a disrespectful wave of his hand and stomped noisily out the door.

With some semblance of order restored, they slogged through the remaining articles, making only a few alterations. Sherman saw relief in Washington's face as he struck his gavel and barked, "Adjourned."

"GOOD AFTERNOON, MR. HAMILTON."

Sherman and Baldwin had ventured across the street from the State House for lemonade.

"I'd have thought you'd be pursuing stronger refreshment," Baldwin said, affecting a Southern accent.

"I'm waiting for the general."

Baldwin put his muscle-hardened arm around Hamilton's narrow shoulder. "Then you may buy us lemonade."

"Abe, do you ever buy your own drinks?" Hamilton asked.

"Never in your presence."

"New Yorkers don't squander their money on backcountry ne'er-do-wells." Despite the disclaimer, Hamilton slapped a heavy Pennsylvania coin onto the cross board. "By the way, when did you lose your Yankee accent?"

"When I ran for office in Georgia." Baldwin wore a huge grin.

The men wandered out of earshot and stood under a tree. "I hear you intend to write a series of papers," Sherman said.

"Yes, I'll call it *The Federalist.*"

"Federalist?" Baldwin sounded perplexed. "The Articles are a federation of the states. It's a stretch to use that term with this Constitution."

"We need to mold public perception. We'll claim the name Federalist so we can call our opponents Anti-Federalists. Hamilton smiled. "First to trough, first to eat."

"You sly devil." Baldwin saluted with his lemonade. "No wonder you're a banker."

Hamilton shrugged. "It allows me to buy lemonade for my Yankee friends."

"Whoa!" Baldwin feigned offense. "You can't buy my friendship with a mere glass of refreshment."

As they laughed, Hamilton suddenly became serious. "By the way, we've established the price for unanimity."

"What does Massachusetts want?"

"It will become clear Monday."

"Why not until Monday?"

"One of Gorham's conditions," Hamilton said. "I just wanted to forewarn you."

"You forewarned me of nothing. Should I be concerned?"

Hamilton shook his head. "No. Gorham's reasonable. He could have gotten more." Hamilton handed his glass to Baldwin. "The general has stepped from the State House. I'll see you men later."

Sherman watched Hamilton's back as he dodged the carriages to cross the street. "That was ominous," Sherman said.

"The man's too clever by half," Baldwin said.

"I don't like surprises."

"What are you going to do?"

"Nothing. It's too late."

WHEN RANDOLPH RECEIVED THE floor on Saturday, he walked to the front of the chamber wearing a theatrical expression of solemnity. "I feel great pain to differ from my fellow delegates on the close of our great labors, but I make a final motion that amendments to the plan can be offered by state conventions."

An audible groan filled the chamber, but Randolph pushed on. "Should this proposition lose, it will be impossible for me to put my name to this instrument. I don't know if I shall oppose it afterwards, but I cannot deprive myself of the freedom to do so."

Mason seconded Randolph and gave his own speech. Sherman had never seen Mason look so haughty or use a more condescending tone. Both traits were personal attributes, but most of the time he kept them in check. Sherman wondered if he was seeing the true George Mason or an extremely frustrated patriot.

When the votes were called on Randolph's motion, all the states sharply answered—no!

Sherman saw Mason accept defeat with a frown and his arms folded tightly against his chest.

Elbridge Gerry felt obliged to state why he would withhold his name from the Constitution. He accused the convention of proposing a system that could make any law it chose by declaring it "necessary and proper."

When Gerry took his seat, Washington gave a gentle rap with his gavel and said in a loud, clear voice, "On the question to agree to the Constitution, as amended, will the states please mark their votes."

The assembly quieted in less than two minutes and then faced the front of the chamber with an air of expectancy. Washington, as dictated by tradition, called the roll of states from north to south.

"New Hampshire?"

"New Hampshire votes aye."

"Massachusetts?"

Rufus King proudly said, "Massachusetts votes aye.""

"Connecticut?"

Roger Sherman stood, paused a heartbeat, and said, "Aye."

"New Jersey?"

"New Jersey votes aye."

"Pennsylvania?"

Benjamin Franklin struggled to his gout-ridden feet. "Pennsylvania votes a hearty aye."

Applause sprinkled the chamber as Franklin sat. Sherman didn't know if it was to honor a great man or the vote.

When the applause subsided, Washington called, "Delaware?"

"The great state of Delaware votes aye." When George Read sat down, the applause grew more pronounced.

"Maryland?"

"Aye." The trend had now been set, and the applause became steady.

"Virginia?"

"Virginia votes aye." The applause strengthened, and James Madison wore the smile of the truly joyful.

"North Carolina?"

"Aye."

Up to now, Sherman had been clapping perfunctorily, but he caught the enthusiasm of the room and started to pound his hands with rare delight.

"South Carolina?"

Charles Pinckney rose and gave Gen. Washington an aristocratic bow, flourishing his arm across his midsection and dipping his right shoulder just a bit deeper than his left. "Sir, the great and sovereign state of South Carolina votes aye."

When the applause grew loud and sustained, Pinckney turned toward the delegates and bowed as if they were honoring him.

"Georgia?"

Abraham Baldwin stood slowly, paused, bowed graciously toward the general, turned, and then boomed in a heavy Southern accent, "Gentlemen, it is my great honor to announce that Georgia votes AYE!"

Sherman leaped to his feet banging his cupped hands and yelling a Revolutionary cheer. He felt a slap on his back and turned, expecting to see Gouverneur Morris, but it was a beaming James Wilson. Sherman grabbed his hand, but they shook quickly so they could resume clapping. Turning toward Ellsworth, he started to reach out his hand but instead clasped him in a fraternal hug. When he broke free, everywhere about him was pandemonium. Delegates clapped, yelled, hugged, and some cried. Washington sat on his dais with a smile and his hand purposely laid flat on the table away from his gavel.

Sherman shouldered through the crowd, trying to get to Madison. Backslapping, handshakes, and emotional embraces slowed his progress toward the Virginia table. As he shuffled through the jostling crowd, he noticed that three men remained seated in steadfast defiance. He reached Madison to find Franklin enveloping the little man in his beefy arms. When they broke, Sherman muscled his way past a couple of well-wishers and caught the eye of the little genius from Virginia. He took Madison's delicate hand within his own huge palm and covered the combined fist with his left hand.

Holding Madison more with his eyes than with his hands, Sherman said, "Congratulations, Mr. Madison, you shall have your republic."

Madison didn't speak, but the mist in the corner of his eye said everything. Just when the moment was about to get awkward, Sherman heard the sharp rap of the gavel. "Gentlemen, please take your seats." Another firm, but benevolent, rap of the gavel sent the men scurrying back to their tables.

Instead of the room becoming quiet, the men, back at their tables, started congratulating their state colleagues. It took several more respectful raps of the gavel to regain order.

Washington assumed a businesslike tone. "Fellow delegates, it is my honor to announce that this Federal Convention, by the unanimous consent of the states present, does commend this Constitution to the people for ratification."

The entire room, save three people, stood and applauded. This time, instead of rambunctious exuberance, the formal announcement elicited a respectful and firm ovation. As the clapping subsided, Gerry marched proudly out of the chamber. Sherman respected Randolph and Mason for remaining at the Virginia table.

When everyone else sat, Washington solemnly remained standing, and in a theatrical voice, gave the command they all wanted to hear. "The plan, as amended, is ordered engrossed."

40

Monday, September 17, 1787

Madison sat in his customary place with folded hands resting on the table. He didn't intend to take notes today. In fact, he didn't intend to take any more notes on any day. This signing ceremony would be the final act of the convention.

Madison noticed that his ink-stained hands looked prayerful. He thought this fitting because a reverential spirit suffused the assembly. The chamber remained hushed as the secretary read the engrossed Constitution in its entirety. At the conclusion, Franklin rose with a speech in his hand.

"Mr. President, I confess there are several parts of this Constitution I don't like, but I'm not sure I won't later approve of them. Most men believe they possess all truth and that whoever differs from them is in error. The older I grow, the more I doubt my own judgment and the more I pay attention to the judgment of others.

"When you assemble a group of men to take advantage of their collective wisdom, you inevitably bring together all their prejudices, passions, and selfish views. From such an assembly, can one expect perfection? It astonishes me that this system approaches so near perfection.

"Thus, I consent to this Constitution because I'm not sure that it's not the best. My reservations were born within these walls and here they'll die. I'll never whisper a syllable about my uncertainties. I hope we all heartily recommend this Constitution. My wish is that any member who still harbors objections will, with me, doubt his own infallibility and put his name to this document."

Franklin dropped his papers to his side and spoke in a commanding voice. "I move the Constitution be signed."

The old man had made a fine last attempt to pull the three dissenters along, but Madison doubted that it would work. They would have to settle for artifice; *by the unanimous consent of the states present* ignored the two missing states and the seven delegates—counting those who had left—who dissented.

Gorham, looking nervous, asked for the floor. "Gentlemen, I wish that the clause declaring, 'the number of Representatives shall not exceed one for every forty thousand,' be changed to 'thirty thousand.'" Hamilton immediately seconded the motion.

Washington rose to put the question to a vote, hesitated, and then expressed his opinion for the first time. "Although I have hitherto restrained myself, my wish is that the proposal be approved. Many consider the small proportion of representatives insufficient to secure the rights and interests of the people. Late as the present moment is, it will give me great satisfaction to see this amendment adopted."

Madison turned to see Sherman's reaction. Ellsworth tapped his forearm, but Sherman just smiled and made a flick of his hand. Sherman couldn't countermand the sole wish expressed by the great hero of the Revolution, but Madison wished he had been rewarded with a flash of anger or at least surprise.

Without debate, the amendment was approved—in the manner so dear to Gen. Washington's heart—unanimously.

Madison expected this to be the end, but Randolph urgently asked for the floor. Bristling with indignation, he stared at the Pennsylvania table. "I resent the allusions to myself by Dr. Franklin." Randolph turned toward Washington. "I apologize for refusing to sign the Constitution. I don't mean by this refusal to oppose the Constitution beyond these doors. I only mean to keep myself free to be governed by future judgments."

Gerry felt obliged to explain his refusal. "This is painful, and I won't offer any further observations. The outcome has been decided. While the plan was in debate, I offered my opinions freely, but I'm now bound to treat it with the respect due an act of the convention. I hope that I'm not violating that respect by declaring I fear a civil war might erupt from these proceedings."

Gerry gave a disrespectful glance toward the Pennsylvania table. "As for Dr. Franklin's remarks, I cannot but view them as leveled at myself and the other gentlemen who mean not to sign."

Pinckney had lost his normal composure, but none of his arrogance. "We're not going to gain any more converts. Let's sign the document."

King interrupted the initiation of the signing ceremony. "I suggest that the journals of the convention be destroyed or deposited in the custody of the president. If it becomes public, those who wish to prevent the adoption of the Constitution will put it to bad use."

"I prefer the second expedient." Wilson looked directly at Gerry. "Some may make false representations of our proceedings, and we'll need evidence to contradict them."

The last hour confirmed Madison's suspicion that the fight for ratification would be divisive and mean-spirited.

The motion passed to deposit the journals into the hands of Washington.

Finally, all other business completed, Washington formally called on the delegates to sign the Constitution. The secretary had arranged the Syng inkstand that had been used to sign the Declaration of Independence on a green baize-covered table. Washington walked around the table and signed first. He then called the states from north to south. The delegates remained silent and reverential as they approached the low dais to apply their signatures.

When Virginia was called, Madison felt a tightening in his stomach. This Constitution would permanently bind his beloved country. When he picked up the pen, he looked at Washington, who stood respectfully to the side, instead of behind the table. The precedents set by this man would seal these words. Madison grabbed the pen, dipped it in the inkwell, and signed with confidence. When he looked up, Washington gave him a nod that made Madison think he had read his mind.

Despite his illness, Franklin had remained standing after he signed, shaking hands with delegates and whispering an occasional aside. While the last members were signing, tears glistened in Franklin's eyes. With an obvious struggle to control his emotions, he began to speak in a stronger than normal voice.

"Gentlemen, have you observed the half sun painted on the back of the president's chair? Artists find it difficult to distinguish a rising from a setting sun. In these many months, I have been unable to tell which it was. Now, I'm happy to exclaim that it is a rising, not a setting sun."

Once the last signature was in place, no one wanted to spend another moment in this room that had dominated their lives for so many months. Besides, John Dickinson had left a banknote with George Read to pay for a celebratory dinner at the City Tavern.

Because of the momentous day, Franklin had abandoned his rented prisoners and intended to walk out of the State House. Madison grabbed one elbow, and Wilson took the opposite side to help the old man out of the chamber. Madison hoped he could protect Franklin from being jostled by the bubbling delegates, but Washington took a point position in front of their little group, and the crowd parted like the Red Sea.

"I want to thank you gentlemen for helping an enfeebled and diminished old man," Franklin said.

"I witnessed your diminished capacity these many months," Madison said. He became puzzled when this somehow evoked a hearty chuckle from Franklin.

The doctor glanced between Madison and Wilson. "I'm usually assisted by the inmates of Walnut Street Prison. It occurs to me that you men have been prisoners in this chamber." Franklin chuckled again. "With the power vested in me by the State of Pennsylvania, I pardon and set you free."

At that precise moment, with theatrics that seemed natural to Washington, the sentries threw open the doors to the State House, and Madison was assaulted by bright sunlight and a deafening roar. Hundreds of people cheered, clapped, and whistled at the sight of Gen. George Washington framed by the great double doors of the State House.

The threesome stopped a respectful distance behind Washington. This crowd was not going to part so easily. In fact, the sentries had skipped down the three steps and joined arms to hold back the surge of people.

"Our rambunctious session on Saturday told our fair citizens that we had concluded our business," Franklin observed.

"Are you riding with the general?" Madison asked.

"Relax, boys. The general will know the exact moment to step off the stoop."

True to Franklin's prediction, Washington gauged the crowd's mood perfectly, and when he stepped down, they gave the men a narrow path to Washington's beautiful new carriage.

As they followed in the general's footsteps, the people continued to cheer and applaud. A woman leaned her head past Madison to yell, "Dr. Franklin, what is it to be? A republic or a monarchy?"

The doctor hesitated in his step and looked over the throng of anxious people. His answer came in a firm, loud voice.

"A republic—if you can keep it."

Part 7

Inauguration

41

Thursday, April 23, 1789

"HELLO, MR. MADISON. NICE weather."

"Thank goodness. I get frightful seasick."

Sherman looked to the sky. "I believe we'll have a smooth sail."

"Portentous?"

"I suspect the luck of our president. Even the weather does his bidding."

"Still an ordinary citizen. I can't wait for this inaugural celebration to be over."

Sherman and Madison, part of the Congressional Welcoming Committee, stood at the railing of a barge that was nearly fifty feet long. Thirteen pilots in crisp white suits rowed the freshly whitewashed barge toward Elizabeth Town, New Jersey.

The general had left Mount Vernon on April 18ᵗ and in six days, had traveled two hundred and eighty miles through five states, soon to be six when he entered New York. Washington was due on the opposite shore in a few hours, and the barge would float him and his entourage the fifteen miles back to Manhattan. As they plowed along the Hudson, a multitude of ships, sloops, and barges took positions alongside to witness the event.

Federal Hall, the temporary seat of the new government, sat at the corner of Wall and Broad streets. The First Congress had been meeting there since early April, but they had marked time by establishing parliamentary rules and electing officers. Their only real accomplishment had been to plan the inauguration. The original date to induct the new president had been March 4, but Congress didn't have a quorum until April, so their first order of business had been to reset the date to April 30.

"Clinton looks as if he's in charge of this event," Sherman said.

"He has no right," Madison said. "We barely nudged by his obstructionism."

George Clinton and John Adams monopolized the greeting end of the barge. Adams, as the elected vice president, deserved the place of honor. Clinton, a massive man who had been a massive nuisance, had elbowed his way to the front.

Ratification had been fought in the newspapers first. After the convention, Madison had immediately returned to New York and found himself drafted to write *The Federalist* essays with Hamilton and John Jay. George Mason wrote *Objections to the Proposed Federal Constitution* and said that the convention was a conclave of "monarchymen." Luther Martin wrote *The Genuine Information* and disclosed some of their sensitive voting. To the joy of printers in all thirteen states, the Federalists and Anti-Federalists fought this second revolution with words instead of swords. A few heroes of the first revolution, like Sam Adams, Patrick Henry, and Richard Henry Lee, opposed the new Constitution and made the contest agonizingly tight.

The strongest Anti-Federalist argument was that the Constitution granted unrestrained power to a national government. The strongest Federalist argument was that the Anti-Federalists had no alternative design. Within five months, Delaware, New Jersey, Pennsylvania, Georgia, Connecticut, and Massachusetts ratified—six of the nine needed states. In April and May, Maryland and South Carolina ratified, but even though the number had grown to eight, the vital states of Virginia and New York wavered. New York tried delaying for political leverage but rushed into the union after Virginia ratified in June. The hottest debates occurred at the Virginia Ratification Convention, with every contestant convinced that the outcome in Richmond would dictate the outcome for the nation.

"I haven't had a chance to congratulate you on ratification," Sherman said. "It's a shame you didn't have the honor of being the ninth state."

Madison smiled. "New Hampshire beat us by three days, but we didn't know it. We believed the future of America rested on *our* vote."

"It did. Your ratification moved our corpulent friend up there, and I can't imagine a United States divided by Virginia or New York." Sherman squeezed back to let someone move past. "I heard debates were contentious."

"Henry's a great speaker."

"Someone once told me that Patrick Henry had been speaking for three hours and he had to urinate so bad it hurt, but he stayed because he was afraid he'd miss something."

"Thank God, logic and need won in the end."

"You're being modest." Sherman leaned his buttocks against the railing. "Is it true Henry called the wrath of God down on you?"

Madison laughed. "Literally. He had been speaking all morning, and in his summation, he called on God to punish those who would inflict this tyranny on his beloved country. At that very instant, a great crack of thunder echoed through the hall, and a deluge followed within minutes. Frightening."

"You should be president. The general defeated only the British Empire."

"No, thank you." Madison shook his head as if trying to fling off a bug that had just landed in his hair. "The general has his hands full with an unruly bunch like us."

Roger Sherman and James Madison had been elected to the first House of Representatives. Other members of the Federal Convention, now commonly called the Constitutional Convention, had also secured important posts in the new government. Elbridge Gerry, Abraham Baldwin, and several others had been elected to the House of Representatives. Rufus King, Oliver Ellsworth, William Paterson, Robert Morris, George Read, William Blount, Pierce Butler, and others had secured appointments from their state legislatures to the Senate. Charles Pinckney had won his race for governor of South Carolina.

It was common knowledge that Washington would appoint Alexander Hamilton Secretary of the Treasury, and James Wilson and John Rutledge would get seats on the Supreme Court. The enigmatic Gouverneur Morris had ventured off to France and the French Revolution, an offspring of the subversive American spirit that had caught the European capitals unaware.

"We may prove the least of the general's challenges," Sherman said.

"Foreign intrigue?"

"I was referring to his cabinet."

"Jefferson and Hamilton. You might be right."

"And Randolph." Edmund Randolph was to be attorney general.

"We needed his support for ratification," Madison said defensively. "Did you know Clinton wrote him a letter inviting him to form a devilish pact? He didn't know the general had already seduced our dear governor back to the side of virtue and light."

Sherman took a long look toward the approaching shoreline of New Jersey. "Sometimes I think we were both pawns."

"Excuse me?"

"The general pulled our strings."

"Not mine," Madison demurred.

"Perhaps not, but for someone who spoke only once, he orchestrated events to a remarkable degree."

"To what purpose?"

"Union."

Madison seemed contemplative. "An honorable goal. One I shared."

"As did I. At least after the first weeks." Sherman tried to catch Madison's flitting eyes. "You were masterful in *The Federalist* papers."

"Thank you, but again, I was but a part."

"No. The papers you wrote were incisive."

"As were the others. Hamilton hid his objections."

"As you did your Southern roots."

"Hamilton's admonition. He wanted New Yorkers, but Duer wrote poorly and Jay became ill. Were you *Letters of a Landholder*?"

"That was Oliver. I helped some."

"I expect you did." Madison's eyes settled for a moment. "No wonder you recognized Washington's behind-the-scene maneuvers."

Sherman had to laugh. "Our papers were prosaic; yours were brilliant."

Madison smiled with genuine joy. "Jefferson said they were the best commentary on government ever written. My father wrote that Publius had done a magnificent job."

"What did he say when you revealed you were Publius?"

"I haven't told him."

"Why not?"

"He would withdraw the praise." Madison looked toward shore. "Steady." The barge bumped against the shore with enough force to cause both men to stumble forward.

"Damn," Madison said. "Clinton's handhold kept him from tumbling into the mud."

Sherman, and several men within earshot, burst out laughing when they imagined Clinton greeting the future president in a mud-splattered suit. Madison looked embarrassed to have caused the gaiety, but Sherman patted his shoulder to let him know that a respite of humor was hardly inappropriate.

Within minutes, a rider galloped from the woods and sharply pulled his horse up sideways to expertly stop the animal parallel to the front of the barge. "They're a half hour behind me."

The barge pilots immediately went to work. Wood planks had been positioned on the bed of the barge. These were now scooted out and laid on the beach to make a hard surface entry for the general's carriage. The welcoming committee of city and state dignitaries and congressional representatives disembarked and lined the wooden pathway. Governor Clinton took the position of honor at the head of the reception line.

In less than thirty minutes, a lone rider trotted from the woods. Washington, sitting rigidly astride a great white mare, led the procession that included his empty carriage. Sherman and Madison joined the other dignitaries in sharp applause as the general dismounted with an élan born of a countless number of official receptions. Washington formally greeted each man with a deft combination of dignity and brotherhood.

When he reached Madison, the general shed some of the stiffness and clasped

Madison with both hands. "Thank you, Jemmy. You're a true patriot." Madison managed only a nod of acknowledgment.

Washington then grasped Sherman in the same fraternal manner. "Mr. Sherman, to an extent the nation may never know, we owe this day to you."

"I only did my part."

"A vital part." And he was off greeting the rest of the entourage.

After they had all boarded the barge, Washington began to rotate among the dignitaries with the aplomb of a seasoned politician, and Sherman and Madison retook their position along the rail.

"Look at all these boats," Madison said. It seemed that the entire Hudson was filled with vessels elaborately decorated with patriotic bunting and flags.

"This is historic," Sherman said.

"Not since Greece."

"'If we can keep it,' in the words of Franklin."

As they neared Bedloe's Island, a sloop appeared and drew to within ten feet of the barge. About twenty men and women, in neat columns and matching dress, began to sing an honorific ode set to the tune of "God Save the King."

"We really must cultivate our own composers," Madison said.

"I shall speak to John Dickinson," Sherman quipped. Dickinson had written "Liberty Song," the most popular Revolutionary tune. "He told me that on occasion indifferent songs are powerful."

"This would be one of those occasions," Madison said. "It would be especially powerful if the melody didn't evoke British royalty."

"People feel they can treat Washington like royalty because he has no kingly ambitions."

"The Anti-Federalists still look for anything that hints of monarchy."

"The general's demeanor will keep them at bay."

"You're wrong, Roger. In the months ahead, nothing will restrain a fervent opposition from surfacing."

Sherman looked to the sea because of shouts to his left and right. "It seems something else has surfaced at the moment."

Immediately alongside the barge, a school of porpoises suddenly bobbed up and down as though they were part of the official welcoming celebration. "The man has an uncanny knack for theatrics," Madison said in awe.

The porpoises disappeared for the moment and then resurfaced in front of the barge, as if leading the flotilla to port. As they drew parallel to the tip of Manhattan, the Battery let loose thirteen cannons that rocked the barge and deafened the passengers.

At the wharf, another thirteen-gun salute welcomed the future president. More dignitaries stood in stiff lines along Murray's Wharf at the foot of Wall Street, and an even larger crowd extended up the street. When Washington stepped from the barge, the citizenry clapped, whistled, yelled, and frantically waved flags and banners. Washington stopped and, before shaking hands with the officials, bowed deferentially toward the cheering throng. After the formal greetings, the general pulled himself ramrod straight and followed the young maidens scattering flowers along the crimson-carpeted steps that led to the street.

When Madison and Sherman reached the top of the steps, they saw Gen. Washington returning the salute of an army officer.

"General, your orders, sir."

"I shall proceed as I am directed." Washington almost made a complete turn to view the crushing crowd of well-wishers. "But, sir, after this reception, don't bother yourself further. The affection of my fellow citizens is all the guard I need."

With that polite dismissal, Washington climbed into the carriage that would take him to Franklin House on Cherry Street, which served as the temporary executive mansion.

"Where are you headed?" Madison asked.

"For a nap," Sherman said.

"Walk with me down Wall Street; I want to buy some souvenirs."

"James, those are for spectators; you're a participant."

"One with many friends in Virginia. I recommend that you don't return to New Haven empty-handed."

"How simple can I be? My children and grandchildren would disown me."

"Not likely," Madison chuckled. "I'm sure they're conditioned to your forgetfulness."

"Your foil has pierced a vital organ."

"Difficult, considering the size of your heart."

"Ouch."

"Help me dicker. I'm terrible."

"Very well." Sherman extended his hand. "Lead on."

They sauntered up Wall Street and soon encountered vendors sandwiched into every cranny of the narrow thoroughfare. They stopped midblock, where three vendors tried to bark sales spiels louder than their elbow-rubbing competitors. Madison picked up a souvenir tankard and turned it so Sherman could read the inscription—March 4, 1789.

Showing it to the vendor, Madison said, "Wrong date."

"Not my fault, gov. Blame that muddleheaded Congress. They can't get the first thing right."

"Bunch of parasites, I suspect," Sherman said.

"Got that right, gov, but don't you worry, the general'll get 'em lined up. Read the back of the tankard."

Madison turned it and read out loud. "President George Washington, The Greatest Man on Earth."

"Now or for all time?" Sherman asked, straightfaced.

The vendor cocked an eye at Sherman, "You a damned Anti-Federalist?"

"No, sir," Sherman responded. "I support the Constitution."

"Damn the Constitution. These souvenirs honor the inauguration. Humph. Should've been a coronation."

Madison held the tankard aloft. "How much?"

"Priceless," the vendor snipped.

"Outside our range. Good day, sir," Sherman said.

"Just a minute, gov. Two dollars."

"Still outside our range," Sherman said.

"A dollar and a half." This came from the vendor at the next table.

"Ignore that knave, his brother's a Tory."

"I'm not interested in a tankard," Madison said.

"Then I can make you a good deal on these buttons, medals, or brooches. How about a watch fob or a commemorative plate?"

Madison picked up the watch fob. "How much?"

"One dollar. Quality silver."

"How much for ten?"

"Ten?" The vendor scratched his head. "I don't know if I want to sell my whole stock."

"Someone else can handle the order," Sherman said.

"Eight dollars."

"New York money?" Madison asked.

"Do I look like a bank?"

"James, you'll need to wait for the greatest man on earth to fix the money issue."

This remark earned Sherman a nasty glare from the vendor. After they had finished bartering, Madison had bought ten watch fobs, four plates, and dozens of buttons. Sherman had bought one plate for Rebecca's sideboard and a few other items to spread around the household.

"What are you going to do with all those souvenirs?" Sherman asked.

"Friends in Virginia. I'll use the buttons for gratuities: they'll be more valuable than money."

"Good idea."

Madison hefted his load. "These trinkets increase in value the further they get from New York."

"And further in time," Sherman mused. "Perhaps I should reconsider."

"Madison gets Sherman to reconsider." Madison smiled. "This is indeed a memorable day."

ON APRIL 30, MADISON and Sherman went to Franklin House with other congressional delegates to accompany Washington to the inauguration. They had been wakened at dawn by cannon salutes, followed by church bells that rang incessantly.

Dark clouds had hovered over the city in the morning, but by noon, as Washington's luck would have it, the skies had cleared to a radiant blue. When the escort delegation arrived at the residence, an orderly crowd had already gathered in the street. Washington greeted them dressed in a dark brown coat with brass buttons decorated with spread eagles, brown waistcoat and breeches, white silk stockings, and shoes with simple silver buckles. Freshly powdered hair and his dress sword set off his otherwise modest attire.

The entourage included three carriages. Sherman and Madison had been assigned to the last coach in the matched set. As they crowded into their seats, Sherman said, "The general chose plain civilian dress."

"A sharp contrast to his normal hint of a military uniform. I understand he insisted that every article be made from American cloth."

"Good for the New England vote."

"He spent last week visiting every member of Congress and others with influence. You'd never know he was elected unanimously."

"Four years can be short," Sherman said.

"He doesn't want a second term."

"He said he didn't want a first."

"Who'd follow?" Madison asked.

"Adams?"

"God, I hope not."

A line of militiamen extended through Federal Hall to the Senate Chamber. As he strode past the men he had once commanded, Washington looked as if he were marching to his doom. When he entered the chamber, John Adams formally greeted him. After a series of introductions, Washington said, "I'm ready to proceed."

Adams bowed and led Washington to a half-enclosed balcony overlooking Wall and Broad streets. Sherman, Madison, Gerry, Baldwin, King, Ellsworth, Paterson, Read, Butler, Robert Morris, and others squeezed onto the balcony. It was a tight fit.

The streets were even more crowded. When Washington appeared, a great shout went up from the spectators. Every window, balcony, and rooftop was packed with spectators. Someone close by mumbled, "One could traverse the block by walking on the heads of people."

Washington gallantly put a hand over his heart and bowed several times. When people refused to stop cheering, he took a seat in an armchair and waited. Eventually, the audience hushed, and Washington rose and went to the railing.

On a small red-draped table, a Bible rested on a crimson velvet cushion. Robert R. Livingston, the presiding judge of New York's highest court, had been designated to administer the oath. Livingston came forward, and Washington reverently placed his hand on the Bible and looked Livingston directly in the eye.

Repeating after Livingston, Washington took the thirty-five-word oath prescribed by the Constitution: "I do solemnly swear that I will faithfully execute the office of President of the United States, and will to the best of my ability, preserve, protect and defend the Constitution of the United States." Washington then added four more words, "so help me God," and leaned over to kiss the Bible.

"It's done," Livingston said. He turned to the spectators and shouted, "Long live George Washington, president of the United States."

The crowd immediately took up the cry and then shifted to wild cheers and huzzahs. A flag was raised on the cupola, and thirteen cannons went off at the Battery. Church bells tolled in every steeple in the city. The United States had just peacefully transitioned to an entirely new government and inaugurated its first duly elected chief executive. No one in this crowd, including those on the balcony, could remain silent or reserved.

President George Washington bowed several times, and then, before the audience calmed, he retreated into the Senate Chamber. When Madison and Sherman made their own way into the chamber, Washington had already taken his seat on the dais to wait for people to take their places. Ignoring protocol, members of both houses scrambled for the few seats in an atmosphere of confusion and happy chatter.

When Washington finally rose to give his inaugural address, the sound of scraping chairs filled the chamber as everyone stood.

Washington spoke in a shaky voice that conveyed both modesty and embarrassment. He reminded Congress about his lack of experience but promised to execute his duties to the best of his abilities. He then expressed anxiety over the weight of responsibility, saying that he would have preferred to remain at his beloved Mount Vernon.

"I was summoned by my country, whose voice I can never hear but with veneration and love."

He then moved to a highly religious tone and said that he saw divine guidance in America. Throughout the address, Washington constantly shifted the manuscript of his speech from hand to hand and never overcame his tremulous delivery. A weak finish didn't dampen the rousing applause or the exuberant congratulations that took most of an hour.

Special services were scheduled at St. Paul's Church. The entire Congress intended to accompany the president, but the crowd outside prohibited bringing up carriages and even blocked the senators and representatives from leaving the building. When Madison and Sherman finally made it to the street, they asked the whereabouts of the president.

"He walked."

"Seven blocks?"

"He insisted."

Madison looked at Sherman. Sherman shrugged and said, "Let's walk."

People thinned after a few blocks, and Madison said, "Good speech."

"I understand you wrote it."

"Editing would be a better description."

"A fine job, just the same. It moved some to tears."

"He originally made a big point of being childless."

"Childless?"

"He wanted the country to understand that there was no way he could create a hereditary monarchy."

"The country would check that."

"That's why I deleted it. By the way, did you know the Bible came from St. John's Masonic lodge?"

"God's word comes from him alone."

Madison looked embarrassed. "The president looked nervous and unsure."

"If the country hadn't called Washington to other vocations, he would've been our greatest thespian."

Madison looked startled. "Are you saying he feigned modesty?"

"I'm saying George Washington is precisely the man the country needs at this moment."

"MR. SHERMAN, MAY I have a word?"

Sherman turned from Abraham Baldwin to face Madison. "Of course, James."

"Do you need privacy?" Baldwin asked.

"Good morning, Abe," Madison said, reaching around to shake hands with both men. "Yes, if it wouldn't be too inconvenient."

The three men stood in the cloakroom to the house chamber prior to their first session since the inauguration. Sherman put one hand on Madison's shoulder and extended his other arm toward a corner. "Let's step over there."

After they had moved away from the milling representatives, Sherman asked, "What's on your mind?"

"A bill of rights."

"A worthy goal."

"I believe it should be our first order of business."

Sherman glanced around at the other representatives. "We have many serious issues before us."

"None more serious," Madison said.

"Abe would disagree. Georgia needs protection against the Spanish and the Indians."

"Commitments were made to achieve ratification."

"By whom?"

"Myself—among others. Ratification wouldn't have been possible otherwise."

"We can address rights later. First, we need to resolve our finances and security."

Madison looked nervous. "If we don't address rights immediately, we may never get to them. There will always be pressing matters."

"James, personal liberty is not threatened at the moment. Farms and our territorial sovereignty are. The public wants us to solve the nation's problems."

"This won't take long. I've brought a revision with me."

"What kind of revision?"

"I've incorporated the rights into the text of the Constitution."

"James!"

"What?"

"That will require another convention and ratification."

"I kept everything identical except for adding rights in the appropriate place."

"If we change the Constitution, our opponents will seize the event to reopen the debate. We barely eked out this one."

"Look at it before you judge."

Sherman looked anxiously around. "Why did you come to me?"

"I need your help."

"I oppose what you want done."

"You oppose the timing. The country fears this new government. What better way to gain time than to give them a statement of their rights."

"I can't let you discard our accomplishments by opening the Constitution. It must remain sacrosanct."

"Are you saying we may never have a bill of rights?"

"They must be amendments, proposed and ratified according to Article V."

Madison hesitated. "If I concede that point, will you help?"

Now it was Sherman's turn to pause. The bell signaling the start of the session rang. "Mr. Madison, I must admit that you have a knack for knowing what must be done."

"And Mr. Sherman, you have a knack for knowing how to get it done."

Both men looked at each other for a long moment, and then Sherman put his lanky arm around the narrow shoulders of Madison. "The country seems to have more work for us."

Madison's darting eyes caught Sherman's, and then moved away. "I'll be happy as long as my country needs me."

As both men moved toward the door, Sherman lightly gripped Madison's elbow. "Jemmy, it'll be a sad day when America no longer needs men like you."

Shoulder to shoulder, Sherman and Madison walked through the double doors and into the House of Representatives.

Epilogue

I laid my steel-tipped pen aside and tried to shake the cramp out of my hand. James Madison looked as if he had dozed off once again, so I closed my inkwell, content that we had completed a good day's work.

"I believe we're done." The old man had not twitched a single muscle except to open his eyes.

That had used to startle me, but I had grown accustomed to his determined stillness. "I agree. This has been an unusually long day. You should get some rest. We can begin again in the morning."

"I mean our collaboration is done. You have your material."

"Mr. President, please, I have so many questions."

"Everything else is a matter of public record. Well documented."

"At least tell me what happened to the Ohio and Scioto companies."

Madison sighed. "Very well. The Scioto Company advanced the Ohio Company about one hundred and fifty thousand dollars toward their first installment of five hundred thousand. The Ohio Company founded Marietta, Ohio, but never came up with the remaining money. I believe it went defunct in 1796. The Scioto Company was a complete bust. They sold land in Europe, but the money disappeared." Madison chuckled. "Hard to imagine now, but there was too much land for too few people."

"What about the Revolutionary War bonds?"

"Mr. Witherspoon, I refuse to go into that subject, or any other for that matter. You are welcome to remain a few days to organize your notes, but this interview has drawn to a close."

"Mr. President, you and Jefferson quarreled with Hamilton over those bonds. The resulting chasm gave us our two-party system. Surely, you can enlighten the public record."

"I refuse to spend my final days reliving that episode."

The old man's eyes told me the issue was nonnegotiable. As Washington's Secretary of the Treasury, Hamilton had created a national bank and retired the bonds at face value. These actions had inflamed Jefferson and triggered Madison to insist that the Constitution did not authorize a government bank. Years later, Madison was accused of duplicity when he championed a less literal interpretation. I decided that could wait because there was something more important I needed to probe. "You promised to discuss slavery."

"I think I explained the slave issue." As he spoke, his eyes wandered over my shoulder. "Have you come to fetch me for my nap?"

"You must excuse us, Mr. Witherspoon." I craned my head around at the sound of Dolley's voice. She glided around my chair and put a hand on her husband's shoulder. "James needs his rest."

"Will we talk again, Mr. President?"

"I have nothing further to say."

"I want to talk about the present. I believe abolition achievable."

"As do I. It is the price that has held my hand."

I bent forward. "I support a new tax to compensate slaveholders."

Madison spoke in an even softer voice. "If the North tries to mandate emancipation, war will ensue. The republic will not survive. Not then, not now."

"I don't believe that."

"Do you think you can simply pass an amendment?" Dolley asked.

Not knowing whom to address, I shifted my gaze between the two Madisons. "Well, yes."

Madison didn't answer immediately. "Mr. Witherspoon, the price of union in 1787 was the accommodation of slavery. The price of abolition in 1835 will be disunion."

"We shouldn't be faced with this quandary. Was there no other choice in 1787?"

"Yes. Two nations: one slave, one free."

"Perhaps a better choice."

"That would only assuage your guilt."

I had started to lean back in my chair, but Madison's words made my back as stiff as a seasoned plank. "I beg your pardon. I'm guiltless."

"You are a citizen of a slaveholding nation."

I crossed my legs and let my glance flit between the two. "Times change. You're a slaveholder and the father of the Constitution. Your endorsement of an abolition amendment would carry enormous weight."

"I'll not instigate an armed conflict."

"You support the Constitution with all its defects?"

"I took an oath to protect the Constitution."

"I thought that expired with your term."

"I don't believe so."

"Mr. President, in time, we'll secure an amendment. You can make it sooner."

"The country isn't ready."

"Why did you make the amendment process so difficult?"

"There were fifty-five men in the chamber. We designed a system to give voice to every faction, while restraining any single interest group from gaining dominance."

"With all due respect, you're mistaken. You endorsed the oppression of one faction by another. You gave slaveholders a constitutional right to maintain their status as masters."

Madison remained still as a wary cat. I began to fear I had overstepped, when his lips curled up in an unruffled smile. "Did you bring any other clothes?"

I looked down at my threadbare wool suit. "Only my travel garments."

"Well, put them on, and my overseer will give you a tour of Montpelier."

"Are our discussions over?"

"You must excuse me. I fatigue easily."

Dolley stood and guided me by the elbow out of the great man's presence.

I HAD JUST BUTTONED my waistcoat when Paul softly knocked on my door.

"The president asked me to see if you needed assistance."

"No, thank you. I can dress myself."

He started to retreat when I stopped him with a question, "Paul, do you envy the free Negroes in the North?"

"I know nothing of their predicament."

"You accompanied the president to Washington, did you not?"

"I've been with Master James my entire life."

"There are free Negroes in Washington."

"I stick to my own."

"You mean fellow slaves."

"I mean the Madison family."

"Surely, you must occasionally desire freedom?"

"I'm doing what I want."

I realized Madison had sent Paul to answer questions. "What will happen to you when the president dies?"

"My wish is to be buried as close to him as possible."

Maybe I had found a weakness. "That shan't be very close."

"I'll find a permanent home at Montpelier. That's all I ask."

"You see yourself as part of the family?"

"Excuse me, sir, if you have no need of my services, I have other duties."

Before I could grant permission, Paul was gone. I shrugged. For every house-slave, hundreds toiled in the fields. I hurried out of the house to find a cobalt sky that signaled a harsh winter on the near horizon.

"Mr. Witherspoon, I'm John Watson, manager of Montpelier."

"I'm pleased to meet you. Am I dressed appropriately?"

"It'll do. This is your mount."

The man had been holding the reins of two horses and now, with an extended right arm, pulled one horse around for me. As I stepped up into the saddle, I asked, "Will I have an opportunity to talk to slaves?"

"If you wish."

"How many hours does a field hand work?"

"Mostly twelve-hour days, a few more during harvest. The problem is how to keep them productive in the winter."

"Difficult problem, I'm sure. Distressing how they eat every day."

Watson threw me a hard stare. "You don't think much of our way of life, do you?"

"I am unconcerned about your way of life. It's the slave's way of life that distresses me."

"The mill girls in Lowell live a more restrictive life."

"They choose to work in the mills, and they can choose to leave."

"Yes, of course they can. Shall we proceed?"

We rode around the plantation, but I was disappointed to see that late fall didn't require work in the fields.

"Mrs. Madison tells me you're an abolitionist," Watson said.

"Yes."

"Montpelier is a large, well-run plantation. We do not abuse our slaves."

"You mean you take care of your property."

"Exactly."

"I meant that sarcastically."

"I know."

"Do you believe treating a Negro as well as a horse condones slavery?"

"We're all slaves, to one degree or another."

"Then the degree matters."

Watson turned in his saddle to look at me. "Interference from soppy abolitionists will incite armed conflict."

"You're suggesting the South would go to war?"

"I'm not suggesting."

"Were you instructed to give me this advice?"

"I was instructed to show you Montpelier."

"Not much to see."

"We'll go to the ironworks."

We rode up to a large shed and dismounted. Inside, the dark interior brought a little warmth from the forges scattered around the periphery of the earthen floor. About eight black men labored at different tasks, and the hammering, the protesting hiss of hot iron dipped in water, and the snap of embers gave the place a bustling atmosphere.

"Montpelier has the largest blacksmith operation in Orange County. Take a look around. I'll be back in a moment."

Watson walked over to a white man just entering the shed. "Hello, Mr. Caster. What can we do for you today?"

"Nails. I also want to settle my account."

"I hope that means you had a good crop."

"Middling, but one of my niggers grew into a strapping buck that brought a good price."

I saw a hooded look from the black man standing a respectful distance behind Caster and realized he was not a Montpelier slave.

"Let's step over to the ledger," Watson said.

As Caster followed Watson to a writing shelf along the wall, he pointed and said, "Sam, carry one of those kegs out to the wagon."

The keg of nails looked anchored to the floor, and I knew that I could never lift it. Sam crouched and, winding his lanky arms around the keg, with a grunt brought it up to his chest. As he shuffled toward the door, he suddenly stumbled and dropped the keg, spewing nails in every direction. Sam immediately dropped to his knees to gather up the nails, but once he had a double handful, he looked forlornly at the burst wooden keg.

Caster flew across the shed and kicked Sam in the rear, splaying him across the nail-strewn floor. "You imbecile!"

I stepped forward, but Watson held up a restraining hand. "Mr. Caster, no harm. We'll get you another keg in respect for your business."

Caster hovered over his slave, and for a second, I thought he might give him another kick, but instead he made a dismissive wave of his arm. "Sam, you thank Mr. Watson for savin' you a whippin' and make sure to gather up every one of those damn nails."

"Yas suh, and thank you, Mr. Watson."

I wanted to help Sam pick up the nails, but a stern look from Watson dissuaded me.

After the incident, we left the shed and rode back to the mansion in silence. Dismounting, I couldn't help but throw one more barb. "Mr. Watson, would the South fight to protect men like Caster?"

"The South will fight to protect Virginia's right to choose her own way. Good day, Mr. Witherspoon."

I FOUND THE MADISONS in the parlor, sitting side by side with an unoccupied chair facing them. I took the chair and leaned in to rub my hands in front of the crackling fire. An involuntary shudder tried to chase away my chill and distress.

"Tea or coffee, sir?" This came from Sukey, who had materialized behind me.

"Coffee, please." I twisted in my chair to see her face, but she had disappeared.

"I see it hasn't warmed up," Madison said.

"No, there's a crispness that brittles your bones."

"Well, warm yourself," Dolley said. "We'll have coffee for you in a moment."

"Thank you." I soon felt flushed and leaned back in my chair. "Mr. President, Mrs. Madison, may I speak bluntly?"

This caused Dolley to laugh merrily. "I thought you had been speaking bluntly."

This took me aback, but I plunged ahead anyway. "At your ironworks, I witnessed an atrocity perpetrated by one of your neighbors. The man physically and verbally abused his slave."

"Who?" Madison asked.

"Mr. Caster."

"Ah, yes," was all he said.

"You know him?"

"Of course. Most slaveholders own fewer than five slaves. They're hardscrabble planters, and Caster is typical of the breed. An unseemly lot."

"So most slaves are owned by harsh masters?"

In answer, Madison simply turned his teacup in its saucer.

"I'm sorry, sir, but just because you're a humane master does not make you better than Caster. You should free your slaves."

"You probably believe me rich, but my debts far exceed the value of Montpelier. The liens—"

"How will you survive?" I had thrown the question at Dolley, surprised by how quickly I had grown fond of her.

"I'll publish James's notes from the Constitutional Convention. The world has waited fifty years for them."

"Is that why I can't read them?"

"I assure you, you need not wait long." Madison smiled. "If I may continue?"

"Of course."

"The liens against my estate include my slaves. You may think me an incompetent planter, but I assure you that my predicament is common."

"That's why you can't free your slaves?"

"I was making a larger point. Abolition will cause a financial collapse."

"I never believed abolition would leave the South intact."

"Intact? Abolition will destroy the South: its plantations, social order, financial institutions, and governments. Absolute devastation."

"So, we should do nothing?"

"I once thought the wound would heal itself, but I've come to believe that only a cataclysm will wipe this scourge from our land. Fifty years ago, your grandfather asked me to end slavery. I could not. So I promised to end the slave trade. There were many difficulties, but I managed to get a prohibition put into the Constitution."

"It didn't take effect until 1808."

"I got what I could."

"And in the intervening years?"

Madison coughed, holding a tiny fist in front of his mouth. "The past is immutable." Madison gave Dolley a glance. "If emancipation comes, your generation, or one following, must endure the cost." He rubbed his gnarled knuckles. "You say you're an abolitionist, but are you willing to sacrifice the lives of your relatives to this cause?" When I hesitated, Madison added, "You cannot defeat the South by yourself. It will take your family and all your neighbors."

I spent many moments pondering his question. "I might sacrifice one generation to free countless generations, but I'm not convinced it must come to war."

Madison struggled to lift himself, and Dolley quickly helped him rise to his feet. The old man seemed especially frail, and I could barely hear him mutter, "The bane of slavery has afflicted me all my life. I shall soon be free."

"You still have time." I had to make one last plea. "Write a letter to the nation. People will listen to James Madison."

"No. I intend to abide by the bargain we struck in Philadelphia. With my passing, we'll all be dead, and I shan't violate their trust in my last days." Madison made a few feeble steps toward the door. "I'll go to my grave satisfied that I bequeath a lasting republic to my countrymen."

"A republic with a basic flaw."

Madison interrupted his halting shuffle to look at me with taunting eyes. "We provided the necessary mechanisms for change."

Madison leaned on Dolley and extended a tiny, emaciated hand. I stepped forward and gently shook his hand for the first time. It was startlingly weak. I looked hard at this mortal man who had carried into history such immortal aspirations. When he grappled with the world and endless generations, his egalitarian mind intended nothing but good, but within the confines of his home, he acquiesced to unconscionable tyranny.

"It's been a pleasure, Mr. Witherspoon." Dolley gave me a smile and assisted the last of the founding fathers out of my presence.

I reached down to pick up my notes when I heard his familiar voice. "We also bequeathed a loftiness of purpose that will continue to expand liberty."

And then he was gone.

Author's Note

There are many excellent history books about the Federal Convention. This novel is not one of them. A historical novel has its own strengths and limitations. I chose the novel format because the drama and characters begged to be brought to life. A novel also provides a vehicle to fill gaps in official records. For every journey away from the documentation, I took care to ensure that sufficient circumstantial evidence exists to justify my conjecture. Errors have undoubtedly occurred, and *Tempest at Dawn* should not be viewed as a definitive source.

Certain literary license was required. Sherman did not arrive in Philadelphia until May 29, the third day of the convention. Others delegates at Benjamin Franklin's preconvention party also had not arrived. Unlike an eighteenth-century convention, a novel must get its players on stage when the story requires, not when they meander into town.

Everything said in the State House chamber is accurate, but the debates have been rearranged for clarity. Madison's record of the convention is 231,000 words, so obviously the deliberations have been severely abridged. In addition, the language has been modernized, the sequence adjusted in some circumstances, and, at times, two or more days have been blended for brevity. The actual debates meandered in a fashion not conducive to fiction. With Madison's hard work, we have a near-verbatim record that can be pursued by those interested.

In order not to confuse the reader with too many characters, some actual quotes are attributed to a delegate already active in the story. In most situations, I used a character from the same state as the person who actually made the statement. One serious deviation, however, is Paterson's angry speech on June 30. This speech was actually delivered by Gunning Bedford of Delaware.

Benjamin Franklin, due to age and ill health, was too feeble to make his own speeches. He wrote them out for James Wilson to read. Oliver Ellsworth left the convention in late August and was not present for the signing. He actively supported ratification. The Reverend Doctor John Witherspoon was present for the Presbyterian Convention prior to the Federal Convention but may not have stayed through the summer. The Montpelier ironworks, as described in the epilogue, no longer existed in 1835. Due to wood rot, the State House steeple was removed in 1781 and not replaced until 1824.

Seven delegates refused to sign the Constitution. John Lansing, Jr., and Robert Yates, of New York, left the convention in protest in July. Luther Martin and John Francis Mercer, of Maryland, left just prior to the signing ceremony. George Mason and Edmund Randolph, of Virginia, and Elbridge Gerry, of Massachusetts, were present at the ceremony but refused to sign. William Blount, of North Carolina, said he signed only to attest that the states were unanimous.

The delegates from other states feared that Virginians wanted to dominate the new nation. Their fears may have been justified. The District of Columbia found a home on the Virginia border, and Virginians controlled the presidency for thirty-two of the nation's first thirty-six years.

The Connecticut Compromise proved only a temporary truce. Sherman proposed the compromise to protect the small states, but the South immediately recognized that the Senate could protect slavery. The next seventy-three years saw compromise piled on compromise, until the divisions between the North and South escalated into civil war.

Breinigsville, PA USA
06 October 2010

246797BV00003B/3/P